P9-DGR-078

PRAISE FOR TESTIMONY

"[An] engrossing new page-turner...In this shift to an international stage, with its complex web of alliances and deceptions, Turow has created a compelling, all-consuming drama that maintains the themes that thread through his fiction: the contradictions and conflicts of characters with secrets, often from themselves, and how idealism can be shaken when law, politics, and capitalism mix to distort fairness and justice."

—*National Book Review*

"The real pleasure of the new novel lies not so much in solving the mystery of the massacre as in watching Turow knock down assumption after assumption made by Boom—and the reader. In fact, I can't think of another novel in which so many givens end up being exposed as either honest mistakes or outright lies."

—*Washington Post*

"Scott Turow's latest legal thriller goes international and is a page turner not to be missed!"

—Daniel Silva, #1 *New York Times* bestselling author of *The Black Widow*

"Takes us from the gritty familiarity of his beloved Kindle County into a mysterious world of international intrigue. It's the best kind of thriller, which stimulates the mind as well as thrilling the heart."

—Jeffrey Toobin, *New York Times* bestselling author of *American Heiress*

"TESTIMONY [is] one for the beach bag…This is a guy who knows what he's doing: Turow has been crafting intricate, best-selling legal thrillers dating back to his blockbuster wifedunit, *Presumed Innocent* (30 years ago!)."

—*USA Today*

"Turow writes with zest and authority…TESTIMONY unfolds in highly descriptive prose and is sprinkled with colorful characters."

—*Atlanta Journal-Constitution*

"Turow guides readers through a minefield of a plot until everything finally becomes clear. It's complicated but will hold anybody who ventures in."

—*St. Louis Post-Dispatch*

"Turow applies the same storytelling magic to the ICC that has drawn scores of readers into his Kindle County courtrooms, weaving fascinating details about the challenges of prosecuting war crimes into a suspenseful story of redemption and the complexities of justice."

—*Booklist*

"Follows twists and turns, shifting alliances, and a near-fatal confrontation…[TESTIMONY] is exciting and consistent with Turow's prior novels."

—*The Missourian*

"Tightly written action."   —*Kirkus Reviews*

"A complex and haunting tale of war crimes that will not only satisfy his courtroom drama devotees but also readers of international thrillers."   —*Library Journal*

"Bestseller Turow (*Identical*) movingly evokes the horrors of the Balkan wars in this gripping thriller."
—*Publishers Weekly*

"TESTIMONY is an absolutely crackerjack read, and again leaves us wishing that Turow would haul out his typewriter a tad more often."
—*Winnipeg Free Press*

"A thriller yarn with many twists and turns."
—*Chicago Sun-Times*

"Raises important questions of responsibility, patriotism, corruption and the role of military power. And even as it confronts these weighty issues, it keeps the reader engaged in a page-turning thriller...Turow is back on his game in TESTIMONY."
—*Illinois Times*

"Fast-paced...Scott Turow is first and foremost a storyteller, and that's what propels the action, that and trying to figure out the truth...another fine book by this very fine writer."
—*Washington Times*

"[A] smart, demanding thriller."
—*Washington Post*, "17 Thrillers and Mysteries Worth Toting to the Beach"

"Scott Turow has done the impossible: Making the International Criminal Court in The Hague interesting...in TESTIMONY it is a hotbed of intrigue and infighting involving a massacre of Roma people in former Yugoslavia and the travails of an American prosecutor."
—Bloomberg.com, "Our Favorite Summer Reads"

"TESTIMONY shows the great human toll when an entire section of the world descends into chaos...this novel is a legal thriller on a grand stage...Turow's descriptions of the causes and aftermath of the Bosnian war are both substantive and compassionate...sheds an unwavering light on the devastating human toll and the still-reverberating political aftershocks."

—*The ARTery*, WBUR

"Brilliant? Yes. Compelling? Yes. Complex? Yes. Fraught with misperceptions, twists and turns? Yes....Turow knows how to tell a good story."

—*Free Lance-Star* (VA)

"Engrossing...never without surprises and thrills."

—*Toronto Star*

"A suspenseful globe-trotter...Turow deftly explores identity as a theme both overt and subtle."

—*Writer's Digest*

"Turow weaves a tale of intrigue...there is never a dull moment."

—*News Herald* (MI)

"Satisfying and politically topical."   —*The Guardian*

"As always, Turow knows how to keep the story moving and keep the reader guessing as pieces fall into place or new questions arise."

—*Omnivoracious*

"I couldn't put this book down. It's simply terrific, intense, and comes right out of today's headlines…stunning!"

—*Providence Journal*

"Turow takes a bold step…TESTIMONY is a natural progression in Bill ten Boom's story and one that adds a deep complexity to his character. Rather than present just another case in the same old setting, Turow reinvents his protagonist by taking him out of his element. At the same time, Turow reinvents himself and reasserts his own mastery of the genre."

—*BookPage*

TESTIMONY

ALSO BY SCOTT TUROW

Testimony

Identical

Innocent

Limitations

Ordinary Heroes

Ultimate Punishment

Reversible Errors

Personal Injuries

The Laws of Our Fathers

Pleading Guilty

The Burden of Proof

Presumed Innocent

One L

TESTIMONY

SCOTT TUROW

GRAND CENTRAL
PUBLISHING

New York   Boston

PF
Turow

This book is a work of fiction. Names, characters, places, and incidents are the product of the author's imagination or are used fictitiously. Any resemblance to actual events, locales, or persons, living or dead, is coincidental.

Copyright © 2017 by Scott Turow
Cover design by Flag
Cover background image by EschCollection
Cover photograph of running man © Mark Owen/Trevillion Images
Cover photograph of paper background by Larry Washburn/Getty Images
Cover copyright © 2018 by Hachette Book Group, Inc.

Hachette Book Group supports the right to free expression and the value of copyright. The purpose of copyright is to encourage writers and artists to produce the creative works that enrich our culture.

The scanning, uploading, and distribution of this book without permission is a theft of the author's intellectual property. If you would like permission to use material from the book (other than for review purposes), please contact permissions@hbgusa.com. Thank you for your support of the author's rights.

Grand Central Publishing
Hachette Book Group
1290 Avenue of the Americas, New York, NY 10104
grandcentralpublishing.com
twitter.com/grandcentralpub

Originally published in hardcover and ebook by Grand Central Publishing in May 2017

First Mass Market Edition: November 2018

Grand Central Publishing is a division of Hachette Book Group, Inc. The Grand Central Publishing name and logo is a trademark of Hachette Book Group, Inc.

The publisher is not responsible for websites (or their content) that are not owned by the publisher.

The Hachette Speakers Bureau provides a wide range of authors for speaking events. To find out more, go to www.hachettespeakersbureau.com or call (866) 376-6591.

Library of Congress Cataloging-in-Publication Data

Names: Turow, Scott, author.
Title: Testimony / Scott Turow.
Description: First edition. | New York : Grand Central Publishing, 2017.
Identifiers: LCCN 2016057513| ISBN 9781455553549 (hardcover) | ISBN 9781455571185 (large print) | ISBN 9781478926900 (audio download) | ISBN 9781478926917 (audio book) | ISBN 9781455553525 (ebook)
Subjects: LCSH: War crimes—Bosnia and Herzegovina—Fiction. | Genocide—Bosnia and Herzegovina—Fiction. | Missing Persons—Investigation—Fiction. | BISAC: FICTION / Legal. | FICTION / Crime. | FICTION / General. | GSAFD: Suspense fiction. | Mystery fiction. | Legal stories.
Classification: LCC PS3570.U754 T47 2017 | DDC 813/.54—dc23 LC record available at https://lccn.loc.gov/2016057513

ISBN: 978-1-4555-5354-9 (hardcover), 978-1-5387-5996-7 (signed edition), 978-1-4555-7118-5 (large print hardcover), 978-1-4555-5352-5 (ebook), 978-1-4789-1849-3 (international paperback), 978-1-4555-5353-2 (trade paperback), 978-1-4555-5355-6 (mass market)

Printed in the United States of America
OPM
10 9 8 7 6 5 4 3 2 1

For Adriane

TESTIMONY

PROLOGUE

5 March 2015

"There were men," said the witness. He was lean and dark, the color of an acorn, and seated beside his lawyer at the small table reserved for testimony, he appeared as tense as a sprinter on the starting line.

"How many men?" I said.

"Eighteen?" he asked himself. "More. Twenty? Twenty," he agreed.

The witness's name was Ferko Rincic, but in the records of the International Criminal Court, he would be identified solely as Witness 1. To protect him, a shade closed off the spectators' section in the large courtroom, and electronically distorted versions of Ferko's voice and image were being transmitted to the few onlookers, as well as over the Internet. Standing several feet away at the prosecutor's table, I had just commenced my examination with the customary preliminaries: Ferko's age—thirty-eight, he said, although he looked far older—and where he lived on April 27, 2004, which was the place they called Barupra in Bosnia.

"And about Barupra," I said. "Did anyone share your house with you?"

Ferko was still turning to the right at the sound of the translator's voice in his headphones.

"My woman. Three daughters. And my son."

"How many children in all did you have?"

"Six. But two daughters, they already had men and lived with their families."

I picked up a tiny photo, creased and forlorn with wear.

"And did you provide me with an old photograph of your family when you arrived this morning?"

Rincic agreed. I announced that the photo would be marked as Exhibit P38.

"Thirty-eight?" asked Judge Gautam, who was presiding. She was one of three judges on the bench, all watching impassively in their black robes, resplendent with cuffs and sashes of royal blue. Following the Continental custom, the same odd white linen cravat I also wore, called a 'jabot,' was tied beneath their chins.

"Now let me call your attention to the computer screen in front of you. Is that photo there, P38, a fair resemblance to how your family looked on April 27, 2004?"

"Daughter third, she was already much taller. Taller still than her mother."

"But is that generally how you all appeared back then, you and your wife and those of your children still at home?"

He peered at the monitor again, his expression shrinking in stages to some form of resignation before at last saying yes.

I began another question, but Rincic suddenly stood up behind the witness table and waved at me, remonstrating in Romany, words the translator was too surprised to bother with. It took me an instant, therefore, to realize he was concerned about his photo. Esma Czarni, the English barrister *who had initially brought Ferko's complaint here to the International Criminal Court, rose beside him, drawing her torrents of dark hair close enough to briefly obscure Ferko while she sought to calm him. In the meantime, I asked the deputy registrar to return the old snapshot. When she had, Ferko studied it another second, holding it in both hands, before sliding the picture into his shirt pocket and resuming his place next to Esma.*

"And in P38, is that your house directly behind you?"

He nodded, and Judge Gautam asked him to answer out loud, so the court reporter could record his response.

"And what about these other structures in the background?" I asked. "Who lived in those houses?" 'House' was generous. The dwellings shown were no better than lean-tos, each jerry-rigged from whatever the residents of Barupra had salvaged. Timbers or old iron posts had been forced into the ground and then draped most commonly with blue canvas tarpaulins or plastic sheeting. There were also chunks of building materials, especially pieces of old roofs, which had been scavenged from the wreckage of nearby houses destroyed in the Bosnian War. That war had been over for nine years in 2004, but there was still no shortage of debris, because no one knew which sites had been booby-trapped or mined.

"The People," answered Ferko, about his neighbors.

"And is the word in Romany for 'the People' 'Roma'?"

He nodded again.

"And to be clear for the record, a more vulgar word in English for the Roma is 'Gypsies'?"

"'Gypsy,'" Ferko repeated with a decisive nod. That might well have been the only word of English he knew.

"Well, we'll say 'Roma.' Was it only Roma who lived in Barupra?"

"Yes, all Roma."

"*How many persons approximately?*"

"*Four hundred about.*"

"*And now let me ask you to look again at the computer screen. This will be Exhibit P46, Your Honors. Is that roughly how the village of Barupra appeared during the time you lived there?*"

Esma had secured a couple of photos of Barupra and the surrounding area, taken in 2000 by one of the international aid agencies. The picture I was displaying showed the camp from a distance, a collection of ragged dwellings clinging together at the edge of a forbidding drop-off.

"*And how long had you and the other Roma lived there?*"

Ferko seesawed his head. "*Five years?*"

"*And where had you and your family and the other people in Barupra—where had you been before that, if you can say?*"

"*Kosovo. We ran from there, 1999.*"

"*Because of the Kosovo War?*"

"*Because of the Albanians,*" he answered with another dismal wobble of his head.

"*So let us return then to the late hours of 27 April, 2004. About twenty men appeared in the Roma refugee camp at Barupra in Bosnia, correct?*" We waited again for the laborious process of translation to unfold a floor above the courtroom, where the interpreters were positioned behind a window. My questions were transformed first from English to French—the International Criminal Court's other official language—and then by a second translator into Romany, the Roma's own tongue. The answer came back the same way, like a wave rippling off the shore, finally reaching me in the female translator's plummy British accent. This time, though, the process was short-circuited.

"Va," answered Rincic in Romany as soon as he heard the question in his language, adding an emphatic nod. We all understood that.

"And what nature of men were they?" I asked. "Did they appear to have any profession?"

"Chetniks."

"And please describe to the Court what you mean by that word."

I leaned down to Goos, the tall red-faced investigator assigned to the case, who was seated next to me at the foremost prosecutor's desk.

"What the hell is a Chetnik?" I whispered. Up until that moment I had thought I was doing fairly well, having been on the job all of three days. There was nothing here I was familiar with—the courtroom, my colleagues, or the rigmarole of the International Criminal Court with its air of grave formality. The black robe I wore and the little doily of a tie beneath my chin made me feel as if I were in a high school play. This was also the first time in my life I had examined my own witness without the opportunity to speak to him in advance. I had first met Ferko Rincic in the corridor, only seconds before Esma escorted him into the courtroom. He had gripped the hand I offered merely by the fingertips in a mood of obvious distrust. I did not need anyone to tell me he would rather not have been here.

"They are supposed to be soldiers," said Ferko of the Chetniks. "Mostly they are just killers."

By now, Goos had inscribed his own note concerning the Chetniks in his uneven script on the pad between us: "Serb paramilitaries."

"And how were these Chetniks dressed?" At the witness table, Rincic himself wore weathered twill trousers, a collarless white shirt, a dark vest, and a yellowish porkpie hat,

*which none of us had thought to tell him to remove in the
courtroom. All of it—his long crooked nose that appeared to
have been broken several times, his hat, and his thick black
mustache, which might have been a smear of greasepaint—
made Ferko resemble a lost child of the Marx brothers.*

"*Army uniform. Fatigues. Flak jackets,*" *Ferko said.*

"*Were there any insignia or other identification on their
uniforms?*"

"*Not so I remember.*"

"*Were you able to see their faces?*"

"*No, no. They were masked. Chetniks.*"

"*What kind of masks? Could you make out any of their
features?*"

"*Balaclavas. Black. For skiing. You saw only the eyes.*"

"*Were they armed?*"

*Again Rincic nodded. To reemphasize the need to an-
swer aloud, Judge Gautam created a broadcast thump by
tapping on the silver microphone stalk that rose in front
of her, as well before Rincic and me, and at forty other
seats in the rows of desks ringing the bench. Those spots were
normally reserved for defense lawyers and victims' representatives, but they had no occupants for today's pre-trial
proceeding, in which the prosecutor was the lone party.*

*The large courtroom was a pristine exercise in Dutch
Modern, perhaps a hundred feet wide, with a bamboo floor,
and furnishings and wainscoting in yellowish birch, the
color of spicy mustard. The design impulse had favored the
basic over the grand. Decorative elements were no more
elaborate than wooden screens on the closed fronts of the desks
and on the wall behind the judges, where the round white
seal of the International Criminal Court also appeared.*

*Once Ferko had said yes, I asked, "Did you recognize the
weapons they carried?"*

"AKs," he answered. "Zastavas."

"Would that be the Zastava M70?" It was the Yugoslav Army version of the AK-47.

"And how is it that you can recognize a Zastava, sir?"

Ferko raised his hands futilely, while his face once more swam through a series of bereft expressions.

"We lived in those times," he said.

Goos called up a photo of the weapon on the computer screens, which rose around the courtroom, beside the microphones. It was a Kalashnikov-style assault rifle with a folding stock and a long wooden handguard above the curved ammunition magazine that projected with phallic menace. I had first seen Zastavas years ago in Kindle County, when I was prosecuting street gangs who were frequently better armed than the police.

"Now when the Chetniks arrived, where were you situated? Were you in your house?"

"No. I was in the privy." I already suspected the translator, with her upper-class accent, was significantly enhancing Ferko's grammar and word choice. Based on my very brief impression of him, I was fairly certain he had not said anything remotely like 'privy.'

"And why were you in the privy?"

When this question finally reached Ferko, he jolted back in surprise and slowly lifted his palms. Laughter followed throughout the courtroom—from the bench, the registry staff seated below the judges, and my new colleagues from the Office of the Prosecutor, a dozen of whom were at the desks behind me to watch this unprecedented hearing.

"Let me withdraw that silly question, Your Honors."

Goos, with his ruddy round face, was smiling up at me in good fellowship. The moment of comedy seemed to have suited everyone well.

"If I may lead, Your Honors: Had a need awakened you, Mr. Witness, and brought you to the privy in the middle of the night?"

"Va," said Rincic and patted his tummy.

"Now, if you were in the privy, sir, how were you able to see these Chetniks?"

"At the top of the door, there is a space. For air. There is a footstool in the privy. When I first heard the commotion as they came into the village, I opened the door a slice. But once I saw it was Chetniks, I locked the door and stood on the stool to watch."

"Was there any light in the area?"

"On the privy, yes, there was a small light with a battery. But there was some moon that night, too."

"And were you alone in the privy throughout the time you saw or heard the Chetniks?"

Several people around the courtroom giggled again, thinking I had once more stubbed my toe on the obvious.

"At first," Ferko said. "When the running and screaming started, I saw my son wander by. He was lost and crying, and I opened the door very quick and brought him in there with me."

"And how old was your son?"

"Three years."

"And once you had grabbed your son, what did you do?"

"I covered his mouth to keep him quiet, but once he knew he couldn't talk, I stood again on the stool."

"I want to ask you about that point in time when the screaming started. But before I do, let me turn to other things you might have heard. First of all, these Chetnik soldiers, did they speak at all?"

"Va."

"To the People or to themselves or both?"

"Both."

"All right. Now how did they speak to the People?"

"One had an electronic horn." He meant a power bullhorn.

"And what language did that soldier speak?"

"Bosnian."

"Do you speak Bosnian?"

He shrugged. "I understand. It is somewhat like they speak in Kosovo. Not the same. But I understand mostly."

"And did he sound like other Bosnians you had heard speaking?"

"Not completely. Right words. Like a schoolteacher. But still, on my ear, it was not right."

"Are you saying he had a foreign accent?"

"Va."

"And did the Chetniks speak to one another?"

"Very little. Mostly it was with the hands." Ferko raised his own slim fingers and beckoned in the air to demonstrate.

"They used hand signals?" There was a pause overhead. The term 'hand signal' apparently did not have an obvious equivalent in Romany. Eventually, though, Ferko again said yes.

"Did you hear the soldiers say anything to one another?" I asked.

"A few whispers when they were near the privy."

"And these words—what language was that?"

"I don't know."

"Was it any dialect of Serbo-Croatian? Croatian, Bosnian, Serbian? Do you understand those dialects?"

"Enough."

"And were the words you heard in any of those tongues?"

"No, no, I don't think so. To me, I thought it was foreign. Something foreign. I didn't recognize. But it was very few words."

"*And the man with the horn. What did he say first in Bosnian?*"

"*He said, 'Come out of your houses. Dress quick and assemble here. You are returning to Kosovo. Gather the valuables you can carry. Do not worry about other personal possessions. We will collect them all and transport them to Kosovo with you.' He repeated that many times.*"

"*Now, you say screaming started. Tell us about that, please.*"

"*The soldier continued yelling into the horn, but the other Chetniks went from house to house with their rifles and electric torches, waking everyone. They were very well organized. Two would enter, while other Chetniks made a circle outside with their rifles pointed.*"

Judge Gautam interrupted. She was about fifty, with a pleasant settled affect and long black hair in a contemporary flip. I had been warned, however, that she was not nearly as mild as she appeared.

"*Excuse me, Mr. Ten Boom,*" she said to me.

"*Your Honor?*"

"*The witness has just testified that the soldiers were speaking a foreign language and that it was not Croatian, Bosnian, or Serbian. That surely does not sound like Chetniks, does it?*"

"*I wouldn't know, Your Honor. I never heard the word before today.*"

Again the sounds of hilarity cascaded through the courtroom, most heartily behind me from the prosecutors. Both of the other judges laughed. Gautam herself managed a bare smile.

"*May I ask the witness a question or two to clarify?*" she said.

I swept a hand out grandly. There was not a courtroom

in the world where a lawyer could tell a judge to keep her thoughts to herself.

"You testified, Mr. Witness, that the soldiers were in fatigues. Was that camouflage garb?"

"Va."

"The same for each soldier or different?"

Ferko looked up to reflect. "The same, probably."

"And over the years in Kosovo and Bosnia, had you seen many soldiers in camouflage fatigues?"

"Many."

"And had you noticed that different armies and different military branches each had their own fatigues, with distinctive camouflage patterns and coloring?"

Ferko nodded.

"And on that night in 2004, when you saw these soldiers in fatigues, could you recognize the army or military branch they belonged to?"

Ferko again lifted his palms haplessly. "Yugoslav maybe?"

"But over the years had you noticed the fatigues of different countries sometimes resembled each other? Had you seen, for example, the similarity in the camouflage outfits of the Yugoslav National Army and the United States Air Force?"

Ferko gazed at the ceiling for a second, then waved his hands around vaguely.

"But in the dark, could you say whether these soldiers wore the Yugoslav uniforms or the American uniforms?"

Once the question reached him, Ferko shook his head and made a face.

"No," he said simply.

Judge Gautam nodded sagely. "Now Mr. Ten Boom," she said to me, "would you care to follow up in any way on my questions?"

On my notepad, Goos, who'd worked throughout the Balkans a decade ago, had written, 'NO USAF in Bosnia then.' Olivier Cayat, the law school friend who'd recruited me for the ICC, had briefed me on Judge Gautam. A former UN official in Palestine who had never actually practiced law, she was known to be part of the clique within the ICC disturbed that an American prosecutor had been assigned this case. But her insinuation that I might have been covering up for my countrymen was insulting—and unwarranted. She had just heard me go to considerable lengths to make sure Ferko mentioned that the gunmen were speaking a language he didn't know.

Having resumed my seat during the judge's questions, I took a second to adjust my robe as I again stood, preparing to ask Ferko if he'd seen even one member of the US Air Force on the ground in Bosnia at that time. From behind, Olivier discreetly pushed a folded note in front of me, which I opened below the level of the desk. 'IGNORE her,' it read. 'A trap.'

The attention of the courtroom was already focused on me, and I stood in silence before I understood. If I asked that question, Judge Gautam, who was guaranteed to have the last word, would add some public comment branding me as an apologist for the US. I ticked my chin down slightly to let Olivier know I'd gotten the point. The formal air of the ICC felt genteel as velvet, but the currents below were treacherous.

"No follow-up," I said.

"Well," the judge said, "given the witness's answers, and without objection from my colleagues, we will ask him to refrain from describing these men as 'Chetniks' and to refer to them simply as 'soldiers.' And would you do the same, please, Mr. Ten Boom?"

She attempted to smile pleasantly, but there was a lethal glimmer from her black eyes.

In the meantime, Esma slid her chair from the end of the desk and leaned close to Ferko again to explain the judge's direction. I had first met Esma last night, when we'd conferred about what I could expect Ferko to say. At one point, I had asked her to limit her conferences with Rincic in front of the court. His testimony would count for little if it looked like he was merely the mouthpiece for an experienced barrister. She had reassured me with a tart little smirk, amused that I thought I needed to school her about the dynamics of the courtroom. She'd proven her savvy by leaving behind the designer attire she'd worn yesterday, coming to court in a simple blue jumper and only a bit of makeup and jewelry.

I turned again to Ferko.

"Now you said, sir, there was screaming?"

"The women were yelling and carrying on to have strange men see them when they were not dressed. The children began crying. The men were angry. They rushed from the houses, sometimes wearing only shoes and underwear, cursing at the soldiers."

"And do you remember anything the people in Barupra said to these soldiers?"

"Sometimes the women cried out, 'Dear God, where would we be moving? We have no other home. This is our home now. We cannot move.' And some of the soldiers yelled, 'Poslusaj!'"

With Goos's help, I had Ferko explain that the term meant 'Do as we say.'

"In each house," Ferko said then, "the soldiers gave the People only a minute to leave. Then two or three soldiers would go in with their assault rifles pointed to check that

the place was empty. Often they just tore the house down as they swung the light of their torches this way and that."

I asked, "Now, had you ever heard before about any plans to move the residents of Barupra back to Kosovo?"

"When we came first, yes. But then, no more. Not for years."

"Did you yourself—did you want to go back to Kosovo?"

"No."

"Why?"

"Because the Albanians would kill the People. They had tried already. That was why we had come all the way to Bosnia. To be near the US base. We thought that close to the Americans we would be safe." He stopped for a second to reflect on that expectation.

"And by that you mean Eagle Base, established near Tuzla by the US Army, as part of NATO's peacekeeping efforts?"

A bridge too far. When the translation reached him, Ferko again stared comically and once more raised his palms, short of words.

"American soldiers. NATO. I know only that."

"Now, as the soldiers cleared the houses and the residents gathered in various collection points, what happened?" I asked.

"There were trucks that drove up from below."

"How many trucks?"

"Fifteen?"

"What kind of trucks?"

"For cargo. With metal sides. And the canvas over."

"Did you recognize the make?"

"Yugoslav, I thought. From the shape of the cab. But I didn't see for sure. They were military trucks."

"Now, as the vehicles arrived, did anything else unusual occur?"

"You mean the shooting?"

"Was there a shooting, Mr.—" I stopped. I had been about to use his name. "Please tell these judges of this Pre-Trial Chamber about the shooting."

With that, I turned to face the bench, the first time I had nakedly surveyed the court. Judge watching is usually a furtive exercise, since jurists, at least in the US, resent being studied for signs of their impressions. The three judges, all intent, occupied a bench raised only a couple of steps, a longer version of the Bauhausy yellow closed-panel desks in the well of the court. Beside Judge Gautam on her right sat Judge Agata Hallstrom, a lean sixtyish blonde who had been a civil court judge in Sweden, and on the left, Judge Nikolas Goodenough from Trinidad, the former chief justice of their Supreme Court. He never stopped scribbling notes.

"As they went from house to house," Ferko said, "the People would argue. They would shout, 'I'm not moving.' The women especially. The soldiers grabbed them and forced them out, and if they resisted, the soldiers struck them with their rifles, the butts or the barrels. Twice, the soldiers fired their guns in the air in warning. Once, a soldier shot his rifle and a woman would still not move, and I then heard her scream as she rushed out: 'He burned me with his gun. He put the muzzle on me while it was still hot. I am marked for life.' There was much screaming and running about. But the soldiers, especially those in the outer circle, they remained—" Again a pause ensued as the translator searched for a word. "Stoic," she came up with at last, probably a million miles from what Ferko had actually said. "They stayed in position with their weapons pointed. But near the privy, one man, Boldo, when they got to his house, he stormed out with an AK of his own."

"Do you know why Boldo owned an AK?"

"Because he had the money to buy one," Ferko said, which produced another ripple of laughter in the courtroom. Bosnia, even in 2004, was not a place where a person could be entirely sanguine about being unarmed.

"And did Boldo say anything?"

"Oh yes. He was shouting, 'We are not going. You cannot make us and we are not going.' The two soldiers who had been clearing his house fell to the ground. They yelled in Bosnian, 'Spusti! Spusti!'"

There was another silence as the translator came to a dead end, not knowing Bosnian. Below me, Goos muttered, "Put it down." For all his amiability, speaking Serbo-Croatian was, so far as I could tell, the only visible talent Goos brought to the job.

"Were they yelling 'Put it down' in Bosnian?"

"Va."

"And did he put it down?"

"No, no. He kept waving the AK around. The soldier in charge, who had the horn, he yelled again."

"In what language?"

"Bosnian. Then he counted, one, two, three, and fired. Boom boom boom. Boldo exploded with blood and fell like he had been chopped down. Then his son came running out of the house. The soldiers yelled again, 'Stani!'"

"Stay back," whispered Goos.

"The soldiers kept telling the son to stay away from the body and the gun, but of course it was his father, and when the son went forward there was gunfire from the other side. Two or three shots. He fell, too."

"And how old was Boldo's son?"

"Fourteen? A boy." Again, Ferko worried his head about in mournful wonder. "Finally, Boldo's brother ran up from his house. He was screaming and cursing. 'How could you shoot my family? What did they do?' He was weeping and carrying on. He fell to the ground, near the bodies. And he picked up Boldo's AK. After the two shootings, the soldier who seemed to be in charge, the one who killed Boldo, he ran up and waved and gave orders. He pushed the soldier who had shot Boldo's son away. And he ordered other soldiers forward to grab Boldo's brother. They wrestled with him quite a while. The brother was screaming and he would not let go of the AK. They hit him with their rifle butts a few times, but on the last occasion, the blow hit one of the other soldiers instead of Boldo's brother and that soldier fell. At that point, the commander ordered the soldiers back and he said to Boldo's brother, like Boldo, that if he did not drop the AK before the count of three, he would be shot. Instead, Boldo's brother raised the AK, and the commander shot him, too. Just once. In the side. The brother fell down and held his side and made terrible sounds."

"Did they administer medical treatment to him?"

"No, he was there moaning the whole time."

"And what became of Boldo's brother?"

"He died. He was still there in a large circle of blood in the dirt when I came out of the privy later."

"And about the words the commander yelled to his troops—did you understand them?"

"No, no. But there was much shouting. The People were screaming to get back. And take cover."

"And after the gunfire stopped, what was the mood in the camp, if you can say?"

"Quiet. Like in church. The People went to the trucks. They didn't yell. They didn't want to get killed. The soldiers helped them up. As the houses were cleared, the trucks drove off. The camp was empty in perhaps twenty minutes after the last shots."

"*Now when the trucks drove off, in what direction were they going?*"

"*They went west, down toward the mine.*"

I had a topographical map, which I doubted Ferko would understand. It depicted the valley adjacent to Barupra and the switchback gravel road that descended to where a large pit had been excavated.

"*And what kind of mine was in the valley?*"

"*Coal, they said. It closed because of the war.*"

"*And what variety of coal mine was it? With shafts or open pit?*"

"*They dug for coal. Scraped up the earth. It was the brown coal.*"

"*And how far from the village was the mining area?*"

"*A kilometer perhaps, down the road.*"

"*Now, once the trucks left, did you ever hear the horn again?*"

"*Yes, I heard the horn again. It echoed back off the hill.*"

"*What was said?*"

"'*Get out of the trucks. You will wait here in the Cave for the buses that will take you to Kosovo. We will go pick up your belongings now and they will follow you in the trucks.*'"

"*And by 'the Cave,' what did you understand the bullhorn to be referring to?*"

"*The Cave,*" said Ferko.

"*What cave was that?*"

"*The cave he was talking about.*"

Beside me, Goos pinched his mouth to keep from laughing.

"*Part of the mine was an area the People called the Cave?*"

"*Va.*"

"*Now, calling your attention again to the computer screen at your desk—this will be P76, Your Honors—does that photograph depict the Cave more or less as it was in April 2004?*"

This was another photo that Esma had turned up, in this case from the New York Times. The picture had been snapped from a distance in January 2002. It showed dozens of people scavenging coal in the harsh winter with their bare hands, many of them stout older women in headscarves, crawling along the incline below Barupra. We had enlarged and cropped the photograph to better depict the landscape. Apparently, years before, a vein of coal had been discovered in the hillside, and heavy equipment had gouged out a deep oblong opening. That was the Cave. With its huge overhang, the site did not look especially stable, and in fact there were yellow signs in Bosnian telling people to keep out: ZABRANJEN ULAZ.

"*How large was the Cave? Can you estimate its measurements?*"

"*Several hundred meters across.*"

"*And how deep into the hill did it go?*"

"*Fifty meters. At least.*"

"*Was it large enough that everyone from Barupra could stand inside the Cave?*"

"*More or less.*"

"*Now, did you hear anything further from the horn?*"

"*Yes. Eventually, he started repeating, 'Step back. Crowd in. Everyone into the Cave. Everyone. No exceptions. We need to count you and take your names. We will let you out one by one to do a census. Stay put. Stay put. You will be there only a few minutes.'*"

"*Now when these instructions were given, where were you?*"

"*Once the trucks and the People were all gone, I came out of the privy. My son and I hid in what remained of one house where I could look down into the valley.*"

"*And could you see the Cave?*"

"*Not so much. I could see the headlamps of the trucks better. In that light, I saw them pushing the People back.*"

"*And what happened with the vehicles?*"

"*The trucks? After several minutes, they started to move again. I thought they were going to come back up to collect everyone's belongings, as the horn had said. I picked up my son and was ready to run back to the privy, but I saw the lights going off in the other direction, further down to the valley floor, and then across it to the other road.*"

"*West?*" I asked.

He simply threw his hand out to indicate the direction.

"*And did you hear the horn at all after the trucks moved?*"

"*Yes, but it seemed fainter.*"

"*What was the horn saying?*"

"*The same. 'Stay put. Stay put.'*" This time Ferko repeated the words in Bosnian. "*'Ostanite na svojim mjestima.'*"

"*And what did you observe next?*"

"*Next?*" He waited. For the first time, a tremble of emotion moved through Ferko's long face. He grabbed the bridge of his nose before starting again. "*Next, I saw flashes on the hill above the Cave and heard the explosions. Six or seven. And I could hear the hill tumbling down.*" Without being asked, Ferko waved his hands over his head and imitated the sound, like a motorcycle's rumble. "*The earth and the rock rushing down were almost as loud as the explosions. It went in waves. The roar lasted a full minute.*"

"*Did you believe that the explosions had started a landslide?*"

"Va."

"And what did you do next?"

"What could I do? I was terrified and I had my son. I hid with him under a tarp in case the soldiers came back. Half an hour perhaps I waited. It was suddenly so still. Every now and then there was the sound of wind. Under the tarp, I could feel the dust still settling out of the sky."

"Now after that half an hour, what did you do?"

"I told my son to remain under the plastic. Then I ran down into the valley."

"Did you go to the Cave?"

"Of course. But it was gone. The hill above it had tumbled down. The Cave was almost completely filled in and rocks now blocked the road."

"And what did you do then?"

"What could I do?" He shook his head miserably. He was weeping now, in spite of himself. He wiped his nose and eyes against his sleeve. "I called my woman's name and my children's names. I called for my brother and his children. I called and called and scrambled over the rocks, climbing and calling and pulling at the rocks. God himself only knows how long. But there was no point. I knew there was no point. I could claw at the rock the rest of my life and get no closer. I knew the truth."

"And what truth was that, sir?"

"They were dead. My woman. My children. All the People. They were dead. Buried alive. All four hundred of them."

Although virtually everyone in the courtroom—the judges, the rows of prosecutors, the court personnel, the spectators behind the glass, and the few reporters with them—although almost all of us knew what the answer to that question was going to be, there was nonetheless a terrible

*drama to hearing the facts spoken aloud. Silence en-
shrouded the room as if a warning finger had been raised,
and all of us, every person, seemed to sink into ourselves,
into the crater of fear and loneliness where the face of evil
inevitably casts us.*

*So here you are, I thought suddenly, as the moment lin-
gered. Now you are here.*

I.

The Hague

1.

Reset—8 January 2015

At the age of fifty, I had decided to start my life again. That was far from a conscious plan, but in the next four years, I left my home, my marriage, my job, and finally my country.

These choices were greeted with alarm or ridicule by virtually everyone close to me. My sister thought I was still recovering from the deaths in quick succession of our parents. My law partners believed I had never adjusted to life outside the spotlight. My ex dismissed it all as an extended form of middle-aged madness. And my sons were alternately flabbergasted and enraged that their stolid father had become as flighty as a teenager just when they seemed to have found their own footing as adults. I ignored them all, because my life had crashed against the rock of a large truth. For all of my success, in looking back I couldn't identify a moment when, at core, I had felt fully at home with myself.

My exile to Holland and the International Criminal

Court was not a guaranteed solution, but it was the proverbial door that opened as another one closed. What had actually appeared in my doorway was my law school friend, Roger Clewey.

"Boom!" he screamed and, on his way to seize my hand, picked a path among the open cardboard boxes that blocked most of the floor in my corner office. For three days now, I had been sitting with a trash can between my legs, largely stalled in my efforts to move out. Effective January 1, 2015, I had resigned as a partner at DeWitt Royster, where I had worked for the last fourteen years, heading the firm's white-collar criminal defense practice. Someone with a more ruthless nature could have packed up in a matter of hours, but I found myself lingering over virtually everything I touched—law books, desktop tchotchkes, photos of my sons at various ages, and dozens of plaques and pen sets and hunks of crystal I'd been awarded during my four-year stint, a decade and a half back, as United States Attorney, the chief federal prosecutor here in Kindle County. Walloped by emotion and the force of time, I'd return from my memories to find myself staring down forty floors at the snowy patchwork of the Tri-Cities and the thread of gray that was the River Kindle, frozen over in yet another lousy winter in our new climate of greenhouse extremes.

"They say you've cashed out here," Roger said.

"Retired before they threw me out is more the truth of it."

"Not their version. Your sons okay?"

"From what they tell me. Pete's engaged now."

"You expected that," Roger said, correctly. "What's with *your* personal life?" he asked. "Still enjoying the post-divorce fuckfest?"

"I think I'm past it," I answered, a more convenient reply than telling him I had never quite gotten started.

Roger and I had met at Easton Law School more than thirty years ago. From there, Rog had entered the Foreign Service, acting as the legal officer attached to several embassies. For a while I thought I knew what he was doing. Then his assignments in various hotspots, like the Balkans, Afghanistan, and Iraq, left him with duties he could never discuss. Over time, I'd taken it for granted that he was a spook, although I was never sure which agency he worked for. Recently, his story was that he was back at the State Department, although if you'd been using a diplomatic cover, I'm not sure you could ever renounce it. He had the habit of turning up in Kindle County with little warning and an uncanny ability to know when I was in town, which I eventually realized might have been more than good luck.

"And what happens now?" he asked.

"God knows. I think I'm going to give myself a year of summer, follow the sun around the world. Swim and hike, work out every day, look up old buds, dine al fresco at sunset, then spend the evening reading everything I've always meant to."

"Alone?"

"To start. Maybe I'll meet someone along the way. I'm sure the boys will take a couple of trips, if the destination is neat enough. And I pay."

"Want to know what I think?"

"You're going to tell me anyway."

"You'll be bored and lonely in a month, a sour gloomy Dutchman wondering what the fuck he did."

I shrugged. I was pretty sure it was going to be better than that.

"Besides," said Roger, "there's a terrific opportunity for you. Any chance you've spoken to Olivier in the last couple of hours?"

Olivier Cayat was another law school classmate. He had been far closer with Roger back then, but about ten years ago he had come down to Kindle County from Montreal to join me in the defense of a Canadian executive who'd shown striking imagination in the ways he'd pilfered his corporation's treasury. We'd lost the trial but become far better friends. More recently, Olivier had gone off on a midlife frolic of his own to the Netherlands, where he'd consistently reported himself to be quite happy.

Roger said, "Olivier claims you've been ignoring his messages for a week."

At year-end, I'd created automated replies on the firm's voice and e-mail systems explaining that I'd resigned effective January 1 and would no longer be checking in regularly, which, at least for the first week, meant I had not checked at all. I thought it was better to go cold turkey. Nonetheless, with Roger watching, I turned to the computer behind me and poked at the keyboard until I'd located the first of what proved to be four e-mails from Olivier starting New Year's Day.

"*Mon ami*," it read, "please call. I have something to discuss that might excite you."

I revolved again toward Roger.

"And remind me, Rog. Where the hell is Olivier working in Holland?"

"The International Criminal Court in The Hague. It's a permanent war crimes tribunal. He's one of the top prosecutors there, but Hélène wants him home." Roger allowed himself a meaningful pause and then added, "Olivier thinks you're the right guy to replace him."

After a pause of my own, I asked, "So your big idea for me is to go back to being a prosecutor?" I had been chosen as United States Attorney in Kindle County by pure fortuity in 1997, largely so our senior senator, who made the recommendation to the White House, didn't have to pick between two other candidates, both political heavyweights who hated each other's guts. By then I'd been a prosecutor in the office for close to twelve years, including two as first assistant, the top deputy. Yet at thirty-seven, I was a decade too young for the responsibility and had to quell my terror of messing up every morning for months. With time, I came to feel I had the greatest job possible for a trial lawyer—electric, challenging, and consequential. Nevertheless, I told Roger I had no interest in moving backward. That Greek philosopher had it right when he said you couldn't step in the same stream twice.

"No, no," he said. "This would be different. They prosecute mass atrocities. Genocide. Ethnic cleansing. Mutilation, rape, and torture as instruments of war. That kind of stuff."

"Rog, I don't know a damn thing about cases like that."

"Oh, bullshit. It's all witnesses and documents and forensics, just on a larger scale. The crimes are horrible. But evidence is evidence."

He'd moved a box and plunked himself down in an armchair, going at me as comfortably as he had for thirty years. These days his trousers were pushed below his belly, and his hair was a curly white horseshoe with a couple of those embarrassing untrimmed wires sticking straight out of his glossy scalp. He had taken on that middle-aged WASP thing of looking like he'd worn the same suit every day for the last twenty years, as if it were plebeian to care much about his appearance. His shoes, sturdy and expensive when purchased, had not been polished since then. And I doubted he owned more than two or three ties. It was just a uniform he donned each morning. He played for a team whose stars were nondescript.

"And Rog, why is it you're in my office carrying Olivier's water? Do you have a professional interest in this of your own?"

"Some," he said. "There's a case over there that the government of the United States would hate to see end up in the wrong hands."

"What kind of case?"

"Do you know where Bosnia is?" he asked.

"East of anyplace I've been."

"In 2004, there was a refugee camp outside of Tuzla. All Romas."

"Gypsies?"

"If we're not being PC."

"Okay. Some Gypsies," I said.

"Four hundred. All murdered."

"At once?"

"So they say."

"By?"

Roger drew back. "Well, that's where things get opaque."

"Okay. And 2004—is the Bosnian War over by now?"

"Oh yeah. For years. The Dayton Accords ended the war in 1995. Nine years later, the Serbs and the Croats and the Bosniaks, meaning the Muslims, have pretty much stopped killing each other. And NATO is there enforcing the agreement, which amounts to rounding up tons of weapons and chasing down the war criminals wanted for trial in The Hague. The NATO force includes about eighteen hundred US troops in a ring of camps near Tuzla."

"I.e., close to the Gypsies."

"Very close. Couple miles."

"And why would a bunch of American kids, who are there to keep the peace, want to kill four hundred Gypsies?"

"They didn't. Stake my life on it."

"Who did?"

"You know, to take down four hundred people at once, that's some serious firepower. So it's not a long list of other suspects. Serb paramilitaries are most likely. Maybe rogue cops. Maybe organized crime. A lot of that back then. And some leftover jihadis, too, who'd shown up in Bosnia originally to defend the Bosnian Muslims from the Serbs."

"Well, it doesn't sound like the American military has much to worry about."

"Not so fast. Now we enter the realm of diplomacy and politics."

I groaned reflexively. Politics and prosecution never mixed well.

"The ICC," said Roger, "was established by a treaty negotiated by most of the UN member states, including the US. Clinton signed it in 2000, but the Bushies hated the whole idea, especially Dick Cheney, who supposedly was afraid he'd get prosecuted for authorizing waterboarding. So Bush announced in 2002 that he's unsigning the ICC treaty."

"Can you do that? Unsign?"

"Do you think that mattered? Instead, the Republicans, who controlled Congress, passed something called the American Service-Members' Protection Act, which basically says if you try to put our troops on trial, we'll invade your fucking country and take them home."

"Literally?"

"I don't think they used the word 'fucking.' Otherwise, that's a reasonably accurate legislative summary. In Western Europe, they call it 'The Hague Invasion Act.'"

"So you're saying that if the ICC charges American troops, we're going to war with the Netherlands?"

"Let's just say it risks creating very serious rifts with our closest allies. The mere thought gives angina to whole floors in the Departments of State and Defense."

"Is that why the case is still hanging around after eleven years? Because people like you have been trying to obstruct it?"

"First, for the record," said Roger, with a coquettish grin, "I object to the word 'obstruct.' We have simply expressed our point of view to various authorities. And a lot of the delay had nothing to do with us. Even the Roma organizations didn't start investigating for several years, because the only survivor was hiding under his bed, trying to shovel the poop out of his trousers. And frankly, if you ask me, I haven't been able to obstruct the damn thing well enough. Several weeks ago, the prosecutor's office at the ICC applied to the Court to open a formal investigation, largely because the flipping Roma activists keep screaming, How can four hundred people get massacred and nobody even looks into it?"

"Sorry, Rog, but that sounds like a pretty good question."

Roger tipped a shoulder. He didn't really disagree. On the other hand, he had a job to do.

"And what do we mean by 'Roma activists'?" I asked.

"How much do you know about the Roma?" he asked.

I let my eyes rise to the fluorescent panels in my office ceiling and concluded that an honest answer was, "Next to nothing."

"Well, it's not the kind of contest anybody wants to win, but even taking account of the genocides of the Armenians and the Kurds and of course the Jews, there may not have been another group of white people on earth who have had the shit kicked out of them more consistently for the last millennium than the Roma." Roger hunkered forward and lowered his voice. "Basically, they've been the niggers of Europe." He meant that was how they'd been treated. "They were slaves in Romania for four hundred years. Did you know that?"

"The Gypsies?"

"It never stops with them. Hitler tried to wipe them out. Ninety thousand fled Kosovo. And Sarkozy just booted a couple thousand out of France a few years back. Everybody from Athens to Oslo hates their guts."

"They're thieves, right?"

"You mean every single one of them?"

"No, just enough to get them hated."

"Enough for that. Pickpockets, scam artists, credit card fraudsters, child gangs, car thieves, phony beggars. The Gypsy caravan rolls through town and a lot of crap disappears. That's the old story. On the other hand, they can barely get jobs or go to school, so I don't know what else is gonna happen."

"Okay," I said, "so now I feel sorry for the Gypsies, but I still don't see a starring role in this drama for me."

"I'm getting there," he answered. "The ICC is ambivalent about the USA. They hate us for not joining. But they need us in the long run. An operation like theirs is never going to be on solid ground without the support of the most powerful nation on earth. So they'd rather not piss us off irreparably. Which means there's been a lot of back-channel stuff."

"And 'back channel' means Olivier and you?"

"It means we've been the messenger boys between our bosses. But after weeks of discussion, everyone seems to believe that the best option would be if the ICC investigation was led by a senior American prosecutor."

"Sort of a special prosecutor?"

"Sort of. But no formal title like that. It has to be the right person. Not a patsy. Somebody they respect and we respect. For us, that means a quality guy whose reputation is bulletproof when some yahoo in Congress wants to foment a world crisis just because there's an inquiry occurring at the ICC."

"And that's me?" I said, with genuine incredulity. "The man with built-in body armor?"

"You still have a lot of fans on both sides of the aisle in DC, Boom."

That was an exaggeration for the sake of flattery. I'd gotten along well with the Attorney General during her prior stint as deputy AG and also had a college friend who was now a Republican senator from Kentucky.

"Rog, have I read about this case?"

"Not really. The major papers haven't tumbled to it. Couple items in the blogosphere. The Roma advocates, they've tried to gin something up, but the massacre is old news, and so far you can't name a bad guy, so it doesn't make good copy. All fine with us."

"And how long will this investigation last?"

He tossed up a hand to show he couldn't say, but acknowledged that such matters often moved slowly.

"But because of that," he said, "cases over there are like buses. People get on and off. Whenever you're fed up, you can leave."

I laid a finger across my lips to think.

"Wait," Roger said. "I haven't even sold the Dutch part. I thought you'd love the whole *Roots* thing. You've never spent any real time in the Netherlands, right?"

"No," I said, "my folks never wanted to go back." I had yet to tell Roger the larger, more complicated story of my heritage. Now, however, was not the moment.

Instead, I sat back in my big leather desk chair, doing my best to be lawyerly, calculating all the angles and scrutinizing Roger. The competitive side of our relationship meant he'd never fully reveal what he was up to. But as a friend of decades, he knew I'd find the job intriguing. Even after I'd announced my retirement here, I'd sensed I was not done with the law. I didn't think practice mixed well with capitalism, but I still liked what lawyers did and was immediately attracted to the idea of plying a trade I knew overseas.

"Look, Rog. We'll ignore the fact that you're selling a job you have no right to offer. Olivier and his people will have to speak up for themselves. But it's obvious you want to replace one friend of yours with another. So I'm not even going to dial The Hague unless you look at me and say that I'll be doing this straight up, chips fall where they may."

Roger sat forward again and let me see his soft eyes deep within the sad little pouches of aging flesh.

"Wherever Jesus flings 'em," he said.

2.

The Hague—2 March 2015

By the end of January, after many calls with Olivier, often two or three a day, I had accepted a formal job offer from the International Criminal Court. It required another month to wind things up in Kindle County—rent my condo, store my stuff—and to square things with Willem and Piet, my sons. (Ellen and I had given our boys Dutch names, thinking it would inspire my parents to educate the boys about their heritage. That hope proved misplaced, and my sons had started calling themselves Will and Pete by the time they entered first grade.) Now both seemed disconcerted by the prospect of my departure, which frustrated me privately. For the last several years, while my sons worked out their anger with me for ending my marriage, they had acted like it was a form of forced labor to share my company for a meal every couple of weeks.

On Sunday, March 1, I boarded an overnight flight to Schiphol, Amsterdam's international airport. I was several days ahead of my original schedule, because the Pre-Trial Chamber had unexpectedly ordered the Office of the Prosecutor to present Ferko's testimony later that week. At Schiphol, I found the Intercity, the blue-and-yellow fast train that connects Holland's major cities. An hour later, I was sitting in The Hague's central square, the Plein, absorbing the morning pace of Dutch life and trying to quell my jet lag with coffee and what passed for daylight.

Once I was in the Netherlands, I began to understand why their transcendent painters, say Rembrandt or Vermeer, were obsessed with light and shadow. The winter gloom was even worse than in Kindle County, which I always described as like living under a pot lid. On the day I arrived, the wind blustered through a sky of dun scraps.

Despite the weather, The Hague struck me as an elegant dowager of a town with a cheerful cosmopolitan air. In its old center, stout brown-brick buildings, with their steep slate roofs and brightly trimmed windows, dated back centuries and created a feeling akin to heavy wool. Across the open stretches of the Plein, beyond the ever-present bicyclers, I saw an old palace, the Ridderzaal, whose pointed turrets like witches' hats were vaguely reminiscent of Disneyland. I rolled my suitcase a block and stopped on a bridge to watch the ice-skaters whiz along on a canal below, their heavy scarves flying behind them as they braved the ice despite the temperature in the low 40s. I loved the place on sight.

Eventually, I took a taxi to the chain hotel the ICC uses to stash visitors, where the cramped lobby seemed to aspire to a youthful affect with overhead accent lights of optic lime and mauve. Upstairs, in a room smaller than some high-end refrigerators, I called Olivier to reconfirm our meeting at the Court, then opened my case and started shaking out my suits.

As I learned in time, one of the defining characteristics of the Dutch was that they adhere proudly to what others might regard as eccentricities. Thus, I found that in a country about the size of Maryland, two cities shared the traditional functions of a capital. Amsterdam played that role by law. But The Hague had long been the seat of government. While Amsterdam was a renowned commercial center, in The Hague the main business was, basically, idealism. About 150 different international entities were situated there, including various organs of the UN and the European Union, and scads of international NGOs: the Organisation for the Prohibition of Chemical Weapons, the African Diaspora Policy Centre. High-minded stuff like that. The city was also home to more than a hundred embassies and consulates. As a result, perhaps as many as an eighth of the one million inhabitants in The Hague's metro area were expats. English was spoken virtually everywhere as a second language.

Over time, The Hague's status as a unique international center had led to a new growth industry—global justice. Nine different independent international tribunals operated there. The International Court of Justice, just to name one, was where countries sued each other. The newest additions were criminal courts, established in recent decades by the United Nations to prosecute atrocities in different wars—Cambodia, Lebanon, Sierra Leone, Rwanda. When I arrived, all of these tribunals, even those that were decades old, were still working on prosecutions, offering silent tribute to the unwillingness of any bureaucracy to go out of business.

By many standards, the most successful of the ad hoc criminal courts was the International Criminal Tribunal for the Former Yugoslavia, which laid charges against 160 of the Serbian, Croatian, Bosniak, and Kosovar leaders who perpetrated the mass slaughters and other horrors of the Balkan wars. Although the Yugoslav court was still working its way through pending trials, it closed its doors to new cases in 2004. The International Criminal Court, which opened in 2002, became in every practical sense, from inherited personnel—including judges, lawyers, and administrators—to shared procedures, the Yugoslav Tribunal's far larger offspring.

By the late 1990s, the UN had recognized that the proliferation of special criminal forums in The Hague bespoke one sad fact: Genocide and wartime atrocities were not about to end. Negotiations commenced on a global treaty to establish a permanent war crimes court, the ICC. Yet as those talks wore on, more and more of the world's powers recognized the perils of submitting to criminal penalties controlled by foreigners. Not only the US, but also Russia, China, Israel, India, Pakistan, North Korea, and most of the Arab nations refused to join. The Europeans, the Latin nations, and the Africans signed on, all deeply chagrined with the US and other countries for backing out.

An hour later, I presented myself at the prison-like entry to the ICC. At the foot of two conjoined white high-rises, the security checkpoint was closed off on three sides by ten-foot iron gates, buttressed by chain link and topped by five taut lines of barbed wire.

Eventually, Olivier appeared in his shirt and tie, but with no jacket. Without Hélène around regularly to keep

an eye on him, he had gained at least thirty pounds.
His fine features were now puddled in flesh and his mid-
section looked like a globe was hidden under his shirt.
His warm, emphatic manner, however, was unaltered,
and he lit up like a boy as soon as he saw me, hugging
me strongly once I'd been buzzed through the revolving
doors.

He ushered me upstairs to the spartan office that in
a matter of days would become mine. We sat at a small
table just inside the door, chatting about our kids and
my departure from Kindle County, before turning to the
job.

"It will frustrate you at times," he said then. "I
shouldn't pretend. Do you know the phrase 'With great
power comes great responsibility'? At the ICC you get
great responsibility and no power. You are investigating
the worst crimes committed on earth, with little if any
functional authority to compel witnesses to speak to
you—even the victims—or documents to be surren-
dered." He sat back in his Aeron chair and rested his
hands behind the shrub of graying hair that ringed his
bare scalp. "I must admit to you that if the decision were
mine, I probably would not have moved forward on this
Roma case."

"Now you tell me," I said, smiling. On the phone,
Olivier had actually said more than once that the case
would be 'a challenge.'

"One problem," said Olivier, "which you surely understand, is that the event in question took place eleven
years ago. These investigations—'situations' as they call
them here, to be delicate—are like trying to chase an
echo in the best of circumstances. You charge a general
and at trial he pretends to have been a nun: 'Show me

the order that says "Shoot." Or "Burn." Or "Rape."'
Now, when memories are stale and records are gone, the
problems of proof in your case are likely to be insur-
mountable.

"But the largest obstacle will be the US military. The
Service-Members' Protection Act prohibits any American assistance in an ICC investigation, even to point the
finger at someone else. Since the US Army was in control of this area where the alleged massacre occurred, it
is guaranteed that a mass of significant evidence will be
beyond you."

"So then why did the powers-that-be here decide to
proceed?"

He smiled mystically, while the back of his hand
trailed off in space in that worldly French way.

"The prosecutor and the chief deputy felt no obligation to explain to me," he said. "But many here would
regard declining to investigate as rewarding American in-
transigence. Also, I'm sure you have noticed where all
thirty-six of the defendants this Court has charged happen to reside."

I had. Every case the Court had brought in its
thirteen-year history arose in Africa—Congo, Kenya, the
Ivory Coast, Libya as examples. Failing to pursue an investigation that could culminate in charges against white
folks risked deepening the outrage about the ICC on the
African continent.

"But," said Olivier, raising a finger, "I have one positive note." He sat forward, folding his pudgy hands, as
if this truth required some formality. "I regard this as
the best job I've ever had as a lawyer, even better than
my years as a crown prosecutor. If I could dislodge
Hélène from Montreal, I would stay another decade."

"And what's the good part? The mission?"

"Yes, the overall mission is noble. For most of recorded history, the victors in wars have not even pretended to do justice. They simply executed the vanquished. But beyond that, the stakes here are so high that you will never question the value of your labors, as we all often do in private practice. You are responsible for bringing justice to four hundred souls. When you leave, stand in front of the Court and count the pedestrians going by until you reach that number. It will take a while. The importance of what you are doing, and the limited tools to accomplish it, will require extraordinary imagination from you. You will inspire yourself." He chortled a little at his own description, then slapped the desk.

"But now," he said, "work begins." He handed over the two-page order, which the Court had issued last week, requiring Ferko to testify before the Pre-Trial Chamber a couple of days from now.

In the US, a grand jury was supposed to supervise the investigative work of the prosecutor. At the ICC, the judges of the Pre-Trial Chamber played that role. Until the chamber approved, the Office of the Prosecutor— 'the OTP'—could not so much as ask a direct question of a potential witness. Before that, the only information on a case was what third parties, like newspapers or human rights organizations, had gathered.

In the last few weeks, I had read the ICC treaty, all the Court's rules, and the vast majority of its decisions. One fact stood out now: The Pre-Trial Chamber had never before called for live testimony in passing on an OTP application to investigate.

"True," Olivier said, "but we've all agreed it has some

validity. That is why we asked you to rush here early. In our cases, ordinarily there are hundreds of victims. In this one, there is a single survivor. The Court wants to be certain that he is truly willing to give testimony—and will make sense when he does. No point inviting controversy if it turns out he's missing a few tiles."

I accepted that, but confessed that I was less comfortable with the European practice that required me to present Witness 1's testimony without talking to him in advance, relying instead on a few prior statements.

"You will want to meet with this barrister, Esma Czarni," Olivier said. "She's from the European Roma Alliance, and found this gentleman in the first place. She's planning to be here." He rooted around on his desk and eventually handed over a Post-it with her number. He lifted a finger in warning. "You will find her disarming. Very bright. *Très jolie*," he said, accompanied by a little French wiggle of his eyebrows. "But very single-minded about the Roma cause."

By way of summation, he offered another hearty laugh, then turned with great enthusiasm to discussing our options for dinner.

3.

Going to Work—March 3–4

I spent most of Tuesday morning in an administrator's office at the Court, receiving manuals and signing forms. Despite being a relatively new organization, the ICC had already developed an encrusted bureaucracy, albeit one fairly typical of Western Europe, where clerks often act as if history will stop if certain documents are not properly executed.

The most pleasant surprise was my salary—€152,800 with various cost-of-living adjustments—which, somewhat embarrassingly, I'd never bothered to ask about. I still thought of myself as a frugal person of modest tastes, but money had ceased being an issue in my life a while ago. For more than a decade, I had earned more than $1 million a year at DeWitt Royster—often much more—even though I never really understood what lawyers did that was worth that kind of money. When I divorced, Ellen got the larger share of our savings, but it was easy for me to be generous because my parents had left behind a fortune. The millions my father had silently accumulated through decades of adept stock picking stunned both my sister Marla and me, but by then we'd both come to recognize our parents' intensely secretive nature.

In the afternoon, Olivier took me office to office, introducing me to colleagues, including the prosecutor himself, Badu Danquah, a former judge from Ghana, and Akemi Moriguchi, the porcupine-haired chief deputy, who barely seemed to speak.

Wednesday was dedicated to what little preparation I could undertake before the hearing the next day. I reread the petition the OTP had presented to the Court summarizing Witness 1's prospective testimony, as well as the office's internal file, compiled by the so-called situation analysts, which was not much more than a stack of articles about the political situation in Bosnia in 2004 and the history of the beleaguered Roma community there and in Kosovo.

Late that afternoon, I was finally able to meet with Esma Czarni. I had called her London mobile number right after receiving it from Olivier. She was in New York as it turned out, trying a case, and could not get to The Hague until very early Wednesday. She had already promised to spend most of the day with Ferko but agreed to see me afterward at 4 p.m. at her hotel.

The bright yellow Hotel Des Indes was a refuge of secure elegance. Square pillars of Carrera marble, along with dark wood and heavy brocades, dominated the lobby into which Esma bustled, a few minutes late. She came straight toward me.

"Bill ten Boom? You look just like your photos on the Internet." There were zillions from my prosecutor days.

She shook with a strong grip. "So, so sorry to have kept you. Have you been waiting long? Your witness was unsettled. First time he's even been close to an aeroplane."

She had not stopped moving, and waved me behind her to the elevator. She had a rich Oxbridge accent, like the older newsreaders on the BBC. Upper class.

"I have everything laid out," she said. "We can work and I shall order dinner when you care to. My appetite is several time zones behind us, but regrettably, I know it will catch up."

In Esma's corner suite, she threw off her coat and took mine, while I admired the room and, to be honest, Esma. I had heard Olivier say she was very pretty, but when I'd looked her up on the net, she'd proved camera shy. In person, she was striking, not exactly a cover girl but quite good-looking in an unconventional way. Framed within a great mass of fried-up black hair was a broad face of South Asian darkness, with supersize features: fleshy lips, an aquiline nose, feline cheekbones, and huge, imposing black eyes. In her designer suit, her figure was shapely if a trifle ample, and her large jewelry jingled as she moved around the room.

Esma offered me a drink, which I declined, but she was still dopey from travel and called down for coffee, which arrived almost instantly. Esma poured for each of us, and then we assumed seats in little round dressing-room chairs with upholstered skirts, beside the small round glass-topped table where Esma had piled her files.

I took a second for bridge-building, asking about her offices in London—'chambers,' as the Brits say. It turned out, as I'd hoped, that I knew another lawyer there, George Landruff, whose voice, loud enough to shake the pictures off the walls, provoked laughter from both of us when I referred to him as "soft-spoken." With that, it felt safe to ask about Witness 1 and what to expect with his testimony.

"Ferko?" It was the first time I'd heard his true name, which was blacked out in the situation analysts' file. "He is a simple man."

"Still terrified?"

"I believe I've calmed him." With members of the Court's Victims and Witnesses Unit, Esma had shown Ferko the courtroom and explained the basics. Judges. Lawyers. "You should find him well prepared to give evidence," she told me. "I went over his prior statements with him quite carefully. He understands that he should listen to your questions and attempt to answer directly. The Romany people, you know, don't like imparting information about themselves to the *gadje*—outsiders—so I expect you'll get concise replies."

"And how was it that you first met him?"

"With great persistence. I've been active with Roma organizations since I got to university. Self-interest, of course."

"You are Roma?"

"Raised in a caravan in the north of England." That meant she had exercised what the Brits regard as a right of the educated classes and had taken on today's posh accent in school. "In 2007, I joined the board of the European Roma Alliance. By then, rumors had reached Paris of a massacre of Roma in Bosnia a few years before. I went off to Tuzla to find out what I could. People had heard this tale of hundreds buried alive in a coal mine. But no one seemed to know more. Or even if it was true.

"Eventually, I went to a Roma village and was informed that a single survivor of Barupra remained in the vicinity. I received Ferko's mobile number, but he was too terrified to talk. I must have called him once a month for a year. I had all but given up and had decided to go to Kosovo, where the residents of Barupra came from. My thought was to prove the massacre circumstantially, by finding relatives who would confirm that all communications from Barupra ceased abruptly in April 2004. But I was spared the trip when Ferko at last decided to meet."

For the next hour, as I tapped furiously on my tablet, Esma read me line by line the notes of her many conversations with Ferko since 2008. Over the years, he had contradicted himself on some minor details—the time the trucks appeared, or how he found his son. That was normal with witnesses. If they tell you a story exactly the same way time after time, they often prove to have been coached or lying.

Midway through this recitation, Esma kicked off her high strappy heels and plunged down onto a sofa nearby, perching her legs on the scarlet cushions. She said she was one of those people who can't sleep on airplanes, and by now was going on roughly forty hours awake.

Esma's suite, like the rest of Des Indes, featured horse-hair furnishings the color of fresh blood, big mirrors with mahogany frames, and windows draped with French embroidery. It was a large room but without partition, so her bed was visible across the way.

In the meantime, I looked through the other information she had supplied the Court to corroborate Ferko's story. Using photographs and UN refugee reports, she'd established the presence of a Roma refugee camp of four hundred persons on the outskirts of Tuzla in April 2004. Their sudden disappearance was confirmed by affidavits from local police, provincial officials, and two nearby

Orthodox priests, who baptized the children and buried the dead in Barupra. Photographs showed the changes to the landscape of the coal mine below the camp in April 2004, and she'd obtained reports from two different seismographic stations that recorded a ground disturbance late on April 27. Finally, several residents of the nearest town, Vica Donja, had described, under oath, a truck convoy racing away from the mine in the wake of the explosion. Although it had taken eleven years to get to this point, the need to investigate seemed unassailable.

While I was reading this material, Esma announced she was hungry. She called down to room service, then covered the extension long enough to ask what I'd like. I requested fish.

"You did an impressive job with all this," I told Esma when she returned. Just as the greatness of many scientists lay in the design of their experiments, good lawyering required considerable inventiveness in assembling proof.

"You are kind to say so," she replied. "Not that it helped gain much interest from anyone with the authority to investigate further." She described a long journey of frustration. The Yugoslav Tribunal eventually concluded the case was outside the time limits on their jurisdiction. The prosecutors in Bosnia fiddled with the matter until 2013, but clearly feared antagonizing the US and worsening divisions in their fractured nation. Instead, the government of Bosnia and Herzegovina— BiH—referred the case to the ICC, empowering the Court to act with any legal authority BiH would have. Despite that, the file languished at the ICC until Esma threatened to stage demonstrations.

"But I cannot pretend to be surprised," she said. "The

truth, Bill, is that very few persons on this continent can be bothered with the Roma. The most literate, progressive, tolerant people will comment without self-consciousness about 'the dirty Gypsies.' You will see."

I asked how she explained such deep-seated prejudice. The question energized her, and she swung upright.

"I will not tell you, Bill, that the Roma have done nothing to inspire those attitudes. 'Roma' means 'the People.' Accordingly, you"—she pointed a polished nail at me—"are a nonperson against whom misbehavior—theft, fraud, even violence—requires no apology within the group. I daresay that attitude is inexcusable.

"But," she said, "we have been among you for more than a thousand years, since the Roma first migrated from India into Greece. And generation after generation, what has most infuriated Europeans about the 'Gitanos' or 'Celo' or 'Tziganes,' by whichever of a thousand names we are called, is our absolute stubborn insistence on living by our values, not yours. As a child, Bill, I was not taught to tell time. I never saw a Rom man wearing a watch. We go when all are ready. A small matter seemingly, but not if you wish to attend school or keep a job. Millions of us have assimilated to one degree or another, most notably in the US. But less so here in Europe."

Her mention of American Gypsies suddenly summoned a childhood memory of the tinker who pushed his cart down the streets of Kewahnee, where I was raised, singing out unintelligible syllables in an alluring melody. He carried a grinding wheel operated with a pedal, and I sometimes stood nearby and watched the sparks fly as he sharpened my mother's knives. In a rumpled tweed coat and a county cap, he was the color of tarnished brass, like a candlestick my mother once asked him to polish. But he knew his place. He did not even approach the doorways. The women of the neighborhood brought their cutlery or pans to him—and kept one hand on their children.

"And this commitment to remaining different has drawn from the *gadje* unrelenting persecution. Slavery. Floggings. Brandings. Organized arrests and executions. Towns we were forbidden to enter and settlements we were forbidden to leave. And a mythology of sins: That we are filthy, when the inside of a Rom house is spotless. That we steal children, when the hard truth is that Roma have often been forced to part with their offspring. That the women are whores, when in fact purity is prized."

With a knock, the waiter in a long frog-buttoned coat arrived, pushing a dining cart. I gallantly pulled out my credit card to pay, but Esma waved it aside, at which I felt some relief, since my training at the ICC had not gotten as far as expense reports.

After extending the sides of the cart to form a table and uncovering the meal, the waiter pulled the cork on a bottle of Entre-Deux-Mers and poured each of us a glass before I had time to object. The sole Esma had ordered for me was delicious and I thanked her.

"Oh yes. This is a lovely place." She buttered a roll and ate with relish. There was no delicacy in the way she attacked her food or waved her wine glass at me to refill it. "So tell me, Bill. What is your story?"

I started on my résumé, but she threw up the back of her hand.

"No, Bill. How does a successful American lawyer uproot himself and come to The Hague? Is it acceptable if I call you 'Bill'?"

"'Boom' is better. I haven't heard much of Bill since I was in junior high school." The pals who'd started calling me Boom in sixth or seventh grade were practicing irony. I was a quiet kid. But Esma wrinkled her nose at my nickname.

"I shall stay with 'Bill,' if you don't mind. And how was it that you decided to come here?"

I told her what I was only beginning to understand about myself, that I more or less started again at the age of fifty.

"The all-knowing Internet says you are divorced," she said.

"Four years plus," I answered.

"And was that bloody or mild?"

"Mild by the end."

"She more or less agreed?"

"Not at first. But once she reconnected with her high school boyfriend, about six months after I moved out, the divorce decree couldn't be entered soon enough."

"So no Other Woman?"

There had not been. Just terminal ennui.

"And how long were you married?" Now that we had roamed to the personal, Esma's black eyes were penetrating.

"Nearly twenty-five years when I left."

"Was the approaching anniversary the reason?"

"Not consciously. My younger son was about to graduate college. We'd teamed up to create this family and done it pretty well, I thought, in large measure due to Ellen, but now there didn't seem to be much to look forward to together."

"And since, Bill?" she asked. She produced a slightly naughty smile. "Many romances?"

I shrugged.

"Do you mind that I'm asking?"

"It seems a little one-sided."

"Yes, but my story is either an entire evening or a few words. No husbands, no children, a legion of lovers and none pending. Is that better?"

I shrugged about that, too.

"I've met a lot of nice people," I said. "But no one who's felt for very long that we could go the distance."

"And is that what you want? To go the distance?"

"I seem to have had that in mind when my marriage ended: doing better with someone else. But it's complicated. When you get to middle age, it turns out a lot of people are single for a reason. Including me, of course."

"And me as well," she said. "Although I think I'm rather quick to grow bored. And now the ladies are calling you, I wager?"

I lifted my shoulders one more time. "Being a successful middle-aged man who is suddenly single is a little like being the water boy for the football team who finds that a magic genie has turned him into prom king."

Esma clearly knew a lot about American culture, because she enjoyed the joke. But I was being honest about my distrust of my sudden rise on the social scale. Admittedly, in the fifties looks mattered less, because everyone had been damaged by time. I still had my lank blondish hair and remained tall and fairly fit. But I had thick features, and in high school and college knew I was not up to the pretty girls. In my senior year at Easton College, I'd been stunned that Ellen, who was clearly far above me in the mating order—smarter, cute by all measures, and a varsity runner—had been willing to go out with me, let alone stick with it. I still believe she felt a small egotistical thrill that she'd made a discovery other girls had missed; namely, that despite my occasional reserve, I could be an amusing wise guy.

Esma finally seemed to accede to my discomfort at this turn in the conversation and went off to the bathroom for a minute. When she returned, she got no farther than her bed. She stopped and flopped down on it dramatically, her arms thrown wide.

"I am entirely knackered," she said.

I apologized.

"My own fault," she said. "I should have held off on that third glass of wine."

As I was gathering my papers, I asked if she'd interviewed Ferko's son. She had, but the young man remembered nothing of these events, which had occurred when he was only three years old.

"And what was the local scuttlebutt," I asked, while I was zipping my briefcase, "when you first went to Tuzla about who was responsible for this massacre?"

"No more than idle guesses. The Serbs. The Americans."

"Any mention of organized crime?"

"Once or twice. Supposedly a few Roma in Barupra were involved in a car-theft ring and the local mob resented the competition."

"What about jihadis?"

Still prone across the room, she drew her hand to her forehead to think and said that had not come up.

"And what motives," I asked, "did the Americans or the Serb paramilitaries supposedly have for killing four hundred people?"

She hummed tunelessly, trying to recall.

"There was always a bit of speculation that the Roma were slaughtered in reprisal for a bungled American attempt to capture Laza Kajevic earlier in April 2004. Do you know who he is?"

"The former leader of the Bosnian Serbs? Of course."

A lawyer by training, Kajevic had the same talent as Hitler, making his gargantuan self-importance a proxy for his country's and his rantings the voice of his people's long-suppressed rage. Connecting Kajevic to the Roma's murders, however, sounded a little like blaming the bogeyman. I said that to Esma, who nodded vigorously.

"Kajevic and his henchmen inflicted the only combat fatalities the US suffered in its entire time in Bosnia. But this is an old tradition in Europe: Something awful happens and the Gypsies are at fault. Certainly, Ferko has never mentioned Kajevic."

She had propped herself on an elbow for my final questions, but now plunged to her back again.

"Bill, you must forgive me, but if you hear me say another word, I shall be speaking in my sleep. And we don't quite know each other well enough for that yet."

Laughing, I thanked her for dinner and promised to reciprocate. We talked momentarily about having another meal after tomorrow's hearing.

Outside, I strolled in an oddly buoyant mood to catch the Sprinter, the train that would drop me a block from my hotel. The street, Lange Voorhout, was a broad avenue, with a center esplanade of tall old trees, and lined on either side by stately residences, many now converted to embassies and consulates, according to the big brass plates beside their large front doors. The Hague at 10 p.m. on a weeknight was quiet. A few couples huddled as they strode along in the fierce sea breeze, while isolated bikers whizzed by in their stocking caps, making only grudging allowance for pedestrians.

Leaving Esma felt a lot like coming in out of an equatorial sun, with my skin still tingling in the shade. She was very bright and disarmingly frank, one of those women whose native attractiveness I inevitably found magnified by her smarts and unapologetic self-confidence. She was sui generis, defiantly herself, which might have been due to her heritage. I hunched up my shoulders in the cold and laughed out loud. It was the first moment that week when I had a solid conviction that I had done the right thing by coming to The Hague.

II.

Moving

4.

The Order

COUR PÉNALE INTERNATIONAL

INTERNATIONAL CRIMINAL COURT

Original: English
No.: ICC-04/15
Date: 9 March 2015

PRE-TRIAL CHAMBER IV

Before: Judge Joita Gautam, Presiding
Judge, Judge Nikolas Goodenough, Judge
Agata Hallstrom

SITUATION IN THE REPUBLIC OF BOSNIA AND HERZEGOVINA

Public Document

<u>Decision Pursuant to Article 15 of the Rome Statute on the Authorization of an Investigation</u>

PRE-TRIAL CHAMBER IV (the "Chamber") of the International Criminal Court (the "Court"), to which the situation in the Republic of Bosnia and Herzegovina has been assigned, issues the present decision pursuant to article 15(4) of the Rome Statute (the "Statute") on the "Request for authorisation of an investigation pursuant to Article 15" (the "Prosecutor's Request"), submitted by the Prosecutor on 14 November 2014.

On due consideration of the Prosecutor's Request, and the testimony of Witness 1, the Pre-Trial Chamber finds as follows:

There is a reasonable basis to proceed with an investigation of the Situation under the material temporal and territorial scope set forth in the Prosecutor's Request.

Full opinion to follow.

This brief ruling was a departure from the Court's usual practice, by which it wouldn't say even hello or good-bye in fewer than fifty pages, with hundreds of footnotes. That long opinion with the intricate legal discussion would come later, but the quick turnaround acknowledged that too much time had passed in the case already and was tantamount to an instruction to the OTP, and me, to get moving.

This was hardly an unanticipated victory. No matter how much Judge Gautam disagreed with putting an American in charge, there was no doubt she would allow the investigation to proceed. Nonetheless, a win's a win. My new colleagues in the OTP drifted by all day to offer congratulations, and I was briefly received in Badu's office to allow him to pat my back as well.

Goos, my investigator, took it as an occasion to invite me out for a drink at the end of the day. He was a former Belgian policeman who had first come to The Hague to work for the Yugoslav Tribunal. From there, like so many others, he had recently migrated to the ICC and was assigned to my case the day after I arrived, because he had learned some Serbo-Croatian, which was bound to be of use with Bosnian documents or witnesses.

As a prosecutor, I learned quickly that I was only as good as my investigators, the cops or federal agents whose ability to uncover reliable evidence determined the success of my cases, much more than any of my courtroom performances. But Goos seemed entirely unpromising. He was about my age, tall and beer-bellied, with bloodshot cheeks and a blond thatch that stood straight up like the coat of a hedgehog. He wore a trim goatee fading to gray, which, being accustomed to FBI agents, I considered just a little unprofessional. In fact, the first time I visited his office to introduce myself, the day before Ferko's testimony, I found him stuck to his computer, amusing himself with clips on YouTube. My years in the US Attorney's Office had taught me that the comfortable nature of government employment often dulled ambitions, and on first impression, Goos appeared to be someone in search of an early retirement, bright and affable but thoroughly uninspired.

Around five that afternoon, we crossed Maanweg, the broad boulevard in front of the Court, and meandered to a stylish little bar in Voorburg. In a matter of two blocks, we traveled from a familiar Western metropolis of big sleek buildings and speeding cars to old Holland, with tortuous cobbled streets and chunky brick buildings with awnings protecting the storefronts.

Talking over our next steps, we agreed that we needed to go to the scene of the crime in Bosnia. Yet under the Court's rigid rules, the ICC's diplomatic arm, the Complementarity Section, was required to give the Bosnians thirty days to change their minds about conducting the investigation themselves. For the moment, we could only plan.

"First off, mate," Goos said, "we'll want a squizz at that grave Ferko dug for Boldo and his family. See if there's forensics to be done on the remains."

Given Goos's name, and the bit I'd learned in advance about his background, I'd expected a Flemish accent when we met. Instead, Goos spoke Aussie English. He said he'd been raised in 'Oz,' where his father managed Australian operations for a Belgian coffee importer. In Sydney, he'd been known as Gus until he moved back to Belgium for university at the age of nineteen.

"What about exhuming the Cave?" I asked.

Goos visibly ricocheted off the idea.

"That's heavy equipment, mate, and bunches of blokes to sort through the rubble. Registrar would spit the dummy if we proposed spending tens of thousands of Euros straightaway. Have to be absolutely sure of Ferko first."

We made notes about several other investigative ideas, and I asked Goos what he knew about the incident with

Kajevic in April 2004, since Goos had been visiting Bosnia regularly during that period.

"Big news at the time," he said. "Bunch of Americans shot up. Four dead, as I recall. Everyone in NATO was cranky. But never heard a word about Roma."

After we'd finished our first beer, Goos asked my impressions of The Hague and the Court.

"So far, so good," I said, "except my hotel room, which could double as a coffin." Goos had stayed in the same place when we arrived and grimaced at the memory, as if it had been a dental extraction. I asked how The Hague had worn on him over a much longer period.

"Like it most of the time." He hunkered down and lowered his voice. "Suppose I don't need to tell you about the Dutch."

Americans were often mystified or impressed by 'Ten Boom.' These days, most guessed that I was Native American. (I'd never had the guts to ask if the senator was under the same misimpression when he chose me as US Attorney.) But 'Ten Boom,' like many European last names, simply designated a place. It meant 'at tree' in Dutch, like Atwater or Stonehouse in English.

"My parents were both born here," I told Goos, "but they were thoroughly Americanized. They never spoke Dutch, never returned. They didn't even seem to like windmills."

Goos laughed heartily. I was pleased he had a sense of humor.

"Dutch are nice enough," he said. "Let everyone be. You can see that with the pot bars and the molls putting themselves on display in the shop windows. But they're to themselves and keep very tight with their own ways." He made a fist. "Look up at the windows as you go walking.

No curtains. That's because a person should have nothing to hide. Don't conceal their thoughts either. If I run across some neighbor I haven't seen in a while, I want to go the other way on sight, because the bloke'll say something to me like, 'Oh my, your beard is getting so gray!' As if I might not own a mirror. *Baise moi l'ail!*" said Goos. French was another of the languages of Belgium. The derelict remnants of my high school education allowed me to puzzle out the phrase: 'Kiss my garlic bulb.' I guffawed once I understood.

"But all told," said Goos, "it's come good for me here. Nice salary. Comfy little flat. And less time for the wife and me to growl at each other at home. She stayed back in Brussels." He glanced up from his beer glass. The alcohol had summoned color to his face, accentuating the contrast with the fair hair standing straight up on his head. His expression was impenetrable, almost as if he himself didn't know how he felt about the living situation with his wife.

I was starting to like Goos. His strengths as a drinking companion were clear, although I still hadn't seen much focus from him as an investigator. As I would have guessed, he wasn't ready to depart when I slid off my barstool and grabbed my briefcase. I thanked him for the drink and left by myself.

The next afternoon, I called Esma with the news of the order. She had come to mind somewhat unwillingly over the weekend, and picking up the phone yesterday I had felt an odd lurch of feeling that had actually made me delay. With very little contact, we had already arrived on a strange footing.

Despite my promise to reciprocate for dinner, we did

not get together after the hearing. On the way to court that morning, I had mentioned to Akemi, the deputy prosecutor, that Esma had briefed me the prior evening at her hotel. A tiny middle-aged woman with witchy stiff black hair shot with gray, Akemi was a person of few words, but she passed me a black look, which I took as reproof. Reflecting, I understood her point. Even though my initial meeting with Esma had been planned solely for business, future defendants would feel free to question my objectivity if I made a habit of private dinners with the prime advocate for the victims. Rather than explain my reservations to Esma when she approached me in the robing room after the hearing, I had relied on the lame excuse of having forgotten other plans.

'Another time then,' she answered cheerfully. She gave me a fleet Continental buss on each cheek before departing.

Now I offered to send a hard copy of the order to her chambers in London, but she said an e-mail would suffice. She asked about next moves in the investigation.

"He won't like it," Esma answered, when I explained that we'd want Ferko to show us Boldo's grave in Barupra. "I told him that once he gave evidence, it would be the last he'd hear of this for quite some time. Returning to Barupra will be traumatic for him."

"His testimony isn't worth much, Esma, if we can't corroborate it."

"I shall have to persuade him," she answered. "Please stay in touch about the schedule." She was about to hang up, when she added lightly, "And when will the winds blow you to London or New York, Bill? I have not forgotten that you owe me dinner."

With that, she rung off, leaving me staring at the

handset. Having been single for going on five years, I was no longer completely blind to the signals if a woman was available and interested. But I was still reluctant to believe it of Esma. With her exotic looks and high style, she was well outside my range, more the kind of glamorous companion customarily seen on the arm of a billionaire or a senator, men of standing who had enough self-respect to pass on thirty-year-olds. The truth was that with her imposing self-assurance, Esma somehow seemed like too much for me. Cradling the receiver, I was actually a bit sheepish, because when I recalled the professional issues that were a barrier between us, I realized I felt relief.

5.

Settling In—March 11–April 8

I spent the next couple of days reading about the raid nearly eleven years earlier, on April 10, 2004, in which US forces under NATO command had failed to capture Laza Kajevic. By early 2004, the American troops were in their last days in Bosnia, because President Bush needed more boots in Iraq. In fact, the NATO Supreme Allied Commander, General Layton Merriwell, who had gone on to become a figure of some note, if not for reasons he would have chosen, had already been appointed to lead the coalition forces in Baghdad and was on the verge of departure from Europe.

As for Kajevic, he was universally regarded these days as the motive force of the Bosnian carnage. In line with his epic self-conception, he presented a somewhat majestic figure, large and imposing, with a virtual monument of black hair, distinguished by a wide skunk stripe that might have been the work of a hairdresser. The coiffure swept across his forehead down to eye level, in the fashion of an old-time rock 'n' roller, and was the subject of frequent comment since it remained utterly undisturbed no matter how vehemently he delivered his race-baiting speeches.

In 1992, Kajevic had stood before the Bosnian parliament and basically threatened genocide of Bosnian Muslims if Bosnia voted for independence from Yugoslavia, as it ultimately did. For the next three years, Kajevic did his utmost to make good on his dark promise. The Yugoslav National Army and the Serb paramilitaries, allied with roving gangs of thugs, shelled and shot, raped and burned, and laid mines in all areas not populated by Serbs. Ultimately, in Srebrenica, eight thousand captured Muslim men and boys were summarily executed on Kajevic's orders. After Dayton, in 1996, he was charged at the Yugoslav Tribunal. He'd been on the run ever since, becoming the most wanted man in Europe.

In late March 2004, US Army Intelligence received word that Kajevic and his band of two dozen bodyguards had taken refuge in a shattered portion of Doboj, which by virtue of ethnic cleansing had become a Serb enclave near Tuzla. He was more or less hiding under the Americans' noses.

According to the accounts I read, Kajevic was supported by a secret network throughout Serbia and Bosnia that operated like the Ku Klux Klan in the US decades ago. He was guarded by ex–Arkan Tigers, the most reviled and feared of the Chetnik paramilitaries. In order to provide for Kajevic, the Tigers had evolved into a crime gang that smuggled gasoline and drugs and sex slaves, and also, reputedly, carried out paid assassinations for Russian mobsters.

For General Layton Merriwell, the capture of Kajevic

would have been the ultimate emblem of the success of
NATO's peacemaking efforts in Bosnia. The operation
was planned carefully, and the remaining Special Forces
troops in country—who had spearheaded the apprehension of many fugitives—were summoned.

On April 10, a perimeter force surrounded the abandoned tenement where Kajevic was said to be hiding,
while two squads entered the ground floor from different doors. They were inside for no more than a few
seconds when at least two rocket-propelled grenades,
fired from above, lit up the building. Snipers waiting on
adjoining rooftops fired on the Special Forces soldiers
as they fled.

The Serbian ambush left four American troops dead
and eight others wounded. Never actually sighted, Kajevic and his Arkan bodyguards were presumed to have
escaped in one of two stolen US Army trucks seen speeding from the scene.

These deaths, the only US combat fatalities in more
than eight years in Bosnia, made a sour end to Merriwell's time there, and front-page news at home. In
perhaps the most famous quote about the episode, an
American NCO snarled into a network camera, "We
didn't come here to die for these [*bleep*]ing people."

After three days, I'd read every article and blog post
I could find online concerning Kajevic's escape, and I'd
also enlisted the aid of the Court's research librarians.
There was no mention of 'Roma' or 'Gypsies' or
'Barupra' in anything written about the firefight.

On Tuesday the following week, Goos came into my
office with a piece of paper. I had taken over Olivier's
space a few days before, although I was still getting ac-

customed to its barren feel. The furnishing was spare—
a round-nose pedestal computer console of blond wood
adhered to a bank of white laminate cabinetry. The
Dutch, as it turned out, frowned on personal displays in
public space, and the off-white walls held nothing but a
colored map of Sierra Leone that Olivier had taped up
by its corners, and which I left, as a low-rent rebellion
against monotony. It was a far cry from the Wall of Respect I had at DeWitt Royster, with the photos of three
different presidents shaking my hand, the courtroom
sketches of my most famous trials, and various important
documents—diplomas, bar admissions, and my US Attorney's Letters Patent—in expensive leather frames.

"A sheila I know over at the Yugoslav," Goos said,
meaning a woman, "defense lawyer, says she and her husband might have a room to let for a couple of months." In
idle hours, I'd been looking at apartments online, but most
required a multiyear lease. A short-term rental would let
me escape the monk's cell I was confined in while I got a
feel for The Hague, before making a longer commitment.

After work, Goos accompanied me on the Sprinter
back to the center of town. Following a short walk, we
found the building, its entry jammed with bikes locked
to the radiator.

The two-story flat was tidy and dustless, sparely furnished with older modern pieces that looked as if they
might have been inherited. My potential landlady was
named Narawanda Logan, Indonesian by heritage but a
resident of The Hague most of her life. She was tiny and
narrow as a bird, with raven bangs and large eyeglasses,
round black frames that seemed to cover half of her face.
Based on the dates when she said she'd done a graduate
law degree at NYU, I figured her for her late thirties, al-

though she had the kind of dainty looks that could lead her to be mistaken for someone much younger.

Her husband, Lew, was an American whom she'd met in grad school. Recently, the international aid organization he worked for had posted him to Manhattan for temporary duties promised to last no more than six months. But the dizzy rents in New York were stretching the Logans' finances and they'd decided to let an empty bedroom. The room was upstairs and small by US standards, albeit spacious compared to my hotel. It had the large windows that are typical of the Dutch in their quest for light, and its own tiny powder room, which had been carved out of a closet years ago as an accommodation for an elderly relative.

Mrs. Logan said she woke early and returned late, and that use of the kitchen would be largely mine because she never cooked. The relative privacy of the entire arrangement was instantly appealing. Beyond all that, the location was choice, only a couple blocks off Frederikstraat, 'the Fred,' with its fancy shops and nice cafés. Knowing myself, I realized that if I couldn't just stumble out the door to find diversion, I'd never leave the apartment.

Goos had told me the rent—€550 a month—was a bargain—and I said yes at once and moved in the next evening.

On Monday, March 23, word came that the Bosnians had reaffirmed the referral of the investigation to the ICC. After eleven years, less one month, a criminal inquiry into the massacre at Barupra could begin.

I was not surprised that Roger, who knew all, called me late in the day.

"So I read you won your hearing."

"It's a little hard to claim victory, Rog, where there's no one on the other side."

"Whatever. Now that you're investigating, how would you like to come to DC to have a conversation with Layton Merriwell?"

"General Merriwell?"

"He's willing to talk to you one-on-one."

"About the case?"

"No, about raising dwarf ponies. Of course about your case. He's also been reading about it." The Court's order had produced the first publicity in the US about Barupra, a small article in the back pages of the *New York Times*. The paper had mentioned that the massacre had occurred in an area under US Army control. I could understand why that would have caught the attention of the NATO supreme commander at the time. "The general wants you to hear his point of view," Rog said. "Tell you what he knows. Which is next to nothing."

I nearly asked Roger what was in this for General Merriwell, but that was peering straight into the mouth of the gift horse. Instead, after hanging up, I sat at my desk trying to answer the question on my own. I didn't doubt that Roger was my friend—he had flown fourteen hours to get to the funeral of my mother, who had cooked him countless meals during law school, and he was far more attentive to me than almost anyone else had been after I decided to leave Ellen. Yet he subscribed, like many guys, probably including me, to a view of friendship that barred no holds in competition. On the squash court, Roger had virtually maimed me through the years, running me over, driving the squash ball into my ass at 80 mph, and—usually when he was behind—swinging wide enough to strike me with his racket. All in the game, he'd say.

So I tried to fathom the game now. Roger was a public servant of the United States. Accordingly, whatever Layton Merriwell had to say was going to serve American interests, which, naturally, were in absolving US military forces.

I walked down the hall to Goos.

"Fair suck of the sav," said Goos, which I took it meant he was as surprised as I about Merriwell. Goos's English had basically been preserved in amber and was spoken as if he were still nineteen, the age when he left Australia.

The ICC's protocols called for the prosecution of leaders rather than grunts who would claim they were just following orders. Therefore, if several hundred Roma had been massacred by American troops, General Merriwell would be our top target. Accordingly, his offer to speak to me contradicted what any good criminal lawyer—including me—would have told him, namely, Keep your mouth shut. The penitentiaries were full of guys who'd boosted their proclaimed innocence with lies that led them to the slammer.

"We can't say no," said Goos. In an investigation in which US law barred any cooperation from the American military, it would be impossible to refuse even one self-serving interview. "But," he added, "this is going to make the old man very, very nervous."

He was referring to Badu. The prosecutor, as well as the president of the Court—a judge who served as the chief executive—were chosen by the member countries, which meant Badu was best off avoiding controversies that might inflame any faction. The Pre-Trial Chamber's order in my "Situation" had authorized the investigation to proceed only within the "territorial scope" of the OTP application, which naturally made no mention of the US. In fact, given the Service-Members' Act, conducting an ICC investigation on US soil was probably illegal.

I called back Roger to make these points, but within twenty-four hours he had proposed that Merriwell and I meet in a conference room in the BiH Embassy in DC, which under international law was sovereign Bosnian territory. The Bosnians, like many others, revered Merriwell and would never deny him so simple a request.

With that, I scheduled a meeting with Badu and Akemi in hopes of gaining their approval. We sat in Badu's corner office at a white conference table beside a wall of floor-length windows. Badu was at the head, while Akemi placed herself in the corner, with a legal pad. With her dark face always seemingly engraved by worry, Akemi was at the Court, with her door open, no matter how early I arrived or how late I left, usually scribbling like mad on the stacks of documents in front of her. Although she was my supervisor, my conversations with her were rare, since she was frugal with words and difficult to understand anyway. She spoke that Japanese version of English, cultivated at their universities, which is largely a dialect unto itself. Although Akemi's office was only two doors down, I had taken to e-mailing her about virtually everything.

Badu was equally inscrutable for far different reasons. He was a large, amiable man, past seventy, hefty and bald, and a renowned authority on international law. He spoke beautiful, musical English and was composed and charming in his aloof way, clearly fit for the ceremonial aspect of his job, in which he received the diplomatic representatives of various nations. But beyond amiable chatter, virtually everything he said seemed to miss the point. He was the master of the grave nod or understanding chuckle, both of which he applied at deft intervals when his subordinates spoke. But he rarely responded directly to questions or suggestions. When I explained the possibility of seeing Merriwell, Badu kept repeating, "Very unusual, very unusual," and then added his light laugh, without offering more.

It was widely assumed around the Court that most critical decisions within the OTP were actually made by Akemi. As an example, I was told that it was she who had finally pushed through the encrusted layers of resistance to investigating Barupra. But she was reluctant about me interviewing Merriwell. She agreed that a conversation with the general in the Bosnian Embassy was technically lawful, but she said the Court, whose expenses were annually audited by the UN, could never pay for an investigatory trip to the US.

Ordinarily, that would have been definitive. But for weeks, my ex–law partners had been nagging me to return to the Tri-Cities to discuss a criminal price-fixing investigation of Kindle County's oil refiners, who for decades had charged the highest prices in the country. It took a few days, but my former clients confirmed that they would be only too happy to pay for the best seat on the plane. When I explained I could make the trip with no expense to the Court, Akemi had no way to refuse permission.

So I prepared to head home. There was also family business waiting for me. Not long after I'd announced my plans to move to The Hague, my younger son, Pete, and his girlfriend, Brandi, had come to tell me they were engaged. Ellen and I had tried to schedule a celebratory dinner with Brandi's parents, but the Rosenbergs were still wintering in Florida when I left. Now I called my ex to see if we could make arrangements for Saturday night, April 11, which worked out. Roger, in the meantime, said Merriwell could see me at 3 p.m. on April 10, a couple of hours after I landed at Dulles.

The last step was to ask Esma to notify Ferko that we would need to see him in Barupra, where I would head from the US. She had called me a number of times in the interval, ostensibly to see what we had heard from the Bosnians. Because of the time difference with New York, we ended up connecting at the end of her court day, which was late at night in The Hague. Once we'd dealt with business, Esma inevitably prolonged the conversations with questions about my kids or stories about herself.

I especially enjoyed her anecdotes about growing up with four sibs in a motor home. She described her father as a con who preyed on the elderly, and a brute who beat his wife and children. Her revenge was to go to school wherever they camped. Because it was forbidden for Roma girls to associate with *gadjos* after puberty, her father had her expelled from the Gypsy nation when she went to university. She claimed not to have cared.

Interesting as Esma was, the perils with her remained obvious and I found myself trying to limit our phone calls to five minutes. This time I resorted to e-mail, but my cell rang moments later.

"Ferko will show you the grave, but he requires me to be there to accompany him," she said.

It hadn't dawned on me that she would make the trip, and my heart squirmed around for a second.

"There's really no need," I said, even though I realized she had every right to be there, if that's what Ferko preferred.

"Bill," she said, "I doubt you will see Ferko without my help. And he struggles with Serbo-Croatian. I can translate from Romany."

I accepted her decision and took a second to explain that I'd be arriving from the US. In response to her usual curiosity, I outlined my plans.

"You and your ex-wife are comfortable at the same table?"

"Completely. Now that we're no longer responsible for one another's happiness, we get along swimmingly. I'm actually going to stay Saturday night with Ellen and her husband."

"Dear me," said Esma, which, truth told, reflected some of my own ambivalence about that detail. "You can tell me more in Tuzla. I shall see you Thursday week. The Blue Lamp?" Goos had already said the hotel was by a considerable margin the best choice in Tuzla.

After ringing off, I sat in my new office, drilled by a hard truth that broke through often in the wake of my conversations with Esma: I was lonely. Worse, approaching fifty-five, I remained unsettled in fundamental ways. I still approved of my choices in the last few months, but I'd made a large wager with my future—and my sense of who I was. Sitting there, I felt the cold void I'd stumble into if things didn't turn out well.

6.

Merriwell—April 10

The Embassy of the Republic of Bosnia and Herze-govina occupied a flat-faced futurist building near Twenty-First and E Street NW, not far from the US State Department. The neighborhood, Foggy Bottom, was a quieter part of town where the eighteenth- and nineteenth-century buildings now housed embassies and museums and hotels, as well as upscale residences, along the leafy streets.

I arrived near 3 p.m., wheeling my luggage with me because I had come straight from Dulles. Inside, grim-faced Bosnian security police treated me—like every other visitor, I'm sure—as a potential terrorist. After I passed through the metal detector, my luggage was im-pounded and my briefcase was searched. Without apol-ogy, my cell phone and tablet were removed for the duration of the visit, along with two pens. Roger had phoned last night to tell me that I couldn't take notes during the meeting.

Over the years, my job as a lawyer had led me into confrontations with lots of supposedly important people—the Catholic archbishop in Kindle County, countless CEOs, the Senate Judiciary Committee that grilled me about my appointment as US Attorney. Yet minutes away from my interview, I found myself unusually nervous.

General Layton Merriwell had achieved that distinctive public profile lately referred to as 'iconic.' He was arguably the most decorated soldier of his day, and had been briefly—but seriously—promoted as a candidate for president of the United States. All that said, his notoriety had increased substantially when he joined the long march of American males of great power and achievement who wandered dick-first into disgrace.

When I was growing up, the popular image of a successful Army officer was Patton, someone who supposedly had balls the size of eggplants, who addressed God by first name, and who could inspire his troops to latitudes of courage they had never foreseen in themselves. Personally, I had virtually no firsthand experience with the US military, since I was of that social class which, in my time, didn't get involved in defending their country, much like the five-hundred-plus members of Congress who had voted to authorize the invasion of Iraq and then as a group sent a single child to fight there when the war started. But over time, I'd developed the clear impression that the men and women who rose to the top in our armed services were far more nuanced figures than Patton.

Certainly that appeared to be the case with Layton Merriwell. He represented the fourth generation of his family to attend West Point, and he had graduated number two in his class before training further as an infantry officer and parachutist. Over the years, Merriwell had moved back and forth between the Pentagon, the field, and academic assignments, teaching Tactics at the Army War College and also spending semesters at MIT, where he was completing a doctorate in Game Theory.

His strategic views were not complex and had been often quoted: "Fight only when absolutely necessary, and then with overwhelming force." His battlefield record was glorious: Grenada, Panama, Haiti. During Desert Storm, he was chief of staff to General Schwarzkopf, planning the hundred-hour ground operation that followed our unrelenting air assault.

All of that had led him to the Balkans, where he was the first commander of the US forces in the NATO Stabilization Force in Bosnia. He was reassigned after the peacekeeping mission was well established, but returned as supreme commander of NATO forces during the bombing of the Serbs in Kosovo and the ensuing pacification of that country and Bosnia. Finally, in 2004, on the recommendation of his friend Colin Powell, he was dispatched to lead the Central Command in Iraq. He had some success in neutralizing Al Qaeda, only to confront the Sadrite insurgency. After eighteen months he asked to be relieved, reportedly convinced that there was no near-term prospect of a democratic Iraq. Instead, he supposedly recommended to the president that we double our force to fully subdue and disarm the many malcontents, much as in Bosnia, and then withdraw.

Once he was back in the US, Merriwell took leave to finish his doctorate, while reports of his misgivings about the war circulated widely. Early in 2007, several prominent Democrats floated his name as a presidential candidate for the 2008 election, until Merriwell announced he would not leave the service. Three years later, in 2010, President Obama nominated Layton Merriwell to become the next chair of the Joint Chiefs of Staff.

Within forty-eight hours of that announcement, both the *Washington Post* and the *New York Times* published front-page accounts, probably based on leaks from Bushites eager to get even, of Merriwell's long affair with his aide-de-camp at NATO. When the relationship started, Captain Jamie St. John, who was half the general's age, was unmarried, a gifted West Point graduate, and the daughter of one of Merriwell's academy classmates. Whatever this young woman had offered Merriwell proved to be something he was unwilling to forsake. He brought her with him to Iraq, but there the relationship foundered. She requested a transfer, which he'd tried unsuccessfully to block, while he continued to e-mail her, his messages growing more and more abject and profane. Finally, after her engagement to a fellow officer much closer to her age, he had sent a series of ridiculous threats—most composed late at night and admittedly under the influence of far too much alcohol—claiming he would end her Army career unless she returned to him.

Both the affair and the turbulent aftermath had been over for roughly four years by the time it became news; in the interval, Merriwell had apologized to now Major St. John in writing several times. Nevertheless, he resigned from the service the week the story broke, while his wife of forty years tossed him out of their house in McLean and his two daughters publicly spurned him. He was now the CEO of Distance Communications, a hi-tech manufacturer of the electronic components for various weapons systems, part of that immense gray world of military contracting where billions were made and little was publicly known.

Merriwell's downfall had come as I was in the waning days of my marriage, and it fascinated me more than those of Bill Clinton or Sol Wachtler or Eliot Spitzer or the hundreds of other men of standing who'd been shamed this way in recent decades. The common understanding of all of them was that they were idiots who proved yet again that a male is just a human being chained to a maniac. But to me there was a deeper enigma: Why had each of these men found desire more powerful than their attachment to everything else in life they had struggled so long to attain? As a group, their behavior said, in substance, something that reverberated with me: With everything gained, huge success was still not enough. Something essential remained missing. Perhaps all humans feel like this and men of power simply have the means to follow the siren's call. Or perhaps this phenomenon reflected the fact that the drive of big power guys was the result of a permanent lack of contentment.

Each case probably had its own answers, including that for many of these men the only thing new was that they had gotten caught. But the profiles of Merriwell included countless testimonials from friends who insisted that these events almost certainly had no precedent. And yet in his last desperate messages to Major St. John, Merriwell had promised to abandon his wife and to leave his Army career behind. Merriwell's story was ultimately most striking to me, not because he felt such intense longing for something missing in his life but rather because he seemed to think he had found it.

When I approached the conference room, through the glass panel in the door I saw Layton Merriwell waiting. He was impeccable but abstracted, a man very much alone at that moment, as he looked off with his legs crossed, one glossy Oxford jiggling idly beneath the knife-edge crease in his trousers. As I entered, he came to his feet and offered his hand. He was a bit smaller and slighter than he looked on TV, with sharp features and trim gray hair, still long enough to comb over. For a person of his age—sixty-eight, according to the net—his cheeks were unusually rosy, probably a remnant of drinking. His hands, pale and perhaps even manicured, seemed unexpectedly refined for a soldier.

Still standing, we talked a little bit about Roger. General Merriwell told me they had served in the same places several times, and we exchanged a couple of light remarks about Roger's intense nature. Merriwell made me laugh out loud by briefly imitating the way Roger screwed up his whole face when he was bearing down on things. Then the general gestured to a chair. We sat on the same side of the long conference table.

"So what can I tell you, Mr. Ten Boom?" He smiled a bit, understanding the ambiguity of his remark.

"Many things, I'm sure, General, but first we need to get through some preliminaries."

"You're going to tell me that I have the right to have a lawyer present?"

"I was and you do."

"As you would expect, Mr. Ten Boom, my attorneys have already told me not to talk to you." Merriwell by now had plenty of experience with lawyers, since the revelation of his affair had led to both a congressional investigation and a brief grand jury probe that went nowhere because the alleged victim insisted she had never taken any of his threats seriously. I already recognized that his preconditions—that he would meet only alone, off the record and without notes—reflected a lawyer's advice, since those in effect inoculated him from any subsequent use of his words against him.

"We both know that I don't face much practical peril here, Mr. Ten Boom. If the ICC ever tried to charge me, our government would do whatever was required to save me."

"Ah yes." I smiled. "The Hague Invasion Act."

General Merriwell smiled, too, but without parting his lips. We were facing each other in two adjoining high-back executive chairs upholstered with uncommonly rich blue leather. There were eighteen of them surrounding the beech table, its pinkish undertone revealed in the late April light entering through the large windows. The paneling was also beech, and the room was double height, three baubled chandeliers suspended over the table. At the far end, the blue flag of Bosnia and Herzegovina, with its yellow wedge and white stars, as well as the Stars and Stripes, stood on staffs on either side of the obsidian face of a large-screen TV that presumably served for occasional diplomatic teleconferences, as well as viewing satellite broadcasts of the soccer leagues back home.

"You know, Mr. Ten Boom, I don't want to start out on the wrong foot, but what you are doing here is exactly what the armed forces feared about the International Criminal Court. The other countries negotiating the ICC treaty refused to exempt peacekeeping troops, like the ones we had in the Balkans, from prosecution."

Given his NATO role at the time, Merriwell obviously was speaking with firsthand knowledge.

"General, how can you give anyone immunity for committing crimes against humanity? The British and the French and the Germans all had peacekeeping troops in Bosnia, and they joined the ICC."

"The British and the French and the Germans are not the same targets our country is, Mr. Ten Boom. And those governments agreed in Dayton that our troops could only be prosecuted by us under American law. Apparently the ICC doesn't regard itself as bound by that stipulation."

"The Court never signed that agreement, General. But you're raising a very good point." The compliment caught him off guard and he raised a faint eyebrow. "Do you know," I asked, "if the Army has done any investigation of this alleged massacre?"

Merriwell lingered before answering.

"Not while I was in the service. Since then, I wouldn't know. But no one would share the results with you anyway, Mr. Ten Boom."

"That's not really why I'm asking. The way the ICC works, the Court is authorized to investigate crimes only when the nations involved can't or won't do that. As you just pointed out, the US Army always retains the power to prosecute its soldiers. So a thorough inquiry by the Judge Advocate General's Corps and a public report of the findings would have prevented the ICC from going anywhere near this case. I don't understand why that hasn't happened."

"Mr. Ten Boom, the US military is not about to let any international body tell them to investigate our troops when there's no basis to do so. Or to reveal its findings when there is. It's hard enough to persuade the American people to allow our military to intervene overseas, without having to tell parents that their sons and daughters will be subject to the moralizing whims of a court thousands of miles from home with procedures nothing like our own."

"It's the same justice everywhere, General. Sealing four hundred men, women, and children in a coal mine without any provocation is a crime in any land, and I doubt you truly view the prosecution of an atrocity like that as 'moralizing.'"

Despite the jousting, our tone was pleasant, even amused, with occasional quick smiles that were only a little bit short of winking. We both knew the arguments. It was probably not a surprise that a military man and a trial lawyer each relished this kind of back-and-forth as a way to get acquainted. But my last challenge to Merriwell brought a more somber look.

"I certainly do not, Mr. Ten Boom. I was newly commissioned during the revelations of the My Lai massacre in Vietnam, and they've always stayed with me. War is hell. And hellish things happen. Although there is an industry of those who don't like to mention it, soldiers in combat are desperately scared and fighting for their lives, and that does not always bring out the best in human beings. But there is no excuse for murdering four hundred unarmed human beings. If that were what happened. But it is not."

The general lowered his chin just a bit to deliver a flinty look. The persistent intensity of his gray eyes, which I'd noticed since starting, was redoubled. We were now down to business.

"And on what basis, General, do you feel such confidence?"

"In the last week, I've spoken to every senior officer I had in Bosnia at the time. To a person, they told me there was not a scintilla of truth to this charge."

"I'm sure if you were I, General, you'd say you would rather speak to those officers yourself."

"If I were you, Mr. Ten Boom, I'd think I was doing very well having a word with the top commander, especially when US law prohibits it."

I was silent, basically conceding the point. Nevertheless, he'd reinforced my long-running curiosity about why he was here.

"Let me be obnoxious and lawyerly, General. Are you saying that you know nothing about a massacre in Barupra, based either on anything you witnessed or were told?"

"That's exactly what I am saying. This is a fabrication."

"And what part is made up—that a massacre occurred or that American forces had anything to do with it?"

"Certainly the latter. But if I understand the allegations, a truck convoy and a couple dozen troops moved through an area under our control, then blew up a coal mine and annihilated four hundred people in the process. Unless I was a complete failure as a commander, that could not have happened without an American soldier noticing something and reporting it up the chain."

Whatever it is that people believe about one another within the first instants of meeting can prove unwarranted—just ask anyone who's been on a second date—but I liked General Merriwell, mostly because he radiated discipline in the face of the truth. His bearing said that he was neither self-deceived nor willing to lie about what he knew.

"General, it's beyond dispute that the entire population of that village disappeared overnight in April 2004."

"This wouldn't be the first time that Gypsies have acted like Gypsies, Mr. Ten Boom, and moved on."

"I thought you were just saying that four hundred people couldn't march through the circle of several US camps without our troops knowing and reporting something?"

"I was talking about a foreign military operation and an explosion, Mr. Ten Boom. Large movements among the civilian population, on the other hand, were common. In Bosnia in 2004, there was little work and dramatic shortages of food. People were out foraging for edibles or coal, collecting scrap iron, hunting. Not to mention thousands of refugees still returning home. A few hundred people going down the road might not have attracted much attention."

"But, General, the people in Barupra lacked the physical means to go anywhere, other than on foot. Those Roma were living under plastic sheeting for the most part."

"My memory, Mr. Ten Boom, is that a few of those Gypsies were known car thieves."

"To move four hundred people, General, you'd have to steal dozens and dozens of vehicles, which would create big issues with the Bosnian police. Not to mention the fact that there is not one report of anyone in the world seeing or hearing from those people since that night eleven years ago."

Merriwell sat back to study me. I took his silence, like mine a second ago, as a concession that I had the better arguments on this point.

"And finally, sir," I said, "all these alternate theories fly in the face of something neither of us has mentioned yet: I have a witness, General, a man who lived in Barupra, who says that everyone there was sealed in that cave."

"I realize that."

"Have you read his testimony?"

"As it happens, I have. Roger sent it to me." At the Court, I had heard nothing about any requests for a transcript, which meant Roger's agency had copied the broadcast from the Internet. No surprise. Roger had been clear from the start that they were monitoring the case.

"Frankly, Mr. Ten Boom, I couldn't comprehend why you were not on your feet screaming for the life of Jesus about what that witch of a judge was doing. There were only a handful of US airmen ever on the ground in Bosnia and they'd been gone for years."

I explained that I thought Judge Gautam's game had been to discredit me, more than the US. That was not, of course, something I cared to hear repeated, but I wanted to let my pants down a little with the general, in hopes that he might do the same. From his intent look, I took it that my reasoning made sense to him as a game theorist.

"But leaving the judge aside, General, are you telling me you weren't impressed with the witness's testimony?"

"You'll forgive my lapse in political correctness, but I'll share a lesson I've learned around the world: Gypsies lie, Mr. Ten Boom. It is not really lying to them. They have no written history. Instead, the past is constantly recreated to fit each moment's needs. Furthermore, when they are dealing with us, it's self-protective. Lying keeps the majority world at arm's length."

"I won't quarrel with you on social anthropology,

General. That's not my field. I'm going to Barupra next week, but thus far this man seems very well corroborated." I took some time to describe the photos and affidavits and seismic reports Esma had gathered originally. "That evidence, General, supports the claim of a massacre. And as you acknowledged before, it is very hard to believe that an explosion or a paramilitary operation could have occurred without American soldiers knowing. And inasmuch as no US troops reported anything to superiors, one reason might be because they were involved."

I had realized as soon as Merriwell conceded that someone under his command would have to have known about Barupra that he had demonstrated why his lawyers told him not to speak to me. Some arguments, as they say in the courtroom, prove too much and end up serving the other side.

Turning the general's point against him set him back. He stood to reach a silver carafe in the middle of the table. He poured water for both of us and adjusted each trouser leg before resuming his seat.

"How much do you know about the war in the Balkans, Mr. Ten Boom?"

I told him the truth, that my recent reading had left me astonished about how little I'd absorbed at the time.

"You were hardly the only one who failed to appreciate events," the general answered. "Our allies in Europe initially viewed the fighting in Bosnia as no more than the continuation of ethnic rivalries that had been going on since the fourteenth century, when the Ottomans first entered this region. But what the Serbs were inflicting on the Muslims in Bosnia was nothing less than genocide, as intentional as the Nazis' effort to exterminate the Jews, and, although blessedly of a much smaller scope, even more savage. Twenty thousand Bosnian women were sexually assaulted, many of them in rape camps aimed at impregnating them with Serbian children. In the rest of the five hundred concentration camps the Serbs operated—ten times as many as the Croats and Muslims combined—the inmates were systematically starved and worked to death. Not to mention the hundreds of mass executions that were carried out.

"All of that, Mr. Ten Boom, was happening less than six hundred miles from Dachau, on the same continent and in the same century, despite all our vows of 'Never again.' But horrible as that was, as slow as we were to see what was happening—despite the repeated alarms raised by your friend Roger, by the way, among a few others— the United States of America finally saw the truth, responded, and put a halt to the atrocities. Bosnia was the first actual military operation NATO ever engaged in. And it was a stunning success.

"We separated three warring ethnic groups. And, as important, we removed the means for them to start killing one another again. At the time Yugoslavia shattered, Marshal Tito had built the third largest army in Europe. We seized eight hundred fifty thousand weapons, most from paramilitaries and jihadists and vigilantes who were quite unhappy to surrender them, and we did it without fatalities. We also arrested twenty-nine war criminals, most of them Serbian but also a few Croats and Bosniaks and Kosovars wanted in The Hague.

"I look back with only two regrets. The biggest occurred on 9/11 when it was suddenly clear that we should have done far, far more to ballyhoo our salvation of the Bosniaks and Albanians throughout the Muslim world.

"Nevertheless, for those, like me, whose lives are dedicated to the belief that military force is also an instrument of peace, our role in the Balkans is a supreme moment."

Merriwell had spoken with slow-fused passion. I'd listened without questions, both to be polite and also because I was certain I would get his point sooner or later.

"General, you're not the kind of guy who needs a pat on the back, and least of all from me. So I wish I knew what you were trying to suggest."

"I'm trying to give you a sense of the stakes involved in your investigation, Mr. Ten Boom."

"Four hundred deaths gave me a sense of the stakes a while ago, General. And I know you're not suggesting that because thousands of lives were saved, a few hundred murdered Gypsies don't matter."

"I surely am not. But there are consequences to your investigation, especially if these allegations gain more attention, which I hope you'll bear in mind. Even a false accusation of this nature fortifies those who say we should save our tax money and stay home and let the world take care of itself. And that gratifies the many around the globe—the Russians, the Chinese, the Venezuelans, ISIS, Iran, and all the extremists of many stripes—who are very happy when we don't project our power abroad."

"I can tell you right now, General, I hope that thought never enters my mind."

Merriwell recoiled visibly.

"My job in The Hague, General, is the same as it was fifteen years ago in Kindle County: Investigate crimes and prosecute when the evidence is strong and the violations of the law are serious. I indicted our Catholic archbishop for looting church coffers to support a child he'd fathered."

"I recall the case," said Merriwell.

"Before we brought the charges, a papal envoy showed up in Kindle County to tell me that my actions would cause thousands of people to lose their faith. And I'll say to you what I said to him: 'The last thing you want me doing is your job.' He was in charge of ministering to the faithful, and folks like Roger and you can worry about American foreign and military policy. I'm just a glorified Joe Friday."

The comparison brought a small smile and a brief toss of Merriwell's head in disagreement. We'd reached another caesura. He allowed himself a moment of distraction with his handheld. I asked if he needed a longer break, but he was ready to go on, except for a second glass of water.

"General, you said you had two major regrets. I assume the other was failing to capture Laza Kajevic?"

Just the mention of Kajevic caused Merriwell to wince. It was the most emphatic emotion he'd shown.

"The man was a monster," Merriwell said. "Given the opportunity, he would have slaughtered as many as Stalin and Hitler and Pol Pot. He was never a political leader— just a sadistic thug with a dormant conscience and an ego that could dwarf Jupiter."

"I'm sure you were horrified by the casualties in Doboj, when you tried to capture him."

"The hardest part of being a battlefield commander, Mr. Ten Boom, is always the loss of life, especially your own soldiers. We spent eight years in Bosnia without a combat fatality. To see four soldiers die and eight others wounded, three quite seriously, while a malignancy like

Kajevic went free made for one of the saddest moments
in my career."

"And how was it that he got the drop on your forces?
I assume there was an intelligence failure."

"'Failure' is too strong. Even diligent efforts in that
arena don't always succeed. As was reported at that
time, we badly underestimated how well armed they
would be. We'd missed Kajevic only a month before,
and in order to escape in disguise, they had abandoned
almost all their weapons."

"But they also seem to have known exactly when you
were coming."

"So it appears."

"And how did they get that information?"

"If I knew, Mr. Ten Boom, I would not be at liberty
to tell you. I can assure you, however, that we didn't repeat prior mistakes." In my reading, I'd been astonished
by reports that the French had sabotaged a number of
earlier efforts to capture Kajevic, believing that would
push the Serbs toward the Russians. "The operational
details of our plan to arrest Kajevic in Doboj were probably the most closely guarded secret of my time at Mons,"
he said, referring to the city in Belgium where Allied
Command Operations was located. The French, in other
words, had been frozen out.

"Then what's your best guess about how Kajevic
knew?"

"Conjecture only? Something happened on the
ground that betrayed our plan. We tried to respect the
local Bosnian authorities. There were Muslim leaders
who didn't want Kajevic captured, for fear that it would
set off the whole fracas again. And of course he had
plants in every police force. All I can tell you, Mr. Ten

Boom, is that we investigated the hell out of that question. There was not an American serving in Bosnia who wasn't deeply upset by the casualties at Doboj."

"Upset enough to kill four hundred Roma?"

Merriwell again drew back, the same skinny eyebrow elevated once more. I continued in the face of his silence.

"There is a well-trod story around Tuzla that the massacre at Barupra was related to the failed capture of Kajevic."

Merriwell shook his head before he answered.

"Again, Mr. Ten Boom, we are getting into intelligence information, which I am not free to disclose."

I was trolling here, but I had learned on cross-examination that one key to success was to continue at the same pace and with no change of expression. Merriwell's last answer suggested there might be something to tell about the Roma's role.

"Well, in thinking very hard about this, General, and asking myself what the Roma might have done in connection with the Kajevic raid that would get them all killed, one clear possibility is that they assisted the Americans somehow."

Merriwell hesitated a second longer, making me surer I was onto something. In the end, he smiled broadly.

"Let me see, Mr. Ten Boom. How many traps does that question artfully set? First, I've told you that I don't believe there was a massacre. And I've also said that I can't comment on intelligence."

"But if you were wrong about a massacre occurring, General, without asking you to disclose any classified specifics, would your first suspicion be of Kajevic and his followers?"

He thought that through with his mouth knotted.

"By character, of course. Killing hundreds in vengeance would be a trifle to him. But we looked intensively for Kajevic in the area around Tuzla throughout the last weeks of April in 2004, and it would seem foolhardy of him to return."

"Or spectacularly arrogant."

After a beat, Merriwell dipped his chin to acknowledge the point. I knew he could say no more, but his demeanor continued to suggest I was on the right track.

Throughout the interview, I had not glanced at the single page of notes Roger had said I could bring. I reached into my vest pocket now to be sure I hadn't forgotten anything.

In trying to figure out why Roger had wanted to arrange this interview, I'd finally realized it offered one clear plus for the US. When the OTP filed the required public report with the Court at the end of our investigation, we could no longer say that the US military had completely stonewalled us. Yet if that was what they wanted, it made sense to press for more cooperation from the Army, and I did.

"I'm not hopeful of that, Mr. Ten Boom."

"But if it's as important as you say that there be no false insinuation of US involvement, then the only way Americans are going to be cleared is if we find other perpetrators or, failing that, if we get the evidence the Army possesses that would exonerate your troops."

"Isn't it hard to prove a negative, Mr. Ten Boom?"

"I'm not a military expert, but things like truck logs and duty rosters could shed a lot of light. If the military documents reflect no troop movements, that could be significant. But the fact that the Army isn't even willing to say publicly that it's examined all those records troubles me. It feels like they won't look because they don't want to see what's there. And that means your troops will always be suspects."

Merriwell's gray eyes, which had begun to remind me of two pencil points, fell to his lap as he calculated.

"I hear you, Mr. Ten Boom, but we're well past the time when such matters were within my control. Is there more?"

He stood then and I followed. The general offered to walk out with me.

It was cherry blossom time in DC and the city was a display of soft-focus beauty. At the Tidal Basin, the Japanese trees were a nimbus of pink. Even in this neighborhood some were in bloom, and their small pale petals decorated every breeze, a showy reminder, after our discussion of mayhem and force, of the delicate things that still enhance life.

I was rolling my bag behind me, and the general asked whether I was headed for the airport. I explained that because I'd been unsure how long our meeting would take, I'd arranged to stay in DC overnight before heading to Kindle County early tomorrow.

"And what are your plans this evening, if I may ask?"

"I'm going to my hotel to write down as much as I can remember of our conversation, and then make a few calls to The Hague before I crash."

"I can offer you dinner, if you like. Get you on your way by nine. I have an early plane myself in the morning."

"That's very kind," I said.

"Not really. I end up eating alone too often at the end of the day. Many friends meet me for lunch. But I'm not quite as welcome for dinner with the wives." He gave a terse smile that was a little too pained to be fully humorous. "Besides, I like lawyers, Mr. Ten Boom."

"You don't hear that said very often, General."

"My grandfather was Chief Justice of the US Court of Military Appeals. He was a very honorable man. Perhaps it's his influence, but I'm engaged by the way lawyers think, in part because it is so different from the way a soldier views problems. You reason your way to core principles. We concern ourselves most with effects.

"I guarantee," he added, "that our interview ended when we walked out of the Bosnian Embassy, just as the law requires. And I assure you I don't dine grandly enough to constitute a bribe."

I laughed. "No, General, the Roma advocate already paid for my dinner last month."

"Would that be Ms. Czarni? Is that her name? Then clearly you owe me the same opportunity. Although from what I'm told, I won't be quite as compelling."

"She's very attractive, if that's what you mean, General. And very, very smart. And quite determined." I experienced a familiar trill of feeling in speaking of Esma. "She's a five-tool player, if you know that term."

He laughed out loud for the first time.

"I do indeed. I love baseball. So we won't be hard-pressed for conversation. We can talk about the prospects for this season. Any dietary restrictions?"

"I only eat what's dead. I draw the line at slaughter. Otherwise, I'm a lifelong member of the Clean Plate Club."

He smiled again and said, "Seven?" He gave me the address before walking off.

7.

Dining

The general's place was at the vast white Watergate complex, and he greeted me at the door to his sixth-floor apartment. Merriwell had removed his jacket but was still in his white shirt and his tie, with a half-consumed whiskey in his left hand.

While Merriwell was hanging my suit jacket, I heard a clatter from the kitchen. My first thought was that he was living with someone, but then I remembered his remark about eating alone. A servant appeared in an instant, a small Asian man in a white coat, to offer a drink. The general introduced him as Paul and explained that the general's older brother, a Marine officer, had gotten Paul out of Saigon as a young man.

"He has four children now," said Merriwell. "The youngest just graduated from Easton Law. That's where you met Roger, isn't it?" The general still had a fond hand on Paul's shoulder. "We have a great country, Mr. Ten Boom," he said.

I held a native suspicion of American jingoism, but a month and a half away from the US had enhanced my appreciation for our country, and I experienced an emotional surge with the general's remark. In this nation, we did a lot of very big things far better than anyone else.

Paul returned with my drink, and a second for the general, then Merriwell showed me around the apartment. The decoration was sparse. The attractions were out the long windows. He had a fine view of the Potomac and the monuments. But the real treasury turned out to be his study. The room had a precise order I found intimidating, since I couldn't keep a space as small as my briefcase that well organized. Merriwell had a collection of Army relics—the insignia of the units he'd served with and the ranks he'd passed through—and a wall of signed photos that made what I'd once been proud of in my office silly by comparison. Layton Merriwell had met virtually everyone in power in Washington in his time. He was pictured beside each president going back to Reagan, often with the incumbent secretary of defense and the leaders of the House and Senate Armed Services Committees. Colin Powell was in a number of pictures. All 8-by-10s, the photographs were arranged evenly on one wall from ceiling to floor, except for a blank spot in the lower right corner.

"And who goes there?" I pointed. He opened his top drawer and removed an autographed picture of himself shaking with Alex Rodriguez, the Yankees star who was coming off a year's suspension for using various performance-enhancing chemicals.

"I've just reacquired this, Bill. Is 'Bill' all right now that we're off duty?"

"I answer more quickly to 'Boom.'"

" 'Merry,' " he said, tapping his shirt. I suspected his nickname had been awarded in the same spirit of adolescent irony as mine. Then again, he might have been far more cheerful years ago.

He said, "It only took eighteen months of negotiations between the lawyers to get a few things from my study at home. You've been down this road, Roger tells me."

I instantly understood the true motive for my dinner invitation. Divorce after a long marriage is not an isolated phenomenon, but you join a minority for whom there are limited sympathizers.

"At any rate, Paul's just finished rearranging all the photographs so we can hang up Mr. Rodriguez tomorrow."

I laughed because I'd misunderstood. "I thought you'd just taken it down."

"Not at all. People who live in glass houses," said the general. "I can't imagine how many photos of me came off of walls in this city, Boom."

He forced up a game little smile and replaced the picture in the open drawer, but when he turned back his look was unfocused and he remained quiet for a second, staring at the blank spot on the wall. Unexpectedly, I felt full flush the magnitude of the general's shame, far more poignantly than I had up until now. Layton Merriwell had been figuratively marched naked down Pennsylvania Avenue in front of a jeering throng. The major papers had been too decorous to publish most of his plaintive e-mails to his former mistress, but the lurid Internet sites that reveled in that sort of thing trotted out every word—angry, tormented, beseeching, and all too often, pornographic. He'd endured having all the teeming internal stuff most of us never share displayed to the entire world, knowing it would always come to mind with his name.

I was saved from attempting a comforting remark, because Paul announced dinner. A bowl of crab soup was curling steam on the old mahogany table.

The general proved to be a fine raconteur. As he'd promised, we talked about baseball. Merry had plenty of stories, insider stuff garnered from his relationships with a number of team owners and general managers. The anecdotes were funny, or more often inspirational, about the athletes who responded to their great success with unusual humility or generosity. Merriwell also possessed a remarkable memory for statistics. He had high hopes for the Yankees this year. Coming from Kindle County, a lifelong Trappers fan, I had no hope at all.

When Paul removed the dinner plates, the general waved me back down the hall to his study, where he asked me to hold his scotch—the fourth, by my count—while he used a mahogany library stool to reach the top of a closed cabinet. He climbed down balancing two huge leather display cases with silver latches. He opened them both on his desk to reveal a remarkable collection of autographed baseballs. In every velvet-lined square compartment, the balls were turned precisely to reveal the signatures across their equators by the greats of the game going back to Napoleon Lajoie, who became a star near the end of the nineteenth century. He had signed balls from Honus Wagner, whose career statistics I'd known since I was a boy, as well as record-breaking hitters like Ty Cobb and Rogers Hornsby. Merriwell's second case was devoted solely to Yankee stars of the last century—Ruth, Gehrig, DiMaggio, Mantle, Dickey, Reggie Jackson, Dave Winfield, Jeter, and A-Rod.

I wowed for several seconds, while the general extracted a pair of white livery gloves from a drawer. He put on one and used it to remove the Gehrig ball. Merry offered me the other, and then the baseball. Struck with ALS, Lou Gehrig had declared himself "the luckiest man in the world" on the day he retired. He, clearly, was the kind of guy a soldier would admire.

"I have been all over the world in temporary quarters," Merriwell said, "where I had nothing besides my uniforms. So I was surprised how much I missed these things. Of course, I still don't have what I wanted most."

"Which is?"

"The photos of my children, which were in my study at home. Florence claims them, too." He shook his head in wonder at the tidal wave of bitterness that now engulfed his life.

I explained that Ellen and I had divorced in relative peace.

"I went through enough, though," I said, "to know that five years of divorce litigation is worse than torture."

My sympathy was real, although it would not have been very hard to write a brief for Mrs. Merriwell. She'd held house and home together for forty years, while Merry was out being great, and had probably believed that she had the relatively contented marriage with all its sharp compromises and reluctant acceptance that many couples know. Then she picked up the morning paper. There she discovered not only that her husband had achieved some hitherto unknown peak of satisfaction with another woman, but that the female in question was younger than one of their daughters, and even worse, that he had ultimately begged that girl for the chance to throw over Mrs. Merriwell, to whom he referred repeatedly in unrefined terms. Perhaps the most painful revelation of all was that he regarded his time with his wife in the wake of the affair as a barren purgatory to which he was now confined as some kind of poetic punishment for the rapture he'd briefly experienced.

"No end to that case in sight?" I asked.

"I've wanted to negotiate. None of us—my wife, my daughters, or me—needs to provide the press with another field day by going to court, but I'm losing hope. I'm earning a large income for the first time in my life and Florence gets half of it as long as she holds out." He glanced up, with that whimsical smile that had first begun to emerge near the end of our meeting at the embassy. "There is a reason people hate lawyers, Boom.

"And, of course," he added, "while nothing is resolved, my daughters seem to feel obliged to side with their mother. I had a granddaughter last year, whom I'm yet to meet." He'd had too much to drink to remain completely stoical with that remark, and his gray eyes shifted south for a second. "But I received that photo at Christmas. So there's hope." I admired the picture of a beautiful, tow-headed lump framed at the very epicenter of his desk.

"And what about your life now?" I asked. "How are you finding dating?"

"Oh," said Merriwell. "There's been none of that. My lawyer believes it would only add fuel to the fire, since it will inevitably be a public event. And I'm not sure I'm ready anyway."

"After five years, Merry, you're probably as ready as you're going to get."

"Ten, really." I didn't understand for a second. Then I realized that he was referring to Major St. John. "It's bound to involve compromises that I don't want to face." A crippling bolt of emotion, sped by alcohol, palsied his features for only a second and he refused to look my way as I took in the fact that the man remained heartbroken. Merry gazed into his drink.

"I lived a life of discipline," he said. "And then I could summon it no longer. I wish I could say that with hindsight I would never do it again. I am devastated by the pain I caused everyone else. But I have a far better idea now of who I am. I would never want to have lived without learning that." He peeked up at last. "Is that shocking?"

"Of course not," I said, although I wasn't positive I meant that. "I'm just trying to add it all up, Merry."

"And what does it come to?"

"I doubt my impressions are worth much."

"No excuses," he said. "Something seems to have struck you."

I turned it all over for a second more.

"I'm sure I'm way out of place, and probably wrong," I said, "but you seem to be giving everybody permission to punish you, starting with yourself, as if that will make up for the value you attach to that experience. I think it's time to move on and take advantage of what you've learned. I have no clue where I'm going, but I feel a lot better moving ahead than I did during the years I seemed to be standing still."

In all likelihood, I was the one thousandth person to tell Layton Merriwell something like this. But that didn't mean the other 999 had been heard. He stared at me as if it were the Annunciation.

"Thank you," he said at last. Nine had just passed. I called a car and removed my jacket from his closet. We stood together at the door.

"I've enjoyed meeting you, Boom. I hope it's not the last occasion."

"Same here, Merry."

Life, of course, is full of people you discover you like a lot and then never see again. It's one of the many small tragedies of going around only once. We both seemed to be contemplating that fact.

"I wish you luck with your investigation, Boom. I truly do. I don't know what you will find. But I'm certain what you won't." He opened the door and extended his hand, which I took. To my surprise, Merriwell held on for a second.

"I did give some thought to what you said about the Army's records absolving all of us. And there's one aspect you may not have considered. The control of the documents you'd like to see, Boom, is more complicated than you may have recognized. Our troops were operating under NATO command. So some are NATO's papers, others are duplicated in NATO's files. If I were you, I'd look carefully at NATO's Status of Forces Agreement and pay attention to the provisions about assistance in investigating crimes."

As soon as he said this, I knew it was a revelation unlikely ever to have struck me. Except for the US, all the countries in NATO had signed the ICC treaty, which meant they would be obliged to cooperate with a document request from the Court.

I looked at him levelly for a minute before saying thank you.

III.
Bosnia

8.

Attila—April 11–15

My weekend in Kindle County, as I probably could have predicted, proved frequently charged. Being back made me recognize how persistent my sense of foreignness had been in The Hague, where I knew from waking to sleeping that layers of meaning lay in virtually every word and gesture that were simply beyond me. The contrasting realization that I no longer lived in the Tri-Cities left me feeling slightly off-balance at all times.

On Saturday, my younger son, Pete, who could magically score tickets for any sporting event, bought seats for himself and his brother and me for the Trappers game, the home opener. I pretended to be thrilled, but I'd given up on Opening Day two decades before, because it was almost never baseball weather in Kindle County. As I expected, the temperature did not reach 40, and after braving five innings, we adjourned to a nearby tavern, where we took turns making fun of each other, usually two on one, more often both boys against me.

In The Hague, I'd had standing phone dates with each of my sons, 6 a.m. on Tuesday and Thursday, respectively, when I was reaching them at the end of their days in the Midwest. They'd sounded good, but the reassurance of seeing them in the flesh now was uplifting.

The Saturday night dinner with the Rosenbergs was a success, with warm toasts and nearly constant laughter. Pete and Brandi had been together since high school, and after years of misgivings from all four parents, we had all come to recognize what the couple had seen long before: They were a durable, loving match.

Afterward, I went home with my ex and her husband, Howard, an engineer who'd become unfathomably rich as one of the original patent trolls. Having a former spouse with whom you get along is a little like acquiring another sibling, someone who knows you intimately and with indelible affection. On the other hand, most of us would go screaming in the other direction at the thought of again living under the same roof with a sib, and the prospect of even a single night here filled me with apprehension. I'd accepted because Ellen, in her usual direct style, had made an unassailable argument: "Who else are you going to barge in on at eleven p.m. on Saturday night? The boys don't have room."

I'm sure Ellen had wanted to show off the splendor of her new life in the mansion on Lake Fowler that Howard had built with his first wife, who'd died of cancer more than six years ago. But my stay proved calm and companionable. I enjoyed the comforts of their guest house, then moved down to Center City on Sunday morning to begin my labors with my former partners and clients.

After two days of listening to oil executives make unconvincing excuses, I was happy to depart.

I arrived in Bosnia at dusk Wednesday. From Kindle County, I'd had a nine-hour flight to Istanbul and a layover there in the terminal, which is stylish, but thronged and airless as a casket. In Sarajevo, I emerged into what was no bigger than a regional airport in the US, with robin's-egg signs declaring *DOBRODOSLI U SARAJEVO*.

Before I had taken my job in The Hague, Bosnia, to me, like most Americans, had always seemed remote, baffling, and largely irrelevant. The Cyrillic alphabet, which was used frequently, was indecipherable to me; the language, Serbo-Croatian, bore no resemblance to the Western languages I knew; and I understood next to nothing about the two largest religions, Islam and Serbian Orthodox. I arrived prepared for something very different, and found that expectation immediately met.

Goos had flown into Tuzla through Austria that morning in order to complete arrangements for our trip to Barupra tomorrow, but had promised to send a car for me. I didn't see my name on the placards carried by three or four dark-suited drivers, but I suddenly heard someone calling, "Boom." The person waving was not only nobody I knew, but also weirdly unrecognizable on a more basic level.

This is what I saw: someone rangy and lean, about five foot nine, with a springy mass of brown hair, dressed in oversize worn jeans cinched at the waist and a round-necked Members Only windbreaker at least two decades old, smiling exuberantly as if we were meeting again after years apart. I was feeling out-of-body due to the travel and the unfamiliar locale, and my mind spun like an old disc drive as it grasped for a fundamental category, namely, gender. I thought immediately of Pat, a sketch character on *Saturday Night Live* who appeared for several seasons, eluding the intrepid but fruitless efforts of everyone else to determine if Pat was a boy or a girl.

"Attila Doby." A sinewy hand was extended in welcome. Attila was a male name, but the voice was thinner and sounded like a woman's. The jacket was open but the blue button-down shirt was too loose to reveal if there were skinny breasts beneath. "Merry said you was on your way. So I told my guys who were fetchin you to stay home and I'd zip down from Tuzla myself."

Attila's racial origins were also uncertain. There was the freckly complexion of people who years ago were called 'High Yeller,' but Attila's eyes were muddy green, even if the nose had an African breadth. 'American' was the only biographical detail I was certain of after he or she had spoken the first words.

Attila grabbed my bag and wheeled it along, waving me to follow across the small parking lot. Attila had a jerky, knock-kneed walk, elbows held away from the body, shoulders peaked as a result. Ultimately, he—that was my best guess—opened the door to a cushy Audi A8, into whose trunk he tossed my luggage.

"So," Attila said from the driver's seat, hiking around to back out, "you're thinking, 'What in the fuck have I got here?' Right?" Attila's eyes hit me briefly before turning forward to put the car in drive. "Don't bother apologizing. I go through this shit every day. That's what you're thinking, true?"

"Right," I said, realizing I had no way out.

"A woman, okay? Married to a woman. And dress however the fuck I please. But last time I had a skirt on, I was thirteen. Played with the boys since I was three.

Okay?" Attila smiled throughout all of this, as if it was all a good-natured joke at her expense.

"And yes," she said, "the name is Attila. Etelka, actually, but Attila is the closest thing in English. Mom is Hungarian. Dad was a US Army lifer, master sergeant, born in Alabama and passed until his daughter came out a little toasty looking, after which everybody pretended like they didn't notice. So yeah, I'm one big fuckin freak, and now we got that out of the way, okay?"

"Okay," I answered, and started laughing. Giddy from jet lag, I couldn't figure whether I should have been quite this amused by Attila's candor. "Did you say that General Merriwell sent you?"

"No, I talked to Merry, but it was your guy who ordered a car. Swan?"

"Goos?"

"Goos, shit. Any kind of vehicle for hire—truck, half-track, limousine—that's my business. One of them anyway."

We were entering Sarajevo proper, where Tito-era apartment buildings, concrete blocks that resembled high-rise prisons, stood beside contemporary glass towers dressed up with garish Shanghai-style lights. The city I was seeing was no longer the shell-ravaged wreck of twenty years ago, but reconstructing the buildings was probably a lot easier than recovering from the trauma.

"And how is it you know Merry?" I asked.

"He was my senior commanding officer close to half my time in service. Sergeant Major Attila Doby," she said, sticking a thumb into her sternum, "US Army retired. Twenty years in and a whole fruit salad on my chest. I served under Merry in Desert Storm and he brought me along when he come to Bosnia. I was the top noncombat NCO here—Quartermaster's Corps. Shit's always the same in the Army, but QC's worse. Senior officers were all in Virginia signing contracts and managing future requirements. But you wanted so much as a sheet of toilet paper to wipe your heinie, then better call me.

"My twenty come up in 2000. I mustered out, but the US, man, fifteen years ago—black and queer? People didn't know what to do with me. I ended up back here a couple years later to straighten out CoroDyn. You know what that is?"

I said no. Attila took a second, nodding to herself as she looked out the auto windshield.

"So here," she said. "Merry was a great field commander for a lot of reasons, but one of the most important was that he wasn't afraid to change things. He sort of invented using private defense contractors to take on noncombat functions. It's a volunteer army, so you need to stretch the troops. Why have your privates doing KP when they can be out toting a bang-bang? CoroDyn was the contractor here, and when I was in service, I was the Army liaison, making sure they did what-all they were supposed to.

"But Bosnia, after the war, there just wasn't any normal here. And a lot of CoroDyn employees were into sex slaves, twelve-, fifteen-year-old girls they were fucking on the job and trading back and forth. The press got wind of that when Merry was at NATO CENTCOM. After he'd just about choked their CEO to death, he called me up personal and said, 'How much do I gotta make these monkeys pay you to get you to come back here and run it all?'

"We basically did everything on base that didn't require shooting. Fed the troops. Ran the buses. Washed the clothes. Provided the trucks and drove them. Stockpiled captured weapons. Handled all the trash. And did most of the bookkeeping. We were like the stage crew and the soldiers were the actors."

Attila had taken a detour on our way to the highway to show me City Library, an extraordinary structure built in Austro-Hungarian times. The masonry alternated stripes of salmon and rust, while the roof sported a Moorish dome and a line of decorative crenellations. According to Attila, the whole thing had been resurrected from rubble.

"And why is it you're still here?" I asked. "Your wife?"

"Nope. Met my wife here, but she's a hell of a lot happier in the US. I gotta go home to see her, isn't that somethin? Why I'm still here is cause the US Army had hired thousands of Bosnian civilians. Speak English. Clean records. Security clearances. And best, most of them are Muslims, which means they know the rules in Islamic countries. So after the US withdrew, I basically set up an employment agency. I supply Bosnian workers for US military support operations all over the Mideast. Iraq, Afghanistan. Kuwait, Saudi. My people make a good buck and so do I. They work for a year, come back, fuck the wife and buy a house or a car, and then take another assignment. I had four thousand people on my payroll at one point; still more than fifteen hundred. And in the meantime, I bought all the vehicles CoroDyn had no more use for in Bosnia and I rent them out. Like I said, I'm rich, man."

"And you stay in touch with General Merriwell?"

"Try. Merry was never one of those generals who didn't know the names of his NCOs. He give me a call two weeks ago about this massacre bullshit, when he was deciding whether to talk to you, and I phoned him back today to hear how it went. And he says he thinks we should be helping you out. That's all I need to know. I'll tell you this about Layton Merriwell. I'd lay down my life for the motherfucker. How many generals you think there were in the US Army that'd look at a bull dyke cross-dressing half-breed and say, 'That's one fuckin smart soldier, I got her back'? I'm here in Bosnia livin like a king, I got a wife at home in a goddamn mansion, and I owe it all to Merry. So he says help you, here I am."

I laughed again, enjoying Attila, who seemed to equate speaking with pageantry. I thought she might give me an honest answer to one persistent riddle.

"And why is Merriwell doing that? Trying to help? Do you understand?"

"Well, he didn't say nothin to explain, but I kinda think I get it. You know, one day everybody from the president of the US on down is suckin your dick and sayin you're the greatest military commander since Eisenhower, and then all the sudden it's a headline that you're this dogbreath jerk that wouldn't be welcome in most alleys. Try telling yourself you don't care what people think of you then. So Merry—this is how I figure— Merry is all about his reputation as a commander. Okay, he stuck his pecker in a meat grinder, and everybody laughs instead of salutes when he walks by, but what he's thinking is, History's on my side. Eventually, it won't be about who he was fucking, but the way he led our troops. But not if there's this story going around that NATO's first-ever combat operation included burying four hundred people alive in a coal mine. Then he's just a flat-ass fuckin failure."

Attila's theory about Merriwell seemed fairly convincing, although the desire for historical redemption could almost as easily lead the general to lie. But assuming Attila was correct, it made even more remarkable what Merriwell had said to me a few nights back—that when it came to Jamie St. John, he would do it all again.

I asked if Attila had known the major.

"Jamie? Sure. You knew Merriwell, you knew her. She was all the time as close behind him as a fart. Smart, nice shape, no beauty queen. Really good soldier. And always treated me with respect. She was a real person. And Merriwell and her, man, they had it going on. You would have needed the Jaws of Life to extract him from that pussy. He was gettin it like he'd never gotten it before. And good for him, too. Why die wondering, you know?"

Why, indeed. The Jaws of Life had never had to be applied to me, at least not at any time in my memory. I doubted I was better off for that.

"You hungry anyway?" Attila asked. "There won't be anything open by the time we get to Tuzla. Nice city, but not exactly Manhattan."

We stopped at a roadside place Attila knew for *cevapi*, which occupied the same space in the Bosnian diet as a hamburger in the US. They were highly seasoned little logs of ground lamb and beef, served like a gyros on pita with onions and sauce. I enjoyed the *cevapi* a great deal, but not the trip to the squat toilet in the restaurant, which immediately ensued. There is nothing like the plumbing fixtures to remind you that you're not in Kansas anymore.

By the time we were back in the car, night was full upon us. In the dark, this part of Bosnia, which I could see only in outline, seemed to resemble Colorado, with mountains of fir trees and A-frame houses, steep-roofed to shed the snow. I was starting to fight sleep, as I still needed to spend some time with Goos once we got to Tuzla. In order to stay awake, I wanted to keep Attila talking, which did not seem like much of a task.

"You mentioned a while ago the 'bullshit' I'm investigating."

"That wasn't personal, you know. It's just bullshit."

"What is?"

"That Americans had anything to do with killing Gypsies."

"And what about the Roma being massacred? Do you believe that happened?"

"Well, they're sure as shit gone. You know, with several thousand locals as employees, I heard all kinda stories. As soon as folks noticed that Barupra was a ghost town, the rumor started in that Kajevic got some old Arkans to bury those Gypsies alive. That bunch, the Tigers, they'd seal Granny in a cave if Kajevic said so."

"And when was it you began hearing that?"

"Shit, I don't know for sure. When did this supposedly happen? Spring 2004? By late summer, then. Maybe the fall."

"And why would Kajevic kill four hundred Roma?"

Attila glanced over from the wheel with a telltale smile.

"You're asking what folks were sayin, right? Cause this security clearance I got is very dear to me. I lose it, and I go back to Kentucky to shovel horse poop and do everything else on the honey-do list. Whatever I know from work, which ain't much, I couldn't tell you."

"Understood. Just what you heard from the locals."

"They was sayin it was the Roma who tipped the Army about where Kajevic was."

I took just a second with that, so I didn't lose my inquisitorial pace. But this pretty clearly was the fact Merriwell had been circling around.

"And how did the Roma know that?"

"Like I said. If I knew and I told ya, I'd have to poison your next *cevapi*." She smiled broadly. "But don't you have some big fuckin secret witness who supposedly was there? Ask him."

The problem was that Ferko—at least according to Esma—knew nothing about any Roma involvement with Kajevic.

"And Kajevic," I said. "He would really kill four hundred people for revenge? Women? Children?"

Attila just snorted.

"The guy's been on the loose fifteen years now. You think that's just because he's got the right camouflage gear? He's made it so if he walks into a supermarket in downtown Sarajevo, everybody turns to face the wall and acts like it would be worse than staring at Jehovah. Killing four hundred people, that's as good as putting up a billboard that says, Talk and die."

I said to Attila, "General Merriwell believes there is no way a massacre like that could have happened without American forces knowing."

Attila responded by making the raspberries.

"Generals," she said. "I mean, even that general. Sometimes they'd drink their own piss and think it was lemonade."

I laughed in spite of myself.

"But in April 2004," I asked, "you were working around the American base, if I understand?"

"Every damn day."

"And at that point—not in the summer, but in the spring—you never heard any Americans talk about the Roma disappearing from Barupra?"

"Not as how I recall." I took a second to mull on that, and Attila looked over again from the wheel. "You don't believe me?"

"Well, Attila, it's strange. There's no argument there was a big explosion in Barupra in the middle of the night. With four American camps within a few miles, it's hard to figure that no US troops heard that or asked about it."

"I didn't say nobody heard it. What I will tell you is that explosions around Eagle Base were nothin to talk about. Bosnia was the most heavily land-mined area on earth. The Serbs had done it to keep the Muslims from returning to their villages. Which generally worked. I mean, talk about a pathetic sight: These poor folks in rags come back to their houses after a couple years, and you got a whole family sometimes down on their knees, sticking pencils in the ground every three inches, delicate enough to be fucking Tinker Bell. And you know, as soon as they move back in, somebody steps on a square inch they missed, and the house is gone and half the folks in the family have no legs. Around here to this day, you don't go walkin without someone can tell you what's safe. And you better pay attention, too." She looked from the road to be sure I grasped the warning.

"And land mines weren't all," Attila added. "Do you know what the main industry is around there?"

I told her I had no idea.

"Mining. Digging for stone. Coal. Salt. 'Tuzla' means 'salt' in Turkish. By 2004, they were trying to get back

to business, which means people were all the time blowing these mountainsides to hell."

"In the middle of the night?"

"Safest time to do it. Everyone's inside, sheltered from
debris. The only thing I'd a done after an explosion from
the direction of a coal mine would be cover my head."

"And what did you think in the fall, when you finally
learned that the Roma in Barupra were all gone?"

"Truth? What I thought was, Don't let the door hit
you in the ass. Those people were just always trouble.
Capital T. Rhymes with P. And that stands for 'puke.'"

"And it was okay if Kajevic killed four hundred of
them?"

"Course not. But with the Roma, you never know
what to believe. The only thing for sure is that whatever
they're tellin you isn't true."

I gave Attila a dim look and asked, "But as far as
you know, no one from NATO investigated this rumored
massacre?"

"That wasn't our job no more. The Bosnians were
back in charge."

It was exactly as Esma said: Four hundred dead Gypsies were just four hundred fewer problems.

"Besides, you need to understand Bosnia, Boom. This
was hell on earth. Even in 2004, there was still horrible
shit being discovered every day—mass graves or bones
washing up on riverbanks. I know what-all this sounds
like when I talk about the Gypsies," she said. "Having
people hate you for no reason? That is my fuckin autobiography. But by 2004, me and just about everyone
else was up to here with them in Barupra. I mean, I was
around when they first got here in June '99. You know
that story?"

By now, I'd read reports. Like tens of thousands of other Roma in Kosovo, they had been driven from their homes, usually by the Albanians, who took them as Serb allies because they practiced the Serbian Orthodox faith. This particular group had been placed in a refugee camp in a town called Mitrovica in Kosovo, right after the NATO bombardment had forced the Serbs to retreat. Within days, the Albanians marched across the main bridge there, surrounded the camp, and set fire to it. Only the intervention of the US ambassador saved the Roma, who then begged the UN to move them close to the US bases in Bosnia, assuming—ironically—they would be safest there. Somehow the UN trucks carrying the Roma refugees arrived at a deserted US installation, Camp Bedrock, before their resettlement had been approved by US commanders.

"One day," said Attila, "Camp Bedrock is this empty yellow rock, full of weeds and garbage, and the next day all these grimy-looking Gypsies are putting together their shabby-ass tent city. That's what 'Barupra' means in Romany—'Bedrock.' Sorta. MPs come out and tell the Blue Hats—you know, the UN guys—Take them back where you got 'em. Like that was gonna work with the UN. Those dickless twerps are probably still driving around trying to find their way back to Kosovo.

"And you know," Attila said, "your heart hurt for those folks. Run out of one country and livin like dirt in another? The kids especially, they all have these huge dark eyes.

"Merry was the commander here back then, and I was still in service, quartermastering, and he's like, 'Attila, see what you can do for these poor wretches.' So I go over to CoroDyn, asking to find a few of them jobs. Mind you, eighty percent of the Bosnians have got no work. But these Gypsy motherfuckers are truly starving to death. And do you think they show up for work? They breeze in at noon for the eight a.m. shift and then tell you they don't like paving roads or washing trucks.

"Don't ask what's wrong with me. Must be I got a heart bigger than my head, but once I come back from Stateside and was in charge of CoroDyn, and all those folks were still living so bad in Barupra, I decided to try it again. Gypsies all think they know cars like they know horses. So I said to a couple, Tell you what, you don't want to wash the truck, how about you drive it? They liked that well enough. But they always showed up with a few kids. I could say no all I wanted. Guy's there every morning with his thirteen-year-old and his ten-year-old, instead of sending them to school, and whenever I turn my back, he's letting the little one drive a half-track. And if all that wasn't enough, the bastards started stealing the equipment. You'd send a Gypsy out with a truck in the morning and that was the last you'd see of any of it, them and the truck and whatever was in it. I just had enough finally. I fired them all. God only knows how many millions in shit was missing."

We were going up and down through the mountains, whizzing past open fields where the patchy snow weakly reflected the starlight, slowing periodically for the little villages in which there was almost always a tiny roadside restaurant with a Bavarian look, a steep shake roof and whitewashed sides.

"And by the way," said Attila, "just so you understand, I got some great Roma folks that work for me to this day. Smart as hell, all of them. Maybe that's how come the Roma have lasted this long, because they're so fuckin clever. But the ones I hire, they've been to school, they wear watches, they speak the language. But them in Barupra? They didn't want to leave the reservation, if you know what I mean."

That was the last I heard. I fell asleep with my forehead against the frigid car window.

9.

The Blue Lamp

Attila shook me awake in Tuzla. "Hat up," she said. Down the curve of a street that bore the narrow dimensions of a road first built for carts, I could see the hotel sign. BLUE LAMP, it read, BOUTIQUE HOTEL. Attila walked ahead with my luggage. The cool night, in the high 40s if I'd done the conversion from Celsius correctly, refreshed me slightly. There was a small shop on the corner that looked to be a convenience store, and some young men in their close-fitting leather jackets milled in the doorway, waving cigarettes at one another and jiving the way young men always do. There was no other traffic. The tranquil domestic air of Tuzla was a testimonial to how wrong Hobbes had been. The natural state of man is peace.

Buzzed into the hotel lobby, Attila immediately got into laughing byplay in Bosnian with the young man and woman who were behind the front desk.

"They say I'm the king around here," Attila told me.

"You should be honored I'm carrying your luggage." She gave me her card and told me to call if I needed anything.

As soon as Attila was gone, I detected a gesture from my right. Over my shoulder, there was a small lounge area with coffee tables and black leather armchairs. I was not surprised to see Goos with a beer glass in his hand, which he tipped in my direction. Once I had my room key, I plunged down beside him. The chair had the gleam and soft feel of the furniture in the embassy in DC. Leather, I took it, was a Bosnian thing.

"Welcome," said Goos.

"I'm on another planet," I told him. The mix of grogginess and jet lag made me feel like half my body was still in Kindle County.

"Drink?" Goos asked.

One of the desk clerks came over to pour a scotch for me, which I asked for as silent acknowledgment of Merriwell, who remained in mind after my talk with Attila. The clerk set down another beer for Goos at the same time, already familiar with his routine.

"Who was your driver?" Goos asked.

He laughed out loud in response to Attila's name.

"Wanted to hire a few blokes to help out tomorrow," said Goos, "and everybody says 'Call Attila.' Been trying to get hold of him all day."

"Her, actually."

Goos stared at the front door, through which Attila had departed.

"Really?" he asked.

"She said you sent her to pick me up, by the way."

"Did she now? Not as how I reckon. Finally rang a taxi service to go get you."

"I guess she owns it."

"Tell you one thing, mate," said Goos. "We won't be using her as a translator. Those young folks over there said, 'You think you're the king around here, and here you are toting the man's luggage,' and he turned it all around so you should be honored. She," Goos added.

The Blue Lamp had a contemporary appearance, comfortable but not fancy, with dark mahogany trim and white laminate fixtures in the compact spaces. A little breakfast area with a few white tables was visible behind Goos. Over the angled front desk, a large-screen TV displayed a slide show of Bosnian scenes—mountain glades, the Grand Mosque in Sarajevo, and an old Roman castle somewhere near Tuzla. The same images played on a smaller TV screen on the wall beside us.

I had e-mailed Goos over the weekend about the notion of going through NATO to get the US Army's records. Before leaving The Hague, he had dug up the Status of Forces Agreement that Merry had referred to. Goos read it to me now off his phone.

" 'The receiving and sending States shall assist each other in the carrying out of all necessary investigations into offences,' blah blah blah, 'including producing evidence.' Blah blah blah."

"That's pretty good," I told him. "We can stand in the shoes of the Bosnians to demand the documents."

Goos nodded. "Course, you lawyers will do what you always do, say none of those words mean what they say. Might be ten years before we're close as cooee to those papers. But still, good thinking, Boom."

"It wasn't my idea," I said. Given the legal issues, I had been careful about what I put on paper concerning my meeting with Merriwell. Goos straightened when I told him that the guidance about going via NATO had come from the general.

"The other helpful thing I got from him," I told Goos, "was that he didn't deny that the Roma in Barupra had assisted the Army somehow in their attempt to capture Kajevic. Attila said the local gossip was that the Gypsies gave the US Kajevic's location. But I'm having a hard time making sense of that."

"Because?"

"Well, I reread my file on that whole mess with Kajevic in Doboj on the plane. And I can't imagine why a bunch of threadbare Gypsies would know more about Laza Kajevic than NATO Intelligence."

"I believe that's why they call us investigators, Boom." Goos smiled.

Like me, Goos was also puzzled by Merriwell's helpfulness. I shared Attila's theory that after disgracing himself, Layton Merriwell now had a large stake in clearing himself and his soldiers. Remote from the American press and its obsessions, Goos knew nothing of Merriwell's affair. I summarized the story and also told him about my dinner with Merriwell, which I characterized as an invitation offered so I could commiserate about the hardships of middle-aged divorce. Apparently I hadn't said much to Goos before this about the demise of my own marriage, and he responded by looking deep into his pilsner glass for a moment.

"I could never quite reckon on divorce," he said. "Couldn't see how it would make anything much better."

He finished the second half of his beer in a single gulp and lifted a finger to the desk clerk for a refill. Goos had been sitting down here drinking long enough to have acquired his own conversational momentum.

"It's just the facts, mate," he said. "Seven billion people on the planet and I wake up with the same one every day? Everybody after a long time is bound to feel stuck. Just a matter of how you react to it."

I understood that attitude, the fatalistic approach to marriage. Ellen and I had been unable to settle for boredom. Instead it was accompanied on both sides by a relentless, grinding resentment.

"Cobber of mine," Goos said, "says beer's a better companion than a woman anyway. Always there. Know how you'll feel after one or two or five. And how you feel is always better than when you started."

He smiled equivocally as he pondered that observation, while a ruckus rose up at the door. Esma Czarni, followed by a driver laboring with two large suitcases, arrived at the reception desk. She paid the driver, while one of the young desk clerks, who greeted her by name, welcomed her back and stepped around to help with the bags. Esma had not dressed down for travel. The collar on her Burberry mackintosh was turned up against the chill, and a furry purple scarf was stylishly doubled over her bosom. Her skirt was short to show off her legs in her glossy high-heeled boots.

She summoned an effusive smile as soon as she saw me, and advanced at once.

"Bill!" She delivered Continental kisses, while I reintroduced her to Goos. He took a second to brief us both on the schedule for the morning.

"Are we drinking?" Esma asked, motioning at our glasses with a hand heavy with several gold rings I hadn't noticed before.

I explained that my scotch had left me close to dizzy and that I was ready to retire.

"Good thought," she said. "Truth told, I'm rather

weary myself. I'll walk you upstairs." Goos, as usual, said he was going to stay on for another beer, although he gave me a fleeting look, too quick to read.

My room was on what the Europeans call the first floor, the second to us. In one of those Continental efficiencies that make you embarrassed at our profligacy, the overhead fluorescents were controlled by energy-saving motion detectors, and they sprang on as we ascended, giving us light as we arrived at the corridor that led down to my room. Standing there, we did another second's worth of business as I asked Esma to question Ferko one more time to see if he had any idea how someone in Barupra might have known where Laza Kajevic was hiding. Then, as I was about to turn away, she cast an appraising look at me.

"I must say, Bill, that I'm rather pleased to see you. You've been on my mind."

"It's good to see you, too, Esma."

She averted her dark face slightly and delivered a hooded look from her eyes, large within the dusky shadow, adding a trifling smile. The communication was on the order of something one of my high school teachers liked to say: Don't kid a kidder.

I waited just a second, then decided, despite my trepidation, that the moment was at hand.

"Esma, I'm as tired as you were the night we met, and not as good as you without sleep. So I'm probably going way out over my skis, and if so, I apologize. But when I was about twenty, I was struck by what seemed to me to be a very sad truth. When I find a woman enormously attractive, other men do as well. Which means you don't need to hear me repeat what you've undoubtedly heard a thousand times."

She smiled hugely, a glamorous display of large, perfect teeth.

"Some things never become trite, Bill," she answered. I smiled as well.

"But nothing can happen here, Esma." I used my right hand to etch the air between us.

"You've become involved?" she asked.

"It's not that, Esma. You're an advocate for a client whose claims I'm supposed to objectively assess as the prosecutor in this case."

"Ferko is not my client. I was appointed to assist him for a single hearing, which is now over."

"If he's not your client, Esma, why else are you here? And besides, the technicalities don't change the appearances. You're far too good a lawyer not to understand what I'm saying."

As before, the compliment pleased her, if only briefly.

"I'm not sure I see it that way, Bill. I'm as conscious as you of the professional commandments. But I had the thought that we could be good for each other."

"But not at the moment, Esma. Who we are in this case can't help being entangled in who we'd be to one another."

That was the self-deception that Layton Merriwell or Bill Clinton or hundreds of other men had practiced, and the reason people mocked them: The power that proved so seductive to certain women was not actually theirs; it was a gift entrusted to them temporarily and for much different purposes.

But Esma shook her head slightly.

"I don't come to the same conclusion, Bill. Yes, the professional informs the personal. But there is nothing false about it. Do I misperceive you? I take you as a man who has given up a comfortable life, who has come thousands of miles from home, so he can know that his energies as a person are devoted to making large wrongs right. That is very attractive to me, you're correct. That kind of conviction is a rarer quality than you think."

As she spoke, the lights blinked out again. In the shadows, I became suddenly conscious of her perfume, a power scent, full of sweetness and allure, which I had heretofore absorbed merely as part and parcel of her strong sensual presence.

I knew Esma was far too nimble intellectually for me to triumph via argument. I went with trump.

"I can't, Esma," I said. I thought I was speaking from principle, but with the words, I experienced, strangely, a sense of my own weakness. I realized again that I was in some way afraid of Esma.

For a second the hotel was still around us, then a door slammed resonantly a floor above.

"Very well, Bill. I shan't push myself on you." In the weak light, she stared up at me a second longer, then approached to kiss my cheeks as she had downstairs, a bit more slowly this time. "But I foresee that in the future you will change your mind."

" 'Foresee'?" The word amused me. "Do you tell fortunes, Esma, like the Gypsy women in their wagons?"

"I am somewhat psychic," she said. "Most Roma women are. Don't smile either. That is a truth."

I nodded rather than disagree.

"Certainly I know minds," she said. "I know your mind—what you do not care to say or even know you need." She was utterly serious, without a hint of irony, and quite commanding. "And I foresee that you will have a change of heart." She had laid her hand on my arm as she was kissing my cheeks, but now removed it.

"Perhaps, Esma. But sadly for me that will be far in the future."

She turned then, and with her sudden movement, the fluorescents powered on again. In the painful brightness, she offered a gallant little wave and turned away.

I dragged my bags into my room. The door closed solidly behind me, a fatal definiteness to the sound. Alone, recoiling, I felt regretful and forlorn, but opened my case to find what little I would need for sleep.

All my life, my unconscious has expressed itself in song. Habitually I'd find myself humming a tune for reasons I was slow to recognize. Now, as I lifted the stacks of clothing into the dresser drawers, I was tootling a soul ballad Pete had introduced me to a few years back. It took its title from the first line of the chorus that rose up amid big horn flourishes. I da-da-da'd until the words came back to me. It was called "Don't Make Me Do Wrong."

10.

Barupra—April 16

At nine in the morning, we arrived on the yellow rock of Barupra. Traveling in caravan, we were led by a line of squat Bosnian police cars that had been waiting for us outside the hotel when we departed. The tubby little captain insisted with great animation that the Bosnian government wanted to do everything possible to assist the Court.

"A pig's arse 'assist us,'" said Goos, as soon as we had closed the door to our little Ford.

"What else would they be doing?"

"They're watching us, buddy. This is still a country with factions within its factions. You have three different national governments here, and every cop will be reporting to somebody else." Goos shifted gears somewhat emphatically and pointed at me. "A fit job for the lawyer will be to get rid of them. Ferko won't fancy lairing around in front of coppers." Esma had already made the same point to me. The loyalties of any single Bosnian policeman were always open to doubt.

The police now led us on what seemed to be the back route out of town. We rose into the hills on residential streets that reminded me of the canyons of West LA. There are rich people everywhere and in Tuzla this seemed to be their hangout. The country roads onto which we eventually emerged doubled back as they ascended, with impressive vistas of the city below occasionally peeking through the trees beginning to leaf. After about twenty minutes, we reached flatlands, still dotted with snow, and buzzed past farms and little whitewashed houses that could have been home to Hansel and Gretel.

On this highland south of Tuzla, the US, after Dayton, set up a base with a network of six camps. Predictably, the US military installations stood at the border between areas controlled by Muslims and Croats on one hand, and on the other, the territory of the Serbian Bosnians that became their autonomous enclave of Republika Srpska. The Army's air base at Camp Comanche subsumed a former MiG landing strip of the Yugoslav Army, which years later became Tuzla's civilian airport, where flights arrived on two commercial airlines several mornings a week.

Due east of Comanche, on the other side of the hills, Camp Bedrock had been built on the waste of two adjacent open-pit coal mines. The brown-black slag had been bleached by sun and wind to a color like whole-grain mustard and was piled high to create a rocky prominence looking out over the Tuzla valley in the distance and the Rejka coal mine immediately below. It was the kind of highpoint that armies going back to the Romans had prized, trading stark exposure to the elements for virtual invincibility to ground assault.

The cop cars led us onto the former camp, turning

down a rocky dirt road that ran behind the old wire-
fenced perimeter, past an old basketball court on which
the asphalt was now split by weeds. I got out of the car.
This was Barupra.

In the eleven years since the Roma had disappeared,
the site had become a town garbage dump, perhaps as a
gesture of good riddance. Between the large gray rocks,
most of the area was covered by what appeared to be
construction waste, especially scraps of shredded plasterboard, amid the usual hardy detritus of dusty bottles,
aerosol cans, and of course the ubiquitous and indestruc-
tible bright plastic bags that will blow through empty
spaces for centuries to come and for which the millennia
to follow will curse us.

Aside from Goos and me and the police, there was another small car in the cavalcade, containing three laborers
Goos had hired from Attila's company. Accompanied by
her driver from last night, Esma arrived last. She was still
dressed like a lady, her lone concession to the landscape
a pair of flat-heeled boots.

Once we stopped, all of the police officers left their vehicles to light on their fenders. Goos had it right. They
were here to spy.

I approached the captain. After several minutes, I convinced him that the protocols established between the
Court and the Bosnian government required us to work
unobserved. Even then, Esma insisted that Ferko would
also be unwilling to speak in front of the three laborers,
whom we ended up dispatching to Vica Donja, the nearest town, to find a coffee, which you could seemingly
obtain on even the remotest mountaintop in Bosnia. Only
then did Esma take out her cell to summon Ferko, whom
she had called earlier and now had waiting nearby.

He appeared about ten minutes later in a red wreck of a car, an Opel sedan, perhaps from the 1990s, with a rust hole in the front fender and a line of duct tape applied vertically to hold on a rear door. Unfolding himself from the red car, Ferko seemed taller and thinner than I had recalled against the stark landscape, especially next to Esma, who, without her high heels, proved rather short. Esma gripped his arm at the elbow, almost as if she were escorting a prisoner. Ferko had on a pair of plaid pants, the same vest and hat he had worn to testify, and beneath his open winter coat, a large-collared orange shirt. Goos stepped forward to welcome him, but Ferko was still speaking to Esma with wide gestures and Goos, in a purple windbreaker, stopped and peered back at me with something of a vexed look.

At last, Ferko was ready and the four of us tromped across the stones and swales of Barupra as Ferko relived his narrative. He showed us where the lean-to he called a house had stood, about a hundred yards into the camp, and then across the village the outhouse in which he'd hidden when the masked raiders arrived. For whatever reason, I had imagined a wooden structure, but what remained had walls of cinder block, meaning it was the lone structure still standing, even though the roof and door were gone after more than a decade. He then pointed out the spot where Boldo and his son and brother had been slain.

After that, Ferko led us to the back of the camp, overlooking the village, where he'd watched the destruction of his family and everyone he knew. The mine plunged down dramatically below us, a steep drop of several hundred feet. I had never been a fan of heights, and the falloff left me feeling somewhat imperiled, even as I appreciated the majesty of the vista of the surrounding green hills, which wore hats of white at their upper reaches. The wind flapped Ferko's wide trousers as he gestured to the switchbacks on the gravel road below. Perhaps a quarter of a mile down, a slope of dark coal and lighter-colored rock lazed over what had once been the Cave and was now a secret burial ground. Staring out solemnly, Ferko delivered a single shake of his head.

We hiked back into the former site of the village. Ferko showed us the approximate location where his son and he had concealed themselves following the murders. Finally, he again led us slowly toward the road until reaching a depression where he said he'd buried the bodies of the three men who had been gunned down. He had built a cairn of white rocks to mark the place. It had been kicked over by passersby or playing children, but several stones were still massed there, making him sure this was the spot.

Goos stooped to examine one of the rocks and kept it in his hand. He gave Ferko a surprisingly hard look.

"Long way to drag three bodies," he said.

As soon as Esma translated, Ferko stomped one of his running shoes on the ground to bolster his point.

"He agrees," Esma said, "but it was not easy to find a place soft enough to dig."

Ferko already had taken a few steps back toward the red car that had delivered him.

"How far down are the bodies?" asked Goos.

Esma and Ferko had a bit of an exchange.

"He says he only dug far enough to keep the bodies from being consumed by animals. No more than two feet, probably less. With the wind over ten years, it may not be much more than a foot to the bones."

Ferko raised a hand weakly then and turned his back on us. Esma walked along with him.

I sidled close to Goos.

"You heard something just as he arrived you didn't like."

"Ah yes." He bowed to the memory. "They were jabbering in Romany, but he used a word or two of Serbo-Croatian for emphasis. *Ste obecali.* 'You promised.' Kept saying that. 'I want what you promised.' Better not be that she's paying him on the side, Boom. His evidence isn't worth a thing if it's bought."

I promised to raise the issue with Esma later. As soon as Ferko was gone, Goos called the diggers back. While he was on his cell with them, another problem suddenly struck me.

"We can't really just scrape up this ground, can we, Goos? Don't we need a forensic anthropologist to do this right?"

He'd been half turned from me, to shield his phone from the wind, but he revolved in my direction at an inching pace, his thin mouth slightly parted.

"Mate," he said at last, "I *am* a forensic anthropologist." Ordinarily easygoing, Goos had grown increasingly sour this morning for reasons I did not understand, and now he appeared totally disgusted with me.

I wanted to say the obvious: No one told me. That was true, but we both seemed to recognize a deeper insult, the implication that I'd somehow not taken him seriously enough to find out.

He turned away to await his crew.

In the small hollow that Ferko had brought us to, a few spots of snow remained, latticed with grime. Beside them, the inspiring green sprigs of some early grasses had nosed out of the earth. Goos's crew arrived with shovels and canvas bags apparently bearing other tools. He unzipped a bag and stepped into white coveralls and donned a surgical cap and plastic gloves. Then he crouched over the low point, studying the spot as if it contained something metaphysical, pushing through the loose earth until he scooped up a handful of dirt, which he deposited in a sealable plastic bag.

I asked what his purpose was.

"So we can check the mix of subsoil and topsoil." He was still grouchy and answered in a bare grumble. He looked down into the duffel and extracted a small video camera, handing it to me.

"Make yourself useful. Record the dig so nobody can say we planted evidence."

It took me a while to master the buttons, but Goos got to work at once. He started with a stainless steel T-bar, three feet long and with a pointed end, which he hoisted over his head and then suddenly stabbed into the ground. He called for a measuring tape, which he used to determine the depth of his probe, making a notation in a little spiral notebook he kept in his back pocket. Then he motioned for another tool, as long as the first but with a pair of vertical lips near the bottom. He twisted it into the ground to extract another soil sample, which he levered free with a simple wooden chopstick, like the kind that comes with Chinese carryout. He said nothing to me except for calling out measurements loudly enough for the camera to record them.

Eventually, he had the laborers spread four large blue tarpaulins on all sides of the depression. He gave each worker a small garden spade and demonstrated how to scoop shallowly, depositing the diggings on the tarp. With his chopstick, Goos picked through what they uncovered.

I'd been silent a good twenty minutes, when I finally asked what he was searching for. It still took a second for him to answer.

"Bullet fragments for one thing," he said. "They slip out of the bodies as they decompose. If we recover any, we'll want to do ballistics."

With the small tools, the dig went at a laborious pace, but finally, after another quarter hour, Goos abruptly raised his gloved hand and snapped a halogen light on an elastic band over his forehead. He loosened the ground with a new set of chopsticks, then used a small brush, sweeping decorously until I could see a brownish lump the color of a toadstool. I realized he was excavating a hip bone.

These remains, just the first sight of them, affected me more strongly than I had been prepared for. Lawyers—all lawyers—live in a land of concepts and words, with precious little physical reality intruding. In the years I was a prosecutor, hearing a judge pronounce sentence and watching a US deputy marshal clap cuffs on the defendant and lead him to the lockup tended to distress me. It was only then that I seemed to fully appreciate that my efforts were aimed not simply at accomplishing that abstraction I called justice, but more concretely, at caging a human being for a good portion of his remaining life.

Goos had exposed most of the pelvis and the top of the femur, when Attila's A8 bumped down the road, raising dust as it came. I was relieved to have a reason to leave the gravesite and handed the camera to one of the day laborers.

Esma, who'd also kept her distance, approached me.

"Finding anything?"

I nodded.

"I don't like blood or bones," she said.

"I'm with you," I said.

She laughed and threw her arm through mine as we moved up toward Attila. I made introductions.

"The famous Attila," said Esma. Her driver, seemingly like half the working people in Tuzla, was in Attila's employ.

"Not half as big a prick as they say," she answered. "If you ask me."

"On the contrary, you're very well liked."

Attila beamed. Being shunned so often had undoubtedly left her vulnerable to any compliment. After a minute, Attila, with her rolling, slightly pigeon-toed walk and her oddly erect posture, strolled over to the gravesite to confer with Goos, just to be sure he was getting the help he needed. While she was gone, I had an inspiration for something useful I could do that would get me away from the boneyard.

"Esma, didn't you tell me that you first heard about Ferko in a Roma village?"

"Indeed. I've been back now and then."

"Is it far?"

"Lijce? I'm not sure."

Given the closed circuitry of the Rom community, I thought we were likely to find the best information about Barupra there. When Attila came back, she said the town was no more than twenty minutes and offered to drive me.

I returned to Goos. He'd already felt his way to a second skeleton, but at the moment he'd fixed a fine tungsten carbide needle to a hand pick to loosen the dirt on the first set of leg bones, examining them for signs of trauma.

He listened to me long enough to agree with the plan. As I turned away, Goos said behind me, "Wasn't trying to up myself on you, Boom." He was apologizing for being pretentious.

"Hardly," I replied. "Fault was all mine. I should have known." He nodded, apparently satisfied by that answer.

When I returned to Esma and Attila, I found that Esma was preparing to dismiss her driver and come with Atilla and me. All Roma were her people, to whom she had a proprietary connection, and Esma was known in Lijce. Even so, I was reluctant to have her present, since confirming Ferko was one principal reason to go. I drew her aside to explain that.

"Do you speak Romany?" she replied. "Because many of those people are fluent in no other language."

She had me there. I checked back with Goos, who thought overall she could help more than hurt, at least on an exploratory visit. We could always come back with our own translator later.

11.

Lijce

Attila drove us back to Tuzla, since Esma wanted to stop to buy small things for the children in Lijce.

"They are so desperately poor," she said, "and it will also make the *gadje* more welcome."

In the meantime, Attila walked me a few blocks to a steel bridge over the highway to point out Lake Pannonica, a local curiosity. Late in the twentieth century, the hundreds of years of extracting the briny water beneath Tuzla in order to produce salt took its toll and the downtown area began to sink. Salt production ceased, but after the war, the former pools, where the subterranean waters had been stored, were turned into a recreational facility, becoming a network of saltwater lakes, an inland sea with graveled shores that were thronged in the summers.

When we returned to the main square, Esma was waiting with two bulging plastic bags. We drove from town, passing the immense site of Tuzla Elektrik, with smokestacks in the sky like the arms of a cheering crowd, and hourglass-shaped vents, stories high, wafting steam.

Soon we were ascending again. It was a lovely country of green mountains. Haystacks, with the silage spun around a pole, lay in some of the fields looking like huge tops. Esma, far shorter than I, had volunteered for the backseat. She leaned forward to hear Attila, supporting herself when we sped through the switchbacks by applying her strong hand to my shoulder.

"Salt mine," Attila said, pointing right, where large white storage tanks loomed on a hilltop. Two narrow pipelines, yellow and green, ran parallel to the road.

In another twenty minutes, we turned down a yellow dirt path to enter the Roma town of Lijce. We had barely reached the first house when a little boy recognized Esma, whose prior largesse obviously had made an impression. He let loose a joyful shout, which brought more than a dozen kids running our way, preventing Attila from driving farther. The children were waifish, dusty from playing in the street and dressed in ill-matched faded old clothes, but seemed nourished and happy, leaving aside one boy who had an open sore on his face, rimmed in green. The boys wore shorts and a variety of footwear, mostly open plastic sandals or Velcroed running shoes, none with socks.

Esma exited, laughing as the kids jumped around her. She questioned each child about her or his family, and then distributed gifts based on her estimate of needs. Attila rolled down the window, chatting with the kids in Bosnian.

"What are they saying?" I asked.

"What would you expect? 'Give us money.' They're bargaining. Just one keim," she said, naming the Bosnian currency. It was officially half a Euro, meaning the kids were asking for about fifty cents. Attila handed out all the change she had. The boy with the sore insisted that he would accept a bill.

It was Thursday now, a little after noon, and once Esma was back in the car, I said, "Why aren't these children in school?"

She smiled. "Ask. See if you get the same answer twice. Some barely speak Bosnian, though. Throughout Europe, people lament that the Roma won't send their children to school, but in very few places have the local authorities tried to teach in our own language, or with respect for our customs. After puberty, Rom beliefs require students to separate by gender, which the *gadje* will not indulge. Because of that, even the children who get some education won't go much beyond the first form." Age eleven or twelve.

Once Attila was parked, I stepped out to view the town. The road ran through two rises on which sat no more than thirty houses, almost all with yards that had become dumping grounds. Hillocks of refuse, including most frequently the rusted pieces of old cars, were piled beside silted-up garbage, old shoes without laces, discarded appliances, bedsprings, used pots, pieces of building material—a remarkable goulash of items, seemingly preserved because they might have some future use. As for the houses, a few looked quite substantial, with stucco or cinder-block bases and frame exteriors, although in those cases the siding was unfinished, as if the wood had been slapped up before anyone arrived to take it back. Beside the bigger places, late-model cars were sometimes parked, and on three or four houses I saw satellite dishes mounted at the rooflines. But most of the dwellings in Lijce were tiny, built of stone or concrete blocks and roofed in overlapping pieces of salvaged corrugated steel.

After a few minutes, several people ventured a few steps from their houses, staring darkly at us. Finally, one voice rang out, singing, "*Ays-Ma*," and with no more, the residents began surging forward. In a matter of seconds, there was a circle surrounding us, all women, usually heavyset with long skirts and colorful head scarves that framed scraps of black hair and coppery faces. They were clearly intrigued by Esma and, given their prior acquaintance, touched her garments with no hesitation, especially the wooly, fringed lavender scarf around her throat. Esma took this well, laughing and thanking the women for their compliments, before turning to me.

"Gypsy women," she said. "They want to know how many children I have, as if the answer might have changed since I was last here a couple of years ago. Also, they wish to know why you have come."

"Please tell them," I said, "that I am here to learn about the Roma who lived in the town of Barupra."

The question, once translated, provoked an outcry of high-pitched laments and wide gestures, which Esma did her best to relay, along with Attila, since the answers were in both Romany and Bosnian. Soon the women of Lijce were quarreling among themselves.

"That woman says they are gone," said Esma. "This lady agrees and says the army murdered them and dumped their bodies in the river."

"Ask which army, please."

"The Bosnian Army. With the Americans exiting, the Bosnians wanted the land from the camp back."

An older woman appeared irritated by that theory.

"She says the Bosniaks wouldn't kill the Roma because the Rom men fought for this country. But the other says that the people in Barupra were Orthodox and to the Muslims no different than the Serbs. And those two women"—Esma pointed—"are laughing at the rest and saying the Americans murdered the people in Barupra because they thought the Roma had helped Kajevic kill their soldiers."

I tried to get specifics on what the Roma had done for Kajevic, but the women were mystified themselves.

I turned to Attila on the other side of the circle for further translation.

"Most," Attila explained, "say it was Arkan Tigers sent by Kajevic, although that lady thinks the Barupra people just went back to Kosovo."

I'd never heard that one, and Attila grinned about the notion.

"Nobody hears word-fucking-one in eleven years? Even with cell phones? All them here, they're oxygen thieves," said Attila. "None of them have a clue really. They're Gypsies. They answer because they enjoy telling stories."

I expected Esma to take offense but instead she laughed with Attila. In the meantime, the oldest lady, stout and bent but with an evident strength that might have been sheer durability, made a noise and waved her hand as she wandered away.

"Where are the men, by the way?" I asked Attila and Esma. "Working?"

"Some," said Attila. "I've hired a couple, sent them to Saudi, if I recall. Always been a large gray market in Bosnia, smuggled goods bartered and sold, which the Gypsies are good at. Some are in town running scams. Most are out picking iron."

"A few also are in prison," said Esma, didactic as ever. "The Roma are the most imprisoned men in Europe."

I focused on Attila. "What do you mean 'picking iron'?"

"Gathering scrap metal," she said. "Steel. Aluminum. They sell it to dealers. Anything will do. Old bedsprings, cans, any junk. That's what most of the men in Barupra did."

A few minutes later, a man, short and wide, burst through the circle of females to introduce himself to me. He spoke some English.

"Am mayor here. Tobar." Missing three upper front teeth, Tobar was about five foot four with a broad white belt that circled his enormous belly. His hairdo, with greasy strands spilling down from his bald crown, looked like someone had dropped a bowl of soup on his head. There were three large gold rings on his fingers when he extended his hand to shake. But when he caught sight of Esma, I lost his attention. He gasped and bowed from the waist and actually kissed her hand.

"The beautiful lady!"

Esma laughed out loud.

"Gypsy men are always on the make," she told me.

Even Esma lost some of Tobar's interest when Attila returned, having wandered off to take a call. She and Tobar greeted each other heartily in Bosnian, amid rounds of shoulder slapping.

"Tobar used to work at Camp Comanche," Attila told us. "He ran the laundry."

I explained to Tobar that we were here to ask about the Roma at Barupra. He took a step back, while he wrinkled up his face as if there were a bad smell.

"No good *baxt*." Esma said that word referred to luck or good fortune.

"Why?"

"They are ghosts now," Esma translated, once Tobar switched to Romany. "It is bad to disturb them."

I asked what had happened, but Tobar waved his palms as if it was all too complicated for understanding. Instead, he insisted on giving us a tour of the town. As it was no more than two blocks long, there seemed no reason to decline. The first stop was his house, which he pointed out from the road.

"Very big," he said, and it was surely the largest here, with two satellite dishes. Tobar, who'd been impressed into the Bosnian Army during the war, had received a grant from the government afterward to help with the construction. The second floor was demarcated by a white wooden balustrade, knobbed in the classical style, atop which Tobar had affixed a line of plastic swans, the kind you might have seen on lawns in Florida in the 1950s. In addition, perhaps for safekeeping, the front half of the body of a twenty-year-old Impala was perched on the second floor, not far from the birds.

From there, Tobar took us down to the river, a beautiful fast-running stream. This was the source of fresh water for the town, which had no plumbing. Eventually, we returned to Tobar's house, where he offered us coffee. Esma nodded to indicate that we should accept, and we sat outside in the chill at a picnic table. Mrs. Tobar emerged with a steaming plastic pitcher of tar-black liquid, while Esma showed me how to drink Roma-fashion, without letting the cup touch my lips.

Eventually, I directed the conversation back to Barupra.

"Are the Roma who lived there dead?" I asked Tobar.

"What else?"

"Why? With what excuse?"

"They are Roma." He was repeating himself in both Bosnian and Romany, and Esma and Attila were taking turns converting what he said to English, with Tobar adding a word or two now and then. "When have the *gadje* needed an excuse to kill Roma? But it is a bad business. When sad things happen, one must not dwell on them." Tobar nodded weightily at his own wisdom.

I said, "One of the women we spoke to when we arrived believed that the Americans thought the Roma in Barupra had helped Kajevic."

Tobar shook his strange hairdo around, then hunkered down and lowered his voice.

"Never," Tobar said. "The Roma all despise Kajevic. When the Serbs captured several Muslims, they would look next for one or two Roma. The Serbians would force the Gypsies at gunpoint to dig two holes, one large, one small. Then the Serbs shot them all, the Roma included."

"Why two holes?" I asked.

"Because the Roma were not good enough to bury in the first hole," Tobar said. Esma shot me a look to make sure I had fully registered the prejudice.

I told Tobar that I had heard speculation that the Roma in Barupra were killed by gangsters because the Roma were in competition with them, stealing cars.

"Well, yes," said Tobar, levering his head back and forth. "They were iron pickers, and you know an auto is mostly steel. I have heard that a few in Barupra stole cars. But the mobs would never bother killing these Roma. They would just send the police to arrest them. They own the police." Tobar smoothed his index finger under his thumb.

Attila's cell phone was buzzing every couple of minutes, and while she walked off to handle another call, I took advantage of her absence to ask if Tobar knew Ferko, whom I wouldn't name in Attila's presence.

"Oh yes," said Tobar, "but we met only once. This man was here, who remembers why? Business of some kind. I am the mayor and said hello. He told us he was from Barupra, the only one to live after the Chetniks. The next year this fine lady comes, asking many questions about Barupra. I told her it is a bad business, but she wanted this fellow's mobile number. A man cannot decline the request of a woman so beautiful, no?"

Esma pointed to Tobar, instructing me to take heed. All three of us were laughing.

Awaiting Attila, we spent another ten minutes or so with Tobar, who told us about recent troubles in his business, selling telephones.

As we were strolling back to the car, I caught sight of the old woman who had turned away from the circle of women earlier. She was outside, working over an old wooden barrel with a long stick, and I asked Esma to help me speak with her.

The old lady looked a little like an American Indian. Her gray hair under her babushka was braided and both front teeth were broken. Her long patterned skirt brushed the ground but her feet, so callused they appeared gray, were in flip-flops despite the cold.

I had a letter from the Bosnian government introducing me and I removed it from the pocket of my jacket, but the old lady smacked it away.

"She can't read," said Esma quietly. "You'll find that very few of the women can."

Esma did her best to explain about the Court, but the

woman, who had never been far from Lijce, did not seem interested. She was one of those naturally quarrelsome old ladies, and as soon as Attila rejoined us, the old lady directed a remark to her, while pointing at Esma. Attila chuckled but was initially reluctant to translate.

"She says she prefers to speak Bosnian with me," Attila finally explained. "'That one—it hurts my ears to listen to how she speaks Romany.'"

Esma took the complaint with good humor.

"Romany has a million dialects," she said. "And of course, all Roma believe only theirs is correct."

What the old lady had been doing, it turned out, was laundry for herself and her unmarried adult grandson, a swirling stew of clothing amid the mist rising from the barrel. Esma said that the wash would take this woman most of the day, between going to the stream, hauling then heating the water, and washing twice, inasmuch as it was again bad *baxt* if women's clothes and men's ever touched.

The old lady continued working over the steaming tub as Attila translated her ramblings. The house behind her, where she lived with her grandson, was no more than fifteen feet by fifteen and made of mud and sticks.

I asked why the old woman had seemed provoked by what her neighbors were saying about Barupra.

"They talk to hear themselves. No one in this village knows anything. Sinfi there, her sister married a Barupra man. Ask her. She should know, but she knows nothing either." With her knobby arthritic hand, the old lady pointed next door, where a skinny young woman was also washing with her back to us, a baby on her hip.

We started in that direction, but the old woman called us back. After disparaging her neighbors for speaking from ignorance, it turned out the old lady had a theory of her own.

"They will return, those people. It is our way."

When I asked who had told her that, she banged her stick against the inside of the barrel, although it seemed clear she would have preferred using it on me.

Attila said, "She says no one needs to inform her. She is an old woman and knows things."

I looked at Esma. "Gypsy women?"

"Very powerful," she answered. "I have told you."

"Ask, please," I said to Attila, "where the Barupra people are now while they wait to return."

Attila again laughed heartily before relaying her answer.

"She says she has heard that lawyers are smart, but that must not include you, if you expect an old woman to know more than you do."

The three of us moved next door to the house of the young woman, Sinfi. She had disappeared but came to her doorway as we approached, smiling shyly. She still toted her baby as she stood barefoot on the threshold. I had noticed at Tobar's that shoes were not worn indoors. The room I could see behind Sinfi was spotless, furnished with a beaten cupboard and an old rug on the wall, although the ceiling was bowed and showed spots of water damage that might soon lead to its collapse. Sinfi was dressed in a pair of leopard-print trousers and a sweatshirt lettered with a saying in German I didn't understand, aside from the word '*Gesundheit.*' Her black hair strayed around her face, in which her eyes, in something of a rarity, were an arresting bright green. She was bone thin and very pretty, except when she smiled, disclosing a deplorable greenish muddle in her mouth. The baby, a little girl of about nine months, watched all of us avidly, and reached to grasp our fingers when we offered them.

I once more withdrew the letter from my jacket. Sinfi smiled but did not bother with the pretense of looking. As had happened next door, she preferred that Attila be the translator.

Sinfi said her sister had married a Roma boy from Barupra. Sinfi had visited there twice with her parents, before her mother and father left Lijce after Sinfi's paternal grandmother died.

"Did any other people from Lijce marry those in Barupra?"

"Only my sister. Others would not."

"Because they were Orthodox?"

My question amused her. "Because they were so poor. They had nothing."

Esma interjected to explain that in traditional communities, Roma adopted *gadje* religions largely as protective coloration, so priests or imams would assist with burials and births. Their true faith, as Esma described it, sounded like some kind of spiritualism, often involving the ghosts of ancestors.

"My sister's right arm was bad," said Sinfi, "shriveled up. My parents were happy she married. Prako had a lip with the cleft, so they were a good match." She smiled in muted irony. Among the fifty or so souls I'd seen here, the consequences of the inevitable inbreeding had been clear: wall eyes, hare lips, but also, especially among the children, instances of startling beauty, before it was diluted over time by poor diet and other hardships.

"And where is your sister now?" I said.

"They are gone from Barupra. All."

"And where did they go?"

"People say they were murdered."

"Do you think that?"

"I want not to," she said, but shook her head to indicate that her hope was faint. "If God wills," she added.

She explained that after her marriage, her sister called her parents or her every few months on a borrowed cell phone. In another of the customs of India, which the Romany people still maintained a millennium after their exodus, a new wife became part of her husband's family, subordinate to her mother-in-law and somewhat detached from her family of origin.

"At first," Sinfi said, "when we did not hear from her, we tried the number of her friend who had a phone, but there was no answer. After the entire winter passed with no word, my father said we should go to see her. We borrowed a car. But they were not there. No one was. The village was gone. My father went to the police in Vica Donja. They acted like he was crazy to think there had ever been people in Barupra." Sinfi stopped speaking for a second and looked at the ground to retain her composure. "That made my father sure that Kajevic had killed them all."

"Why Kajevic?"

"The last I talked to my sister, that spring, she said a soldier had been there to warn them that Kajevic was going to kill some of the men who lived in Barupra."

"One man? Many men?"

"Many."

"And why?"

"He thought they had talked to the Americans. But my sister said Prako was not worried. It was not his business. He'd had nothing to do with that."

"Did your sister say who in town had talked to the Americans? Or what they had said? Anything like that?"

Sinfi knew no more. Yet this was the first thing I'd heard in Lijce that bore some resemblance to evidence. It was hearsay of several magnitudes, but Sinfi had recounted a concrete event, which, if it actually occurred, would offer a strong suggestion about who'd engineered the massacre.

I asked Sinfi if I could take out my phone to record her, but she said her husband would be angry if he knew she had spoken about Kajevic.

"But you and your parents believe Kajevic's troops killed them all in Barupra?" I asked.

"Me? I think so. My father, too. My mother, no. She had a dream a few years ago that my sister called her. So she hopes." Sinfi's eyes now were pooling.

Before we left, Esma removed her purple scarf, the object of such lavish admiration here, and wrapped it around the baby. As we said good-bye, Sinfi took a step over her threshold to squint at me in the strong sun that had just emerged from the clouds.

"You are going to find who murdered them?" she asked.

"I will try."

"They should be punished," she said to me. "Even Roma should not be treated like that."

12.

Still a Gypsy

So you guys hungry or what?" Attila asked, as we departed from Lijce. "Kind of a cool place, a couple miles on."

It was past four and none of us had eaten since breakfast. Attila stopped at a huge roadside inn erected on a hillside, a series of rustic buildings that could have passed as a dude ranch, enlarged A-frames with shake roofs and cedar sides decorated with old wagon wheels. To enhance the inn's appeal to tourists, the lowest level featured reconstructions of Bosnian life one hundred years ago. In one stall, a wax dummy in vest and fez sorted through a sack of seeds.

On the second floor, we entered an open-air pine dining room, noticeably upscale. Waiters in formal vests and bow ties showed us to a windowside table overlooking another lovely mountain stream one hundred feet below, from which a romantic, rushing burble arose.

Attila, unsurprisingly, was a grand host. She ordered

a white wine from Slovenia, although it turned out she didn't drink. Her focus was on a huge appetizer plate of mild Bosnian cheeses and dried meats, a local delicacy, all accompanied by an unusual brown bread assembled from dozens of layers of thin leaves, a little like the crust of a strudel. While we relaxed, Attila smoked cigarettes without apology and Esma mooched a couple, explaining that she indulged only on the Continent while she drank.

Attila had just ordered the entrée when Esma excused herself for a moment. As soon as she was gone, Attila hunched forward confidentially. She was such a large personality that I was already accustomed to ignoring her odd look, with that big ball of kinky brownish hair, her uneven freckly complexion, her slight shoulders strangely squared, and her pale skinny arms poking from the same short-sleeved button-down shirt she was wearing when she picked me up at the airport yesterday.

"So whatta you think, Boom?" Attila asked. "Looks like Kajevic, right?"

"Maybe. I'm a long way from conclusions, Attila."

"You ask me," said Attila, "a guy sends a messenger boy to say he's gonna kill a whole bunch of you fuckers and they're all dead a week or two later, I got a prime suspect. No?"

"Sure. But it's not the only possibility. What did you make of the lady who thought the Bosnians killed the Roma because they wanted the base back?"

"I thought she was as full of shit as the rest of them— everybody but the last gal. The US had withdrawn. That camp went back to government ownership. If the Bosnians wanted the Roma out, all they had to do was move in with bulldozers. No cause for a massacre."

I sipped my wine, thinking how I wanted to approach the next subject. I had been meaning all day to get a second alone with Attila.

"And I'm not ready to declare the US Army above suspicion either."

As I expected, Attila made a face. "And how do you get to that?"

"Well, Tobar confirmed something that I've heard for weeks now, that a few guys in Barupra were car thieves. As a matter of fact, you told me yesterday that you fired your Roma drivers when they disappeared with some of your trucks. Do I remember correctly?"

"Too true." Attila nodded with her whole upper body.

Last night, I had awoken around 3 a.m., not unusual for me when I was contending with jet lag. I found my heart constricted by some dreamtime reconstruction of my encounter in the corridor with Esma. I had remembered the red nails as her hand rested on my arm, but the dream culminated in agitation and regret, although, as happens so often, once I was up I couldn't recall the events I was sorry for. Eventually, when I settled myself and began to doze, my mind went to our case. It was then, halfway back to sleep, that I made a connection that had been nagging at me since I sat with Goos in the bar.

"Now," I said to Attila, "you told me that all the trucks that NATO used in Bosnia were yours. CoroDyn's. Right?"

"Basically. The operational vehicles were under Transportation Corps command, but they all came out of my pools."

"Okay," I said. "On the plane, I reread my files about that attempt to arrest Kajevic in Doboj. Most press reports said Kajevic fled in trucks stolen from the US

Army. The first time I saw that, I thought that meant that Kajevic and his Tigers hot-wired the vehicles Special Forces had shown up in. But the whole ambush was too well planned to involve an improvised escape. So what I realized—actually in the middle of the night—was that Kajevic already had those trucks."

I'd seized Attila's full attention now. Her thin, un-shaped brows were drawn down toward her small eyes.

"Which means," I said, "that the vehicles Kajevic took off in were stolen from you and CoroDyn. Correct?"

Attila's lips squeezed around before she spoke.

"I told you, Boom. I like you and all, but I'm not fucking up my security clearance."

"It can't be a secret who those trucks belonged to, Attila. They had to be identified so the Bosnian police could look for them."

She shrugged.

"Here's the thing," I said. "It was Roma from Barupra who stole those trucks from you and sold them to Kaje-vic. Right?"

Attila was looking down at the table. When her eyes rose, she reached for another cigarette.

"Boom, you ever talk too much?" she asked, with the flame hovering over her Zippo.

"Occasionally."

"Me?" Attila said. "I been doing that my whole life. Shit comes sailin out of my mouth and I'm like, What the fuck did you go and say that for? And, Boom, I really don't know the answer. I just get caught up in things."

I wasn't going to be distracted by her retrospective regrets.

I said, "But *that's* how the Roma knew where Kajevic and his people were hiding. And that's why they were able to give his location to Army Intelligence."

"I'm not here to lie to you, Boom. But I gotta be a lot more careful what I say."

"Well, maybe you want to respond to this, Attila. If the Roma told me where Kajevic was hiding, and I went there and got ambushed, I'd be mad, maybe killing mad, *especially* when I realized they had sold him the trucks he escaped in. It might have felt to me like one huge double cross."

Attila shook her head decisively.

"That's not how it went down."

"How did it?"

"I can't mess on myself, Boom. I know I ran my mouth, and with a smart guy like you, one thing leads to another. But I can't say no more. Only thing is, you heard that lady was telling you Kajevic swore he was gonna kill those Gypsies."

Attila's phone, which she'd set on the wooden table, started buzzing again, vibrating hard enough that I thought for a second it might fly through the window. She smacked her hand down on the cell as it was skittering away and she answered. I would have bet that Attila rang herself to avoid more questions, but the device had been right in front of me and I could hear a voice speaking Serbo-Croatian on the other end.

"Fuck," said Attila when she was done. She stood up. "Gotta bounce. I need to find five guys who speak Pashto and get them on the way to Kabul by twenty hundred hours tomorrow. And the problem, Boom, is that anybody who speaks Pashto has worked in Afghanistan. And anybody who's worked in Afghanistan would rather get buttfucked than go back. This'll cost me. Be makin calls all night."

She shook my hand and said she'd have a driver here

in an hour to bring Esma and me back to Tuzla when we were ready to go. She'd moved off about five paces, when she circled back and leaned over the table, bringing close her small eyes and bad skin. Her voice was low.

"Tell Esma nice to meet her. But watch yourself, dude. That chick is way too slick. Don't never forget: She's still a Gypsy." She was gone again with a quick wave.

The food—grilled lamb and vegetables crowded onto a large stainless platter—arrived a few minutes later, only seconds before Esma returned. I explained Attila's departure and we both marveled about her for a minute. Esma seemed completely charmed. I noted only now that Esma, who'd been seated across from me while Attila was here, had settled now on my side of the table, close enough to brush elbows.

"So, Boom. Did you learn anything useful today?"

"I need to process," I said. I was still loath to share my thoughts with her about the investigation. Instead, I asked about Lijce, knowing that her passion for her people would distract her.

"The challenge of the Roma, Bill, is to open your society to those Roma, like me, who wish to join it, without imposing your values on the many who don't."

"But how can Roma kids make that choice without an education?"

"The value of schooling is not self-evident to many of my people," said Esma. "In Romany, there are no proper words for 'read' or 'write.' There is wonderful Roma music. But no literature. Whenever my grandmother saw me with a book, she was concerned. '*So keres?*' she would ask me. 'What are you doing?' For my people, knowledge is acquired in social interaction, by talking."

"An oral tradition?"

She smiled a bit, amused by the elusiveness of Rom ways.

"Yes, but do not think of Native American elders repeating legends to circles of young listeners. The Roma, Bill, are a people without a history, with no shared understanding of the past. My grandmother refused to believe it when I told her we did not emerge from Egypt, which is the common misunderstanding that led to this 'Gypsy' name. For us, there is no prevailing myth of creation, no seven days and seven nights. The Gypsy men I grew up with were fierce prizefighters, but there has never been a Gypsy army, because there is no land we have ever been inspired to conquer, or to defend, or even to return to.

"And unlike almost any other group on earth, our sense of identity is not forged on the countless injuries of the past. We do not tell the tales of our centuries as slaves, unlike African Americans or Jews. Instead the Gypsy way is to excel in forgetting. You saw that with Tobar when you asked about Barupra. We live in the present. To Westerners we are as strange as Martians."

Again Esma delivered that huge smile, full of her delight and pride about this legacy of difference.

"And what's the impact on you, Esma? Do you feel caught between two worlds?"

"Not really. I made my choices. To Roma like that old woman we saw in Lijce, I am not Rom at all. That is why she didn't want to speak Romany to me."

"And what about your family? Is your mother more accepting of you than your father?"

"My mother is gone. Cancer. All those cigarettes. She brawled with my father about my schooling, but I always felt that was more to oppose him than because she saw much value in it for me. When I was approaching fifteen, my mother started to talk to me about marriage. She had already spoken to another family. The boy, name of Boris, seemed to have a great fancy for me, but it wasn't mutual. So Boris kidnapped and raped me. That is not unusual among the English Roma, for whom a stiff cock is often tantamount to a marriage proposal. Having had his way with me, Boris would declare we had eloped. But he was furious there was no blood on the bedsheet. His family of course disavowed his intentions toward me, and my father was irate.

"Yet that was my liberation. Since I was now widely regarded as unmarriageable, I was free to continue in school and go on to university."

"Oxford?"

"Cambridge. Caius College."

"And never a marriage?"

"No, no. I am too independent, Bill. I still think about a child in wan moments, but I am not constant enough to be much of a mother."

The food, which we'd been eating as we talked, was excellent, prepared without much fanfare but flavorful and beautifully presented, with a grilled onion in the center of the plate from which banana peppers sprouted like antlers. Idling through the meal, we had started on a second bottle of wine.

When we finished the pastries we ate for dessert, I called for the check, only to find that Attila had beaten me to it. Esma laughed and immediately pointed out that, as a result, I still owed her dinner.

Outside, the limo Attila had promised was waiting, an old Yugoslav tank of a vehicle. Esma and I slid into the backseat and we headed down toward Tuzla, winding through the hills as it grew dark. I was not surprised when Esma, who'd outpaced me with the wine, became silent and heavy-lidded, and then disappeared fully into sleep, with her head tossed back and a small whinny escaping with each breath. A sharp switchback threw her against me, and she lay with her face on my shoulder, while I was caught in the net of sensation. I could caution myself as much as I cared to, but with her fine looks and power persona, Esma's sex appeal felt like a live current, and I was not surprised that the heat and substance of her body so close, her breath on my neck, and the thick air of her perfume left me with a hard-on most of the way to town.

Once we were bumping again over Tuzla's cobbled streets, Esma roused and shook the sleep out of her head. She found her phone, but spoke only for a second in Romany.

"I must meet Ferko," she said when we'd stopped in front of the Blue Lamp. "I told him I would find some time tonight to discuss a few things."

I finally remembered to ask her about what Goos had overheard.

"Goos said Ferko was insisting you give him what you'd promised. Forgive me, please, since I know I don't need to tell you this, but if you're compensating him somehow for his testimony, it's worthless."

She took that with a laugh.

"You do *not* need to tell me that. The only talk we've ever had of money is when I advised him years ago that he might receive reparations from the Court in the distant future if there is ever a conviction. But he hasn't spoken of it since. What I *did* promise Ferko when he agreed to testify was that you would do your utmost to keep him safe. And he was well within his rights to insist that promise be kept. No?"

I nodded. I had to be satisfied with that response.

She said, "I have not yet had a chance to press him again about Kajevic, as you asked, but I'll take that up now and shall report back to you."

Esma had listened to Sinfi, just as I had. It was hard to doubt the young woman, which meant it would be quite peculiar if Ferko—or anyone else living in Barupra—had not heard about Kajevic's threats.

She slid the phone back into her large bag, but took a moment to face me again with one foot in the street.

"Thank you for letting me sleep a minute, Bill," she said. "I was comfortable beside you." She said no more but gave me a long look, frank in its intimacy, before walking off.

Stepping onto the cobbles in front of the hotel, I was reverberating. And suddenly in mind of Layton Merriwell.

13.

Regret

Entering the lobby, I caught sight of Goos. He was in the lounge with his beer glass, as I might have expected, making friends with two middle-aged British women, both short-haired blondes who seemed to be enjoying his company. I shook hands with each, Cindy and Flo, and noted their clear disappointment when I pointed Goos to one of the small two-tops in the breakfast room. His glass was empty and I took it from him.

"You're drinking on me tonight, Goos."

I returned with another for him and bubble water for myself. I'd had enough wine with Esma.

"Sorry to have missed the bulletin on your background, Goos."

"Yep. Doctorate. The whole la-di-da. Probably prouder of it than I ought to be."

I asked the obvious—how he'd ended up a cop.

"Well, you know, I was the typical layabout kid," he

said. "But good at school. So I stayed with it. I fancied anthropology, until I was most of the way through with it and realized I was actually rather keen on police work—truth be told, probably because I'd met up with a few too many cops on a professional basis. Not to say I was any kind of hoon—'hooligan,' you'd say. Just got myself into a little bingle now and then when I was rotten with my mates and had an overnight stay at government expense. But I reckoned that a good officer can make a lot of difference. Had an adviser at Antwerp who said, 'Well, with forensic anthropology, you can probably catch on with a police force.'

"Which I did. You know, my Belgium, that's a pretty orderly place, not even two hundred murders a year and not many bodies to dig up. But still, it got me into homicide. And I was good with it. Found a pretty girl, became a right civilized bloke. But when the Yugoslav Tribunal was established, I thought, There's a place to fully use my skills."

"And what did your skills tell you about that grave in Barupra?"

"Got some bones in a bag, if that's what you mean."

"How'd they look?"

"Seemed right. Three males, two older than the last."

"You can tell gender and age?"

"Hip size and certain bone formations in the pelvis. And bone density. I'll be more certain with my microscope."

"And what about the bullets you were looking for?" I asked.

"A couple. We'll get the ballistics done back home."

"Is there a good crime lab there?"

"Netherlands Forensic Institute? Top notch."

"Okay. We look at the bones, we look at the bullets, then what's next?"

"Well, we should put our heads together on some document requests for our friends at NATO, assuming you can square that with Akemi and Badu. And I'd like to come back here with a geologist. Worked with a professor at Nantes who's very good. Madame Professor Tchitchikov. Love to know if she can tell us how recent that landslide at the Cave is. And I'd want her to have a Captain Cook at that grave for Boldo and them." Goos said the Bosnian cops had returned at the end of the day and, eager to be able to say they'd done something, had been happy to surround the area he'd excavated with evidence tape. They promised to keep an eye.

"I don't know enough about the formations around here," Goos said, when I asked what he wanted Professor Tchitchikov to examine at the gravesite. "Seemed pretty soft if the burial was a decade ago. To my eye, looked to be a mix of topsoil and subsoil there. But you know, that's not my *spécialité*," he said, using the French word.

"But what's the potential significance of a mix of soils?"

"Might mean somebody had been digging in that grave a lot more recently than ten years ago."

"Grave robbers?"

"Possible. Curious locals most likely. Probably kids. But could also be someone wanting a squizz at what we'd be finding."

"You concerned that was Ferko?"

"He still seems a little dodgy to me, but that wasn't my first thought."

"The bones were where he said, Goos."

He nodded, taking my point, then asked about my trip to Lijce. Like me, he was struck by what Sinfi had to say. But the moment when I seemed to have impressed him, probably for the first time, was when I unspooled my deductions about the trucks Kajevic had escaped in, and the possibility that the Americans might have suspected a double cross once the Roma's information led them into an ambush.

"Attila didn't want to own up about the trucks," I said, "but I think she's trying to cover for the American troops. She understands the implications, but she sings from Merriwell's songbook and insists the Americans would never have done it."

"Say this," said Goos, "those American kids I met when I first started coming round Bosnia in '97, they were a cut above. The Russians, the Turks, sometimes you wondered what prison they went to for army recruiting. They were bartering starving young girls food for their families in exchange for sex. But the American lot, those men and women were well disciplined, well trained. Played football and rock music with the local kids and handed out candy. Hard to see them taking a hand in a mass slaughter."

"Group psychology is a funny thing," I answered. I had prosecuted dozens of men and women, corporate executives and commodities traders and government officials, most with a lifelong pattern of blameless behavior, who'd then taken bribes or falsified records or cheated their customers, all offering the same timeworn excuse when they got caught: Everybody else was doing it. The most striking example to me, which I shared with Goos, was a friend of mine from the high school football team, Rocky Whittle, who was indicted while I was US Attorney. Rocky had spent years accepting small payoffs so he could maintain the confidence of the sixty other plumbing inspectors he worked with who all took a great deal more money than he had. Rocky's fundamental decency remained so clear to me decades later that, after recusing myself from the case, I testified as a character witness at his sentencing.

"But there's a limit, Boom. Right? A few dollars in the pocket, or holding on to your job, that's not mass murder. You give me your stories, I'll give you one of mine. Been in mind of it all day. Enough to make me regret coming back here."

He drained his glass in preparation, and I again waved to the desk clerk, who brought another.

"Was a witness I had for the Yugoslav Tribunal," Goos said after a considerable silence, "woman name of Abasa Mensur. Muslim. She lived across the river in Sarajevo, on what all the sudden became the Serbian side. So the Chetniks storm into her house. This is just a few days after her husband was killed at the front a few blocks away. And with the Serbs, after a while you'd know this part without my telling you. They raped her—raped her while her children watched. Whole squad. Then when they were done with her, they started in raping her eleven-year-old daughter. Then just for kicks, they grab the three-month-old baby, Boom, and put the child in the oven, and turned on the broiler while they held guns on all of them. And the baby screams and screams, while one soldier or another is rooting the eleven-year-old. Then finally the crying stops, and when they took that poor little thing out, they laugh and hand it over to the mother and tell her, 'This is what a grilled pig looks like.' A Muslim woman.

"And God love her, Boom, Abasa, she came to The Hague and gave evidence and pointed to the captain who had been in charge. And Boom, I'm a hard-hearted policeman, I seen bad, I know what people can be like, but I sat in the courtroom with tears streaming down my face. And the captain, that man, if you could call his like a man, that man, thank God, is rotting in a prison cell. But of course, there's eleven others who were with him we didn't even bother trying to catch. Some of those blokes, after Dayton, they must have gone home and had babies of their own. And what did they think, Boom, when they held those children? How is it that every one of them just didn't go put a bullet through his brain?

"So group or no group, Boom, I want to say there's some that wouldn't have done it. Because I need to be able to say, Not me either. And not your cobber Rocky, I'd hope. And maybe not those American kids who were in service here and who'd been taught better, and didn't come up listening to all the rellies spilling bilge about the Mohammedan monsters who'd done bad to their ancestors for centuries."

I drained my soda. After that story there was not a lot more to say, and I waited in silence for him to finish his beer. He was leaving in the morning for a long weekend in Belgium, and we agreed to reconnect on Monday in The Hague. Then I went upstairs to start on the e-mails that had accumulated over two days, hoping that work would help me shake off the horror of what Goos had described. Evil of that magnitude was like a dead star, sucking all the light out of life.

I was over my tablet about half an hour, when I heard a light rap on my door. I expected that Goos had forgotten to mention something, but when I opened, Esma was on my threshold. She seemed to have refreshed her makeup and run a comb through her huge nest of hair, and I was taken again by how striking she was. But her expression was all business.

"Might you have one second, Bill?"

I stepped aside to welcome her. I offered her my desk chair and took a seat on the bed. I asked if she'd like something from the tiny minibar, which held tepid beer and water, but she declined.

"I won't be a minute," she said. "But something has come up with Ferko that I know you'd want to hear." She'd told him what Sinfi had said about Kajevic's threats. "He acted as if he was only now remembering it, but he agreed that story had indeed run through the camp. I wasn't pleased, and he could see as much, but he claimed he'd never connected the concerns about Kajevic to the night of April 27 because the Chetniks weren't speaking Serbian."

"Are you convinced by that?"

"I count it as possible but not likely. My suspicion is that he was terrified to mention Kajevic's name."

That made sense. Ferko would not have been the first witness to go skinny on the truth out of fear. And while he may have misled Esma, he hadn't lied in his testimony or his prior statements submitted to the Court. Still, I was concerned. If Ferko was trying to leave out Kajevic, he might have also altered other details, and that could trench on perjury.

"We're going to need another go at him, Esma."

"I understand. But may I suggest waiting a bit? See where your investigation leads and what other questions you might have. He's reluctant as is, and he keeps asking me to promise that he's done with this. We don't need him doing an about-turn and refusing to cooperate at all."

Overall, I thought her advice was good.

"Thank you for letting us know," I said.

She nodded and stood. From her feet, she gave me another of her long looks. She was holding on to something, deliberating, and abruptly sat again, this time beside me on the bed.

"The other reason you'll need to wait to speak to Ferko is that I've just explained to him that I shall no longer be his representative with the Court. When you want to see him again, the Victims and Witnesses people can ring him and, if need be, arrange for other counsel. I now have no connection whatsoever to this case."

She watched me as I gathered the import of what she'd said. The directness of her huge eyes on me was like staring into a leveled rifle—if a rifle could express yearning.

"Is that for my sake?" I asked.

"Well, Bill," she said, with a cute smile, "I rather hope it is for mine." With two fingers, she took hold of the necktie I'd been wearing all day in a silly effort to look official and whispered, "Bill, do you know the literal translation of the Romany words for desire? 'I eat you.' Not 'I want you.' 'I eat you.' Or more poetically, 'I'll devour you.'"

She leaned in slowly and kissed me, not in a grazing or tentative fashion, but delivering her entire self to me in the process. That and the full soft weight of her breasts against me were electrifying. I realized that at some level I had known what was going to happen, whatever my excuses, the minute she came into this room. I was sure she could feel my heart flopping around with the desperation of a landed fish.

"Allow yourself, Bill," she murmured. "You will never know yourself completely unless you have lived the moment when there is nothing of you but pleasure."

With my tie still between her fingers, she drew me to her, while I confronted yet again the weight of being well into the second half of my life. The 'Somedays' accumulated through youth and middle age had become a collection in their own right, a wish list illuminating the boundaries between fantasy and life's many limitations, with their unintended cruelty. 'Someday I will learn to scuba dive.' 'Someday I will travel to Bhutan.' 'Someday I will quit my job and take up woodworking.' 'Someday I will clean up…my office…my closet, the garage, the storeroom, the boxes I never looked at after my mother died.' 'Someday I will learn to fly-fish.' 'Go back to the piano.' 'Someday I will live in Tuscany.' 'Someday I will live in Tuscany and read the works of Beckett and Erving Goffman.'

After fifty-four years, the Someday pile had become mountainous—and with it, the inevitable recognition that almost none of it would occur. Having lived well, I felt little bitterness in knowing that. But in the moment, how can you turn away when Someday can suddenly be real?

'Someday I will be with a woman like that, someone who somehow jolts an entire room by passing through the doorway.' In how many rooms, gazing at how many doorways, had that utterly impossible promise strobed through my mind, a commitment made largely so I could do the polite thing and look away?

Perhaps all Merriwell had meant to tell me—
Merriwell and his many cohorts who'd been dragged
down by the tidal pull of desire—was that at a certain age
the bitterest of all emotions is regret.

IV.

For the Record

14.

Records—April 16–23

Life had taught me a cold truth, that the long-savored dream, when tested by reality, rarely approached expectations. That was never so in Esma's bed.

Despite the porn sites and Internet postings that vividly document the outward doings, none of us will ever really know the internal experience of other humans at these moments. But the extremes of physical pleasure I experienced with Esma were new for me. Whether that was Gypsy magic or because I'd checked all inhibitions when I crossed a professional boundary I still should have observed, at instants I felt I had reached the kernel of life, a place where sensation was so intense that the rest of the world became remote and living was purely a thrill.

Each encounter was novel, starting from the first time, while she was thrown over the arm of another of those beautiful leather chairs in my room. There were never any bars or borders, only whim and inspiration. Usually, Esma engaged in a constant narration, a virtual play-by-play in the most profane and arousing terms—'Oh yes, look at that big thing. Oh yes. I'm going to touch it, would you like that, yes, you know how much you like that, does that please you, yes it pleases you so much'—that gave way now and then to whispered instructions about her own satisfaction. 'There, slowly, please. Please.' 'Pinch.' 'Hard.' 'Harder.'

But better than the ballet maneuvers and machinery to which Esma introduced me, she offered an example in how to revel in desire and its satisfaction. She was remarkably free with her exclamations, and with the earthquake of pleasure that jolted her body with startling frequency. She turned the bed into a delicious, soupy mess, and yet always wanted more, reminding me of another unique truth about sex: You can see the Grand Canyon, exult in its majesty, and strike it off the bucket list. But everyone wants the next orgasm.

Naked, Esma was an inspiration, even though her Rubenesque proportions were not favored in our era. As we undressed one another the first time, she suddenly picked up her silk dress from the bed and draped it across herself, just as her bra was about to slip away.

"Do you like large breasts, Bill?"

"Love them," I said.

"Prepare for paradise," she answered.

The sight of Esma languorously approaching me was always arousing and quickly took me beyond what I had thought were the physical limitations of middle age. But her appeal was far more than corporeal. Years before, I had represented a stripper who worked under the stage name of Lotta Lust and who'd neglected to file federal income tax returns for more than twenty years. There was nothing unusual about Stella's—her real name—appearance, but she'd been in high demand onstage for two decades. It was all about self-confidence, she claimed. 'A girl who believes that every guy she meets is dying to fuck her is almost always right.' Esma made me feel every time that she was bestowing a gift as precious as the secret of alchemy.

Because Goos was returning to Belgium from Tuzla, Esma and I stayed two extra nights at the Blue Lamp, departing Sunday morning. For the first forty-eight hours, I never put on a stitch, relishing that freedom, too. On Friday, Esma got hungry before me and ran out to the *cevapi* place across the street to bring sandwiches back for both of us. While I was waiting for her, I lay still on the bed, enjoying the momentary solitude and taking stock. My entire body still felt like a force field in which the voltage center was my dick, and I was gripped by an intense desiccated thirst that seemed to be the product of coming so often. But I did not want to move. Instead, I exulted in having so thoroughly escaped restraint, even while the ghosts of the Bosnian dead, the rapes, the broilings, and the unhindered savagery seemed to dance darkly somewhere within my joy.

I reached The Hague late Sunday afternoon. When I entered the apartment, there was a suitcase in the middle of the living room, and without trying to snoop, I saw Lew Logan's name on the tag. I recalled that my landlady had said that my trip abroad was conveniently timed, since her husband was set to visit, meaning they'd have their house to themselves. I went to the refrigerator for water and heard a consistent rapping overhead. It took a second to realize that it was their headboard, knocking on the wall. Standing a little longer, I thought I could make out Narawanda Logan's low wail. I listened another second, smiling at them and myself. I intended to go out for a long dinner to give them their privacy, but Esma had exhausted me. I lay down for a nap and woke up about five on Monday morning.

My encounters with my landlady had been as isolated as she had promised, due in part to the apartment's floor plan. The lower level contained a small kitchen and a good-size living and dining area. From there, you went up three steps to the lone full bath. Off that landing, two separate facing staircases ascended, each leading to one of the two bedrooms.

On Tuesdays and Thursdays, when I got up for my 6 a.m. calls with my sons, I would potter toward the kitchen to make coffee and would find Mrs. Logan in the living room, contorted in some yoga pose. She was dressed all in black, in clingy yoga pants and a loose top, very tiny but notably well formed and also unexpectedly graceful. On the weekends, or when she made an early return from work, Narawanda ran. She'd come in dripping and winded, in another all-black outfit, with the addition of a stocking cap and mittens. I was often reading in the living room, but she breezed by with only a muted "Hello." I mentioned once that I'd been a runner myself until shin splints had stopped me several months ago, but I received no more than a courteous nod as she continued to the stairs. Overall, her social affect was slightly off-center, which was more or less what Goos had told me to expect.

When I came down to the kitchen that Monday, after my return from Bosnia, Mrs. Logan was in her yoga clothes, staring down the electric kettle so she could have her tea before getting on to her morning routine. Her husband's luggage was gone.

I expected her to be in the same flushed tonic mood in which I'd awakened, but she was abstracted. She greeted me politely—"Welcome back. Good trip?"—but she was in one of those morning funks in which some people start the day, and she moved off in silence to begin her exercise.

I headed into the office early, prepared for a backlog of paperwork. By the afternoon, Goos and I sat on either side of my pedestal desk planning our document request to NATO. We felt specifics would be the best wedge against the Court's natural inclination to avoid controversy.

Goos's time with the Yugoslav Tribunal had given him a good idea of what might be available, and he'd drafted his own list.

"Armies don't really exist to fight," he told me. "They are there to make records. Everything must be documented."

His top item was duty rosters and related records like mess reports. I understood his logic—a large group on leave might be our 'Chetniks,' playing dress-up on their free time. But I didn't think that would get us very far, given the basic obstacle.

"Under American law, we can't go interview any of those guys, Goos, assuming they're home by now."

"Yay-ay," he said, employing that exaggerated Australian version of 'Yeah,' "but we can check Facebook and YouTube and Twitter, Boom. Been looking over the posts about Eagle Base for some time. Quite a bit, actually, but not much that's interesting to us. But with names, mate, we can search up those former soldiers and try some questions from here. No law against that, and you can't believe what these young people will sometimes disclose over the Internet, stuff you'd never get face-to-face."

I comprehended only now why Goos had been glued to his computer the day we met.

The second request on his draft list was for truck logs and fuel depot records. I understood that we'd want to see if any heavy vehicles had left the base in the middle of the night, but I wasn't clear why he was also asking for mechanics' reports and requisitions for spare parts.

"Driving around in that coal mine in the dark, Boom, a truckie could have broken an axle or damaged a wheel pretty easy."

Next, he'd listed day-of records from the camps' infirmaries and sick bays.

"Aren't going to bully four hundred people onto trucks without somebody throwing a punch at a soldier, or an old gal setting her fingernails to somebody's face, maybe a couple troops getting bashed by a flying rock after the explosion."

I agreed. Ferko had said one of the soldiers was hit with a rifle stock while they were trying to subdue Boldo's brother.

The fourth item would never have occurred to me, given my limited knowledge of our military: aerial surveillance records.

"NATO had planes all over the place, Boom, and spy satellites, trying to make sure there were no troop movements by any side. Frightening the detail they get from outer space."

Goos had a number of other excellent ideas. In combat gear, US troops apparently wore blue GPS transponders that were designed to ping and thus prevent friendly-fire incidents. We decided to ask for all GPS records that might show US troops in or around Barupra on April 27, 2004. NATO Intelligence had probably also recorded all cell phone use and IP addresses registered in the area.

On a separate line, Goos had next written, 'Pictures.'

"Pictures?" I asked.

"Daily photographs. Parade shots. Formations. Can see who's missing, maybe hurt. This was near the end of the US presence. Cameras were probably snapping full-time for auld lang syne."

I nodded in slow wonder. Goos was something.

His last suggestion was the entire NATO file concerning the effort to capture Kajevic in Doboj, everything from US Army Intelligence to operational plans beforehand and the investigative reports in the aftermath: ballistic results, investigators' summaries, even the autopsies. This was the one item on which he and I at first disagreed. If Army Intelligence was anything like the intelligence units I'd dealt with at the FBI and other law enforcement agencies, they'd be adamant about not releasing any information for fear that even a decade later it would compromise techniques or sources. On the other hand, requesting these items would give us room to relent if we got into negotiations. All we really required was records that would show how the US had come to learn of Kajevic's whereabouts and whether there were any later suspicions of a setup, plus all information about the trucks the Roma had stolen from Attila.

As Goos and I were finishing up, my cell pinged. It was a text message from Esma.

In a meeting in London. Just felt the last little
goopy bit of you come sliding out of me.

I sat there in a visible blush, a state I hadn't experienced since my early teens.

I had known from the time Merriwell had advanced the
idea of going to NATO for records that my bosses—
Badu and Akemi—might be, in the end, a bigger obstacle
than the US Army. Caution was a way of life at the
Court. The leaden bureaucracy of the ICC, so foreign
from the freewheeling atmosphere of the prosecutor's office I had worked in before, had only one consolation:
It was essential. Without a permanent constituency, the
Court's sole insulation from the inevitable controversies
was to maintain rigid procedural regularity, even though
I often felt I was being asked to chase bad guys in a fashion as mannered as an equestrian routine. The rest of
the week, my time was consumed by meetings with the
heads of the Office of the Prosecutor's three divisions—
Investigation, Prosecution, and Complementarity—
concerning the document request. No one questioned
my legal analysis. The referral document from the Bosnians, with its wax seal and blue-and-yellow ribbons,
gave the Court the right to acquire any record that
the government of BiH was legally entitled to. But my
colleagues remained reluctant, particularly because this
maneuver was such a clear end-run around US law. I
found the Complementarity people—who were basically
the diplomats—particularly vexing. They were rule wor-
shippers who sometimes seemed as if they'd be perfectly
happy if the Court never prosecuted anybody again, as
long as we avoided any flaps.

The ultimate meeting with the division heads and co-ordinators took place in Badu's office. I kept my eye on the old man throughout. Badu chuckled and nodded and groaned in his graceful way, imparting nothing that indicated that he understood in any depth what had been said. I was beginning to realize that Badu's clueless manner insulated him from everyone outside the Court—and within—seeking to influence him. Near the end of the meeting, Badu said in his beautiful accent, "I have an old chum, Lord Gowen, who is the British ambassador to NATO. I am thinkin to geef him a coal." My initial reaction was panic, fearing Badu could irretrievably screw things up, but after a second I realized that this might be an adroit move. If the other leading nations in NATO—the Brits, the French, the Germans, who were all also members of the Court—acknowledged the legality of our document request in advance, the Americans would have a much harder time resisting.

Within a day, Ambassador Gowen had encouraged Badu to proceed. NATO's supreme commander at the moment was another Brit who, by the standard of other soldiers, was something of a supporter of the Court, and who signaled he would not stand in the way. Badu was careful to get the backing of the full OTP executive committee before I sent the formal document request to NATO. We all knew it was likely to provoke an explosive American response.

Back from Bosnia, I began to settle into a routine. On the mornings I didn't call Will or Pete, I would wake an hour later and linger with my coffee over the *New York Times* online. After that, I often phoned my sister, Marla, for a few minutes of the harmless chatter we'd shared across a lifetime. I was reaching her at about 2 a.m. in Boston, while she sat up in bed, answering e-mails, clipping articles from the day's newspapers to send to her kids, and reading the latest novel for her book club. The lights were burning while her husband, Jer, an orthopod, slept soundly beside her.

I got to the office by 8:30, ahead of many people, and was out by 5:30. I ate dinner in one of the cafés near the apartment and continued making my way through the pile of books I'd shipped to The Hague. Currently, I was rereading John Fowles, *The Magus*.

The day our document request was finally sent to NATO HQ in Belgium, I left the office a little early. It was the first fair weather I'd seen in The Hague. The solemn winter sky had broken into blue and a southern wind gentled the air. For a week now, the new vitality I'd acquired at the Blue Lamp had stimulated a yearning for exercise, of which I'd had next to none in the last few months. My landlady had offered me an old bicycle of her husband's, which was part of the herd locked inside the front door, and I contemplated a ride now, but I still didn't know the city and with my poor sense of direction was afraid of getting lost in some dead zone without cell reception.

When I came in, Narawanda was home early, too, probably also inspired by the weather. She was stretching in the living room for a run, her heel perched on the back of the sofa. It was the first time I'd seen her in shorts, and given the modesty with which we lived, I felt as if I'd walked in on her at an inappropriate moment.

I hustled toward the stairs, then regained myself and circled back.

"How would it be if I followed you for a little while?"

I asked. "I'd just like to see your route. I promise I won't hold you up. But I'd love to get back into running."

She pondered that, almost as if I'd proposed cutting my rent in half, but she finally produced a tiny smile and nodded.

My plan was to run beside her as long as I could, then walk back. Our initial pace was halting as we dodged through the crowded little streets near the flat. But she soon led me on a quicker route, down the leafy esplanade on Lange Voorhout, past the monolithic US Embassy, which looked like a bomb shelter, and then eventually into The Hague's vast park, Haagse Bos.

Based on our experience to date, I didn't expect her to be talkative, but I asked politely about her husband's visit.

"Nice," she answered, which seemed a bit of an understatement given the vigor of the bed-knocking. "Lewis talked all the time about how much he loves New York, how wonderful it has been to be back there." Her English was accurate, if occasionally somewhat stilted, and spoken with a Dutch accent—the rolled r's and long o's and guttural g's—spiced with a little of the rising pitches of Java.

"And you?" I asked. "Do you love New York?"

"To visit? So exciting. To live? So difficult. It is not for me. I am accustomed to The Hague." It felt like we had quickly reached a conversational impasse, but after a moment, she asked several questions about my trip. Her pace was much faster now, and I found every word an effort, but I answered expansively, in hopes of finally having some genuine interaction with her. I talked about my sons, and then BIH, providing a brief travelogue without going into details of the investigation.

Bosnia had been my first visit to a majority-Muslim country, and I had been impressed by how easygoing the version of Islam practiced around Tuzla had felt. The call to prayer had keened out from the minarets five times a day, but most of the women eschewed hijab, for example, and there was alcohol on every restaurant menu. Religion was a private matter, it seemed.

"That is the Islam I grew up with," Narawanda said. "Modernist. My mother covered her head in the mosque, and went every week, when I was little, but she always reminded me of the verse in the Qur'an that says Allah Himself planned for many faiths.'"

I had made my observations about Islam in Bosnia without any thought that Narawanda herself was Muslim. She could see I was a little nonplussed, but waved off my apologies.

"I am more of a lapsed Muslim these days. I have not gone to mosque or done the fasts since Lewis and I married."

"Was that what you two agreed?"

"No, no. Just as it has happened. Actually, at that point, Lewis and I said that if we were ever to have children, we would teach them that tradition."

"And that's changed?" I asked.

She reflected on my question for several strides.

"I really don't know," she said. "Right now, Lewis and I are not so close to having children. We do not even live in the same place."

Given her odd manner, I wasn't sure if she was miffed or just being matter-of-fact, but I could feel my lungs giving out. I waved her on without me, promising to do better if we ran again another time.

15.

Leiden—April 24–26

I spoke to Esma every night—remarkably explicit conversations in which I nearly gasped at some of the things she said before I slid into lascivious giggles. She was due to head back to New York from London the following week, and we agreed that she'd first detour to Holland to meet me for the weekend. I remained concerned about being seen together. Although Esma had relieved herself of any formal role in the case, as an ardent advocate for the alleged victims, she remained an interested party. Esma thought I was being ridiculous, but we agreed on Leiden, about fifteen minutes from The Hague, and I booked a lovely-looking boutique hotel along one of the canals.

I arrived there on the Intercity train about 3:30 Friday afternoon, walking along on a fine day and absorbing the charm of Leiden, a bit of Bruges without the gingerbread. Its network of canals and iron bridges was surrounded by the usual centuries-old brick buildings with steep tile roofs. The center of the city was crowded with young people, students at the university who'd already gotten started on the weekend. After another few minutes, I recognized the green striped awning of the hotel, which I'd seen on the Internet.

At the tiny reception desk, I handed my passport to the bespectacled middle-aged proprietor. He would keep the document for an hour or two, as they routinely do on the Continent in order to fill out forms required by the EU. He had finished work with Esma's British passport already and handed it to me, with its eccentric images of a crown, lion, and unicorn embossed in gold on its crimson cover. Holding tangible evidence of Esma's presence, I felt a lurid thrill below my belt.

In our room, I found her asleep, with the canvas curtains drawn and her eyes hidden beneath a sleep mask. There was enough light, though, to see her. She had kicked away half the covers, revealing those well-turned legs up to her thigh, the rest of her body draped discreetly, as in an old painting. Her face was at the edge of the bed, while one bare arm hung down. In the grip of a dream, her mouth moved over uncertain words and her body twitched slightly.

I undressed quietly, then took hold of the duvet and drew it away slowly from her torso, an inch-by-inch striptease of a sort, relishing everything. The sight had a predictable effect on me and I eventually took my hardened dick and nuzzled it against her cheeks and mouth, slowly pushing away the mask. Deep in sleep, she waved her hand vaguely at first and then finally, without ever opening her eyes, took gentle hold of me, guiding me into her mouth.

I woke Saturday morning, my hand webbed in hers, looking down at that odd collection of rings I'd noticed in Tuzla, which were all on the middle finger of her left hand. I was still staring when she roused herself.

"Is one of those a wedding ring?" I asked, about a plain gold band.

"That?" She laughed and sat up. "Don't worry about that. That is my problem, not yours."

"What does that mean, Esma?"

She tossed around her storm of dark hair and finally went off to the bathroom. When she returned, she said, "Are you concerned you have rivals, Bill?"

"Every man who sees you, Esma, is my rival."

The remark delighted her. She padded to the bed sinuously. Diving down on it, she whispered, "I am with you. Let me show you."

Afterward, we sat outside in our robes. Our room was tiny but stuffed with antiques, much to Esma's liking, with a small terrace outside where the potted plants were already in bloom. I pulled two white iron chairs together and took her hand as we looked out over the rooftops and the adjoining canals. She felt distant for a second.

"Enjoy this part, Bill. Make it last. Don't worry about what comes next."

"What makes you think I'm worried?"

She reared back to look at me in mild reproof. I wasn't sure if I was being scolded for doubting her Gypsy voodoo or just for being dishonest.

"That is your nature." She was right about that. "And I am not very good at the next part anyway."

"You mean life?"

"This too is life, and very much the best of it." She snuck her hand under my robe. "Don't fall in love with me, Bill."

Given my character, which Esma had correctly assayed, I was already reflecting on what I felt. Certainly I was gripped by addictive lust, and great tenderness and gratitude born of its satisfaction. But between us there was a connection, too, I knew that. From our first instants together, I had felt that Esma, with her passionate nature and galloping intellect, fit a yearning space inside me. But love? I wasn't even sure anymore what I thought about that word. Yet whatever this was, my ardor was more revitalizing than anything I'd felt in decades.

"And why do you say that?" I asked. "Because you are unavailable?" I was thinking about the wedding ring.

"No," she said. "But I fear I shall disappoint you, Bill."

"Because?"

"Because I always manage to do that in the end." She was back to being the essential Esma, humorless and intense.

I tried to joke. "Should I leave now?" I asked.

As I hoped, the remark leavened her mood. She reverted to her sensual gaze and her thin dominating smile. She loosened the belt on her robe and threw it open as we sat there in the daylight in the view of many rooftops.

"If you like," she answered.

On Saturday night, Esma and I had our first cross moments. Ellen wanted my approval on the plans for the rehearsal dinner before Pete's wedding, which required three brief conversations between 11 p.m. and midnight. We'd had a call on the same subject the weekend before, while Esma and I were ensconced at the Blue Lamp.

"This is very strange with your ex-wife. You speak to her more than your children."

I explained that Ellen didn't have time for these

projects during the week, when she was working. But Esma's dark face was closed off by a look of open skepticism, expressed primarily through a fleshy pout. I thought of replaying the remarks she'd made to me yesterday about being jealous, but I already knew Esma would never make her emotions slave to logic or consistency.

"And you stayed with her when you went back home," said Esma. "That is strange, too. Is there ex-sex now and then?"

I laughed out loud. "Esma. You've heard these conversations. There is nothing but family business. My ex is no one to worry about."

"Some men can never leave their marriages behind. I have known too many."

"Well, you're reacting to what happened with them. Ellen and I are merely planning our son's wedding, and I consider it a blessing that we can enjoy this together."

To subdue her, I suggested that we go out for a drink. A mime was performing under a streetlight a block from the hotel and she lightened our moods.

On Sunday morning, we both wanted air again and wandered around Hooglandse Kerkgracht, where tony shops lined the narrow brick streets beside a parklike median.

"Look at that," Esma said, as we came out of an antique store, where she had looked over several Japanese ivories called netsuke, animal figures that she said she collected. "Your name in lights, Bill."

She was pointing one hundred feet up to an elegant-looking jewelry store with an oak facade. TEN BOOM appeared in large gilt letters above the shop window. In the lower right corner, the sign read *SINDS 1875.*

The sight turned me to cement.

"I've sometimes thought you made that name up," said Esma.

I finally said, "I forgot they were in Leiden."

"Who?"

"My parents. I'm pretty sure my father worked at that store," I told her. "It was during the Second World War."

"What did he do?"

"He was a watchmaker."

But that was hardly the most important detail, and as we meandered for the next hour beside the canals, I shared most of the tale with Esma. The actuality of the store, emblazoned with our name, had removed my parents' story from the shrouded place I ordinarily kept it to quell my discomfort.

The day I turned forty, my parents asked me to come see them by myself. Like a lot of married people, I rarely visited my mother and father without Ellen or one of the boys as a shock absorber. As a child, I never understood what it was that had infuriated me about my folks, who were in all ways mild and kindly. But getting older, I had recognized that their bond had an intensity that left Marla and me feeling we were forbidden to enter the inner sanctum where they actually lived. As an adult, I preferred not to be alone with them, rather than reexperience that same sense of exclusion.

But I went by myself on my birthday nonetheless. I was fairly certain that they had a family heirloom to pass on, one of the few things they had carried from Holland, perhaps even a piece of jewelry that would find its way to Ellen. I knew my sister had received a diamond necklace that had been in the family since the 1870s when she turned forty, two years before. And my father had made a gift of one of his watches when I reached twenty-one.

Overall, I expected forty to be a good birthday for me. I was on the cusp of middle-aged tranquility, the writhings of youth so far behind me that I couldn't fully recall how it felt. I was the United States Attorney in my hometown, a higher and more esteemed place in the world than I had ever imagined for myself. My two sons were not yet full-throttle teenagers, and I was wise enough to enjoy them while they remained content with their parents. Even my marriage seemed okay. I knew that I bored Ellen in a fundamental way and that she blamed me for it, but she was an interesting, competent woman who shared my passion for our sons, which, at least then, seemed to be enough common ground.

My parents' house was a modest Kindle County bungalow that they bought in the 1950s, and which each of them eventually left for good only on the EMT's rolling stretcher. My mother hugged me at the door to wish me happy birthday, while my father, a master of old-school restraint, shook my hand. Then they led me into the living room from which my sister and I were largely banished growing up. They took places on the flowered sofa, as if they had been preassigned by stage directions. My father's long pale face was rigidly composed. My mother sat close beside him, her plump hands in her ample lap as she gazed toward him, apparently awaiting a sign to begin. They had already been through this two years before with Marla, as it turned out, but even so, it must have been a nightmare revisited for them, realizing that they were again about to place their relationship with one of their children in jeopardy.

"We have decided that we need to tell you something," my mother said. That clearly was her part. The hard line fell to my father.

"We are Jews," he said.

The most important thing my parents were saying, of course, had nothing to do with religion or heritage. They were telling me that they had lied to my sister and me all our lives. In retrospect I was always proud of the way I responded: With nothing else, I began to cry, a man who had not broken down completely since my dog had been run over in front of me when I was thirteen.

I called my sister on my drive back home, and merely from the way I said her name, she knew what was up.

"They told you," she said. "I'm so glad. I've been warning them I couldn't keep this secret much longer."

"What the fuck," I answered.

For Marla, whatever the drama within, the practical adjustments were minimal. She had married Jer, a wonderful guy who happened to be Jewish, and she had raised her three kids in the embrace of the Jewish community in Lexington, Mass. Marla had lived the kind of contented suburban life—the kids, the country club friends, the committed acts of charity—that Ellen regarded as a form of early-onset morbidity, an opinion I more or less shared in those years. Only when my marriage ended another decade later did I tumble to the recognition that my sister was happy, far happier than many other people who arrive in their middle years, including me. Now Marla understood my shock and indignation, but the news had clearly not shaken her as deeply.

When I reached home, Ellen absorbed what I had to say with a river of emotion flowing through her face, culminating in a smile. "Oh my God," she said. "How fascinating. You know, I love them both, you know that, but there's always been something not quite right. How many times have I told you, 'Your parents are strange'?" She thought only a second longer and added, "They have to tell the boys," who were then twelve and fourteen. I do not remember Ellen asking me for many days how this news had affected me.

Although it may be what the psychologists call cognitive dissonance, my enduring reaction was that I was fairly pleased about being Jewish. I had grown up with many Jewish friends and had always felt some envy for their fierce ethnic pride, which contrasted with my parents' reluctance—now far more understandable—about anything Dutch.

On the other hand, I did not tend to talk about this discovery very often. I made no effort to keep it a secret and I don't think I was ashamed to have lost my status as a Real White Person. The hard part was accounting for my mother and father.

By the time they died eight years later in close succession, I had gone through many stages, but I had ultimately given them the benefit of the doubt. It was a considerable sacrifice to part with core elements of your identity.

As for what had happened during the war, Marla eased more details from my mom in the last months of her life, after my dad was gone, when my loyal sister often came to town to sleep on a cot beside our dying mother.

My father's family, then named Bergmann, always distinguished watchmakers, had left Frankfurt for Rotterdam in the 1870s in response to one of the periodic waves of anti-Semitism that swept through Germany. My father's uncles joined them in the 1890s when several proposals were offered in the Reichstag to limit the rights of Jewish citizens, laws that were ultimately adopted decades later once Hitler took power. When that began to happen, in 1933, almost two dozen more cousins came to Rotterdam, joining the diaspora of more than half of Germany's Jews who left in the next few years. Unfortunately, the Nazis were not far behind the Bergmann cousins and rolled through the Netherlands in 1940, bringing their racial laws with them. The German-speaking relatives were a special burden on my father's family, since their poor Dutch made them easily identifiable as Jews. My father knew that as a result, sooner or later, the entire family—now called 'Bergman,' having dropped an n to sound more Dutch—would be rounded up and sent to camps.

In July 1942, Aart and Miep ten Boom of Leiden were killed when a tree collapsed on their car as they were driving through a fierce storm. The Ten Boom family were leaders of the Dutch resistance, which over time hid thousands of Jews from the Nazis through various means. Aart and Miep's surviving relatives decided it would be a fit tribute to suppress all news of their deaths and to allow a young Jewish couple to assume their identities. The Ten Booms were jewelers, with need of a skilled watchmaker in their store. When the offer came, my father and mother left their lives behind—and dozens of doomed relatives. They hid in plain sight in Leiden, with the knowledge of hundreds of local residents who never betrayed them.

The end of the war was trying in its own way. My mother, an only child whose parents had died in their forties, wanted to return to Rotterdam to seek the possible remnants of their community. My father apparently regarded it all as better left behind, given the near-certain capture and annihilation of his family. He convinced her that the greatest safety for them and, far more important, their children was in remaining Aart and Miep rather than chancing the vagaries of history's roulette wheel, in which the Jews' number, along with several other perennial losers, was always coming up black.

The Dutch neighbors who had hidden my parents throughout the war were confused by my father's attitude and even somewhat critical. They had risked their lives because my parents were Jews, not converts, and so for the new Aart and Miep the best choice was to apply to emigrate. In 1950, because of the need for skilled tradesmen in the US, my parents were granted visas.

By now, Esma and I had taken a seat on a concrete bench in a brick plaza called Beestenmarkt. A large old-fashioned windmill, with its white canvas sails, turned a few hundred feet away, while the masonry was wetted by a strange fountain, dozens of piddling streams that shot straight up from buried piping. Several tow-headed children were frolicking on a day that was finally mild enough to be welcomed as spring. They dared the water with small hands, splashing while their parents remonstrated, and after soaking themselves, sprinted away with exhilarated screams.

"This is a more familiar story to me than you may know," said Esma. "There are thousands and thousands of Gypsies, especially lighter-skinned Gypsies in the United States, who have simply melted into the American population without looking back on their Rom ways."

I stared at her, wondering why it was I was so attracted to women without much native empathy. If I ever went back to therapy, I had to put that question near the top of the list.

We began wandering back to the hotel.

"Wars are horrible," said Esma. "They do horrible things to everyone." This seemed a more comforting response and I took the hand she had customarily lapped over my arm. "That was how I died the last time," Esma said. "During World War I."

I stopped. "You're being euphemistic?"

The dark eyes scolded. "Far from it. I was an Ottoman soldier, a poor private from Ayvalik, a tiny town, and not quite eighteen years old. I died of the infection from a shoulder wound at Gallipoli."

I was far less ruffled by this declaration than I might have expected, perhaps because I'd been struggling with my parents' two lives, or because I had already accepted Esma's warning about potential disappointment as meaning that there were important facets of her character I didn't yet know. Discovering these beliefs was a little more complicated than finding out Esma bit her nails, and probably not a good sign for the long run. But for the near term, I was willing to attempt tolerance, since it was part of the journey to foreign terrain I'd started when I let her into my room in Tuzla. Besides, I recognized an opportunity to gather intelligence on the greatest unknown.

"And was death terrible?" I asked her.

"Not so terrible, no. Lonely. Cold. But I was glad to pass beyond pain. I didn't enjoy the feeling of distance. But I realized almost at once that it was temporary."

"I see."

I found myself in an even, if somewhat resigned, mood processing all of this—my parents, Esma, the fundamental unreliability of humans, and the fact that for me there was, in all likelihood, more searching yet ahead. We returned to the hotel and the world of sensation one more time before I walked her to the station.

16.

The Lab—April 29

The following Wednesday, Goos called me from the crime lab. Several results were now available, which, he suggested, would be easier to absorb if I came out there.

"Am I going to have to look at bones?" I asked.

"'Fraid so."

I grumbled, largely for show.

In the milder weather, I'd started using Lew Logan's old bike to get to work, and by now I was up to the forty-minute ride to the outlying neighborhood of Ypenburg. I'd grown accustomed to the eye-rolling and pointing of the local kids when they saw my helmet. Nothing seemed more quintessentially Dutch to me than their scoffing at protective headgear while remaining the world's leaders in training neurosurgeons.

I had no problem finding the immense Netherlands Forensic Institute, a black square of glass built into a grassy hillside that somehow reminded me of Darth

Vader's headpiece. It was a vast enterprise with nearly six hundred professionals on staff. Once inside, I experienced the place as a world of white, with lab coats and microscope lenses and confounding machines visible through the laboratory windows as Goos strolled me down the corridors.

I asked where we were headed.

"Little hard to do this in order," Goos said. "But we have results in five different labs—DNA, Path, Microinvasive, Ballistics, and Fingerprints."

"What's Microinvasive?"

"You'll see. But they have a special microscope here. Developed to look for trace fractures in the engine block of race cars." Goos shook his head about the priorities. "We'll start with your favorite." He gave it an Aussie pronunciation, so that the last syllable came out 'right.'

In the chill Forensic Pathology lab, we donned shower cap–like head coverings and surgical gowns. Goos steered me over to a stainless steel table on which the pieces of three largely complete skeletons had been laid out, the remains of Boldo and his son and brother, if Ferko were to be believed. There were special tungsten bulbs in here that gave the lab an optic clarity that seemed to exceed daylight.

"Okay," said Goos, "so let us remind ourselves of what we are trying to accomplish."

"I'd hope, one, to corroborate Ferko's testimony and two, to find out as much as I can about who killed these people."

From the slow pace at which Goos nodded, I didn't think I'd get much better than a C on the quiz. I'd missed some of the sub-issues, specifically the age of these bones and the causes of death.

"Now how much pathology you familiar with, Boom? Don't want to yabber on, if there's no need."

"Yabber your heart out, Goos. I've been a white-collar guy my whole career. Crimes of greed, not violence. I haven't spent much time in places like this." My one trip to the path lab, while a prosecutor, had come when the Black Saints Disciples had killed a young man who'd agreed to testify for the government. The agents on the case wanted me to see what had been done to our guy, which wasn't pretty.

Goos withdrew a laser pointer from under his gown and showed me various points on the pelvis used to discern both the gender and age of the decedents. In the lab, Goos was expansive and wonky about the scientific refinements in his field since his time as a grad student. DNA had established that these remains were those of three males, while statistical analyses of the changes that occurred over time in the pelvis, legs, and teeth of a broad population (including, per Goos, "the density of blood vessel canalations") allowed for near certainty in determining the men's ages. For all the forensic advances, the result was close to Goos's original estimate by naked eye. Two men were in their forties—forty and forty-five roughly—and the third was an adolescent of about fifteen.

Goos had snapped on plastic gloves as he handled the skeletons. The bones held a soft sheen now, the product of a layer of protective plastic Goos had applied to prevent further degradation. He tilted the top of one skull at me.

"Notice anything about this fella?" There was a hole, almost perfectly round, through the center of his forehead, as well as a network of fine fractures beside it. At the rear, a far larger hole had been blown away.

"Bullet?"

"Yay, counselor, it would be my expert opinion that this poor devil got shot in the head. And at fairly close range." He pushed his pointer into the eye socket so I could see the light through the front bullet hole. "We've a punched-in surface, small pieces of bone missing, and beveling in the outer table.

"Now, we have a larger hole here." He was indicating two ribs on the same skeleton. "So pretty sure he got shot first at longer range. Bullet wobbles more the further it travels, makes a bigger hole."

He highlighted the examinations of the other two skeletons. The 'youngster,' as Goos put it, had been shot first in the hand and then through the chest, where the small entrance wound suggested the bullet had shattered. The third set of bones—apparently those of the brother who'd bled out—showed no bullet holes, which would be consistent with entry wounds through the softer tissues and organs.

"Last thing that's relevant"—Goos tilted open the jawbone on the middle skeleton—"I see some missing teeth on all three, even this young fella. So I'd say these folks had very little dental care."

"Meaning they were poor?"

"Or didn't like the dentist. But let's say poor."

"Like the people in Barupra?"

"Or most of the people on earth, but Barupra, too."

He plunked the skull back on the table so it made a dull knock.

"Done here now," he said and removed his cap.

We walked down the hall to a stairwell. As he passed, Goos greeted several people in lab coats. I suspected a PhD got a lot of more respect in these precincts than the

usual humble cop. On the second floor, we entered a
door labeled TOOLMARKS AND MICRO-ANALYSIS INVASIVE
TRAUMA LAB.

"This is the place with the special microscope?"

"Infinite Focus Microscope it's called." Inside, the first
thing I saw was a vast light table for the display of X-rays
and other slides. Overhead vents hung down, inverted
bells of clear plastic used to whisk away unwanted vapors.
A piece of one of the long bones, whose absence I'd noticed from the first skeleton, was vised below the hot-shit
microscope.

"Now this here is my *domaine royal*." Goos turned
with his long hands raised somewhat grandly. "Taphon-
omy, basically the study of bodily degradation. Without
embalming, a body is skeletonized in about six weeks.
So trying to figure if the bones have been in the earth
five years or five hundred requires looking to other fac-
tors. Bones decompose more slowly than the flesh, but
they do decompose. Tricky thing in this case is, as you
know, there's lots of salt in the earth thereabouts near
Tuzla. That'll degrade the bone surface more quickly,
meaning you might think the remains are older than
they are. Which is where our friendly microscope comes
in. The interior of the bones, once we've sawed them
open, shows decomposition unrelated to contact with
the earth. All told, I'd say these were in the ground ten
years give or take, and Dr. Gerber here at NFI, dog's bol-
locks in this field, he agrees."

I took a second to reflect on what Goos had shown
me thus far.

"Overall, I'd say Ferko's doing pretty well." The
Monday after we'd returned from Tuzla, I'd told Goos
about Ferko's sudden recall of Kajevic's threats. Goos

had reacted largely as I had. It was not a huge problem in itself, but it meant we had to probe Ferko's story with even greater caution. It was heartening, therefore, that the lab results seemed to corroborate him.

"So far," said Goos. "But it's about to get a little thick. Let's talk about the DNA analysis, because that's where our first troubles appear. I can call up the report from this computer." He batted at a keyboard.

I was better versed in DNA than pathology, because that science had proved revealing throughout the entire universe of crimes. You could extract DNA, for example, from a smudged fingerprint on a cashier's check, as had happened to an unfortunate client of mine who'd bribed a county zoning officer by paying a college tuition bill.

"Now, DNA with buried bones is tricky. That's because there's always little critters in the soil who nibble on these bones and leave their own DNA behind." He got a little deep for me in describing the extraction methods that had been developed to reduce soil contamination, but I followed well enough. A comparison between samples from the bone's interior versus its surface helped isolate microbial effects.

"We performed Y-STR and mitochondrial DNA analysis," Goos said.

"Mitochondrial is mother's side and less subject to contamination?" I asked.

"Right you are, Boom. Mother's side shows more than seventy percent of the genome in each man is consistent with Indo-Aryan origins."

"That's what you'd expect if they were Roma, right?"

"That's what the experts here say. Now, the Y-STR, that was a lot more complicated. The good news is that all three exhibit a common Y chromosome, which you'd expect if they were truly father, son, and uncle. But even getting that result was quite the bitzer because of our contamination issues." The classic contamination problem, even in a lab setting, arose from the fact that there was no way to tell the origins of the DNA you were examining. It could be blood or bone or skin from the subject, or a dandruff flake that had scaled off one of the investigators.

"Here, Boom, even when we isolated the microbial effects, the bone crystal cells from the surface showed much more human contamination than the bone crystals from the inside. And if these bones were in the earth for ten years, there's no way that should be the case, unless my blokes and I were a lot less careful with the exhumation than I thought.

"So that result goes hand in hand with what I told you in Barupra, that I was detecting topsoil down in the grave? Madame Professor Tchitchikov, our geologist, has confirmed that. So the boil-over, Boom, is that some other person was digging in that site fairly recently. And probably handling these bones."

"Meaning what?"

"Let me get you to the end of this."

He motioned and we traveled a few steps to the ballistics lab. Through a window at the back, I could see two guys in white hazmat suits getting ready to discharge shotguns at a car door. Goos, who'd gone to see a technician when we entered, now held an envelope out of which he spilled two objects, one an intact bullet about two inches long, the other a squashed-up fragment with a shining interior. The pretty glow, like polished jewelry, on an object that had been lethal to another human, reminded me of the odd beauty of a slide my mother's oncologist showed me of her cancer cells.

"First thing I'd take note of," said Goos, "is that there's nothing about the presumed bullet wounds we were looking at in the path lab inconsistent with these projectiles. They are the remains of what is sometimes called Yugo M67 ammo, which is characteristically used in the Zastava, a full metal-jacketed, sharp-pointed round, 7.62 by 39 millimeters. This was one of Marshal Tito's lasting contributions to humanity, creating a bullet for the Kalashnikov-style rifle that opens a bigger wound when it's destabilized by the body.

"But here's where our results start to go a little wobbly." Goos went to a computer and pulled up a series of photographs of each of these pieces, magnified to about four times what the unaided eye could see. The photos showed the lands and grooves on the bullets, which were left by the raised surfaces in the gun barrel intended to impart spin. "First, they can tell from the rifling that these rounds were discharged by two different Zastavas. But it's the intact bullet"—Goos held up the piece of lead—"that's problematic. These boys and girls here can't square any of the bullet wounds we saw on the remains in the path lab with a bullet of this caliber and power being left intact in a body. And it had to be in the body if we've recovered it from the grave. If this round struck bone, it would show some compression. And if it passed only through flesh, given where Ferko says the Chetniks were positioned, it had to have exited the bodies and thus wouldn't be likely to be buried with the remains. Following?"

I was. But Goos and I both knew that every case had its anomalies, things that the experts found inscrutable and which were accounted for by a universal principle: Shit happened. The most famous example in the world of ballistics was the so-called 'magic bullet' theory of the JFK assassination, in which a single round seemed to have struck Governor Connally and then deflected to hit President Kennedy in a couple of places. I told Goos that, but he shook his head.

"There's more, mate. Let's go look at some finger-prints."

Among the forensic sciences we'd been discussing, I knew prints the best. I was no expert, but I was con-versant with the lingo of ridges and whorls and points of comparison. This lab was less dramatic-looking than some of the places we'd already been—just microscopes, and computers with giant monitors, hooded with black sheet metal to minimize glare. Nonetheless, Goos said, this was one of the most advanced fingerprint labs on the globe. By doing computer analysis of the hundreds of millions of digital prints that had been recorded around the world in the last twenty years, NFI had been able to attach statistical probabilities to ridge patterns, mean-ing they could say how often a given feature appeared in the human population, just as had long been done with DNA. Because of recent scientific disputes about whether fingerprints were actually unique to each per-son, the NFI technique seemed destined to become, with time, the new standard. But the old method, in which fumes of superglue were used to bring out print details, was good enough for present purposes.

"They found two good prints, one on each bullet. Troubling part is that it's from the same digit."

He waited for me to register the significance. Ballistics had already established that the recovered rounds had been fired by two different weapons. It seemed unlikely that the same person would have loaded both rifles. But that appeared to be the only innocent explanation.

"And here's the print from the intact round." After a minute of fiddling, Goos called up the image on the massive computer screen beside him. It was the standard negative image with fuming, but it was rendered in yellow against an indigo background. Goos zoomed the picture so that the place of the print on the bullet was clear. "Notice anything?"

I didn't. It was a nice full print.

Goos used the back end of his laser pointer. "See here?"

I got it now. The print extended below the casing line. That meant the bullet had been handled after it was fired.

"Maybe kids playing around?"

"Don't think that works, Boom. Fact is, this gravesite was tampered with. From the DNA contamination, we're already saying somebody was handling those bones, and given the fingerprints on the bullets and the fact that the intact round doesn't match the wounds we see in those remains, odds are that these bullets were planted—not just touched by some youngster mucking round. Somebody's funning with us, Boom. Could be whoever done it took stuff out as well as dropped stuff in. But somebody's been monkeying with our evidence, Boom. That's the main point."

This was not a welcome development.

"Were they trying to mislead us?" I asked.

"Can't think of another reason to plant bullets, but that doesn't mean there isn't one."

I took all this in silently.

"Next step," said Goos, "involves Madame Professor

Tchitchikov. I'm going to send her a piece of each of the skeletons so she can match the minerals that the bones have absorbed to the soil specimens from the graves. She needs to do the chemistry before she can finish up on-site in Bosnia."

"What about looking at the Cave?"

"She'll do that then, too." Goos, stoical, with his usual watery eyes, stared at me a second. "Enough strange stuff here that you might want to plan to come along."

I groaned. I hadn't expected to go back to Bosnia so soon, especially not to get bad news.

17.

A Meeting—April 27–May 10

So we entered another period of waiting, not only for NATO to respond to our document request, but also for Complementarity to renew our credentials with the government of BiH so we could return, along with the French geologist. While our investigation hung fire, I was asked to assume a supervisory role on two other 'situations' that were in the last stages of investigation, both likely to lead to charges, one in Sudan, one in Congo. With a slow schedule, I took lunch as the occasion to get to know my colleagues, including a couple of the judges who were curious about me.

At night, several times a week, I spoke to Esma, who seemed to have become submerged in New York, twice putting off her anticipated return to the Continent. Her erotic texts continued to thrill and embarrass me, arriving unpredictably, as I was at my desk comparing witness statements or in meetings with the Complementarity folks about the latest communications with Brussels. At night, before I sleep, I hear the sounds you make, the unwilling little whinny of a groan as you finally succumb to pleasure.

After our first outing, Narawanda was willing to accept me as a running companion. Like me, she seemed to be going through a fallow time at work and we took off together at 5:30 or 6:00 most evenings. After the third or fourth time, I managed to keep up with her, although with considerable strain. I urged her not to let me hold her back, and she denied I was, but I tended to doubt it. She was a beautiful runner, with the bird-boned physique of the best long-distance athletes and a perfect gait in which her arm motion and neck angle were exquisitely synced with her stride for maximum efficiency. I, by contrast, was laboring with each step, but I enjoyed the challenge and was pleased that the vulnerable parts of a middle-aged body, especially my knees and lower back, had no complaints, whatever screaming my muscles did when I rolled out the next morning.

It became our routine, when we were done, to stop for something to eat, since the runs inevitably left me famished. Nara was the type who discovered her appetite only when there was food in front of her, at which point she would often consume more than I did. Generally, we stopped at one of the little cafés near the house, where we could sit outside without offending anyone with sweat still rivering off of us. We usually had a beer each and a large bottle of water, most often at a place that quickly became my favorite, a Netherlandish oddity, a fast-food restaurant serving fresh fish. Behind the glass counters, the huge variety of European catch was a pastel display on ice—anchovies, smoked mackerel, shrimp, mussels, calamari, various fish fillets like dorado, skewers of raw fish, and many styles of herring. A sign out-side boasting of NIEUWE HARING had first brought us through the door, since it was a local delicacy Nara in-sisted I try. The herring, boned and partially gutted, was served with chopped onion, then consumed without sil-verware, simply by grasping the tail. My father had been a huge fan of herring, although he had never explained it was a Dutch habit, but the taste now brought back my childhood, when the pungent flavors were a challenge. Now, I found I could put down four or five herring at a sitting.

As for my landlady, I enjoyed her company as I got to know her. Nara turned out to be one of those people who was quiet largely because she never had quite fig-ured out the right thing to say. Her remarks were in-evitably slightly odd, frequently far more candid than her timid nature would seem to allow.

Her parents were both Indonesian. Her father was an engineer who'd worked for Shell and had risen high enough in the company to get dispatched to the Nether-lands, where Nara had been raised. She was an art stu-dent in the early stages of her education, but her mother's side had been caught up in the Indonesian unrest of the mid-'60s, when more than half a mil-lion suspected communist sympathizers were murdered by Suharto and the military, with another million im-prisoned, including all of her mother's brothers. Her mother's grieving accounts of that period had ultimately inspired Nara to switch her studies to law, and to do the master's degree that led to her employment at the Yugoslav Tribunal. She admitted she'd had an ulterior motive, though, for her graduate studies at NYU.

"I stayed in school so my mother didn't marry me

off," she said one evening when we were outside at a stainless steel table. Without her heavy black glasses, Nara had a lighter, prettier look. "She was willing to allow me to finish my studies, but I was so glad when I met Lewis, since Mum already had someone in Jakarta picked out for me."

"And how did your parents react to Lew?"

"Oh, as you might expect in a traditional Javanese family. My mother wrung her hands and said this was what had come of trying to make her children safe by leaving Indonesia. And of course, she was right: I am much more attached to Amsterdam and The Hague than Jakarta, which is really just a place where my grandparents live—and where I would never feel right drinking a beer with dinner." Nara reached for her glass with a sly ironic smile, lips sealed and cheeks round, that I was seeing more and more often.

On May 3, the Court received a formal response from NATO. They had asked the United States to provide most of the documents we had sought, and the Defense Department, citing the Service-Members' Protection Act, had refused.

I met with Akemi and Badu several times to discuss our options.

Legally, the American response was unpersuasive. Generally, in conflict-of-laws situations, treaties trump statutes, meaning that the US's obligations under the North Atlantic treaty were paramount to the Service-Members' Act. But it wasn't clear what kind of appetite the NATO leadership had for a confrontation with their American partners.

"Gowen has been talking about a compromise of

some kind," Badu told me, when I reported back after a couple days of legal research.

I wasn't satisfied with that. Compromise meant that the Americans would turn over documents that weren't damaging, and only enough of them to give Brussels a way to save face. The Court had no rights of its own within NATO, nor did the Bosnians, in whose name we were acting, because neither of us were NATO members. Our only way to litigate was to bring an action in the International Court of Justice, where countries sue each other, in behalf of the Bosnians. That was bound to take years, and the Americans could be expected to pressure BiH to back out.

After several discussions, the OTP leaders decided I should send a long letter to the NATO countries that were also members of the Court, explaining the fallacies of the American position and the importance of defending principles of international law. Badu agreed to present the document in person to each of those nations' ambassadors to The Hague. The hope was to bring more diplomatic pressure on the US, although no one seemed especially optimistic that the American position would change.

The second weekend in May, while this was playing out, Nara went off to meet Lew in London, where he'd been dispatched by his NGO for a few days. I thought of traveling there with her, since Esma had hopes of finally returning from New York. She remained uncertain about her plans, then at about 8 p.m. on Friday, Esma called to say that she was on her way to JFK and would come straight to me on a flight that would get her into Schiphol at 6 a.m. Saturday. I promised to meet her.

Our hotel in Leiden proved to be fully booked, as

were a couple others I tried. Since Esma would have to return to London late on Sunday, I decided we could risk a stay at my place, which I knew Esma would prefer. I was feeling no less uneasy about the proprieties, but after two weeks apart, I was not expecting to spend much time outside.

Esma, and a porter with a mountain of suitcases, burst through the doors of international arrivals not long after six. She approached me languorously and fell into my arms.

"I have missed you so," she whispered.

The Dutch, who were either more secure or more fatalistic, still had luggage storage within Schiphol, and Esma was able to drop her bags there. She retained only a small piece of hand luggage.

"Thinking I won't need much," she said, with a completely wanton look. As always, I tried to assay my feelings about Esma, since the sight and scent and feel of her remained electrifying. Granted, she was eccentric. But there was still something special going on. Sex at its best is a team sport and Esma and I together were all-stars. Between us, there was a level of trust and engagement and union that exceeded easy understanding.

"What in the world is this litigation in New York?" I asked her when we were on the train to The Hague.

"It's a divorce proceeding," she said, "if you must know. The other side is absolutely bonkers. The husband is busily attempting to establish adultery and inhuman treatment rather than consent to a no-fault divorce. It's a bitter, dreadful case."

"And what about your client?"

"Very fond of her actually. Iranian family, exiled with the Shah. She married another Persian, thirty years her senior, but they have slowly driven each other quite mad. It's like watching one of those nature shows on telly, with two animals whose fangs are in each other's throats, neither willing to let go and be the first to die. I met her in London many years ago, and she insisted I become involved in the case. She will be awarded a huge sum eventually, everyone knows that, but her husband wants her to earn it with pain."

When we reached the apartment, Esma went through the entire place, including Narawanda's bedroom, despite my protests about the intrusion.

"Very little sign of her husband in there," Esma said, descending the stairs. "Only photos of the happy couple are down here, more or less for show, I'd say."

"That's the Dutch. Never open about emotions."

"I thought you said she's Indonesian."

"Yes, but raised here, and more Dutch than anything else by now. They seemed to be having quite a good time when he was last here." I told her about the knocking.

"Well, good for them," said Esma. "We must follow their example." She took my hand and led me to my bedroom. From her little bag, Esma produced a U-shaped object, purple and about three inches long. It was latex, and heavier than I expected when I touched it. I raised a questioning eyebrow.

"Have I disappointed you yet?" Esma asked, with a hooded look.

I had never had complaints about my sex life with Ellen. It might have been a little lackluster, but for a couple in their fifties we seemed to be doing far better than many friends who made allusions to fornication as an activity of the past like recreational drugs and singles tennis. After we separated, it had not taken much cruising on the Internet to figure out there was a lot I had not experienced. Some of it had no appeal; in other cases, I was curious about what so many people found fulfilling. But my explorations had advanced by several orders of magnitude after meeting Esma.

We lived Saturday in reverse. After we had amused ourselves at length, Esma fell into a drowse. She mumbled a bit and then disappeared into sleep mid-sentence. I had gotten up at 4:30 a.m. in order to collect her and napped myself, but I was awake again by 11 a.m. and crept down with my laptop to the living room, where I worked for a couple of hours, until Esma peeked cutely around the entrance. I brewed her coffee, then we made love on the sofa, despite my concern about spotting the furniture.

Afterward, I ran out to my fish place for food and bought a couple bottles of white wine on the way back. As we lay upstairs again later that night, Esma asked about the investigation. I told her that we had gotten some lab reports back from our trip to Bosnia.

"Any issues?" she asked.

I waved that off with an ambiguous gesture that did not connote any real worry.

"And what comes next?"

I answered that we were still awaiting what might be the big break in the case, the production of records.

"That could only be from the US Army."

"I really shouldn't say, Esma."

"And why is that?"

"Because it's confidential. The Court is a very formal place. Everything is secret. There are always rules."

"And if you followed them strictly, we would not be lying here."

She was right about that, even though I was perturbed to hear her acknowledge this only now, when it was convenient. On the other hand, the legal principles involved in the document request were not secret. I explained the concepts, without saying explicitly we had acted upon them.

"And the US is rebuffing NATO?"

"NATO doesn't report to me. But that's certainly my impression."

"And no one can force the Americans to comply. Is that the point?"

"We could sue in the International Court of Justice. But the Bosnians probably wouldn't support that. And even if they did, it would take another four to five years to get the records."

"No other options?"

"None that I can think of."

She propped herself up on her elbow and smiled disarmingly.

"The press can be very effective in this kind of situation, you know."

"Badu and Akemi would have a fit. Leaking is not their style. I had to move heaven and earth to get them to do this in the first place."

"You don't need permission to leak, Bill. You need deniability."

As US Attorney, I had been rigid with my staff about leaking. The Federal Rules of Criminal Procedure forbade any disclosure of grand jury matters, and I had no use for the idea that prosecutors should enforce the law by breaking it, no matter how effective it might be. I had to assume that the ICC's Rules of Conduct for prosecutors were the same, although the truth was that

I'd never bothered to look. I promised her that I'd undertake the research, but only so we could change the
subject.

Around 3 a.m., I had come for the fourth time that
day—as to Esma, there was no way to keep track, because
she peaked so often—and she had padded down the
stairs afterward to use the john. I was lolling ecstatically,
amazed with myself, thinking without conclusions about
Merriwell's declaration that he might well do it all again,
when I suddenly froze. I thought I had heard the front
door slam. Nara was not due back until late on Sunday, at
least sixteen hours from now, and I told myself that the
sound must have come from the rear apartment. But I
was still listening intently when I heard the distinct clack
of high heels on the wooden floor of the living room. I
searched my closet desperately for my robe and was still
wrestling it on as I rushed down.

Just below me, a remarkable confrontation was occurring outside the bathroom door. Esma, who wore not
a stitch, had used her hands as cover-ups, one sloshed
across her breasts, the other over the female triangle.
Nara and she were staring at one another, startled but
also somehow unflinching. When I was still a few stairs
away, Esma let her arms fall, in an act of what seemed
both pride and defiance.

I dashed between them and, stupid as it was, made
introductions. Esma smiled a bit at Narawanda, who
was in a silk dress and hosiery and heels, but said not
a word. I grabbed a bath towel out of the john and
offered it to Esma, but she ignored me and turned to
head slowly up the stairs, looking very good while she
was at it.

"I didn't realize you were having a guest," Nara finally managed.

"I didn't either when you left. She arrived unexpectedly this morning. I would have said something had I known."

"Of course."

"I was sure you said you wouldn't be back until late tomorrow." I looked at my watch. "Or today, I guess."

"I did. My plans changed unexpectedly."

"I should have called you. I'm sorry."

"Nonsense. You live here. It is I who should be apologizing to you. I said I would be away."

We looked at each other haplessly for a second, and then Nara picked up her small red suitcase, which had been behind her, and started up her side of the stairs.

Esma, still naked, was propped against the pillows in my bed, smiling subtly, when I arrived. She seemed quite pleased with herself.

"Are you all right?" I asked.

"Of course."

"What did you say to her?"

Esma shook her head slowly. "Not a word. Neither of us spoke. We each knew who the other was. There was no need for introductions."

Given my qualms about the proprieties, I had certainly not told Nara that I was seeing Esma, but I took it that Esma meant that the circumstances had led each to rather quickly appreciate the other's position: the lover, the landlady.

"She had a fight with her husband?" Esma asked.

"She didn't say that."

"A woman arrives home at 3 a.m.? A woman who you've told me likes to be asleep by ten. She left London precipitously. Bill, really. I am constantly flabbergasted by how little you understand about my half of the species." She smiled. "Come lay down. Let's nap awhile and then make the bedposts knock before I must go."

18.

Deal—May 15–28

F ive days later, early Friday morning, I was reading the *New York Times* on my tablet while I stood in the kitchen, drinking coffee. As the lead news bloomed on-screen, I endured one of those instants when your vision throbs and your heart seems to cramp as you realize that the life you know and value has changed against your will.

An article on the lower left side of the page was headlined:

ARMY BLOCKING INTERNATIONAL COURT AND NATO IN ROMA MASSACRE INVESTIGATION

The United States is refusing to comply with a request by the North Atlantic Treaty Organization (NATO) for U.S. Army records being sought as part of an International Criminal Court investigation of the alleged massacre of 400 Roma in Bosnia in 2004. U.S. troops who were acting as NATO peacekeepers in the area are potential suspects in the case.

The U.S. is not a member of the International Criminal Court, and U.S. law bars American cooperation in the court's investigations, but legal experts say that American treaty obligations seem to require the Army to surrender the records to NATO. The U.S. has refused to do so and has reportedly made vehement protests about NATO turning over records from the organization's own files.

The situation is said to have caused serious tensions within NATO's multinational Central Command in Belgium, and considerable consternation at the International Criminal Court, which has no formal means to enforce U.S. compliance.

In March, a survivor of the massacre testified before the court, which is situated in The Hague in the Netherlands, that in April 2004, 400 Roma in the Barupra refugee camp at the edge of a U.S. base were rounded up at gunpoint by masked soldiers and buried alive in the pit of a coal mine. The witness could not identify the soldiers' military affiliation, but said they were not speaking Serbo-Croatian, the language of the local armies and paramilitaries.

The alleged massacre occurred within weeks of the death of four American soldiers and the wounding of eight others during a failed attempt to capture the refugee Bosnian Serb leader, Laza Kajevic. According to NATO sources, the Romas at Barupra were suspected of providing some of the equipment used by Kajevic's forces.

The second half of the article quoted a former general in the Judge Advocate General's Corps and two law professors, all of whom had been asked whether the Army could refuse to provide the records, given the conflicting mandates of the American Service-Members' Protection Act on one hand, and on the other, the NATO treaty, the Dayton Accords, and the NATO Status of Forces Agreement. The former general called it a "close question, but one where the Army might not prevail," while the two law professors believed that the treaty obligations clearly prevailed, especially with regard to records not stored in the US.

I read the piece several times. It claimed to be based on multiple sources, and it was especially notable that someone at NATO, given the chance, had taken the opportunity to piss on the Americans. But there were also details concerning the Court—that there was consternation regarding how to respond to the US refusal—that left me with a nauseating feeling about where the reporter had gotten her start.

My phone rang as I was pondering. The caller ID was blocked, which was not an encouraging sign.

"Well, aren't you a clever motherfucker." It was Roger. By my calculation, it was a little after midnight in DC, which meant the alarm had gone out at State when the *Times* was posted about an hour ago. Roger was the one who'd convinced his colleagues that I was a square guy who'd do it all by the book.

"It wasn't me, Rog."

"Of course it wasn't," he said. "You're too smart for that, Boom. It was that tramp you think is your girlfriend." A couple of words resounded: 'tramp,' of course, and especially 'girlfriend.' Why hadn't I bothered to wonder if the CIA was going to follow me around? Or was it Esma they'd been tailing?

Roger had done a lot of work in an hour and called in some favors. No one at the *Times* would give up Esma's name, but he'd wheedled enough out of somebody—

probably three or four people—that he could triangulate his way to an answer. I had a litigator's response to his harsh tone and was unwilling to concede anything.

"Read the article again," I said. "I have no clue what's going on at NATO in Brussels. So go wake up somebody else."

"Fuck you. Don't play that game with me. You know how this works. One person talks, then somebody else spills so they can spin things their way. But the daisy chain started with Little Miss Gypsy Hotpants. I've got that nailed down. And I know how she works. I'm sure the whole activist network is set to squeal—Human Rights Watch and Amnesty International, along with various leftie congressmen who hate having to pretend that they respect the military. But let me tell you right now: You won't succeed. I didn't think you were this low, Boom."

One thing trial lawyers get used to is fierce fights with close friends. When I was US Attorney, I watched countless former colleagues march to the door of my office in fury, indignant about my decisions regarding their clients. It was part of the job.

"Stop the high-and-mighty routine, Roger. I didn't do it. And it would be nothing compared to the changes you ran on me. You sent me over here with about one percent of the information you actually had. Did you really think I'd miss all the evidence that points at the US troops?"

He took a second. "And why do you say that?"

"Rog, you're not asking me to break any rules about the confidentiality of investigative information, are you?"

"Oh, go fuck yourself."

"Let me ask you something. Is this the first time you've heard that the Roma at Barupra supplied some of the equipment Kajevic used when he killed those four soldiers?"

He was quiet.

"Anybody ever say to you, Rog, that the Roma had actually set up the Americans?"

"You're full of shit," said Roger and hung up.

I phoned Esma next.

"How dare you," I said as soon as I heard her voice. "After all the bullshit you gave me that you were choosing me over your involvement in this case."

"Bill?" she asked. I'd clearly woken her.

"You took advantage of my confidence and our bedroom."

I could hear her breathing, weighing her options. Assuming she'd been sleeping, she couldn't have read the article yet, and thus didn't know how much of her role was betrayed by what had been printed.

"I did what you wanted but couldn't do yourself," she said finally.

I hung up on her.

I pedaled to work feeling like I was going to my beheading. The only positive note was discovering that I really didn't want to lose this job, especially not in disgrace.

I was in my little white office no more than ten minutes when Goos came in and closed the door. He rolled his lips inward, trying not to smile. He was happy, but looked a little haggard. I took it that Thursday was a drinking night in The Hague.

"I'd call that a ripper piece of work, Boom," he said. "Brilliant."

"It might have been, Goos. But I didn't do it."

"Of course you didn't," he answered at once.

"No horse hockey. This may be my fault, but it wasn't anything I intended to set in motion."

He let his head weigh back and forth. He was accustomed to the world of the Court, where there was so little formal power that you took advantage of whatever you had. In the case in Sudan I'd been reviewing, the investigator had smoked out witnesses with a false leak, bought by the papers, that an insider was cooperating with us. But that tactic had been approved at the top.

"Well, I think this will work out rather well, despite that," Goos said.

"If I keep my job."

"Keep your job? Mate, you still have no idea how this place works."

Within the hour, I was summoned to a meeting of the OTP executive committee. We sat around the corner table in Badu's office beside the large windows. As we gathered, the old man was reading what appeared to be a printout of the net version of the article. He set it down when all of us had taken our seats.

"Do we half any idea how this o-ccurred?" Badu asked.

Octavia Bonfurts, a grandmotherly looking former diplomat, who was representing Complementarity today, spoke up before I could even clear my throat.

"This has Gautam's DNA all over it," said Octavia. "I checked the archive. This reporter did a profile of Gautam when she was appointed. Look at the heavy-handed portrait of the evidence against the Americans."

Badu nodded gravely. As the discussion continued, I learned that Badu had felt obliged to advise the president of the Court, one of the judges who serves as the Court's chief executive, about the document request to NATO. She, in turn, was likely to have informed the other two judges on the Court's administrative committee, Judge Gautam being one. Furthermore, now that I considered Octavia's remark, the brief précis of Ferko's testimony did sound just like Gautam. As Roger said, leaking had a bandwagon effect: Once the story was coming out, everyone wanted to tell it his or her way.

Akemi, with her fright-wig hairdo and heavy glasses, was bent close to the page. As always, she was focused on the details.

"These Gypsies provided Kajevic equipment? What kind of equipment?"

I explained what we knew thus far about the trucks, and the motives both the Americans and Kajevic might have had for revenge in the aftermath of the shootout. Around the table, my colleagues made various approving gestures, intrigued and somewhat impressed by what we had discovered. I was so relieved about the way all this was unfolding that I wanted to hug everyone here.

We took a second to discuss the possible American responses to the article. They did not seem to have good alternatives, except thumbing their nose at the world, which was probably not worth it on what was from a global perspective a minor matter.

Badu laid his large hands on the papers in front of him, uttering that throaty chuckle.

"I would say," he said then, "dis has worked out rudder well."

As we adjourned, I suspected that a secret ballot

would show that at least half the people in the room believed Badu was the source of the leak.

I had not seen Narawanda since the incident with Esma
late Saturday night, and I realized that her scarceness was
no accident. When I arrived from work on Friday, she
was in her black Lycra outfit, wearing a knit stocking
cap to ward off the fierce sea wind that had blown in
this afternoon. I'd caught her again with one of her legs
stretched on the back of the sofa. Every time I saw Nara
getting ready to exercise, she looked like someone else.
Today, with her hair completely covered, isolating her
round umber face, she resembled a Buddhist nun. Her
eyes hit the floor as soon as she saw me.

Half turned, she asked, in the especially stilted way
she adopted when she was most uncomfortable, "Shall I
await you?"

"Please." I changed and was back in a minute. She had
put on her gloves in the interval.

"Nara, I need to apologize to you again."

"Oh no." She shook her head with some force but was
still too embarrassed to actually face me. "This is your
home. You must do as you please here. If my head was
not in the clouds, I would have given a call."

We could go on with each of us blaming ourselves for
quite some time. I raised my hands just to indicate it was
a standoff. I started to stretch myself.

"She is the Roma advocate?" Nara asked. "When you
gave me her name, I recognized it from the articles about
your case I read online."

I straightened up. There was a lot contained in that
sentence. For one thing, I was surprised Nara had been
curious enough about me to bother with any research.

More to the point, however, was my concern that she understood Esma's role in my case.

"Do you feel you should report me?"

Nara's mouth parted. "For fucking?"

Narawanda's word choice was often amusing, but this time I couldn't stifle an outright laugh.

"For fucking someone involved in my case."

Nara wobbled her head to show she didn't get the point.

"I don't know the rules of your Court completely, but at our Court she would have no official role right now. And besides, you don't fully understand The Hague. So many people are away from home for long periods. There are always affairs and sneaking around. You would be surprised what gets ignored here."

I wasn't sure other people's infractions did anything to cure mine, but I took her analysis as kindly. I also noticed how instinctively Nara became a defense lawyer.

"She is very handsome," said Nara. "With an impressive physique." This time that tiny ironic grin crept from the shadows for a second. "She has enchanted you?"

"She certainly had. Today I'm very put out with her—and with myself for not staying away."

"Sex is very potent for men," she said. "And willingness. A woman who radiates experience and confidence is very sexy, I think. No?"

"Yes," I answered.

Her face darkened somewhat. "I was a virgin when I married. That was one vow to my mother I could not break. Now of course I regret that." Her eyes again were aimed at the floor. Then she recovered and said we should run.

Nara's remark about her virginity was not wholly shocking, since there really was never any anticipating what precisely was going to come out of her mouth. Nevertheless, as we took off, I was struck by her note of retrospective regret about her sexual history.

As we ran, I was happy I'd followed her example and worn a hat and gloves. The wind off the North Sea today was like an ice pick. Nonetheless, we kept up a good pace through the park for nearly an hour. Afterward, given the weather, we found a corner inside at a café on the Plein.

"So how was London?" I asked.

"Well, clearly not very good, if I was home a day early," she answered. I didn't know if she was annoyed at me for playing dumb, or simply irritated by the memory, but I explained, somewhat apologetically, that I'd had no idea why she was back early, and thought it might have been due to a change in Lew's plans. That remark inspired a bitter smile.

"Well, his plans *have* changed in a way. Lewis asked me to find a job in New York."

"Ah." I said no more.

"We talked about that before we married. Now he acts as if all of those discussions do not count."

"I'm sure he meant what he said when he said it, but it's hard to be away from home," I said. "I enjoy The Hague, but I would need to think hard about making a lifetime commitment."

"He did think hard," she answered. "And besides, how am I to find a position in the US? The job market for lawyers is still not very good. And I love my work here. If they ever capture Kajevic, and they will someday, I'll join his private lawyer as senior counsel on his defense team. Mr. Bozic has already asked me."

"I don't think I'd count on them rounding up Kajevic, Nara. It's been what, fifteen years?"

"Of course. My point is that I have more and more responsibility at the Court and I enjoy that."

Having failed at my own marriage, I did not regard myself as an adept counselor, but she was clearly seeking consolation of some kind.

"People manage marriages in two cities."

"Separated by an ocean? We decided together that we did not want a life apart."

"Then you can trade off five-year blocks—five in New York, five here. I know couples who do that, too."

She moved her head unhappily. Normally stoic, Nara was nearing the point of tears. Despite the frankness of our conversation, there remained some topics that were unapproachable and probably paining her, especially the question of children.

"It is not merely a matter of what or where," she said. "It is the idea that he thinks he can make an announcement. Lewis has always been very self-sufficient. But he threatens me with that."

Nara unfailingly described her husband as insular. My impression was that at the time they married, she found his remoteness a comfortable match for her own reticence, but that compact, and the size of their separate emotional spaces, was starting to trouble her.

I was sympathetic with the problem of having a spouse who felt unreachable at times. In some ways, Nara spoke about her marriage much as I might have talked about mine at the same stage, assuming I would ever have discussed it with the same guileless openness she did. In the long haul, the Logans' relationship was probably not a good bet. But I would have been petrified if anyone had said as much to me, and I would have regarded the prediction as offensive. Perhaps, like Ellen and me, Nara and Lew would have kids and in that satisfaction mend much of the natural breach between them.

"Marriage is hard, Nara. It's a little like Churchill's remark about democracy. It's a terrible idea, except for the alternatives. At least for most people."

She'd had more than her usual one beer as the conversation had worn on, and once we were walking home, she reached up to give me a comradely pat on the back.

"You are a good friend to me, Boom. I am very grateful."

The coverage of the skirmish between the US Defense Department and NATO continued throughout the following week. Because Bosnia was the first actual combat operation NATO had ever engaged in, many questions I would have thought were long resolved had to be decided for the first time. It turned out that most of the records of SFOR—as the Bosnian operation was known at NATO—or digital copies of them, were housed in the NATO archives in Belgium. Although it struck me as one of the idiotic ways the law finds to resolve difficult issues, the physical location of the files was central to the legal analysis, because the Service-Members' Protection Act applied only within the US.

The political scrambling was also going full speed. The White House and the State Department were taking a different tone than DoD, since the story was not unspooling favorably for the US. References were appearing online to 'a new My Lai,' the massacre of five hundred Vietnamese villagers by US forces more than four decades ago, to which Merriwell had referred as a signal event of his days as a newly minted officer. In the ten-second world of broadcast news, the reports were framed as the US Army stonewalling questions our allies wanted answered. The journalists, who by professional bias despised bureaucratic secrecy, were piling on. Badu and Goos were correct: This was working out rather well. The publicity even seemed to light a fire under the Bosnians, who approved our return trip, which would now depend on the convenience of Madame Professor Tchitchikov.

Esma was calling me several times a day but I refused to pick up. Finally, she must have borrowed someone else's phone.

"May I see you in person to discuss this?" she asked.

Her strategy was laughably transparent. Get me in a room and let the little head think for the big one.

"I don't think that's a good idea, Esma. Once burned, twice wise."

"Oh please, Bill. Don't be so fucking dramatic. It was a miscalculation on my part. I thought you would be overjoyed."

"Esma, principle is clearly far less important to you than it is to me."

"Bill, don't condescend. We cannot hash this through on the phone. I can get to The Hague next weekend."

"Don't do that, Esma. You'll be wasting your time."

I hung up, albeit with more than a small pang. A part of me did not want to accept that this was over, particularly the tonic element Esma had added to my life.

On Friday, a week after our talk on the Plein, Nara announced that she'd taken a few days' leave and was going to New York.

"That sounds like a smart idea," I told her.

"I am not very sure of that," she answered. "Lewis is brilliant about using many different words to say the same thing. He rarely changes his mind."

"Then try changing yours a little. You'll never regret giving this your best."

She stood on tiptoe to deliver a fleeting half hug as she departed.

"Okay, asshole, this is how it's going to be." I was in my office at the Court about 3 p.m. the following Wednesday when my personal cell rang.

"Good day to you, too, Rog."

"Let me tell you right now that if it was up to me, I'd tell you to fuck off. The whole thing with these records will be forgotten next week."

I chose not to respond.

"The records," he said, "all the records, will be provided to the NATO Supreme Allied Commander at the time of the alleged incident for his review."

It took me a second. "Layton Merriwell?"

Rog cleared his throat. "I think that was the guy."

"Okay, so the supreme commander, whatever his name was, gets the records. Then what?"

"If he chooses, he may meet with you on US soil. And if he gives you any records, that's his choice, even though it will be a clear violation of the Service-Members' Protection Act."

I didn't get it. "Merry and I get to share a prison cell?"

"There's no criminal provision in that law, hotshot. And as you already know, Merriwell is in favor of opening the books on all of this. But if any American were to be prosecuted in the future on the basis of any of these documents, he or she could claim that the records were produced in violation of the act and therefore are not competent evidence in any court."

It was a clever plan, aimed at reducing the risk that any American soldier could be prosecuted on the basis of these documents. I told Roger I'd need to run it up the flagpole here.

"You may as well just say yes now. Because it won't get any better. You have twenty-four hours before this offer vanishes. The generals will get to someone in Congress by then. If you accept, the State Department, NATO, and the Court will each release their own statements that say the matter has been resolved and not one word more."

Badu and Akemi agreed with me that this was a pretty good deal for us, assuming Merriwell would make a full breast of the documents. But since he was the one who'd suggested going to NATO in the first place, that seemed largely assured.

I called Rog back to go over a couple of nuances and then agreed.

"Deal," I told him.

"Let the record reflect that I resent the shit out of this," Roger said.

"So noted."

Merriwell called the next day.

"So we meet again," he said.

"It will be my pleasure. Are we back at the embassy?"

"No, no. We have to meet on American soil in order to preserve any future claim that the Service-Members' Act has been violated. But the press has gotten interested in me again this week. Any chance we could get together at your house?"

"In Kindle County?" I was about to tell him I didn't have a home there any longer, but I realized instantly how eager Ellen would be to make the guest house available for a matter that had been mentioned on the front page of the *New York Times*. And even the most intrepid reporter was unlikely to follow Merry to the Tri-Cities.

As I expected, Ellen was excited by Merriwell's name, even though I apologized for being unable to explain much about why we were meeting. After comparing calendars, we all agreed that Merry and I would get together at Ellen and Howard's the following Monday. To further complicate things, the French geologist announced she would be available next week for the only time in months. So I made plans to again ping-pong between the continents, going to the US first and then to Bosnia to meet the professor and Goos.

V.
Trouble

19.

Home Run—May 30–June 1

I arrived in Kindle County about two on Saturday afternoon. As soon as I turned on my phone after the long flight, there was another series of messages from Esma—multiple missed calls, a plaintive e-mail, and two texts. I had refused to answer her again after our last brief conversation, and the silence seemed to be driving her to extremes. The most recent SMS read: Bill—I wanted to say this in person, but you must know that try as I must, I think I've fallen in love with you. I simply cannot let go. It is much too late for that. I must see you and try to make this right.

This sounded like dialogue from a 1930s movie, and the subtext seemed to be all about Esma's ego. Esma was in 'love' with me only because I was not in love with her, never mind her own cautions on the subject. Someday, when I finished bringing international justice to the globe, I was going to figure out the connection between self-image and love.

From the airport, I went to the home of close friends, where I was going to spend the night. Sonny Klonsky, now a federal judge, had started in the US Attorney's Office about the same time I had. She had made a happy second marriage to Michael Wiseman, a nationally syndicated columnist, a delightful wise guy with whom I shared a sense of humor. They hosted a barbecue in my honor Saturday evening, to which they invited several old pals of mine, including Sandy Stern, everyone's favorite defense lawyer, who was living in the alternate universe of cancer remission, in which, he admitted, he was never quite sure he was really here.

On Sunday, I left the Wisemans at 5 a.m. so I could fish with Will and Pete. The white bass were running in the River Kindle, and down water the boats were anchored so closely you could have walked shore to shore on their prows. But the boys and I had a secret spot where we fished near shore in waders. It was just below an outcropping in a public park that we reached with a minor act of vandalism requiring pruning shears. The late spring morning was bright and warm, and there were plenty of fish, attracted by another family trick, a bit of red yarn above the lure.

I was proud of my sons, who had both become decent, loving, industrious men, although I always recoiled a bit when I noticed failings of their mother's or mine one or both boys had incorporated—Ellen's judginess, or my occasional remoteness. One of the sayings I live by about families is that children occupy the space provided. Will had taken on my solid manner and was advancing quickly at the Tri-Cities office of a New York firm, where he did the legal engineering for complex currency swaps on the Kindle County exchanges. At twenty-nine, he'd found one of those comfortable niches in the law that was virtually guaranteed to provide a livelihood forever.

Pete, by contrast, had been the brooding child, the one we worried about more. There were drugs in high school and academic struggles in college. He had emerged from that period with a keen interest in computers and had developed three different apps that had been purchased by bigger companies. Will always seemed a bit affronted by the magnitude of Pete's success, although he often joked he was relieved to find out he would not be obligated to support his little brother.

With both sons, there had been a rough time when I left their mother. I knew what it was like to be surprised and disappointed by a parent; and I understood that my sons had lost the home they'd always counted on being able to return to. But their absolute conviction that their feelings were the only ones that mattered became infuriating. After a year, I had declared a rule that once in every conversation they had to ask, "How are you, Dad?" whether or not they really cared about my response.

But all that was now past. My move to The Hague and Pete's imminent marriage had somehow completed cooling all the lava to solid rock. Standing in the shallows, a few feet from shore, we were three independent adults who accepted our mutual connections as indelible.

After fishing, we had lunch while watching the Trappers game in a sports bar, then Will drove me out to Lake Fowler, where he'd already agreed to stay for dinner. Ellen and Howard's house seemed no less stupendous, a decorator's showcase with huge two-story windows looking down on the lake. Once Will was headed back to town, Ellen and Howard and I had one more glass of wine in their kitchen while we compared notes about our sons. The articles in the *Times* had also sparked my hosts' curiosity about my work at the Court. I tried to say little but didn't deny what was obvious, that my meeting with Merriwell was related to that investigation.

"Can I meet him?" Ellen asked, hunching down a bit, almost as if she were ducking from her own adolescent impulses. I gallantly assured her that the general would undoubtedly want to acknowledge their hospitality. I had known from the start that Merry was the kind of figure, a flawed genius in many eyes, likely to be fascinating to Ellen.

The end of our marriage could have been described with the same term pathologists these days apply to someone who dies from old age: multisystem failure. But from my perspective the real trouble had begun more than fifteen years before, when Ellen had become the director of special events at Easton. I saw the job as a strange choice for someone who'd just received her MBA, but the position allowed her to hang with No-belists and the vanguard of world thought leaders, which I discovered was the company Ellen secretly yearned to keep. With friends, she often gushed about the Life of the Mind, which, apparently, was not the life she'd been living with me.

I never pretended to be as flat-out brilliant as my ex. When she was elected to Phi Beta Kappa as an undergrad-uate, I didn't even know how to pronounce it. But once she took her university position, Ellen began to exhibit a fierce need to look down on me intellectually. I knew in-tuitively that I was doing something to provoke this (a point proven beyond doubt when she married Howard, who, while a true engineering wizard, has never found any book ever written more interesting than ESPN). Instead of trying to figure out why I was alienating my wife, I went into private practice, even though I should have known that move would make things worse. With court dates, meetings, depositions, and trials, I was suddenly out of town at least a third of the year. I worked ridiculously long hours, as I had with the government, but Ellen didn't see the point now, since defending wealthy bad guys was a far less noble cause. The lone advantage of my new job— that I was making gobs of money—was actually demeaning in her eyes. The grim fact was that I bored Ellen, bored her to the point of weariness, and bearing the brunt of my wife's judgments left me grinding my teeth whenever I walked into the house. I thought I was doing both of us a great favor when I admitted that we'd lost interest in a life together. The secret of the friendship that we'd forged in the last couple of years was that Ellen was now willing to admit, with whatever irony, that this was one instance when I'd been a lot smarter than her.

Ellen was outside, dressed for work, when Merry's limo turned up their long driveway at 7:00 a.m. She wore a black sheath with pearls, full makeup and high heels, the kind of getup that could double as business attire and something suitable for the cocktail circuit on which she frequently found herself. Ellen remained trim, and she'd always had the tidy blonde looks that get described as 'perky.' I'd never thought about it, but my ex was probably more physically attractive than many of the women I'd dated, even those quite a bit younger, although she'd never had—or aspired to—Esma's sizzle.

"Boom," Merry said, as he rose from the limo. We shook and he slapped me on the shoulder, offering a welcoming smile. I couldn't help wondering how our warmth struck my ex. On the driveway, Ellen hovered in a somewhat starstruck posture, with her hands in the air as if she was afraid to touch anything.

Merriwell reached back into the car for a weathered caramel-colored briefcase and I walked him over to Ellen, whom he thanked several times. She tried to gossip about a mutual friend, a former MIT classmate of Howard's who now taught there, but Merry had little to say on that score, and she realized, with visible disappointment, that she had no option but to say good-bye. I hugged her farewell with profuse thanks of my own. Tonight, I'd be on my way back to Bosnia, via JFK, to meet with Madame Professor Tchitchikov and Goos at Barupra.

Merriwell watched her clack her way down her driveway.

"Truly your ex-wife?"

"Truly."

He shook his head in amazement.

"Not in this lifetime," he said. "And you trust her discretion?"

"Completely." As the wife of a prosecutor and criminal defense lawyer, Ellen took pride in her ability to keep secrets, and even after our divorce she had never spilled any of them, even the juiciest about prominent folks around town.

"And what about you?" I asked Merry. "Are things any better with your ex-to-be?"

"No improvement," he answered wearily, "but despite that, I am far better." He looked it. He sported a vacation tan and appeared far less tired. Gesturing to the guesthouse, he suggested we get started, because he had to head back to the airport in two hours. "As usual the world is falling apart," he said.

The guesthouse was compact and tasteful, clearly the work of the same architect who'd designed the main house. Upstairs there were two small bedrooms, each with its own bath. Downstairs it was all open space off the beautiful kitchen, with its gorgeous hand-tooled cabinetry in some reddish South American wood. The windows were large, to catch the astounding light off the lake, and were dressed in billowing scarlet roman shades raised with surgical precision to half height. A small dining table separated the living area from the kitchen, and there Merriwell and I placed ourselves in leather Breuer chairs with chrome arms.

I served coffee and put out a basket of muffins Ellen, despite my protests, had asked a caterer to deliver this morning. I'd also taken the precaution of borrowing a bottle of scotch, which I'd positioned innocently at the far corner of the kitchen counter, but Merry never even seemed to look that way. He put the briefcase on a chair he pulled beside him. It was one of those wonderful old valise-type bags lawyers used to carry when I started practice, with a hinged brass mouth that opened wider than the compartment below, and a leather strap that fit into the lock on the other side to close it.

To start, I told him that I had not authorized or engineered the leak to the *Times*, but he waved that off. Merriwell was a veteran of domestic political wars as well as the ones we got into overseas, and seemed to regard both the leaking and the denial as part of the game.

As we turned to business, there was a notable change in Merriwell's air, which instantly struck me as not simply businesslike, but dour and solemn. He secured a sheaf of papers about three inches thick from the case.

"I've brought what I've received," he said. "There is more coming, but you'll be interested in what's here. Because time is limited, I'll give you the Cliff Notes version of what you're bound to figure out on your own, so you can ask questions now. No bar on more later."

"Any overall comment?" I asked him.

Merry stopped to frown, a lip puffed up, the expression drawing deeper grooves in his narrow face.

"Overall, I am chagrined and surprised," he said. "And still disbelieving."

The concession was enticing, but I waited politely. From the shiny edges at the top of the stack, I could tell there were a number of 8-by-10 photographs.

"Your request for official photography was quite brilliant," he said.

I told him it wasn't my idea.

"Never fail to take credit for the accomplishments of your staff," he answered, and smiled. "All right," he said. "At Eagle Base they photographed everything, including the playing of reveille, retreat, and taps. Here's taps on April 27, 2004."

It was a flash photo of a bugler at the base of the empty flagpole. The shot was in color, and the figure against the blue night made a striking image, but on first glance the picture seemed otherwise unremarkable.

"Back here," said Merriwell.

At the top of the photograph, rising up the page, there was a line of lights moving off sinuously in the distance.

"Convoy?"

"So it appears."

I looked more closely. The red taillights were visible on one or two of the vehicles, and the headlights appeared as a swath of brightness in front of them. The vehicles—trucks I'd say—were departing. I counted, although the last of them were little more than a blur.

"About twenty?"

"Give or take."

"And what time was this photo taken?"

"Taps is twenty-two hundred hours."

Ferko said the first men arrived at Barupra a little before midnight. Travel time to the village would have been no more than ten or fifteen minutes, even on the bad roads of those days.

"Any theories about what they might have been doing with an extra hour and a half?" I asked.

"I'm happy to explain what you see in front of you, Boom, but I'll have to keep any speculations to myself."

"Well, if I said that was enough time to change uniforms and rehearse an impending operation, is there any obvious reason I'd be wrong?"

He shook his head tersely—either indicating that I was right or that he wouldn't be drawn into commentary—then reached back to the stack.

"Here, I'm afraid, is what will most interest you." He pulled several photos off the piles. They were black and white, clearly enlarged many times. To me, at first it was like looking at an ultrasound, just lines and blurs and dark spots, although one little rectangle looked whiter than the rest.

"This is a satellite photograph," Merry said.

"Wow," I said. "You can get recognizable forms from a hundred miles?"

"It's an impressive technology."

"I'll say."

"You asked for records of the GPS transponders. As you know, they are worn by our troops and were standard issue even then on operational equipment, like trucks or tanks or aircraft. Whenever they are off-base, the satellite will follow the transponders and photograph their location. There are several more photos here, but they all focus on one truck."

"As opposed to the troops?"

"Correct."

"So the soldiers had removed their transponders?"

"Or weren't our soldiers."

"But someone neglected one truck?"

"I don't know why one transponder was left functioning, but by the time the satellite made its next orbit ninety minutes later, there are no photographs."

"Clearly an oversight that got corrected," I said. Merry refused to respond.

Beyond the one truck that was automatically highlighted, the others appeared in the photo as grayer boxes with white bumps in front of them, the projections of their headlamps. When I lowered my nose to the page, I could also make out distinct ant-like grains.

"Are these people?"

"That's my interpretation."

There were hundreds, once I understood how to recognize the forms. And at the top of the photograph was a stripe of black—the valley that led down to the Cave.

"So this is the residents of Barupra being rounded up?"

"Again, I leave the ultimate explanations to you." But his face was pouty and somber.

At the first sight of the photograph my pulse had

quickened considerably. The skeptical piece of me, the trained professional, had yearned for solid proof to back up Ferko. I would have been jubilant if I did not recognize that this was a visual record of four hundred people being marched to their deaths. Merry and I said nothing for a second, as I took on his grave mood.

Although the satellite could have been in range only for a few minutes, there were at least a hundred photos. The last showed three trucks, apparently fully loaded, turning toward the winding dirt road that led down to the Cave.

"What do the truck logs we asked for show?"

"Those," said Merriwell, "you will have to retrieve from our friend Attila. But CoroDyn has been asked to provide them, and Attila called Friday to assure me they should come along shortly. Apparently there were two motor pools, one operational, one logistical. She wanted to know if we needed the records of both and I said yes."

"And do you know if Yugoslavian-made trucks were ever used in the motor pools?" I was thinking of what Ferko had said in his testimony.

"Not for certain. But most of the frontline equipment, which was US manufacture, had already been moved to Iraq. NATO had seized thousands of vehicles from the various combatant forces. So if some were repurposed, I wouldn't be surprised. Again, Attila will know."

"She's been very helpful so far. I have you to thank for that."

Merry shook his head resolutely. "Not me," he said.

"Well, when she picked me up in Sarajevo she said you'd asked her to assist us."

Merry reclined with a small, skeptical smile.

"With Attila, you always have to bear in mind that there's an improvisational side to her character. She called me the morning after we met. She knew you were on the way and asked if I had any idea what you were looking for. I spoke well of you—solid guy, that sort of thing—and I might have said there was no reason not to assist you. You've met Attila, so you understand. She wants to know everyone's business."

I smiled. "She's very loyal to you."

"I appreciate that. And so far as I was concerned, she was indispensable. Do you know the saying, 'Civilians think about strategy, but generals think about logistics'?"

I'd never heard that.

"Well it's a deep truth," said Merriwell. "She is truly a logistical genius. No matter how many moving parts had to be coordinated, she could do it. She was more capable than any officer I had in QC. I actually talked about sending her to OTS, but she wasn't interested while women were excluded from combat. And the truth is that someone as unusual as Attila got a lot less scrutiny as a noncom. But I was a much better commander having her to rely on."

"She doesn't think many of your peers would have been as welcoming."

"Probably not. Her lifestyle was not typical for the Army, especially at that time. But soldiers can be very pragmatic when their lives are at stake. On task, Attila was exceptional."

"A great soldier?"

"I'd say very good." I wasn't surprised that Merry talked about Attila more cold-bloodedly than she did about him. For her, Merriwell occupied that idealized role of mentor and savior. For him, she was a valued cog in a large machine. "She was outstanding when she was at a distance from her commanders and could function with some independence. On the other hand, she was a ridiculous busybody who refused to accept need-to-know limitations. And she has less talent at taking orders. Commands she disagreed with received a very idiosyncratic interpretation. Frankly, I was relieved when she became a civilian employee. I got the benefits of all her abilities, but none of the phone calls and telexes asking me what the hell she was doing now. But she'll have your truck logs, I'm sure, and will be able to answer your questions. Apparently you're headed back to Bosnia?"

"Word travels fast." In preparation, Goos had gotten hold of Attila to secure laborers. Obviously she was Merriwell's source.

I had our letter to NATO out on the small walnut table where we were seated and ticked through the remaining items.

"Duty rosters? Mess reports? Sick bay?"

"Help yourself." Merriwell shoved a couple hundred pages between us.

"This is one day?"

"Two actually. You asked for April 27 and 28."

Goos had correctly assayed the nature of armies and recordkeeping. The first thing I noticed, when I started thumbing through, was that the name of every soldier had been blacked out. I'm sure the look I gave Merry was not kindly.

"I don't recall agreeing to expurgated records," I said.

"I believe the agreement was that you'd get whatever the supreme commander was willing to provide. And the supreme commander is not serving up the heads of any soldiers on a silver plate. If there was a massacre—"

"It's not much of an 'if,' Merry, looking at these photographs."

"*If* that is what happened—and I remain hopeful of other explanations—then there was a chain of command. And at the top of that chain is where responsibility lies, not with privates and PFCs who were following orders and probably didn't realize what was going to occur until it happened. Boom, this is what you're getting."

"We'll have to talk about it back at the Court."

"Our position won't change," he answered.

I had no doubt that removing names had been demanded by the Defense Department. And despite my rigid pose, I knew that after months of his net searches of Facebook and Twitter and LinkedIn and YouTube, Goos had assembled a good list of many of the personnel at Eagle. Complete duty rosters would have been far better, but the key remained finding a former soldier willing to correspond with us.

The pages in my hands were a maze of black and white, columns of names and units, weapons and language training, assignments and dates on duty. There were pages labeled Combat Support Battle Roster and sign-in sheets from the mess for breakfast, lunch, and dinner. There were also stacks of sheets that showed, beside the obscured names, the officers' and enlisted men's units and duties for the day. I focused there.

When I reached the records of the 205th Military Intelligence Brigade, First Battalion, I had something. Against the captain's report for Charlie Company, I matched assignments with the leave column. Every soldier identified as being part of the Second Platoon had been relieved of duty on the second day, April 28.

I could tell that Merriwell was not happy once I'd pieced that together.

"Is that an ordinary development—an entire platoon on leave?" I asked.

"There might be reasons," said Merriwell.

"General, I said 'ordinary.'" I meant to sound testy.

"For a single day, I would not regard it as ordinary."

I went back to the captain's report, counting the platoon members with the metal button on the top of my pen. There were thirty-four lines where the names were blacked out. Ferko said some 'Chetniks' entered Barupra on foot, the rest in the trucks. The numbers seemed right.

"And who was the captain for the company, and the lieutenant for this platoon?"

Merriwell shook his head with his lips sealed.

I made a face.

"Boom, don't be greedy," he said with some exasperation. "You have far, far more information than you did an hour ago."

I left the table with a heavy sigh, but came back with some of the food the caterer had placed in the fridge. Merriwell and I each had small helpings of chicken salad and a can of soda. In the meantime, he latched the strap over his case.

I asked if I could hitch a ride with him to the airport. I was more than five hours early for my first plane, but I had to make my way from LaGuardia to JFK in New York and didn't mind getting started on that now. At JFK, I'd find an Internet connection and get some work done. I grabbed my suitcase and joined Merry on the leather bench in the rear of an old Lincoln sedan. As we traveled, I rebooked for a 10 a.m. flight to LGA, then Merriwell and I talked about baseball and the season's surprises: A-Rod's play was steady so far. More incredibly, the Trappers were winning. By long experience, I was trying to contain my optimism.

"Can I go back to business and ask about one more thing?" I said when we were still a few minutes away from the Tri-Cities airport.

"You can ask."

"Tell me why I shouldn't believe that the people in Barupra were murdered in reprisal for setting up your troops for ambush by Kajevic."

"Because that's not what happened."

"Explain."

"We aren't going to have another conversation about classified material, are we, Boom?" He told me he was still plodding through the files regarding the efforts to capture Kajevic, but that virtually none of them were going to be released, for fear of compromising Special Forces techniques that were still in use. "But I will tell you explicitly that in my review, I have seen no reports even suggesting that the Gypsies conspired to lure our troops into a trap, nor frankly do I have any memory of hearing that at the time."

"You won't deny, General, will you, that it was the Roma who informed Army Intelligence of Kajevic's whereabouts?"

"I won't confirm it either." He turned on the seat to face me. "I'm sorry, Boom, to sound racist, but Army Intelligence—and our Special Forces—knew better than to take Gypsies at their word or to completely depend on them. Assuming the Roma provided information, it would have been corroborated by days of surveillance. And the Roma had no role of any kind in the action, and no advance information about how or when we were going to go after Kajevic. Even if the Gypsies wanted to betray us—which would make no sense given how well we'd treated them—they didn't know enough to do that."

"Yet as we've already discussed, General, there is every appearance that Kajevic was aware you were coming."

"I agree. But not because of anything the Gypsies knew. As I've explained, our forces couldn't close off four square blocks in Doboj without informing the local authorities, all of Serb ethnicity. I've always assumed that was where the leak came from."

When I was US Attorney, we engineered a number of big busts, dozens of federal agents in SWAT gear taking down drug kingpins and gang leaders. But we learned the hard way to be cautious with the Kindle County Unified Police Force. There was never any telling which cops were jumped in to the gangs or on a dealer's pad. So our first call to the Force for backup wasn't made until the battering ram was about to hit the door. Special Forces had to be even more circumspect than we were. Whatever they were obliged to tell the Bosnian Army or the local police would have been passed on far too late to allow Kajevic to set up the elaborate trap that had greeted the American soldiers.

"He had to have known earlier than that, General."

"I take the point, Boom," said Merriwell. "But if that's true, we never established how that happened."

"So what you're saying, Merry, is that you know of no reason that Army elements were furious with the Roma?"

"On what basis do you think they were?"

"On the basis of a dozen photos you just showed me of those people being rounded up and driven to their deaths."

Merriwell pouched up his thin mouth and his face went dark with irritation. It was the closest to angry I'd seen him, although I couldn't tell if he was put out with my persistence, or with himself for not incorporating the implications of the evidence he'd turned over. He also might have been peeved by other thoughts he couldn't share. After a second, he offered another determined toss of his head.

"Boom, I've done what I can to allow you to investigate this matter without interference. As you've told me before, that's your job. So I haven't asked anyone who served under me to explain these materials. But I will never stop believing in the men and women I commanded."

I could see that we'd need the testimony of one of his soldiers before Merriwell accepted that there was an American role in the massacre. Until then, as he'd just acknowledged, he'd assume there were innocent explanations. We had reached the airport anyway.

I was flying from a different terminal than Merry, and the car dropped me first. The general rose from the limo to wish me well, fixing the center button on his suit coat while he stood on the pavement. Overall, I was impressed by how much stronger he seemed, more fit, and even, if it was possible, straighter. Despite his clear unhappiness as we were going over the NATO records, he otherwise seemed buoyed by a self-confidence that had been absent when I had first visited with him, although I wasn't sure I liked him as much without that sad contemplative air.

I told him again how good he seemed.

"Oh yes," he said. "Life is far better, even if a bit more complicated, but I have you to thank for the improvements, I believe. Your advice hit home."

"Just timing. I didn't say anything new."

"And you?" he asked. "Roger seems to think you fell under the spell of the compelling Ms. Czarni."

There was no point denying it.

"Well, Merry, I've learned how deeply a man can long to do something completely stupid." I decided there was no polite way to tell him how often he'd crossed my mind in the process. "It's over now."

He studied me, squinting in the spring sun.

"I suppose, Boom, if it's something you will still remember in your waning days, then it might not have been stupid at all." Merriwell looked at his watch. "To be continued," he said, and slid back into the car.

Merry's last remark stayed with me as I entered the terminal. His personal observations had far more power for me than our back-and-forth about business. After clearing security, I called Esma's New York cell and she picked up on the third ring. I told her that I would be going between airports and could hopscotch through Manhattan and meet for coffee around 1:30.

"I'm in court but I could beg for an early recess," she said. "It's golf season, so this judge is always happy for an afternoon off." She said she was staying at the Carlyle.

"Is there a coffee shop near there?"

"Oh, Boom. Don't be pedantic. You're not going to leave me weeping in a Starbucks, are you?"

She told me to ask for 'the Jahanbani apartment' when I arrived.

No part of America ever seemed as impressively rich to me as the Upper East Side, because the fury of so much of Manhattan is subdued there, almost as if there were border guards posted somewhere in the

Sixties, checking tax returns before anyone was admitted. The doorman at the Carlyle directed me to a separate entrance, where the receptionist called up to announce me.

Esma opened the door and fell on me. I turned my face away, but she still held me for quite some time. She was in her courtroom apparel, deliberately subdued, a loose royal-blue jumper without much of a waist. Her makeup was minimal and her bosk of hair had been tamed in a bun, giving her a schoolmarmish appearance. But the modest look was becoming.

Predictably, I found Esma residing in glamour in a two-bedroom apartment furnished with Francophile elegance. There were antiques in the style of Boulle with gilded decorations on rich woods, a gray velvet sofa with rolled arms, and windows a story and a half high with orange drapes. The artwork was nineteenth-century etchings and watercolors.

"Nice digs," I remarked.

"Ah yes," said Esma. "What lawyer doesn't love rich clients? Madame Jahanbani is allowing me to stay here during the trial."

She offered wine, and I settled for a glass of water from the tap as Esma sat a safe distance from me on the other side of the velvet sofa. She asked where I had been and I explained only that I'd been back in Kindle County to visit.

"Staying again with your ex-wife?" Her eyes were sharp.

"And her husband."

"Ah, Bill. What you don't see."

Esma arranged herself a bit and folded her hands primly in her lap and rolled her lips into her mouth, preparing for launch.

"Where do I begin?" she said then. "I made a mistake, a terrible mistake. I assumed you would be pleased. That was a ridiculous misjudgment on my part, I admit that freely. I promise you, swear to you with my entire heart, that nothing like it will ever occur again. But to end our relationship over this is an even bigger mistake, Bill. I truly feel that way. We have an exceptional connection."

"Esma, I feel ill-used. I couldn't have been clearer. You were acting for the Roma cause. Not for my sake."

"Not at all." Her entire upper body quivered in disagreement. "Not at all."

"Esma, this is exactly what I was afraid of from the start. That the roles would become confused."

She sat calculating.

"So what is your theory, Bill? That I was using you to get information which I would then deploy to further the Roma cause, as you put it?"

"That's a little coarser than I would have it."

"But still a grain of truth?"

"A grain."

"And what does that make me, Bill, if I was sleeping with you for that reason?"

"Mati Hari?"

"'A whore,' is what I'd say, Bill. Free-spirited I have no doubt been. But my body has never been available for a price. It's insulting that you would think that were possible."

"Don't try to turn the tables on me, Esma, and make yourself the injured party. You betrayed my trust."

"Yes of course." She nodded eagerly, virtually bouncing up and down on the sofa. "I understand why you feel that way. And I have explained. But we are in touch, Bill, in a vital way, you and I. A deep way. You don't have to call it love, although on my side, I believe that may be the word. But please don't turn from this because I made a foolish error."

As she'd expected, in Esma's presence I felt her full force, not just the deep sensual appeal but that fierce intelligence that was so deeply engaging to me. In her company, I'd always felt like life was being lived at a faster speed.

"Esma, when I read that newspaper, I realized what I'd known all along—that I was an idiot. Even if I accept your word that there will be no further 'mistakes,' as you put it, that the words 'Barupra' and 'Ferko' will never be uttered between us again, the appearances remain. They compromise me at the Court. I have dodged a bullet somehow, but I'm not going to chance it again. We must end this."

She stopped and looked at her hands and again drew her lips into her mouth for a second, then glanced up trying to be brave.

"You are resolved."

"I am."

She edged closer and reached for my hand.

"Then come to bed with me, please, one last time."

I took a second. "To what end?"

"To make one more remarkable memory. Or are you saying you wouldn't enjoy it?"

"You know better."

"Then come." Still holding my hand, she stood. "Haven't you ever heard of a farewell fuck, Bill? Come fuck me farewell. Come on. And do a good job of it, please."

With the terms so clearly established, there seemed no reason to say no. It was the price she was asking—and yes

I'd heard of such things. The bedrooms were up a spiral staircase. The one she was occupying contained a platform bed, and to my amazement, a mirror on the ceiling. Even when I was on top, it left me feeling that we were being watched, and as ever with Esma, I found a way to enjoy that.

If she thought I would feel sharper regrets, recognizing what I was losing, she was right about that, too. Even if this was not our greatest moment together, it was close enough, and the memories of the others were so much at hand that at the height of things I even thought briefly, You're insane, this is realer than anything else, *this is*. But it became one of many great truths that dissolved within moments of reaching climax.

Afterward, Esma napped. I rose and dressed. In the living room I drank down the rest of my water. Across the way, in the rosewood breakfront, in the intensity of the halogens over the glass shelves, dozens of netsuke, the little Japanese ivories Esma collected, reposed. I admired the intricacy of the detail on several. Then I found a pad in my briefcase and scribbled a note.

> Sorry to run off, but rush hour can be such a mess, and probably better this way anyhow. Will miss you. Truly. Bill.

I couldn't mark the precise start of my relationship with Esma. The intensity had been unrivaled, but the duration was not. Since my divorce, whenever I'd known a woman about two months, Bermuda Triangle forces seemed to exert themselves.

In the elevator down, I thought again about what a remarkable person she was. Then my heart stalled as my mind stumbled over certain details. The mirrored ceiling seemed a bit much for a respectable lady still in the midst of a divorce, and I was also suddenly struck by the collection of little ivories. Who, no matter how eccentric, transports thousands of dollars of antiquities to a temporary residence? Let alone for only a month or two?

This, the place I'd left, was Esma's home. It had to be. But by the time the doors opened into the hushed lobby, I had turned all of that over again. My suspicions made no sense—why bother claiming I was in somebody else's house? I realized instead that my brief unwillingness to take her word was symptomatic of how deeply ingrained my distrust for her had become. It was just as likely that the client, Madame Jahanbani, had stimulated Esma's interest in building a collection of netsuke of her own.

I stood a second longer studying the patterns in the marble floor and absorbing my overriding response to all of this. Esma would always be a person of enigmas. What was striking to me now was the conviction in my core that I no longer cared about figuring her out.

20.

Buried Again—June 2

I flew to Vienna and made an early morning connection to Tuzla, landing at the site of the former Camp Comanche. I was expecting Attila, but she'd sent one of her drivers instead, who had me back in Barupra around 10:30 a.m. Spring had arrived since our last visit. Up here on the rock it was gusty, but the sun was bright and there were shirtsleeve temperatures, the low 70s, which I was already starting to think of as 20 Celsius. Goos was up top to greet me, but he pointed below to the old mine where the French geologist was already at work.

From her name, I had expected Madame Professor Sofia Tchitchikov to be shaped like a refrigerator and sporting a tweed jacket over an estimable bosom. But the woman who was scrambling over the former site of the Cave was an athletic fortysomething with brass curls, dressed in baby-blue zippered coveralls. She waved as she saw me hiking down the mine road beside Goos.

"Halloo," she yodeled and hopped over the hillside of

loose rocks as nimbly as a kid. As soon as I had shaken her hand, she took several pebbles out of a front pocket to show me her initial discovery, the black edging on each of the brown stones.

"Gunpowder?" I asked.

Her English was far better than my French, but with Goos there to translate, she stuck to her native tongue.

"Maybe," Goos said. "Certainly burn marks. She's found dozens of such stones with a little excavation, most of them at a radius of three hundred meters."

"Suggesting an explosion?"

She nodded. Goos said that the ballistics folks at NFI would tell us for sure, and could probably also determine whether there was an explosive agent adhering to the stones. If so, they might even be able to identify the device that had detonated. None of us had any idea whether the gunpowder in US hand grenades was distinguishable from Yugoslav.

"What Sofia can say is that the explosion is not recent," said Goos. "Most of these fragments were several millimeters below the current surface material. This is a windy place up here. So nothing stays on top for much time."

"Any way to tell how long ago the blast occurred?"

The professor and Goos had a long back-and-forth in French. Rocks lasted a lot longer than humans, and geologic time was therefore measured in eons, not years. She could say only that the burn marks on the debris were less than a century old, although the lack of wear suggested a much shorter period.

Madame Tchitchikov moved to the side then to show me the fall line of the hill. Goos translated, although he seemed to understand little more than I of the real meaning of what he was repeating.

"Lignite—the soft coal—is what she calls 'a tertiary rock,' which because of its softness normally lies at five to ten degrees to an incline. The Cave was formed for just that reason, because the coal sank below the Cretaceous rock that surrounded it. But the incline here, composed mostly of exploded lignite, is angled at thirty degrees, meaning that what we are seeing is not a natural formation."

As Goos spoke, Madame Tchitchikov did an accompanying pantomime, rushing her hands through the air to illustrate the explosion and the various angles of repose, which, in her demonstration, involved laying her head on her hands like a sleeping child. Her enthusiasm was charming.

The professor had brought two graduate students with her. Before she was ready to visit the gravesite, she wanted them to assist her with photographs and various measurements, employing portable surveyors' instruments, both a transit and a compass. While they were busying themselves, Goos and I walked back to the top.

In the rear seat of Goos's rental car, I showed him the papers Merry had turned over. The photographs, especially those from the air, naturally drew Goos's attention. On the flight here, I'd gone over the index card–type records from the base infirmary and had found that two soldiers had sought medical attention the next day, one for a human bite, the second for a "poss maxillary fracture due to rifle butt." Their names and service numbers had been blacked out, but not their unit: Both were assigned to the 205th Intelligence Brigade, Charlie Company, Second Platoon, the unit in which each member had been on leave on April 28, 2004.

"What did the general say to all this?"

"He was basically in denial. You've seen it before, Goos. He'd call himself an agnostic, so he didn't look like an idiot, but if the moment came, he'd want last rites. He believes in his troops."

Goos considered that, a hand scratching away at his bearded chin.

"Could be he knows more than he's told you," Goos said.

"I'm sure he does. On many topics. But he seemed flabbergasted by the pictures."

"Must say," said Goos, "I'm very surprised he handed these materials over. I'd have thought once they got a look, they'd've just told us to bugger off."

"I assume, Goos, they agreed to produce the records before they knew what they showed. Don't forget a lot of this was in Brussels."

After another half hour, the professor and her students were ready to move up to the grave. Since Goos had exhumed the remains last month, the local police had stood guard over the site, and there was a single officer on watch today. Goos had driven steel stakes into the ground to hold down heavy plastic sheeting across the opening, and the police had surrounded that with yellow tape. The first thing the professor asked was to remove all of it.

Once that was done, she got down on her belly and hung her head over the edge of the trench. After putting on a plastic glove, she scooped up some of the soil and let it run through her fingers. Then she probed the wall of the opening with a pencil point.

Still lying there, Professor Tchitchikov gave her head a decisive shake and said to Goos, "*Ce n'est pas authentique.*"

I spoke enough French to understand that. "What the

hell?" I said to Goos, but he held up a hand to listen to her. He nodded for quite some time before again giving me his attention.

"So here is what our Sofia says. Normally, exhuming a grave more than a decade old, you expect stratifications in the soil. But what I found here and sent to her for analysis was a mixture of subsoil and surface soil that made her think the grave had been dug—or dug up—more recently."

"You got that right, Goos."

He nodded. "You recall, I then sent Sofia some of our skeletal remains, so she could examine them. As bones decompose, certain trace elements from the surrounding soil more or less merge into them. And what she found ingrained in those bones is of a completely different mineral composition than the fireclay and sandstone of this grave. Magnesium and iron, especially, you'd expect to find in higher concentrations, if the bones had been laying here."

"Meaning?"

"Well, Boom, I reckon this is what's called in the trade a 'secondary grave.' We saw plenty of that with the Yugoslav Tribunal as the armies tried to clear out the mass burial sites before we got to them. Same idea here, only in reverse. Those bones back at NFI, the ones that I dug up here, they were moved from somewhere else. You remember our strange bullets and our DNA contamination? Well, there's your explanation. This grave has been staged, more or less for our consumption."

I struggled to make sense of that and, after a second, argued with him.

"Those three men, they share a Y chromosome. There are bullet holes in those bones consistent with Zastavas.

And we've just looked together at visual evidence of those people being loaded onto trucks."

"Yay. All true. But those bones we have weren't buried here, Boom. Simple as that. Remember, I was questioning Ferko about dragging three bodies all this way? There's plenty of loose lignite down below. He could have mounded over the corpses where they lay to keep the animals away from them, if that was all he was trying to accomplish."

"Then why are they here?"

"Closer to the road, I imagine. Once they brought the remains back, they had no desire to go gallivanting over the rocks. But those skeletons haven't been laying here very long, because the local soils haven't leached into the bones."

"Ferko was lying?" I asked Goos.

"Mate, according to the tale he tells, he was the only soul who knew where those bodies were buried. So unless he buried them, dug them up, and moved them somewhere else for a decade and then reburied the bones here again in the last six months, yay, he was lying."

"Fuck," I said. I was already weighing the implications for the case. This was far more serious than shorting Esma about Kajevic's threat. I couldn't count the number of trials I had been involved in as a prosecutor in which the major witnesses had told substantial lies, but with enough evidentiary backup on the big points that we won convictions anyway. Jurors were rarely perplexed when a scumbag witness acted like a scumbag. But I'd been warned that at the ICC, the atmosphere of moral purity also prevailed in the courtroom. I asked Goos what he thought the damage might be.

"'Uge," he answered, and told me in a state of revived

bitterness about one of his cases at the Yugoslav Tribunal. With enormous effort, they'd developed an insider witness who had worked as a guard at a Croatian-run concentration camp. For whatever reason, the man had kept a diary, and the written record was intricately corroborated.

"Even when the bastard wrote down it was raining, weather records confirmed him. But after the war, he became a drug dealer, and we had to turn over reports that he'd used his thirteen-year-old daughter as a courier to deliver cocaine. Once the judges heard that, they wouldn't even let him finish giving evidence. And tell me the truth, Boom. You remember the part in scripture where the Virgin Mary helped perpetrate mass murder?" He was about to head back down to the professor and asked the last question over his shoulder. He answered his own question with a grunt. "Cause that's who these damn judges seem to expect our witnesses to be."

I sat in the rental car stewing while Goos was aiding Tchitchikov with the rest of her soil sampling around the grave. When Goos returned half an hour later, I said, "Let's find Ferko. We need to know what the hell is going on with him."

Goos eyed me, rubbing his hand over his chin. He was not inclined. Ferko was a protected witness and under Court rules, investigators could not contact him directly; that fell to the Victims and Witnesses section.

"I'm not wasting another three months," I said, "doing the Dance of the Seven Veils with Victims and Witnesses just to see if Ferko picks up the phone when they call. We're here. Let's find him."

"And where would that be, Boom?"

"We know he lives within an hour of here, because Esma was able to whistle him in when we left Tuzla. Remember?"

"Might be he was just staying nearby temporarily."

That was possible, but there wasn't much to lose except the time. The day we went to Lijce, Attila had told me there was another Roma town in the vicinity. I couldn't imagine Ferko choosing to reside away from the People. One of the laborers said this second town, Vo Selo, was about forty kilometers due east, well into the Bosnian Serb enclave, Republika Srpska, near the Drina River. The drive would take about an hour.

Goos shrugged and said to me, "You're the lawyer."

We took off in the rental car, another little Ford, navigating by cell phone GPS. It was about 1 p.m. The main roads were surprisingly navigable, given what I'd heard about winter drives that were sometimes impossible because of potholes and landslides. With the spring sunlight luminous on the high clouds, we both relaxed. For me, sidestepping the Court's iron-headed rules made our trip feel a little like a high school lark.

Once we reached the river, we turned north. As Goos was negotiating a switchback, an immense structure suddenly loomed over us. It appeared so abruptly it seemed like a magic castle, with proportions to match. Erected atop a mountain of gray rock perhaps a thousand feet high, the building, on first impression, seemed to be a fort built to command the river. Then I noticed that the roof's highpoints were Byzantine domes topped with Orthodox crosses.

"What the hell," I said to Goos.

"If you've got data reception on your mobile," said Goos, "check the Internet."

"It's a monastery," I told Goos after a few minutes

of poking around, "first built with the permission of the Ottomans in 1566 on the remains of an old church by the Hrabren family." Within its gargantuan stone walls, the monastery had been a world of its own for centuries, with a winery, guest quarters, a library, and a seminary. Like so many other places, it was also a relic of the region's dismal history. In 1942, the Croatians had raided, tortured the monks, and thrown them into a pit in which they had all slowly died of infection and starvation while the Ustase—the Croatian version of Chetniks—burned most of the buildings to the ground. The monastery was rebuilt, only to be torched again by the Croatians in 1992, as Yugoslavia fell apart. This time the Croatians plundered the treasury and burned all the books, including irreplaceable sixteenth- and seventeenth-century manuscripts. The monastery had risen yet again after the Bosnian war as a stubborn testimonial to the Serbs' dedication to their faith.

"Take a look?" I asked Goos. It was time for lunch anyway.

The town beneath the monastery, Madovic, was small, with cobbled streets built for horse traffic, but it did not have the dusty, depleted look of other little places we had passed through. The merchants seemed to have prospered, supplying the many goods the monks did not produce on their own. While we waited a few minutes for a table in the busiest restaurant, it became apparent that Madovic was also a regional medical center. A three-story hospital stood at the other end of the long main street, and nurses and doctors in their long white coats comprised at least half the clientele who were eating.

Across the way, not long after we sat down, three monks passed by in long brown rassas, as the Orthodox cassocks are called. Bird's-nest beards drooped down their chests, almost reaching the wooden crosses suspended on prayer ropes from their necks. Each monk carried a long shepherd's crook and wore the same exotic cylindrical headdress, a little like a brimless stovepipe hat. They moved in slow, matched paces as they made silent pilgrimage back from the hospital where presumably they had prayed with the sick. I surreptitiously snapped photos and a quick video, in order to e-mail them to my boys, who had implied last weekend that I existed in a state of moral degradation because I'd ventured to a place as exotic as Bosnia without filling Instagram and Facebook with dozens of images. I tried to explain that a criminal investigator generally did not make a visual record of his doings, no matter how many likes I might have attracted. But for this scene I was willing to make a brief exception. I put the phone down when I thought I saw the nearest monk's eyes shift toward me.

Once we were done with lunch—I was yet to get a bad meal in Bosnia—we strolled up and down the main street, just to see what we could and to take a couple of photos of the colossal monastery overhead. It was close to 2:30 when we returned to the car.

As we did, a police officer appeared from the corner behind us. He might have been waiting. In any event, it was clear to me, as he lectured Goos, that the cop was maintaining that we had parked in the wrong place. I walked a few steps while Goos was engaged, but saw nothing that could have been a sign. Traffic shakedowns of tourists were routine in Bosnia, according to Goos, and with my back turned, I located a twenty KM bill in my wallet, a little over ten bucks, which I suspected would be adequate.

The cop was very young, still with acne, and it was possible he was just one of those overeager newbies familiar to police forces all over the world. He was in the police summer dress: blue pants, white hat, white blouse with epaulets, and a white belt that included a holster, so his pistol was also clothed in white, making it all the more noticeable. Goos appeared to be humbling himself appropriately, apologizing for our innocent error, but the cop remained grave, subjecting Goos to surly questions. Ultimately, Goos produced our letter of introduction from the Bosnian government, which explained we were emissaries of the Court. The cop read it over several times, seemingly unconvinced, and then instructed Goos to hold it open between his hands while the policeman took out his old toad-size cell phone and snapped a photo. With that, he walked off without my money.

"What do you think that was about?" I asked Goos, when we were again headed to Vo Selo, the Roma town.

"No idea. I suspect he's going to call someone just to be sure the letter's authentic."

"I thought he was looking for money."

"I as well. Kept waiting for him to come the raw prawn, as they usually do, how he would pay the fine for us so we could be on our way."

Vo Selo turned out to be no more than another fifteen minutes up the road. As we reached the outskirts, Goos rolled down his window and asked a dark fellow, Roma by his looks, if he knew Ferko Rincic.

The man responded by laughing. He waved over his shoulder toward a hill and, according to Goos, said we couldn't miss it. He shouted something else as we pulled away.

"'Mind the dogs,'" Goos said, when I asked for a translation.

"Dogs?"

"He said 'dogs.'"

That made sense. If Ferko lived in fear of retaliation by the people who'd massacred everyone in Barupra, he would want security of some kind.

On the other side of the hill was the town, which appeared even poorer than Lijce. Most of the dwellings were like the shack of the disagreeable old woman I'd talked to, a room or two with grab-bag exteriors— corrugated metal or stucco, but most often mud and twigs. I also saw at least one family huddling in the discarded portion of an old concrete viaduct, and several living only under tarps suspended between a few trees. The lone exception to the prevailing poverty was a house that loomed over Vo Selo almost as dramatically as the monastery we'd just left. It looked a little like a castle, but built not just with palatial grandiosity but also monumental bad taste. There were nine separate turrets, each with a balcony from which, in most instances, the laundry hung. Even from a distance, we could see that scenes had been painted on the stucco walls, and that the top roofs were festooned with animal sculptures, dogs and frogs, atop a gilt railing.

"The mayor's house?" Goos asked.

"*Baro Rom*," I answered, repeating the word Esma had applied to Tobar, the so-called Big Man who had established himself in a place of clan leadership.

On the narrow road through Vo Selo, we stopped again to ask an old lady about Ferko. She responded with emphatic motions up the hill.

"That there," said Goos as he again got behind the

wheel, "is Ferko's house." He was pointing at the little palace.

I processed. "Can't be the same guy."

"I asked her for Ferko Rincic. You heard me. She said we have to be very special because he treats the whole lot of them like they're wackers, not even worth hello."

We drove up the rest of the hill and parked at the side of the road in front of the huge house. Now that we were here, I could see that construction was still incomplete. Electrical wires sprouted from the turret walls. More revealing, an open trench near the road showed a sewer pipe without a connection. For all its grandness, the house seemed to lack indoor plumbing.

The perimeter was guarded by a white stucco wall about eight feet high, capped with pieces of jagged glass cemented in place. Two wooden doors of the same height stood at the center, with an iron lift-latch between them. A stick could have easily secured entry, but no one would dare, since there were three dogs who charged us in fury, barking and snarling, jumping at the breach between the doors and revealing their pink gums and huge teeth slimed with foam. They were all the same breed, brindled but with the pointed faces of Dobermans.

Goos looked around for a while, then suddenly raised a finger and returned to the car. He returned with the little takeaway box in which he had saved the remains of his lunch as a possible snack, and a small branch he'd picked up from the roadside. From the carton, he extracted three logs of *cevapi*, which he held to the gate. The dogs suddenly quieted, bounding against each other for a chance at the scent.

"Prepare to bash off," he said. He shoved me behind him, then lifted the latch with the tree branch. He pulled the gate open, tossing the *cevapi* a good fifty feet toward the road. As the dogs ran off baying for the meat, he jerked me inside and bolted the gate.

We were now in a courtyard. A fire pit, with some speckled graniteware pots thrown beside it, was nearby, and several rugs and a mattress lay before the front doorway, making me think that some or all of the residents slept here. A bell on a string extended near the door, and Goos gave it a jerk. In response, we heard voices and motion on the other side.

The man who threw the door open was in some senses Ferko. It was undoubtedly the same man, with the same broken nose and bad teeth visible when his mouth gaped in surprise. But he was dressed resplendently, as if for date night, had it occurred in the 1990s. He sported a big-collared shirt of chartreuse and turquoise blocks, and it was open almost to his waist, revealing a heavy gold chain that held a watch the size of a sommelier's salver over his pelted chest. When he raised his hand, every finger bore a thick gold ring.

Now that the door was ajar, a hefty woman, whom I instantly recognized as the wife I'd seen in the wrinkled picture Ferko had brought to court, peeked behind him. Clinging to her skirts was a little boy of about four. In the rear of the open passageway that had been revealed, I could see a portrait of a caravan drawn on the stucco in the overripe style of paintings on black velvet.

Ferko looked us up and down one more second, then said something to Goos in Serbo-Croatian and slammed the door.

"He says we don't belong here," Goos told me.

We rang the bell several more times. Goos yelled out in Serbo-Croatian that Ferko was required to speak to us, and finally, as a last gambit, screamed that unless Ferko spoke to us now he could receive no share of the reparations the Court someday might pay on the case. After all of that, Ferko responded with one sentence from the other side of the door that Goos instantly translated.

"He says he has called a neighbor to round up the dogs, and he will set them on us if we don't leave now."

We discovered almost at once that the threat had not been vain. A thuggy-looking fellow, unshaved, with dark greasy hair and a distinctly hostile look, arrived with the dogs tugging him along by the leashes he'd fixed to their collars. He was wearing a black leather jacket, odd garb in this weather, and I thought he might be hiding a gun.

We were in better stead with the dogs, however. The *cevapi* did not seem far from their minds, and only one of them growled a bit as we backed away.

21.

Back to the Salt Mine

S o Ferko is the richest man in town?" I asked Goos when we were under way once more in the small Ford. We were both in a somewhat wounded state and seemed eager to get back to Tuzla to take stock of the day.

As we traveled, we speculated about Ferko, although I offered most of the commentary. Goos's responses were limited, one-word answers or grunts, his mood expressed principally in the vehemence with which he shifted gears.

Given the fact that Ferko could summon a hood to menace us, he was clearly a person of stature in some organization. Drugs seemed the most likely business— there was said to be a lot of meth, often call ice, in Bosnia. Indulging in ethnic stereotypes, it was also possible that Ferko was boss of a gang of child thieves or beggars, or full-grown pickpockets. One thing was sure, though. The fellow who'd come to glower at us didn't have the look of anyone attached to a legitimate businessman.

Taking for granted that Ferko was a crook of some kind, I weighed the implications for our investigation. In order to protect his identity, Ferko had never answered the questions routine for virtually every other witness, stuff like 'Where do you live?' and 'What do you do for a living?' So he hadn't lied about those matters. But between staging the grave and claiming under oath that his wife was dead—assuming my eyesight was good and she wasn't—his testimony was worthless, even by the most forgiving standards.

Deepening my dismay was the realization that I was going to have to call Esma. I took it that today's revelations about Ferko would be news to her, because any trial lawyer puts her entire career in jeopardy by allowing a client to lie under oath. Yet Esma was the only person who might be able to get Ferko to sit down with us again to see if there were any explanations that might help us salvage the investigation. We were facing the law's version of real tragedy: the murder of four hundred people goes unpunished because the lone witness manufactured a bunch of eccentric lies.

Just outside of town, we pulled over in a spot with cell reception in order to get our bearings. We were at the side of a potholed road, just wide enough to qualify as two-laned by Bosnian standards. Beside us, weeds had already grown up thickly, and a stand of firs stood on the other side. I had just set my navigation app for Tuzla when a car pulled in behind us, a white vehicle with the word POLICIJA appearing amid a band of blue. In the sideview, I saw two policemen alight, one heavy-set, one thin.

I assumed they'd stopped to be sure we didn't need help, but Goos had another impression.

"Oh, sweet Jesu," Goos said. "Not again."

He rolled down the window and tried to chat up the fat cop who'd come to the driver's side. In the meantime, the wirier one ambled up to my window, leaning on the door to keep an eye on me and make sure I didn't escape. Goos again pulled out our court credentials, but the cop flicked a hand at us, as if the documents irritated him further.

"He says we both need to get out," said Goos.

We did, and the two leaned us on the fender, frisked us, and took our cell phones, passports, and wallets.

I thought they might look the documents over, but the fat cop simply slipped them in his back pocket. He returned to their car, while his partner watched us, his hand on his pistol, still holstered but with the white covering flap unsnapped.

"What did he say?" I asked.

"He wanted to know what we were doing around here. I told him we were here to talk to a witness, but he said that we could not operate in the Republika Srpska without permission of the local police. He was quite emphatic."

When the cop ambled back, he pointed to their vehicle and told us we were going to have to come with him.

Goos objected several times and even offered to follow them in the rental car, but the cop kept shaking his head. He was heavy enough that the mere stroll back and forth to his car had brought a line of sweat dribbling down from beneath his hat.

"Don't move," Goos said. My suitcase, in the hatchback, made me particularly reluctant to abandon the Ford. Goos kept remonstrating in a patient way, while the fat officer continued pointing to their car and motioning, as if he were directing traffic. Finally the thinner cop took out his gun and pointed across the auto's roof at Goos.

Once we were both in the backseat of the police car, Goos said, "Mate, this doesn't feel right at all."

"Is this Ferko's posse?"

"Damned if I know. Can't say I've made a lot of friends in this part of Bosnia. Might be someone knows my name and wants to pay his respects." He was being sardonic. "But it appears they're getting orders. I saw the big fella on the radio before they decided to haul us in."

"Are we under arrest?"

Goos found this laughable.

"Boom, you are one of the least lawyerly lawyers I've met. Which I appreciate. But, you know, what does it matter what they call it? We're in a police car headed nowhere we know with coppers who don't seem to care about our credentials. To me, that sounds like big mobs of trouble, no matter what the label."

The longer we drove, the more concerned we became. After about twenty minutes, Goos asked again where we were going and the wiry cop told him to shut up. A few minutes later, Goos pointed to a road sign that said we were twenty kilometers from Tuzla, which clearly relieved him. He'd been worried, I think, that they were going to take us into Serbia, where, in many quarters, the international tribunals in The Hague were reviled.

It was now after five, but in this season, the sun was still about two-thirds of the way above the horizon. The recognition that we had several hours of daylight left was mildly comforting, since the thought of traveling with these two in the dark seemed petrifying. As we continued winding through the mountains, Goos tried again to find out where we were headed. This time, the thin guy wheeled back, once more displaying the pistol, the barrel not quite leveled at us. We both subsided to silence. I could see from his pale blank look that Goos had gone from concerned to scared, a place I'd been since the thin cop first pulled out his sidearm.

We drove around more than another hour, until we suddenly parked at a roadside turnout. It was a vista point, looking down on thick hills of green trees, amid which tiny beaches of snow remained in the deepest gloom. I thought one of the policemen might need to piss, as I did, but instead they directed us to leave the car.

"Stay put," Goos told me. He rattled on in Serbo-Croatian. It seemed as if he was now demanding to be taken to a police station at once. The fat cop walked away from him, while the wiry one returned with his pistol drawn and opened the rear door on Goos's side. He was about thirty, with lifeless blue eyes and the pebbled remnants on his face of some skin condition that had gone untreated during the war years. By long experience, I marked him as one of those cops who liked the job because it came with a license to be mean. Goos, probably of the same mind, was aggravated and continued telling him off. The cop seemed to be listening attentively when, with no warning, he smashed Goos in the temple with the gun barrel and pulled him out of the car. Immediately, the fat one opened my door and wrestled me out and pushed me along to the driver's side of the car, where Goos was on all fours in the dust of the roadside. Blood flowed from a small gash at his temple, the steady drip coloring his hand and the ground.

I started screaming when I saw that.

"For God's sake, what is wrong with you people? We

are lawful investigators here, operating with the full authority of your government. And you beat this man? You have created a diplomatic incident. You will all be fired. Don't you understand that?"

The wiry guy responded by motioning with the pistol, instructing me to kneel beside Goos. The cop seemed to understand a little English and was smiling just a bit, revealing craggy yellow teeth. He might as well have said, "Motherfucker, you don't have a clue." He then grabbed me by the shoulder and pushed me down, until I was on all fours. He pointed his gun again, instructing me to look at the dirt, as Goos was doing.

"How are you?" I whispered to Goos.

"A bit whirly," he answered. "'Bout thirty seconds now, I'm going to collapse and make out like he might have hurt me quite badly. Maybe we'll get to a hospital."

Just as he said, Goos shortly reared up, held the side of his head, groaned deeply, and went facedown on the gravel. The thin cop sauntered up and felt the pulse in his neck. When I looked up at him, he slapped me open-palm in the back of the head and pointed down, then walked off at a casual pace. Compared to the way he'd hit Goos, his blow to me was minor, but my front teeth had smashed together and I could feel some lingering pain there.

I was like that as much as half an hour, when I heard footsteps. In front of me, I caught sight of a pair of heavy work boots. I peeked up timidly and as I went south to north, I saw blue jeans and then a rifle barrel with a sight. Lifting my head fully, I found myself facing a man in a flak jacket and a black balaclava. He was holding a Zastava and smiled tauntingly through the stitched mouth of the ski mask.

He beckoned with one finger, indicating I should stand, then ambled over to Goos, who was still lying there, feigning unconsciousness. The Chetnik who'd appeared in front of me suddenly kicked Goos in the ribs, with the velocity of a soccer player striking a ball far downfield. The boots were probably steel toed, and Goos cried out and flew up off the dirt, landing on his side. He went fetal, until two others, also masked and armed with Zastavas, hoisted him up by the elbows with their free hands.

The first one looked beyond me and spoke, and I revolved to see a fourth man in a mask, with his AK pointed toward us. The cops and their car were gone. They must have coasted down the road, because I had not heard their engine.

The man whose gestures had brought me to my feet now spoke in Serbo-Croatian, and I shook my head to show I didn't understand. He repeated himself to Goos, who, while standing, was bowed limply toward the ground, clearly as a means to contend with his pain.

"He says put your hands behind your back," Goos said. His voice was husky and I could tell it hurt him to talk.

"Should I?"

"Suit yourself, Boom. They'll beat you until you do. You fancy our chances two on four, and them with assault rifles?"

Goos tucked his hands behind his waist and I watched as the fourth man slid a white plastic zip tie over Goos's wrists and wrenched it tight. I gave a second to the thought of fighting, largely as a matter of deduction. It was going to be my final chance, but I had learned in the last hour about the sheer terror that flows from the bar-

rel of a gun. I'd never had a firearm aimed at me, and
the fear driving stakes through my heart seemed entirely
out of keeping with the reluctant cooperation and smart
remarks people in the movies mustered in the same situation.

Having tied us, the four masked men walked us over
the crest in the road, about one hundred yards, to two
small square cars with Serbian license plates. They shoved
us roughly into the backseat of one car, while the apparent leader walked ahead to the other vehicle.

I tried to talk myself down from panic, which would
be paralytic. Killing two credentialed investigators from
the International Criminal Court had to be bad juju.
Cell tower records would provide a rough fix on our
whereabouts when we were taken, and dealing with a de-
pendent state like Bosnia, the Western powers behind the
Court would demand accountability. Unless those countries had signed off on this. Perhaps that was why Merry
had turned over the documents? As a cover? No, that
was ludicrous. But I couldn't understand why exposing a
small-timer like Ferko seemed to merit a death sentence.
We didn't even know what we'd found.

"I don't think they're going to kill us," I said to Goos.

The blood flow from his temple had still not fully subsided, accumulating on the front of his shirt and soaking
the collar. The side where he'd been kicked didn't seem
to hurt any less now that we were sitting down. In response to me, he merely shook his head, not agreeing so
much as acknowledging what I'd said.

After a few more minutes on the road, I whispered to
Goos, "Where are we?"

"Near Tuzla," he mouthed.

I couldn't understand the reason to take us back to

where we'd been, except to return us to our hotel, even though logic told me that was unlikely. Did they want it to look like we'd disappeared on our way home? I kept on with thoughts like this, adding things up to mean we'd be safe, and then again, concluding we were in deep trouble.

After another half hour, I saw out the window the same landmarks we'd passed when Goos said we were near Tuzla. I wondered why we were circling, which, on reflection, seemed to be what the cops had been doing as well. The answer, when it came to me, drove another icy shard of terror into me. They were waiting for dark.

By now the sun was declining toward the mountains, the first faint hints of pink starting to color the sky. I tried not to be sentimental or morbid, but wondered whether this was going to be my last sunset. It was probably an illusion, but it felt worse to be dying for reasons I couldn't understand.

As the horizon faded toward purple, we started off in a new direction. The terrain seemed familiar, and for a second my hopes sparked that we were going back to the Blue Lamp after all. Then we made a sharp turn and headed up into the hills, where I knew no good outcome awaited us.

About ten minutes later, we left the paved road to ascend on a dirt path, where the dust clouded up like fog, reflecting in the headlights. We passed through a gate, but the property, whatever it was, seemed heavily forested, leaving aside yellow and green pipelines that ran close to the road, rising and falling with the contour of the earth.

"Ah, Jesus," said Goos.

"What?"

"It's a salt mine."

The words—or Goos's agonized tone—intensified my terror. The old saying, 'Back to the salt mine,' seemed to equate places like this with harsh conditions.

"Are we headed for the bottom of a mine shaft?"

"Not likely," said Goos. "They mine these days with water." He outlined the process briefly. Rigs drilled as if for oil. The dense salt deposits created a sealed chamber under the earth, and freshwater was pumped in through the green pipeline, driving salt-laden water out in the yellow one. The salinated water was stored in the huge white tanks I'd seen before, when we drove by with Attila. The salt water was then shipped to production facilities, in which evaporation produced the celebrated salts of Tuzla.

I was surprised that the two Chetniks in front didn't bother to tell Goos to shut up while he was grunting his way through this explanation. I took it at first as a sign that our situation was completely hopeless—they didn't care what we talked about because there was no way out. Then it dawned on me that they probably had another reason to let us speak.

"English," I mouthed to Goos and nodded toward the front seat. One of them was probably fluent and gaining intelligence just by listening. Goos smiled somewhat bitterly in response. I knew Goos had a better idea than I about what was coming, and that I should ask, but I was beginning to try to find a place of peace.

In another moment, the cars ground to a halt. The four masked gunmen jumped out and tore open our car doors. We were parked beside three enormous white water tanks, each at least a hundred feet high. With AKs pointed, the men instructed us to walk toward the nearest tower. I still had no idea why, until we came around the side, where a narrow ladder ran to the top. Goos took one look and fell to the ground, and I followed suit.

The one who had kicked Goos before did it again. With his hands tied behind him, Goos had no way to protect himself. The guy kicked him twice, the second time with another huge windup. Goos screamed and was left groaning afterward. In the meantime, the leader motioned to one of the men we'd ridden with. As I suspected, he spoke good English and sounded American. It crossed my mind that he might even have spent time in Kindle County, where we had a large Serbian community. I amused myself for a second with the thought of asking him if he knew Rusty Sabich, a judge who was also Serbian and could pass as my friend.

"If you like," the masked man said, "we can beat you so that you'll be glad to be dead, or you can go up the ladder and die like men."

In the wake of the second kick, Goos was lying on his back, coping with his pain. He spoke in a low voice, once he was able to.

"I've had enough, Boom. But suit yourself. No hard feelings either way."

He rolled over at that point and struggled to his feet with the help of one of the Chetniks. I thought about it and followed his lead, but told off the English-speaking guy as they were grabbing my elbows.

"Ferko has no reason to treat us like this," I said. "And he'll never get away with it. They know at the Court that we were in Vo Selo and what we found. If we disappear, Interpol will make Ferko's life a living hell. This is pointless." I added another two-word message to Ferko, which, as they said when I was an adolescent, was not 'Let's dance.'

At the bottom of the ladder, one of the Chetniks held a length of yellow plastic utility rope, which he formed into a noose. He put it around Goos's neck and then, after letting out about six feet, doubled the rope around my throat so that Goos and I could basically be garroted at the same time. Then he sliced through the zip ties on our wrists with a steel box cutter. The two who had driven us here, including the one who spoke English, climbed up first, with their rifles slung across their bodies. The other pair circled their AKs as a sign for Goos and me to follow.

"Ready?" Goos asked me.

I nodded. I still wasn't sure if we were about to be shot, or hanged by tossing us from the top. For the present, the nooses ensured that we couldn't make any attempt at escape by jumping off the ladder as we ascended. Even if we miraculously timed it perfectly and leapt off together, the impact when we fell to the ground might effectively hang at least one of us, maybe both.

Instead, we climbed slowly. The rope went tight enough to choke me each time Goos took another step, and I tried to follow him precisely as he talked me through it, right foot, then left. We paused on each rung. Given my aversion to heights, I made it a point not to look down. My heart was banging so hard I could feel it throbbing in my temples. Our pleasant lunch in the shadow of the monastery seemed a swallow away from forcing itself back up on me, which could prove lethal if Goos or I moved the wrong way in response.

When Goos reached the top, the English-speaking

guy had his automatic rifle pointed. Stepping over the top rung, Goos stumbled. The rope burned into my neck suddenly and for a second I saw black, while my forehead crashed against the ladder. The other Chetnik at the top grabbed the rope to keep me from falling off, then pulled me up as if he were reeling in a fish. Once I had my feet on the top of the tank, I saw that Goos's noose had been removed, but his hands were again zip-tied behind him. They did the same to me. In the meantime, the leader and his lackey arrived.

There was a three-quarter moon, providing considerable light. The dome of the tank was steep, probably to keep rainwater from accumulating, and it was edged with a steel band about six inches high. The surface was studded with little metal footholds that rose in ranks all the way to the top. The leader used them to climb up to a door in the dome, which he propped open.

Goos had sunk to one knee while all this was going on. The temple that had been pistol-whipped was toward me, still glistening at the small laceration. That side of Goos's face was streaked with three lines of clotted blood, black in this light, but it was clearly his side giving him the greater pain.

"Broken ribs?"

He nodded rather than speak. I'd been there once, after a car accident. For an injury that was rarely life-threatening, it was astonishingly painful and left you reluctant to breathe.

"This here is the salt vat," he said. "It's full of water, supersaturated with salt. Hydrochloric acid basically. Won't be much trace of us in a few weeks." He said it almost casually.

So that was the plan. Throw us in with our hands tied.

Let us drown as our flesh was burned away. Maybe the beating would be better. What I really wanted to do was make them shoot me now.

The leader returned and pointed the AK. I sat down beside Goos, causing the fellow with the Zastava to grunt in Serbo-Croatian. He was telling me to stand up and I shook my head no. I saw the rifle barrel coming and ducked under it as it swept over my head, but having gotten down, there was no way to avoid the muzzle as it returned on the backhand swing, catching me solidly on the ear and the temple. It probably wasn't an availing angle for him, because the pain didn't feel overwhelming.

There was some growling around and the English speaker was back.

"If you walk up there, we will shoot you in the head before you go into the tank. Otherwise, we will drag you and throw you in there alive."

"And why should we believe that?" I asked from the ground. These guys weren't humanitarians. If we walked up, I was pretty sure they'd throw us in anyway, while we were still breathing. Maybe they'd stand around for a few minutes to laugh as we screamed.

I took a second trying to figure why they seemed intent on getting us to walk up to the top of the tank, and recognized we finally had some advantage. Dragging a man struggling for his life up an incline was dangerous for them. Even beating us with the fierceness of the blows Goos had received on the ground risked catapulting the assailant right off the dome if he lost his balance. They couldn't shoot us either as we lay there, for fear of blowing holes in the tank, with God knows what consequences. In a while, they'd find solutions for these problems, but right now we were a little safer than we'd been down below. The guy who spoke English walked away to confer with the leader.

"Don't move," I told Goos.

"And I was just about to run for the next tram, mate."

I laughed a little, which had a weird sweetness to it.

The stalemate with our captors continued for a couple of minutes. Then, as I lay there against the steel rim of the tank, I could see lights sweep up the road. I heard gravel spurning, and in a second, the thud of a car door. In the dark, a voice echoed. They had phoned for assistance, apparently.

"Nikolai," a man called below. He repeated the name several times and the leader walked over to the ladder and looked down. The man on the ground said something else and Nikolai protested, but stepped onto the ladder. I could hear the two arguing as Nikolai descended. Their voices quieted once he was on the ground.

When Nikolai climbed back up in a few minutes, he whispered to the others. There was a new plan. All four came over to me first. One of them administered a solid shot with the metal stock of the AK that caught me in the mouth, and they pulled me up to my knees. I was bleeding inside my lip, which within seconds felt like it had grown to the size of a grape. One of them held me upright while another suddenly placed a ski mask over my head. I felt the muzzle of the AK braced hard against my temple as I realized that they'd placed the mask on backward so I couldn't see. It stunk of sweat and cigarette smoke, and my breathing was stifled. I'd been hooded, just like the familiar pictures of men in their final instants before execution. Even now, there was something to learn: Blindfolding the doomed man was not for his

sake. The sudden blackness geared up my fear to an absolute level, where fright itself was physically agonizing.
The mask was meant to spare the executioner the beseeching look of the condemned, to keep any last-minute
fellow feelings from standing in the way.

From the sound of his breathing, I recognized that
Goos had been positioned beside me, both of us kneeling
with our feet against the rim of the tank as we faced the
crown of the dome. I took it they had realized they were
going to have to shoot us here and drag us up to the tank
door themselves. I thought of plunging down on my face
again, but I was satisfied that dying right here was the
best we could do.

In the meantime, I could hear footfalls on the ladder
again and, occasionally, the clanging of a rifle barrel on
the iron. Two or three of our captors were heading
down. They were going to leave one man up here to finish the job. I felt the Zastava pressed harder against my
temple as the executioner, probably the English speaker,
prepared to shoot.

"God no, please," I said, but I didn't get out more,
because I was shocked by the wet heat of my own pee
soaking my lap. I would never say I was concerned
about self-respect at that moment, but I did care about
self. I had come too far in the last few years to die without wrapping both arms around who I was, and I sunk
inward. I had solemn fervent thoughts about my boys,
which rose in my heart like a silver beacon, and then,
as I knelt there waiting for the bullet, I unexpectedly
thought about my father. And what do you say now,
Dad? I suddenly asked him. He'd abandoned who he
was to be safe from the return of history's monsters, and
yet here I was, about to die at the hands of the same

kind of ghouls. In this life, there was no place beyond the reach of evil.

Time wore on. I was amazed by every second. Another, I thought, another. I heard something from the side of the tank that sounded like one of the AKs banging again on the ladder rungs. Then the gravel popped below as one of the cars drove off, quickly followed by a second, even a third, perhaps, judging from the engines' whines.

The night wind whipped across us and I was abruptly aware that my hands were numb from the ties. The urine on my lap and left pants leg was cold now.

"Are you here, Goos?"

"Yay, mate."

"Are they gone?"

Goos spoke up boldly, something in Serbo-Croatian, shouted into the night. The silence afterward lingered.

"Gone," he said. "I just said 'Your mother's cunt is wide as a river from all the men that have been in it.' Would have earned us a proper spanking if they were still here."

"Did you understand anything of what the guy who drove up was saying to Nikolai?"

"Not much. He told him to come down. When Nikolai objected, the other one said it was an order. But I couldn't understand anything they said on the ground, except that they were cross with one another."

"They're not going to kill us?"

"No idea, Boom. Apparently not right now. But I reckon I wouldn't be donning my party hat. We're forty meters off the ground with our hands tied behind us and blindfolded to boot. Best be careful or we'll do the job for them."

Talking it over, we wondered if they might have left some kind of booby trap behind. We decided to lie down again, with our feet braced against the tank rim, so we didn't tumble off blindly. The steel footholds stood high enough to make for painful bedding. Goos had to lie on his other side, which meant he'd landed another couple of feet away from me. I knew he was hurting and I told him to remain still, while I began inching toward him, keeping my feet against the rim as I scooted his way. The footholds cut into my gut as I moved over them, but in time I felt his shoe against mine.

I took a couple of tries at getting my mask off along the edge of a foothold, but that only seemed to be another way to knock out a couple more teeth.

"Can you bend toward me?" I asked Goos.

"Slowly," he answered.

"All the time in the world," I said.

I eased back and Goos doubled over, then I carefully rolled to my other side, a frightening business since I had to remove one foot from the tank rim and really had no idea of exactly where I was heading. But when I'd finished the turn, my hands were facing Goos. I eased back toward him, until I felt him there, then I lifted one leg to the next foothold above and pushed myself up until my fingers behind me grazed Goos's face. I grabbed the mask and climbed up to the next foothold, then one more.

"Can see," he grunted. We worked the mask up a little farther to be sure it didn't slip over his eyes again. Then he slowly straightened up and guided me inch by inch as I made my way back to the safe footing of the tank rim. Once I was there, I bent slowly toward Goos until he had the back of my mask in his teeth. I tried skootching away to help him pull. He got it up as far as the back of my skull, but it seemed stuck there. Finally, he managed to get all the gathered material in his mouth. I had found one of the steel footholds with my hands, which meant I had more support, and after a three count, I jerked my head down. My chin rammed against another foothold, but the mask was up to my crown and then off. I filled my lungs. The air was sweet, but my front teeth hurt a lot.

We both lay there. It was a beautiful night, with a clear country sky, a bright moon, and away from that light, a spill of stars. Life, I thought, life. Out of nowhere, I was reminded of being in Esma's bed, thrilled by my own vitality.

22.

Why—June 3–4

Talking things through on the top of the tank, Goos and I agreed that the best idea would be to get down the ladder and run like hell. But there was a reason that jailers around the world used zip ties. After sawing them against the rough edges of the footholds for at least thirty minutes, we'd accomplished nothing besides cutting our wrists. The rope that had been around our necks had been left behind and I crawled over to it— Goos was much too sore to move much. We figured if we could somehow secure one end up here, and then fasten it around us, we could make the climb down, but the line proved far too short to reach the ground. Without that, descending the ladder with our hands bound behind our backs was pretty much suicidal. However, after more than an hour of working back to back, we had gotten surprisingly adept and managed to loop the yellow strand over a rung of the ladder. We then threaded the ends through the belt loops on our trousers, making the rope a kind of safety harness. This allowed me to explore the top of the dome a bit, although I failed to discover anything that could razor through the ties. We pondered using the hinge of the door on top, the place where we were supposed to die, like a wire cutter, but we decided we were more likely either to cut off part of a hand or fall in. Ultimately, we settled down on either side of the ladder to wait for daylight, in the hope that the workers who were sure to arrive would not shoot us as intruders.

With rest, the adrenal rush was subsiding, making each of us more aware of our discomfort. Goos was much worse off than I was. My mouth hadn't seemed to stop bleeding, and my shoulders were aching from using my hands so much with my arms tied behind my back. Other places hurt, too, but not enough to warrant a lot of attention. Overall, we were both exhausted. Goos lay down to try to sleep and actually dozed for a while.

As our kidnapping was progressing, I had thought only in spurts about why this was happening, and even now I couldn't fully piece things together. I still had no clue what kind of enterprise Ferko held status in. There had always been a mob in Bosnia—they'd been fierce fighters during the war and were the first to commit atrocities against the Serbians—but I couldn't imagine what stake organized crime would have in promoting the story of a massacre at Barupra. Perhaps the mobsters had been the killers, and Ferko was covering for them by blaming 'Chetniks'?

Not long after sunup, two fellows in white jumpsuits drove into the graveled area below in a truck with the logo of the salt mine on the side panel. They parked about a block up, near what I could now see was a small wooden office. I started screaming at them, and Goos woke up and joined me in Serbo-Croatian. They heard us relatively quickly, but couldn't place where the voices were coming from, even as Goos repeatedly shouted "*Ovamo*," meaning, 'Up here.'

When one finally caught sight of us, he immediately demanded we come down. It took a few minutes to persuade him that we were tied up. Instead of rescuing us, the two went off to call somebody else, but the man they summoned, named Walter, sussed things out quickly and was up the ladder with a wire cutter in a matter of minutes. He ordered the two men on the ground to bring up security belts, and once they were fixed on us, we headed down the ladder, latching and unlatching the carabiner clips on each rung. I was a lot weaker than I would have guessed and was glad to be attached.

Walter was a sincere, decent guy, and as soon as he heard our story, he wanted to call the police. Goos and I responded politely that that was not a good idea, which Walter was quick to accept. Instead, he allowed us to use the office phone, from which I dialed Attila.

"Fuck, I must have called both of you six times," she said, as soon as I said hello. She'd wanted to be sure we didn't need more workers. I told her in outline what had happened last night.

"Joke, right?" she said first. She promised to come immediately.

Walter made us coffee while we waited in the small office, which had the dimensions of a trailer. More people were arriving for work now, and each did a turn at the door looking us over. We were a sight. Most of Goos's shirt was black with clotted blood, and the agony in his side left him slumped awkwardly in his chair. My lip was blown up to the size of a squash ball, and a streak of bloody brown ran from the corner of my mouth to my chin. The company had a nurse on call nearby. She took Goos to the small washroom and washed off the wound at his temple, applying gauze and a wrap that went all the way around his head. She also taped his ribs. She pronounced me much better off. My chin was bruised and there was a lump on the side of my head from the rifle barrel, but the only lasting damage was that the bottom third of one of my upper front teeth was gone, with the tooth beside it divoted by a chip. Our wrists were still bleeding, and she treated them with iodine and a sterile wrap. My trousers had dried, but not my underwear, a problem I kept to myself.

Through Goos, Walter explained that he was the deputy chief engineer and lived on the property, but more than a mile away at the motor works, where the enormous pumps operated. Because the water pressure had to remain constant, the machinery was always whining, meaning Walter could hear nothing happening outside. As a result, the mine had been dealing with persistent vandalism since reopening about a decade ago. A security guard was supposed to make rounds every night, but he had not showed up last evening. In front of us, Walter called the guard, who claimed that his wife had taken ill suddenly. Walter fired him on the spot, saying, "You work for crooks, let them pay you."

"He is Orthodox," Walter said, after he put down the phone, "and people here told me not to hire him, but that is not how we were in Tuzla, and how we must never become."

Attila arrived half an hour later.

"Jesus motherfucking Christ," she said, stopping in

her tracks when she saw us. "You've gotta start drinkin in better places."

Our first stop on the way back to the Blue Lamp was a small one-story clinic nearby, equivalent to a rural emergency center, so Goos could be x-rayed. As always, everyone seemed to know Attila, and the doctor, a young man who wore his white coat over his blue jeans, saw Goos ahead of four or five waiting patients.

It was all good news. Goos did not have a skull fracture, and he exhibited no signs of a brain bleed from his pistol-whipping. Three of his ribs were cracked, but none with a through-and-through break that would have required total bed rest for fear of puncturing his lung. A nurse at the clinic put a butterfly on Goos's temple and retaped his ribs and sent us off.

As we were driving, Attila asked us for a full version of the story, beginning from when we left Barupra. Her initial suspicion was that the men who had kidnapped us were the remnants of one of the Serbian *milicija*, the civilian militias, which had it in for Goos and probably had trailed us all day. To me, that didn't add. Our kidnappers never seemed to make any distinctions between the two of us. And they'd had plenty of opportunities to grab us before we reached Vo Selo. Things had gone to hell only after we rang Ferko's bell.

To explain, I told Attila about our encounter with the man I referred to as 'our major witness.' I had gotten as far as describing the house and the dogs, when Attila smashed on the brakes. Goos cried out in the backseat as the seat belt constricted against him, and Attila pulled over at the roadside to be sure Goos was okay. She then surged toward me in the passenger's seat.

"*Fer*-ko? Ferko the Jerko is your big witness?"

I looked back to Goos. He was supposed to be resting with one leg across the rear bench, but his eyes were closed and he was grimacing. I had the feeling that was about more than his ribs.

"How do you know Ferko?" I asked.

"That soup-sandwich motherfucker used to work for me. Just for one thing."

"Doing what?"

"I told you," said Attila. "Remember I told you how I hired Gypsies? Ferko was a driver. Until he started in stealin the trucks. The ungrateful fuckface. He's basically gone Elvis, but I caught sight of him sneakin around Tuzla a few years ago, and he ran like he was in the Olympics. That jagbag knows better than to ever let me catch him."

"But why does he own a big house?"

"Ferko? Ferko's a fuckin car thief. I guess you could say I gave him his start in show business, stealing my flippin trucks. Now he steals cars all over Bosnia, Croatia, Serbia, Montenegro, mostly on order. He can break into a car and drive it away in ten seconds."

"Does he work for the crime gangs?" I remained focused on why he'd been able to deploy the goons who'd captured us.

Attila laughed out loud.

"Ferko sells cars mostly to the Russian mob. Everyone in Russia wants a car. Have you seen the traffic in Moscow? They still have seven families sharing an apartment, but every one of them needs a Buick. That's how they know Putin is better than Stalin. But Ferko's a fuckin butler to those guys. He's small-time. He might pay off the local cops, but nobody's takin orders from Ferko. Or kidnapping anybody for his weak ass."

From the backseat, Goos asked, "He lived in Barupra, did he?"

"When I hired him first, he did."

"Any reason for a man with money to make up a story about a massacre?"

"Hell if I can say," said Attila. "Some Gypsies, scamming is a way of life. All I know is if the Jerko told me it was daytime, I'd run to the window to check."

Goos went silent. I thought he was figuring things through, but the pain meds had caught up with him and when I looked back he was sound asleep, his mouth wide open so I could see the dark evidence of several fillings.

"Ferko," said Attila, still trying to believe it. "You're not really telling me this whole shitstorm is because of Ferko, are you?"

I'd basically missed two nights' sleep, given the fitful slumber of a transatlantic flight, and I felt limp now. In memory, certain sensations, like the wind and the view from atop the water tank, had a high-def quality, but there were already vague spots in my recollection and some disorder about which events happened first. Goos, in the meantime, began snoring.

"By the way," I said to Attila. "You owe me some records."

"I'll give you the records," said Attila, "but hell if I know what for. If Ferko's your big witness, dude, then your case is *so* over."

Right now, I was too tired to care. After apologies, I reclined the deep seat in the A8 and followed Goos into a black sleep.

When we arrived at the Blue Lamp, Attila shook me awake to help with Goos. Now that he had time to stiffen up,

Goos's pain was worsening and he was also woozy from the meds. We walked him up the street, supporting him from each side with his arms slung over our shoulders, like an injured player leaving the field. Once we had him on his bed, I headed down to check into the hotel. With my luggage AWOL, I thought of going out to buy some cosmetics, but I had no energy for that. Attila promised to touch base tomorrow. When the clerk handed me the key card, I smiled. It was the same room where I'd frolicked with Esma. That already seemed far in the past.

Once I was upstairs, I found that my brief sleep in the car had revived me a bit. I sat on my bed, both comforted and terrified now that I was alone. I looked at my hands for some reason, lifted them and studied my fingers and palms. Being alive seemed such a profound mystery.

I was also a bit lost, not only about what had happened, but also about what was ahead. A good part of me wanted to book a flight back to the US and stay there, a feeling I resisted, in part because I realized again I didn't even have a house to return to. The homiest activities I'd undertaken recently were fishing with my sons and eating herring in a café in The Hague with Narawanda.

I decided to check my e-mail. That seemed ludicrously mundane, but that was where much of the comfort of life actually lay for us, in the routine. I considered writing my boys, but knew I'd alarm them if I made even a sideways reference to being safe. Instead, I went down to the bar, drank most of a double scotch at two in the afternoon, and barely made it back upstairs. I finally took off my underwear, then slept until 12 o'clock the next day.

After I woke, I was surprised to find Goos downstairs already. He'd made himself a coffee from the machine in the lobby and was sitting at one of the small tables in the breakfast area, stirring his cup with his left hand. His second dose of hydrocodone had worn off a couple hours ago, he said, so he'd come down for 'brekkie.'

We shared a long look across the white laminate.

"That was something," I said.

"That was something," he agreed. "Thought we were cactus, mate, for sure." He told me about his closest brush before that, which had come while he was a police trainee in Brussels. He'd been called on a domestic—the male was Russian, which was unsurprising since they had a track record of raising hands against their women—but when the wife let Goos in, the guy grabbed Goos from behind and put a butcher's knife to his throat. The stink of alcohol was all over the room. Fortunately, the woman started to go off on her man again, and he released Goos so he could charge her. Goos brought him down with his truncheon.

"I pissed myself when they had us kneeling there," I told Goos. I knew he had to have noticed, so I wasn't confessing much. "But it ended up being a good thing, because it brought me into myself."

"What did you think of?" Goos asked.

I explained about my father. The most shocking part to me was how angry I was at him.

I asked Goos what had been in his mind.

"Ah," he answered. "Wife, kids a little. Mostly, buddy, I couldn't believe I'd been so daft as to come back to Bosnia."

"Are you going to quit?" I asked. From someone else, the question might have suggested cowardice, but we both knew this was only a matter of logic.

"Don't know," Goos answered. "Need to get back and

have a long think. One thing for sure, though, mate. We can't go barracking around here without real protection. We'll need the army if we come back. Badu will have to get on the blower and make that happen."

"Are we coming back?"

"Well, we're going to have to exhume the Cave, aren't we? Ferko's word is no good. And it's been blasted all over the front page of the *New York Times* that we suspect a massacre. So the only way to know if that's so is to look for the bodies."

He was right.

We were still at the table at about 1:30, when Attila breezed in, wheeling my suitcase. She'd sent two of her people to Vo Selo, where they'd picked up the rental car, which was now parked outside. Neither of us had even thought about the vehicle, and we thanked her at length. From under her arm, Attila withdrew an envelope and threw it on the table before making herself a coffee, too. She was wearing her usual rumpled jeans and the old pinstriped short-sleeved shirt. Attila could have vastly improved her fashion presence with a trip to Goodwill.

"What's the report from the medical corps?" she asked.

Except for needing a dentist, and not being able to drink coffee on my right side because of my teeth, I was pretty good. Goos would require a few days.

Attila had told us yesterday she had a close friend on the police force, a lieutenant she'd trust with anything, and with our permission, Attila had gone to the station to have a word with Dalija. The lieutenant had made a few calls in Attila's presence. In a town down the road from Vo Selo, two officers had reported that their car and uniforms had been taken from them at gunpoint the day before yesterday.

"That bag of asses," said Goos. "Steal a police car in a small town where everybody knows everyone's business? A fine way to get beaten with a pipe. No chance that happened."

"You guessed last night that Ferko had financial arrangements with the local cops, didn't you?" I asked.

Attila smiled at that idea.

"I'm sure they shake him down. But nobody's gonna take orders from Ferko. You'd have to have had the numbnuts work for you to understand."

"Well, he was clever enough to steal your trucks, wasn't he?" Goos asked.

"He was playin follow-the-leader. Another Gypsy from Barupra, kind of the Big Man there, Boldo Mirga— he was the only one with the stones to do that."

I looked to Goos, who was playing coy and avoided my eye.

"Okay," I said. "And tell us how this truckjacking went down. I'm not sure we've ever heard the whole story."

Attila hesitated. "Man, I got to be careful here."

"Attila, those were NATO vehicles. If you want, I can send another letter to Brussels tomorrow asking for your records and their interview notes with you. That was all before the Kajevic thing. It can't be classified."

Attila pondered.

"You know, it ain't all that much to tell," she said. "The US was leaving, and Merry wanted to send a bunch more of the military equipment NATO had collected to Iraq. So I sent trucks and drivers down near Mostar to pick some of it up."

"When was this exactly?"

Attila lifted her chin to think. "Late March 2004?"

That would have been two weeks before the Kajevic thing in Doboj, and a month before the people in Barupra disappeared. "In those days, the roads were still crap. I mean you'd be drivin and come to a shell crater and need to build your own bridge with railroad ties you carried with. So it was a long trip, most of a day, and what with the roads, I wasn't surprised that they didn't drive back in the dark. But there was no sign of all of them by noon the next day. About Taps, Boldo and Ferko and the rest of them come strollin in, sayin while they were bivouacked some gang hot-wired six of the trucks and made off with them. The drivers were all Gypsies and they didn't even have their stories straight. I fired them just about on the spot."

"And what happened when it turned out that Kajevic got away in a couple of those trucks, the ones Boldo and Ferko stole?"

"Well, no one knew that for sure at first. It was most of a week after Doboj before the getaway trucks were recovered out in the country."

"But what did those guys have to say for themselves then?"

"Boldo? Testicles of titanium. He just stayed with his story. Must have been the carjackers who sold the trucks to Kajevic."

"And who were they telling that fairy tale to? Bosnian police? NATO?"

"NATO MPs and the Bosnians."

"And did the law enforcement guys believe that?"

"Boom, I keep tellin you: Ain't no one who takes a Gypsy's word. Thing is, the only way to completely disprove what they were puttin out there would be with Kajevic and them. Nobody'd ever tell you Boldo was stupid."

"And is there any chance Boldo's story might have been true—that someone else stole the trucks and sold them to Kajevic and his Tigers?"

"Chance? Sure. The part that didn't never make sense was Boldo dealing with Kajevic. You heard Tobar in Lijce. That's mongoose and cobra. Gypsies hated Kajevic and Kajevic, he'd rather sit down to a meal with a snake and a rat than deal with the Roma."

"And when was the next time you saw Boldo and Ferko?" I asked. Goos's eyes quickly passed my way. He approved of me truth-testing Attila.

"Never. I'd sooner crap bricks than talk to any of them and they knew it. Steal my fuckin trucks? I've told you before. It wasn't until August or September I heard this shit about all the Roma bein gone."

There was a lot of news here, and almost all of it was confusing. One thing was clear, though. If we could ever crowbar the truth out of Ferko, we'd be on a much better footing, even though I'd require an armored vehicle and a box of Depends before heading off to that interview.

"Do you think you could get a phone number for Ferko?" I asked Attila.

"Not if he had any idea it was for me," Attila said. "But I can gumshoe around."

I finally picked up the envelope Attila had thrown on the table and asked about the contents.

"Truck logs from April 26 to 28, 2004."

"Showing?"

"Nothing. No convoys out of either pool."

I was about to tell her she was wrong, that her trucks were on film, when Goos's blue eyes flicked up in warning. Clearly Merriwell hadn't shared anything about the

NATO material with Attila. As he maintained, Merry was keeping his distance and letting us do our jobs.

"Who made the records of vehicle deployments?" asked Goos.

"My people."

Goos nodded and calculated, yet said nothing, but Attila read something in his response.

"Nobody took my trucks without my say-so," she said.

"I thought Boldo stole them," I said.

"That's why I'm so sure. Because after that, I had three guys patrolling each depot. We just about tucked every vehicle into bed at night. That was even before we realized Kajevic had ended up with the trucks."

Something in her last remark struck Attila. She angled her round face. In her eyes, I could see a thought taking her somewhere.

"Did you say you made some photos in Madovic?" Attila asked. "Any chance I could see them?"

I reminded Attila that the Bosnian Friendship Club had stolen our cell phones.

"What about the cloud?" Attila asked.

I removed my tablet from my briefcase, still strapped to my suitcase that remained beside us in the lobby. Until this moment, neither Goos nor I had given any thought to using the 'find my phone' app. We tried now, but no signal registered, implying either that the phones were off or, more likely, destroyed. But the photos and the short video I'd taken in Madovic had uploaded before then.

Attila looked all of it over for quite a while and replayed the video three times, finally spreading her fingers—and her ragged bitten nails—to enlarge the shot of the three monks approaching. I hadn't even caught it in real time, but the one in the center had flicked his dark intense eyes toward us minutely, as we watched them from where we sat. He'd actually stared a bit longer than the nearer monk, whom I'd seen glance in our direction later.

"That's why they were going to take you out," Attila said.

I was astonished. "I had no idea it was forbidden to take pictures of monks."

Attila laughed then and faced us looking a lot like a jack-o'-lantern on Halloween night, the same fiendish gap-toothed grin, appearing as if she were lit from within.

"See that one?" She put her finger on the screen, indicating the monk in the middle. "I'm almost positive you guys just found Laza Kajevic."

VI.
Kajevic

23.

Who's There?—June 4–9

Goos immediately wanted to inform his former colleagues at the Yugoslav Tribunal that we might have located the most wanted war criminal since Nuremberg, but Attila persuaded us that the better course was to contact NATO headquarters in Sarajevo. They were authorized to arrest Kajevic—in fact, hunting for him was probably their most significant remaining duty in Bosnia—and also had the most secure structure to preserve the secret. Attila, who evinced a junior-high giddiness about nabbing such a big-time bad guy, made the introductory call, followed by several coded communications, mostly by text, between Goos and me and various NATO officers. Goos was in a grim mood, which I attributed to pain. I, by contrast, was simply confused. My ability to adjust to dramatic news seemed to be like a broken transmission in which the gear spun without catching.

In the intervals, the three of us sat in the breakfast

room, whispering as we reinterpreted what had gone
down the night before last. Some conclusions seemed
fairly obvious. Once the parking cop in Madovic had
established that the yokelly guys snapping photographs
of the monks and the monastery were from the International Criminal Court in The Hague, word had
filtered back to Kajevic's protectors, who sounded the
alarm. Their plan probably was to take us out ASAP,
before we could report our findings. Following us from
Madovic, Kajevic's cadre almost certainly witnessed our
visit to Ferko before they were able to grab us outside
Vo Selo. During the hours they were awaiting darkness
before throwing us into the salt tank, somebody must
have realized that the ICC and the Yugoslav Tribunal,
where Kajevic was wanted, were not the same institution. Local inquiries would have validated that Goos
and I were present to investigate Barupra, not capture the former president. Coincidentally, my rant that
Ferko would never get away with killing us demonstrated to them that we didn't realize what we'd discovered. At the last minute, some old Arkan commander
had rushed to the salt mine to stop Nikolai rather than
risk the intense manhunt that would have followed our
murders.

Given these insights, though, it seemed likely that the
Arkans would want to keep an eye on us, to be certain
that we remained unsuspecting about the true reason
we'd been kidnapped. Attila called her police friend, who
swept by the hotel a few times in her private vehicle and
confirmed that there were a couple of guys just sitting
around in two different cars, both trained on the hotel.
The news was instantly terrifying to me, and Goos didn't
appear any happier, but we agreed with Attila to await

NATO's input before doing anything to show we were aware of being under watch.

In our communications earlier with the NATO fugitive hunters, we'd set a meeting at Attila's headquarters on the outskirts of Tuzla, where we all would pretend to be attending a business gathering related to our ICC work. We left the Blue Lamp at 6 p.m. Dalija, Attila's cop pal, called to let us know there was a tail—and a fairly clumsy one, just two vehicles following at a short distance, almost as if they were the laggards in a funeral procession. Dalija said she'd keep everybody in sight, just in case.

Attila's headquarters occupied an entire single-story building about the size of a small strip mall, decorated with a seemingly studied effort in the nondescript. Her office had indoor-outdoor carpeting, the color of brown dirt, and louvered vertical blinds. On the desk were several photos of the wife Attila had said she met here, a blue-eyed, black-haired beauty. The shots showed the two of them together, posed beside horses and dogs on their farm in northern Kentucky. Attila's domestic life, which she almost never mentioned, seemed somehow incongruous, but she was pleased by compliments about how gorgeous it all was, house and garden and wife.

"Yeah," Attila answered, "it's amazing how fast a poor girl can get used to spending money."

Not long after dark, the NATO delegation arrived in two pickup trucks bearing the logo of an international construction company. Attila had already made a dozen local calls, designed to put out the word that we were beginning preparations to dig up the Cave. The NATO soldiers were in jeans and windbreakers and hard hats, and all four of them carried clipboards. The commander was a Norwegian general, Ragnhild Moen, accompanied by three senior staffers, a Dutchman, a German, and an American. The general was lean and almost six feet tall, with impossibly long, thin hands. She proved disarmingly personable while remaining quietly authoritative. She had relatives in Minnesota where she had spent a year in high school, and she retained fond memories of Kindle County, which she had visited several times. Her student-exchange group had met the chief federal judge there, Moria Winchell, whom I knew well.

The NATO officers huddled around my tablet and examined the photos several times. No one doubted Attila's identification, especially not after comparing my photographs to pictures of Kajevic obtained in the last several years. The four spoke English among themselves, so for once I could follow the deliberations.

The abiding question was whether our presence in Madovic—or the initial misplaced response of Kajevic's thugs—had been enough to spook him and lead him to move. The monastery offered advantages as a hiding place hard to equal, especially in the Balkans of today where safe harbors for Kajevic were probably dwindling. Commanding that kind of highpoint made it impossible for any large law enforcement or military detail to enter Madovic undetected. Only a single approach led to the mountain compound; even if troops blocked it off and surrounded the place, it was a near certainty, given the history of persecution of the monks, that the rebuilding had included subterranean escape routes, probably through the wine cellars. Finally, entering the monastery to arrest Kajevic was, even if not quite legally forbidden, likely to agitate many people, especially in Serbia, where the Orthodox Church would portray it as a grave violation of a sacred place.

All in all, the general thought it was best to attempt discreet intelligence-gathering in Madovic for several days.

"May I ask you to remain in the area, please?" she said. "We are likely to have further questions for you, if it turns out Mr. Kajevic has not departed."

I could see that Goos was displeased by the request. He'd had enough of Kajevic and his Tigers, but the general promised to assign us an escort while we were in Bosnia, NATO troops in civilian garb, since the sight of military uniforms would be enough to send Kajevic packing. On the other hand, no one would wonder why we'd hired private bodyguards after the other night. In return for staying around, I requested the general's help in replacing our passports and cell phones.

At the end of the meeting, Attila stood at the door to say good-bye to everyone. Despite her initial excitement about identifying Kajevic, after second thoughts she wanted no public role in this operation.

"Still need to do business in this country," she said. "Anything you need on the DL, let me know."

By the time we were back at the Blue Lamp, two soldiers had shown up in jeans and bulletproof vests, with sidearms visible on their hips. I thought the hotel people might object, but to them it was no more than an indication that the establishment was housing dignitaries. As far as handguns went, Bosnia remained the same kind of Wild West as the US, where anybody could carry one with a little paperwork.

Goos still wasn't happy.

"Mate," he said, when we returned to the lounge, "this isn't our show. I don't want to be the wuss," he said, "but our Attila has the right idea. We'd best think carefully before spending the rest of our lives being known as the people who brought that fellow in. Some diehard will pin our faces on his bulletin board."

I understood, but there were certain limiting realities. Merely the jostling on the short drive out to Attila's office had been agonizing for Goos. An eight-hour trip back to The Hague, involving two flights, let alone dragging a bag of rocks from Barupra, wouldn't be possible for him before next week, leaving aside a trip by medevac, an idea Goos immediately dismissed as too grandiose and humiliating.

We spent the following day, Friday, trying to get back to work and to make sense of the information we'd come across this week. Many pieces didn't fit. But the priorities were pretty much as we'd figured: (A) Make arrangements to exhume the Cave; (B) Speak to Ferko; (C) See if Internet searches could help ID the soldiers assigned to the military intelligence unit in April 2004 and establish whether they'd posted anything that might shed light on what had occurred in Barupra.

Goos went back to poking through Facebook and YouTube. My job, which I didn't relish, was to create some kind of report to our bosses in The Hague. The idea was to bring our Court supervisors up to date without being especially forthcoming, either about our kidnapping or whom we'd found, news which in both cases was guaranteed to spiral events out of control.

Late in the day, not long after our replacement phones were delivered, I received a call from Attila. She'd tasked one of her Roma employees, who, she said, lived like "a normal person," to get information on Ferko. The employee had taken the trouble to visit Vo Selo.

"Ferko is *totally* un-assed," Attila said. The story from the locals was that within a couple of hours of our visit to Ferko, four police officers had shown up at his house. They made an immediate impression by shooting all of the dogs. According to the one neighbor who had spoken to Ferko, the cops had punched him around until Ferko had coughed up the fact that he was a witness in a case in which we were the lawyers. Ferko swore he'd told us he wanted nothing more to do with us, which further corroborated that Goos and I weren't looking for Kajevic. Presumably, that was what propelled Nikolai's commander to run to the water tank to prevent our assassination. Back in Vo Selo, as soon as the cops left, Ferko and his family loaded their four cars with everything they could carry. The neighbor believed they were gone for good.

"Any idea where?" I asked.

"None," Attila said. "Apparently he took a hammer to his cell phone right there, so no one could track him. I have the number, in case you want to try anyway."

I went to report all of this to Goos, who was working in the breakfast area. Across from him at the little white table, I dialed the number Attila gave me for Ferko, which produced a long message in the Bosnian dialect of Serbo-Croatian. I handed the device to Goos.

"Not in service?" I asked once he'd clicked off.

"Disconnected."

"Crap." The fact that Ferko had run for his life, probably after dealing with Nikolai's boss and other members of the ex-Arkan gang, did not require explanation, especially for us. But Goos remained baffled about Ferko.

"Here's where I give it away," Goos said. "Why's he

tell this story in the first place, not even to mention moving bones around and planting bullets so we think it's all fair dinkum?"

I wasn't sure if Goos was being rhetorical.

"You think Esma put him up to the whole act?"

"Why's he bother, mate, for Esma or anyone else? That's what I'm saying."

"Maybe because it actually happened? Maybe he lost some people he cared about and wanted justice done?"

"Does that man with the dogs and the rings strike you as a figure of good citizenship? He's telling this story, true or not, because there's something in it for him, but I'll be stuffed if I know what it is."

Our conversation, and the riddles about Ferko brought me back to a place I did not want to go: calling Esma. She was the only person we knew who had any connection to Ferko, and we were also obliged to confront her, as an investigative matter, about who her erstwhile client had proven to be. I wanted to hear her say this was all a surprise to her, just to get a sense of whether it was actually true.

The complications for me in approaching Esma showed yet again why we should have kept our private parts private in the first place. My lack of success in sustaining dating relationships had made me fairly practiced about ending them, and I had learned that cold turkey was the only reliable approach. 'Let's be friends' just prolonged the pain for the party more wounded, who took it as a beachhead for hope.

So it was unfair to call Esma. And understandable that she might not pick up. I felt obliged to explain this to Goos, and to apologize. He passed the back of his hand through the air.

"You won't get a gobful from me, mate, about this. Wouldn't be many single blokes who wouldn't crack on to her."

I didn't need a translation. I'd acted predictably for any male with an unregistered penis.

Adhering to the ethical proprieties, Goos should have been the one to call Esma. But we both knew I was far more likely to get to the truth, if she was inclined to talk.

I started with the most antiseptic approach, a text: Must speak to you briefly. Business issue. Very sorry to have to be in touch.

She didn't reply. On Saturday, I tried e-mail. And on Sunday, I finally called, twice in fact, leaving the same message both times. After that, Goos took over, but I wasn't surprised that she didn't answer either of us. It was the mess I'd made.

Goos and I slept in both days over the weekend. I dug through more e-mails, read more Fowles—I was now on *The French Lieutenant's Woman*—and poked around Tuzla. Also, to be polite, I e-mailed Narawanda to advise her about my schedule, which I thought would bring us back early next week. After some thought, I added, "I hope your trip to New York went well and has made you feel better." I got a one-word reply: "Not."

On Sunday, I decided to venture out for a run. Overall I looked worse than I felt. Except for temperature sensation from my tooth, which shot unexpected streaks of pain through my nose and forehead, I was not in much discomfort. There was still a lump in my lip with the black line of a scab in the middle of it, and a colorful bruise had emerged along my jawline where it had met the rifle stock, and there was a welt on my forehead,

which had collided with the top iron rung of the ladder.
The broken front tooth made me look to myself like
an unruly teenager. But as happens once you get accustomed to running, I felt a physical craving for the
endorphin rush. One of the NATO MPs agreed to drive
along beside me.

Tuzla was pretty, the old center mostly low bright
stucco buildings decorated with white architectural details, like plaster medallions. The population was no
greater than Peoria, but the city had a far more urban
feel, with skyscrapers and minarets visible when I looked
south.

The main square, through which I jogged, was
marked by a geometric arrangement of multicolored tiles
and an Ottoman well, centuries old, from which fresh
water still burbled out of a copper nipple. I headed toward Lake Pannonica, the man-made seashore in the
center of town, circling it several times.

Like the local police lieutenant, NATO recon were
also convinced that we were under surveillance. Some
guy had spent twelve hours at the *cevapi* place across the
street, at a table on the front porch, pretending to read
the paper, only to be replaced on Saturday and Sunday
by a younger fellow doing the same thing at the little café
on the corner, where he nursed countless cups of coffee
while maintaining a direct line of sight to the hotel door.
My bodyguards had been advised to look for a red Yugo,
and it was occasionally visible now when I looked back
while I was running. So long as we continued to give
the impression that we believed it was Ferko, not Kajevic, who was watching us, the Arkan Tiger surveillance
team had no reason to be discreet. A menacing presence,
in fact, might hasten our departure.

I managed to enjoy myself anyway. The sun was bright and it looked like every person in Tuzla was on the sand in their skimpy European bathing suits, the little kids in sun hats dashing back and forth to the water with their buckets. I picked up a brochure about the lake and was astonished to learn that the ersatz seawater in the network of ponds was pumped in from the same tanks where Goos and I were supposed to die, although diluted many times. I struggled with the thought that if things had gone differently, these people might be splashing around amid indistinguishable little molecules of our remains, but it was almost like thinking about getting hit by oncoming traffic as you're driving: It just didn't happen.

For me, the terror was starting to recede, leaving aside a couple of throttling nightmares. As I trotted along, it was nice to feel under my own power again, less dominated by the shadow of trauma and fear. It dawned on me, however, that I had now visited the true Bosnia, sharing a little bit of the abiding national experience.

Monday morning, Goos said, "If you don't mind being a tad impromptu, might be we could start back to The Hague tomorrow. Won't quite be tickety-boo, but I think I can stand it. Know for sure in the a.m. Perhaps you can give the good general a tingle and let her know duty calls."

When I got back to the hotel in the late afternoon following another run, there was a message on my cell from General Moen. I reached her aide-de-camp, who asked if we could come to Sarajevo to meet with the general at 2:00 p.m. tomorrow. The MP bodyguards would drive.

As soon as I relayed the message, I could see Goos was on the verge of saying no. He wanted to go home.

"Any idea what this will be about?" he asked.

"He—the aide—just said the general felt it was important to speak to us again."

"'Important?' Christ the Savior, I don't want to be important." He seemed to give his remark some thought. "All right, let's give it a burl."

"We'll go?"

He nodded.

Sarajevo, which had gone from Olympic city to the site of a harrowing siege, was by appearance, like much of Bosnia, seemingly returned to its former self. The military escort who was driving, a young Norwegian named Andersen, seemed to have developed deep affection for the city in his time here and stopped on an overlook, where, in a postcard shot, Sarajevo reposed beside the spangled Miljacka River, with the southern Alps majestic in the distance. From here, my eye went to the minarets and skyscrapers, the tile roofs, and, most striking, the ranks of stark white tombstones that occupied far more mid-city real estate than in any other urban center I'd visited. Andersen pointed to a large building in the heart of town, an old palace that was a bombed roofless wreck but which, he said, would appear lovely from ground level. He was not the kind of kid who would have said the state of the building was a metaphor, but I think that was why it was so significant to him.

He drove us down into the old section, Bascarsija, where worn paths and walls of stone surrounded the sites rebuilt in the familiar white stucco with brown terracotta roofs. The hotel where we were headed was a couple hundred feet from the national war memorial, dedicated to the dead of World War II. Walking through the pedestrian way, Goos and I stopped to observe the evergreen wreaths with ribbons piled beside an eternal flame. In this country there was no end of carnage to recall. Here, where the population had been besieged because of their faith, there were more women in hijab than I'd noticed in Tuzla.

While the soldiers positioned themselves at the door, Goos and I went to the reception counter. Our cover was that we'd arrived for a business meeting with the same construction company whose logo the NATO folks had sported on their pickup trucks the other night. The clerk, a diffident young man who spoke excellent English, gave us keys and ran down the hotel rules, which included serving no alcohol. At that news, I felt Goos tense instinctively, even though we had no plans to spend the night.

On the third floor, the room keys opened a conference room in which the general and six other soldiers sat, all in civvies. A map had been fastened to a portable bulletin board. Everyone stood as we entered, a show of respect I immediately registered as a forbidding sign.

"You seem better," said the general to Goos.

He answered that he was fine, which was obviously untrue. He was still limping to protect his right side, and the drive had been painful.

"Let us brief you on what we have found," said General Moen. "The good news is the subject does not seem to have departed."

She turned things over to an intelligence officer, an intense Hungarian, long and crew cut, a captain named Ferenc. He referred repeatedly to 'assets,' which made me think much of the allied intelligence apparatus had been called into play, although some of the information he was relaying had been obtained by sending two officers into Madovic to pose as German tourists.

For roughly a year and a half, Ferenc said, the three monks had been appearing in town at noon on weekdays, moving in slow procession to the hospital, where they prayed over the bedridden. Through the centuries, it had been a rarity for monks to leave the monastery, and the change had been the subject of much initial local conversation. The abbot, in his casual dealings with some townspeople, had explained that the three had been displaced by the war and had arrived in Madovic seeking shelter and the opportunity to help heal the sick. Although the three monks were called to a different vocation than the regime of reclusive prayer and contemplation at the monastery, the abbot had granted them refuge indefinitely.

"I know Kajevic isn't going to town for prayer meetings," Goos said.

Ferenc nodded. The actual purpose of the visits, they believed, was to see a Serbian doctor, a radiologist. He relayed messages to and from Kajevic, who still regarded himself as the leader of a nation and remained in control of a large network of supporters. To NATO, the importance of the hospital visits was that they provided an ideal opportunity to bring down Kajevic outside the monastery walls.

"Zere are tactical problems," Captain Ferenc added. His grammar was perfect but his accent was strong. He explained that the two men who were accompanying Kajevic each day were not monks either, but rather bodyguards with automatic weapons concealed under their cassocks. I was intrigued by the technology that had allowed NATO to identify the concealed firearms from a distance, but even going back to my days as US Attorney metal-finding infrared scanners existed, although employing them on US soil for random searches of the civilian population was barred by the Fourth Amendment.

"In hospital, vee know," said Ferenc, "zere is one man, perhaps more, who vould fight for our subject's freedom."

An expectant silence fell over the room, which seemed to signal that it was the general's turn to speak again.

"In order to avoid a repetition of what happened in Doboj eleven years ago," she said, "we need a substantial force at the hospital. We continue to believe that one reason the subject has remained at the monastery is due to the vantage it affords, allowing them to detect any large-scale movement into town. We can infiltrate some soldiers appearing to be tourists with backpacks or guidebooks, but Madovic doesn't ordinarily see more than a few such visitors each week, so a large presence—say a tour bus, which we thought of originally—might prove alarming. Also, troops posing as tourists can hide only pistols. So in order to get a force of combat-ready soldiers into that town, we need to ask for your assistance."

"*Merde*," said Goos.

With the bad news delivered, the captain spoke again.

"Vee have been able to monitor communications. Zey are vatching you. Very helpful."

"For us or you?" Goos asked. No smile. He was prickly.

The general, however, grinned politely.

"Both actually. As we expected, the people we have overheard are not surprised that you now have protection, which they regard as an unfortunate consequence of their overrreaction on Tuesday. But they remain nervous that sooner or later you will correctly guess their true motivations. We take it from the chatter that they successfully encouraged the gentleman you had gone to Vo Selo to visit to leave the area."

"So we understand," I said.

"They hope you will be departing once you learn he is gone."

"Wish is my command," said Goos.

The general again smiled at Goos's venting.

"Here are our thoughts," she said. "We would like to use the situation they created on Tuesday night to ensnare them. Given what followed your last visit to Vo Selo and your witness's response to you, it would be understandable—especially to those who know little about your Court—if you returned to Vo Selo, accompanied, say, by a full squad in combat gear as a way to express your repugnance at this fellow's intimidation."

"And why won't Kajevic bash off as soon as they see NATO troops?" Goos asked.

General Moen nodded. "We have access to Bosnian Army uniforms. I would describe the arrangement as Don't Ask, Don't Tell. At any rate, these 'Bosnian' troops will be there to help you enter the premises and to ensure that your reluctant witness does not use the same measures as last time."

"But he's gone," I said.

"Exactly," said the general. "You will find the house empty. Just as you are about to leave, however, one of you will suffer a serious injury."

"What kind of injury?" asked Goos.

"Feigned of course. Although we must make it convincing. However, because of this mishap, you and your

military escort will rush to the nearest hospital—in
Madovic."

I got it, naturally.

"This injury in Vo Selo," continued the general, "will
take place just as the three monks have departed from
the hospital, around 13:30. Traveling at top speed, you
should be in Madovic in roughly ten minutes. The
monks' procession back to the monastery usually takes
half an hour, although it would be better to apprehend
them in the first fifteen minutes, when they are farther
away and less likely to receive any efforts at aid from the
mountaintop. Four 'tourists' will cut them off from the
rear. If all goes well, the subject can be extracted in a
matter of seconds.

"He will be taken back to The Hague, but I assume
you would rather travel independently, which you can do
on your own or with an escort, as you prefer."

Goos's face was still.

"Why can't one of the soldiers be the injured party?"

The intelligence officer answered. "He vould go to
military hospital."

Goos still had a snarling look. "They'll know, you
realize. Kajevic's people? They'll know it wasn't a coincidence we were there when he was bailed up."

"If you like," said General Moen, "you can proceed to
the hospital for medical treatment. We'll have someone
in place. Or we can have a medic on the scene bandage
you up as a smoke screen."

Goos was shaking his head, and I interrupted.

"General," I said, "we need to talk about this. I'm sure
you understand. And even if we choose to go along, we
probably need to inform our superiors."

"Please let me know. I'm sure we can help with that."

"And when would this take place?" I asked.

She stopped to consider how to deliver the next piece.

"Given the realities, the sooner the better. We are preparing for an operation tomorrow."

Again, no one spoke for some seconds.

"You must understand," she said, "how reluctant we are to ask the assistance of civilians in a matter of this nature, especially given your recent experiences. Unfortunately, you are essential."

Goos left the room without a word. Andersen and a soldier named Greer were at the front doors of the hotel to escort us to the car.

"Look, Goos," I said quietly, when we were in the backseat again, "I'm going to be asking myself only one thing: Do they really need us?"

He replied in a low growl, "You don't have to talk me into this, mate."

"I wasn't going to try." I bowed my head toward the two soldiers in the front seat, but Goos was unconcerned about speaking in front of them. "I just want to think it through."

"They already have," Goos answered. "It's as she said: They don't want to be using civilians for a military operation any more than we care to be used. But they need numbers to do this quickly and to keep anyone from getting killed."

He was surprising me, as usual.

"I still need to think," I answered.

"That you should, buddy," he said. "Because there's a lot that can come a gutser."

After another minute without words, Goos said, "You can skip this one, Boom. They only need one of us and I signed up for this sort of thing a long time ago."

To be precise, neither of us had really signed up. But he meant that when he took his oath in law enforcement he knew he was accepting a measure of physical risk. For lawyers, that was not in the job description. Early in my career as an Assistant US Attorney, I had, for kicks, gone along with the DEA to watch when they arrested Gaucho Hinjosa, a local drug kingpin. My boss, Stan Sennett, reamed me out afterward. 'You want a badge and a gun, then go apply to be a policeman. Would you let an agent give a closing argument? We each have our jobs and an obligation not to get in each other's way.'

Perhaps if Goos were better off physically, I might have been willing to send him on his own. But he didn't seem to be in condition to be falling down in a heap to play a part, or to do whatever else might be required to pass himself off as seriously injured.

I said again that I needed time to think.

"And no matter what," Goos said, "I wouldn't be telling the home office. You know what they say: Better to ask forgiveness than permission. If you need cover, then send Badu an e-mail saying you have an urgent matter."

I laughed out loud. Badu was infamous for never answering his e-mails. He generally responded only to Akemi.

Back at the Blue Lamp, I went immediately to my room and sat alone on the bed to commune with myself, but I soon realized that my decision had been made in January. Both of my sons were well on their way now. I had no life partner to worry about. Far more important, as I had discerned with a Zastava resting on my temple atop that water tank, I had come to The Hague out of a family obligation to subdue the toxic predators who became a cancer on civilization. I was scared utterly shit-less. But my life would not mean what I wanted it to if I didn't help bring justice to the millions in several nations murdered, tortured, raped, starved, and savagely misled by Laza Kajevic.

24.

Now in Person—June 10

I woke on Wednesday after sleeping better than I had anticipated. My feeling-state was a bit like the first morning of trial, when I employed a meditative effort to freeze away my exploding anxieties over all the things I couldn't control. As I dressed, the momentousness of what was at hand seemed to enhance my vision, as if I was seeing a more sharp-edged version of myself when I looked in the mirror. If you were very lucky, you experienced times like this, when what you did mattered to thousands more people than just you, and which, for that reason, you'd remember right to the end.

Goos had gotten himself buttoned together. He sported his usual subtle smile when I greeted him at the breakfast table. We ate quickly and for lack of anything else talked about the news that Obama was going to send five hundred Special Forces troops back to Iraq to fight ISIS.

At 10:00, Andersen and a new MP drove us to

Barupra. The empty basketball court outside the former base was a staging area for a training session intended to be largely fictitious, in clear sight of the road and whatever surveillance vehicles the Arkans would send by. Fourteen soldiers, all members of the NATO Response Force, a special ops unit, had been outfitted in the camo combat fatigues of the Armed Forces of Bosnia and Herzegovina. Seven were German, seven were Danish, twelve men and two women.

The commander was a German colonel, Lothar Ruehl. He was thickset and positive, with a ginger bottle-brush mustache, and greeted us with a quiet word of appreciation passed on from General Moen. The shoulder of his make-believe uniform bore a tan patch with a single star and a line, the insignia of a second lieutenant.

Goos and I, both dressed in jeans and running shoes, were outfitted with ballistic helmets and full body armor, which included a groin panel, half sleeves, and a collar. It was heavy but the Velcro strapping allowed more mobility than I expected.

With Ruehl in charge, we acted out the fake operation. I pretended to knock on Ferko's door, while the squad fanned out to surround the perimeter and then batter its way in. As anticipated, the two local cops guarding the gravesite today wandered up to see what we were doing, but maintained a polite distance. For their sake, a sergeant—who was actually a Danish first lieutenant—went through the charade of shouting out Colonel Ruehl's orders in Bosnian.

After that, we broke for lunch. The NATO field ration pack was French and, astonishingly, included a tin of chicken pâté and a small wheel of Brie, but I was in no state to eat. Ruehl sat with Goos and me and quietly explained the real plan, which, naturally, we couldn't practice around prying eyes. The colonel repeated the details several times, until we understood the deviations from the maneuvers we'd acted out.

At noon precisely, we started for Vo Selo. The military vehicles were all NATO issue, which apparently was not unusual in BiH. The convoy included a boxy blue armored Mercedes SUV, in which Goos and I rode behind Colonel Ruehl; a canopied 4x4 personnel truck; and an armored personnel carrier, which Goos proudly told me was a Belgian design called a BDX. It looked a little like a miniaturized tank, with four tires, camouflage paint on the plating, and a gun turret.

The hope, as General Moen suggested, was that Kajevic's thugs would take the size of this force as a measure of how thoroughly they'd scared the crap out of Goos and me last Tuesday night, which they'd probably view with mean-spirited glee. With any luck, they'd still be laughing when we ended up in the middle of Madovic.

Goos and I rode with our helmets in our laps, largely unspeaking due to the loud radio traffic as Colonel Ruehl exchanged encrypted communications with the troops here and the undercover elements who had spent the night in Madovic. The driver, who spoke Serbo-Croatian, also frequently issued phony orders in perfect Bosnian over the Army's normal channel.

During one of the few quiet moments, I turned to Goos.

"Okay?"

He nodded solidly. "First-class operation," he said.

"I'm wearing adult undergarments," I told him. "Just in case."

He smiled a little less than I'd hoped.

After the fifty-minute ride, we rolled through Vo Selo, where many of the Roma emerged from their tiny sad homes to watch. Up the hill, Ferko's little castle gave all signs of being abandoned. The place was utterly still. The laundry was no longer flapping on the lines on the balconies, and the shutters on the windows, as well as the front gate, were wide open. The dogs' blood remained in brown-black circles on the gravel of the courtyard.

Nonetheless, we went through the whole act. The Danish lieutenant handed an electric megaphone to Goos, who asked Ferko in Serbo-Croatian to come out. After a minute without response, it was my turn to yell. I had memorized two words in Romany, *Gavva na*, which I had been told meant 'Don't hide,' and I screamed them repeatedly while Goos stalked around, calling out more or less what he had last week when Ferko was actually here.

With our signal, the troop truck steamed between the gates and, without stopping, drove right through Ferko's double front doors, which popped off like a Lego toy. From behind, the soldiers in the 4x4 immediately deployed.

While Goos and I flattened ourselves against the stucco walls by the front doors, four soldiers in full combat array, including helmets and the same body armor we wore, ran to cover the rear. Four more fanned out behind us with their weapons pointed, while another foursome ran through the house, shouting in Bosnian as they cleared each room.

After about ten minutes, Colonel Ruehl, at the SUV, circled his hand, which was the sign that the monks had just appeared at the door of the hospital in Madovic, prepared to depart.

Now came my close-up. Behind the house, the Response Force members had covertly planted something like a cherry bomb, meant to sound like a blowout on the armored vehicle. At that bang, one of the soldiers protecting the courtyard was going to pretend to panic and fire his assault rifle toward the front door. One round would supposedly ricochet and strike me in the lower forearm. The uncomfortable part was that combat troops didn't use blanks. Colonel Ruehl assured me that the shooter was a first-class marksman, but there was still going to be live fire within a yard of me, and in the moment, as three bullets suddenly chewed into the stucco, pulverizing it into a fine white dust, I didn't need any acting lessons to scream as loud as I could and spin to the ground.

The lieutenant rushed to me and emptied a vial of blood from inside his sleeve all over my hand, which he then wrapped in his bandanna. The troops on the perimeter ran to the rear and pretended to discover that the explosion was a blowout, not armaments, with the mounting of a spare undertaken with the speedy precision of a pit crew. The soldier who'd supposedly shot me dashed up to the lieutenant and me, pleading for understanding. Playing the sergeant, the lieutenant screamed out orders, still in Bosnian, while Ruehl and Goos and my accidental assailant all grabbed me by the elbows and dragged me to the SUV.

The convoy was in motion immediately, but we were underway only a minute or two when a police car came tearing up. The cop clearly had been watching from someplace below us. The Bosnian speaking sergeant leaned out his window to explain I had been shot accidentally and had suffered an arterial bleed and would be dead shortly unless they got me to a surgeon. Lying across the backseat of the SUV, with my back against the rear passenger's-side door and my hand in the air, I did my part by moaning and crying out, "Jesus, Jesus, Jesus."

I don't know what the cop's orders were—he probably was unwitting and simply reporting to a superior officer—but he bought what he was told completely. He sprinted back to his vehicle and set off his Mars lights and the hee-haw siren to lead us at maximum speed as we tore through Vo Selo and reached the mountain road. The 4x4 was next, with us in the SUV right behind it. The armored vehicle, trailing because of the tire change, arrived at the rear of the speeding convoy. It was impressively nimble and stayed on our tail, even though we were going over 100 kilometers per hour on the straightaways.

In the SUV, Goos and I said very little. The radio screamed at intervals with at least six different voices. Two or three soldiers somewhere were continuing the Bosnian narration of events, but Ruehl now and then switched to a NATO frequency for brief traffic in English. I took it that Kajevic, code-named Vulture, and his bodyguards were so far unsuspecting and still walking in slow procession from the hospital toward the monastery.

We were no more than a minute outside of Madovic when an emergency call barked from the radio.

"Up high, they see us coming and don't like it," Ruehl explained. NATO was all over the radio traffic from the monastery. Whoever watched out for Kajevic had ordered the local police to do what they could to detain us.

As we spun through the last turn on the hillside, we

could see that the cop who'd been leading us had suddenly pulled over with his beacons still spinning. He was out of his car, one hand in a white glove raised to bring us to a halt. With the radio mike to his mouth, Ruehl ordered the convoy to proceed at top speed. The troop truck bore down on the cop and he sprang out of the way at the last second, literally diving off the road, while the vehicle hit his hat, which had gone flying. As we tore by, I could see the officer lying in a bush about six feet below the roadside, with a hand over his head to shelter him from the dust and flying gravel.

We were coming straight downhill and must have reached the turn to Madovic at about 60 miles per hour, skidding around it. One of the strengths of the plan to seize Kajevic on the way back to the monastery was, as General Moen explained, that Vulture could not get any visual directions from the top of the mountain. The infrared surveillance of the bodyguards, which had detected the AKs under the rassas, had shown no radios. But that missed the obvious.

As we flew into Madovic, just above the main square, the three monks were in sight. They had come to a halt a hundred yards in front of us on the narrow road that crossed through the town. One of the three had his cell phone to his ear. Looking back, I saw a black sedan throwing a fog of dust as it raced down from the monastery, while police sirens were suddenly echoing from at least two directions.

Halfway to the monks, our SUV stopped. The 4x4 braked another twenty yards ahead, while the armored vehicle surged to the front, bearing down on Kajevic. Goos and I were supposed to take shelter on the floor, but instead we knelt in the foot wells, our eyes just high enough to see through the windows on Goos's side. The SUV was parked laterally to block the road, and Ruehl and the driver jumped out to take up spots behind the vehicle, the young driver leveling his assault rifle across the hood. Crouched beside him, Ruehl raised the electric megaphone. In front of us the troops flowed out of the rear of the 4x4 in precision, each one rolling as he or she landed and quickly assuming a combat position on their bellies with their rifle sights trained on Kajevic and his bodyguards, only a few yards away. The four supposed tourists, with their hidden pistols now drawn, had crept near the monks to close off the rear.

Through the megaphone, Colonel Ruehl spoke in Serbo-Croatian, reading from a paper in his hand. Goos whispered the translation:

"Laza Kajevic, surrender at once. You are under arrest pursuant to the warrant of the United Nations and the International Criminal Tribunal for the Former Yugoslavia in The Hague." The words echoed off the small buildings of the square. A few residents, initially drawn by the commotion, scattered at the sight of the automatic rifles, retreating indoors. I could hear some of them screaming.

The monk with the cell phone lost his high round hat. He groped under the rassa and suddenly swung up his AK. It was no more than a quarter of the way to horizontal when two separate bursts of automatic fire struck him. The monk flew backward, almost as if hit by a grenade, spattering blood over Kajevic beside him. The other bodyguard raised both his hands and fell to his knees.

In the process of covering up from the gunfire, Kajevic had also dropped his clerical hat. Now he feigned incomprehension, as if he didn't understand the language or perhaps had been mistaken for someone else. But there was no doubt it was he. The infamous hairdo had been shorn to a moderate length and had gone white, or been dyed that color. The untamed beard was real and covered his whole face, including furry patches on his cheeks. He wore heavy black glasses and he was a great deal fatter than in his sleek days of vitriol and menace. But it was Kajevic, with the same wild eyes, and he was clever enough to know he was wanted alive. He ran.

He scampered wide around the armored BDX and dodged between the soldiers on their bellies, who, as he'd expected, hesitated to shoot. Nor could anybody get a hand on him, despite two of the troops' diving efforts. As Kajevic sprinted, he reached into the left pocket of his rassa and produced a Glock pistol, which he held beside his ear, dashing straight toward us in the SUV. Ruehl stood up and yelled to him to stop and Kajevic answered by shooting once at Colonel Ruehl, who screamed out. The driver sank instinctively beside the colonel to attend to him. I had the crazy thought that Kajevic was going to stop to shoot Goos and me, too, but he knew this was his one chance to escape and he was at top speed, clearly headed for the black car that was barreling down from the monastery.

As Kajevic galloped toward us, I ducked in the floor well behind the front seat. I felt Goos lean back against me. Scared stiff, I assumed he was seeking cover, but what he wanted was leverage. As Kajevic drew abreast, running for his life, Goos suddenly kicked open the back door on his side. It caught Kajevic full force. His face smashed against the window and he reeled backward and lost his footing.

The door recoiled but Goos caught it and sprang from the SUV.

I screamed "Goos!" but followed him out. He had thrown himself on top of Kajevic. With his right hand, Goos had Kajevic by the hair, beating his head against the road, while his left hand was on Kajevic's wrist, holding down the Glock. Kajevic gripped it by the stock, apparently intending to use it as a bludgeon. Frightened by the weapon, I had no choice but to stomp Kajevic's gun hand, and then grabbed the pistol by the barrel, forcing his wrist back until he released the sidearm. Just as it came free, half a dozen soldiers fell upon us, easing both Goos and me away. They wrestled Kajevic's hands behind him, zip-tied him, and then picked up the former president by his arms and legs as if he were trussed livestock. Holding him aloft, they ran Kajevic in a bundle up to the truck. The soldiers counted to three in German and tossed Laza Kajevic into the rear like a duffel bag. Several more troops clambered up beside him.

Almost simultaneously, the cop who'd led us from Vo Selo arrived with his siren blaring. He skidded to a stop near the SUV. He was a brave man, clearly angry now, and he sprinted from his car. In the middle of the street, he braced to shooting position with both hands on his pistol, screaming instructions as he confronted a squad of soldiers in battle gear. The armored vehicle had already spun around to pursue Kajevic. It rolled about thirty yards, until it was between the officer and the SUV, at which point the artillery piece on top of the BDX suddenly spat fire, riddling the police car with high-caliber ammunition. The auto jumped around like a bug. Its tires flattened while its windshield disappeared in a downpour of glass. The cop face-planted in the ground again.

A couple of hundred yards behind him, the black sedan, which I'd lost track of, was suddenly facing the BDX's gun. The car had screeched to a stop at the foot of the road up to the monastery, but once the police car was destroyed by gunfire, the sedan slammed into reverse and backed up the hill at top speed without ever turning around.

There was a second of quiet in which I rolled toward Goos, but from across the town square, another police car raced in, with its light bar and siren at work. The vehicle skidded up dust, coming to a halt between the 4x4 and the SUV. The fat cop and the wiry cop we'd first met eight days ago got out shouting, both with shotguns in hand. The fat one was red-faced, spitting as he screamed.

Once Kajevic had been taken, Goos and I had viewed the whirl of activity while sitting in the road beside the SUV, almost as if we were in stadium seats. Now I sprang up so the soldiers could see me, yelling out as I pointed, "Those are the ones who kidnapped us!" Goos immediately grabbed me by the belt and dragged me to the ground before either of the cops could make out my location, even though the wiry one had looked like he might have recognized my voice.

He wheeled toward the SUV with his shotgun raised, only to find the armored vehicle now rolling toward him, as the gun turret revolved in his direction. The fat one yelled something and the two cops scampered back into the police car, squealing the tires as the vehicle tore off through the square, its siren still bleating. One of the supposed backpackers ran behind it, snapping pictures of the license plate with his phone.

When I finally looked down, I was astonished that I still had Kajevic's Glock in my left hand. I laid it on the pavement beside Goos, who was now flat on his back. He was red with pain and grunting with each breath. He clearly had rebroken his ribs.

"Aren't you the fucking hero," I said.

"Pure instinct," he answered. "Good on you with the gun, Boom."

"It was my extensive training watching crime shows on TV," I said. "You already had him." That was true. When I bent the weapon back, Kajevic seemed to have already let go of it. It came away like the stem from a grape.

In the meantime, a medic had appeared, one of the ersatz backpackers. He treated the colonel, who had sustained a wound a bit like the one I had faked, a through-and-through gunshot to the forearm. He did not appear to be bleeding heavily, although from the way he held his arm with his good hand, I took it that the bullet had fractured something.

I sat in the street beside Goos until the medic made his way over. He checked Goos's vitals, then gave him an injection of some painkiller. After that, he had the presence of mind to remember the initial plan and pretended to examine, then bandage, my hand. I nearly objected, having completely forgotten why he was doing that. There was no point to that exercise anyway. Kajevic's people would always remember Goos as the guy who'd flattened the president and ended his last chance to escape.

The medic then returned to Ruehl and hopped into the backseat of the SUV, where the driver placed the colonel while Lothar gave us a gallant smile.

Just then, I noticed a low-flying combat helicopter appearing to hop over the mountains as it passed the monastery. The aircraft had a sharp snout that made it resemble a dragonfly, and at the sides were a patch of tiger stripes and two white missile launchers. It hovered over the square, taking its time to put down so that the residents, who'd begun to creep out again from the buildings, could once more retreat.

After the helicopter landed, the armored vehicle advanced to cover the far side of the square, while several soldiers who'd been guarding the 4x4 and Kajevic fanned out, pointing their weapons to establish a perimeter. The truck rolled forward until it was just outside the overhead circle of the chopper blades. I heard the lieutenant shout out "Clear!" and eight soldiers jumped from the rear, moving double time as they carried Laza Kajevic in the air between them. He was bound hand and foot, gagged and still squirming, with a bloody bandage in the middle of his face—Goos, it turned out, had broken his nose. His coarse brown rassa was gathered at his waist, revealing his blue jeans beneath. The soldiers tossed Kajevic through the open door of the chopper as unceremoniously as he'd gone into the truck. Four of them leapt in beside the prisoner.

Colonel Ruehl had remained in the SUV to command the final step of the operation, but the lieutenant took over then and settled in the front passenger's seat of the chopper. With that, the helicopter was aloft again, soon disappearing behind the mountains.

One old woman came out in its wake and threw both of her shoes in that direction, but I didn't know if her contempt was for Kajevic or us.

25.

Home to The Hague—June 10–13

Despite Goos's remonstrance, he was placed on a stretcher and driven in the 4x4 down to the hospital. The real Bosnian Army was now on the scene, securing the small emergency area so that Ruehl and Goos could be treated. The two patients lay side by side on adjoining stainless steel tables, with blood on a standard being drained into Ruehl's arm. As the Bosnians hustled in and out, including a growing number of civilian officials, there was an increasing hubbub of loud voices and a lot of tense rushing around. I was delighted when General Moen arrived and immediately took the situation in hand. She banished everyone but a few NATO troops and the medical staff from the ER. She explained that the lone radiologist had been detained for questioning, and thus there was a delay as they struggled to find a doctor to look at Ruehl's and Goos's X-rays. After more tape and Demerol, Goos was insisting on going home now.

A private ambulance was summoned, so Goos could lie flat on the trip to Tuzla airport. Andersen, now in uniform, drove me back to the Blue Lamp, where I packed up Goos's room and my own. When I returned to the airfield, a NATO plane had landed. Goos was already aboard on a paramedic's rolling stretcher, and in very good spirits, particularly when he didn't try to move.

We were flown a couple of hours to the NATO air base at Geilenkirchen in Germany near the Dutch border. From there, General Moen had arranged for another ambulance to take us the remaining two hours to The Hague.

When we arrived outside the little condo Goos had bought years ago, he insisted, with considerable effort, on getting to his feet. I understood this was for the benefit of his wife and his older daughter, who'd rushed down from Brussels. The wife, a thickish figure with wavy blonde hair, and the daughter, a mess of tattoos, took over to help him make a halting entry to the building. He took a single step at a time, resting a second before the next effort. His wife never stopped talking a mile a minute in Flemish.

It was midnight when I slipped into my flat. I was stunned to find Nara, in her black running tights, still awake. She was curled in an easy chair in the living room as she read under a shell lamp that provided the only light in the apartment. On sight, she instinctively moved toward me and brought her small hand to my face, where the bruise along my chin and jawline had turned green and yellow.

"Oh my," she said.

"Looks worse than it feels."

I dropped my bag and fell onto the sofa. Now that I

was back, I was suddenly so exhausted that it felt as if even my bones could give way.

"A business thing ended up getting physical," I explained. "Goos was with me. He's worse off. But he's mending."

For many reasons, starting with our continuing safety, Goos and I had agreed to keep our role in Kajevic's capture a vaulted secret. I changed the subject to Nara.

"New York wasn't good?"

"I was in town three days and saw Lewis for all of an hour. We had a furious argument in the hotel lobby and never spoke again while I was there." Her tone in relaying this was characteristically odd—she was surprisingly light, as if the entire trip had been a passing annoyance. On the whole, she seemed upbeat, and in a second I understood why. "Laza Kajevic was arrested today," she announced. "It must be huge news in Bosnia."

"All I heard about," I said.

"He has a private defense lawyer from Belgrade, Bojan Bozic, but I worked with Bozic on General Lojpur's case, and he always promised me I would be senior trial counsel with him if Laza was captured. He will file the papers tomorrow asking for a joint appointment." Her face was ripe with the cute childish light of unsuppressed pride. We both knew as lawyers that it was one of those cases you'd be going to dinner on for the rest of your life.

"Congratulations." I lifted my palm for a genial high five. But I found myself peering at her afterward. There was a lot about this woman I did not understand, because we tended not to talk much about work, given our roles laboring on opposite sides. Yet with Nara, because of her frequently unfiltered responses, I knew I could speak my mind.

"And it won't bother you to defend a monster like this? The camps and executions, the systematic rapes?" In a way, this was a completely galling question coming from me, given the big-league cruds who often had been my clients. Over the years, I had seemed to specialize in ego-drunk CEOs, men in all cases, who'd looted their companies with no more hesitation than they would have exhibited in picking up the loose change from their sock drawers, and who frequently exhibited a variety of loutish behavior toward women. I believed in the mantra that everyone deserved a defense, but I had resolved long ago that the defense didn't necessarily have to be provided by me. Mob clients, for example, were always on my personal Do Not Call list. The unprovoked and conscienceless violence on which their business was erected was too much for me.

"I don't mean to sound like some boor at a cocktail party," I said, "asking how you can stand up for such awful people. But Laza Kajevic is probably a finalist for the title of single worst human being alive."

She actually smiled for a second, before her black eyes drew down more seriously.

"Because I do not know," she said.

"Know what?"

"What I would do in wartime—when the world is all topsy and nothing is right. It is easy to be the prosecutor, Boom, and say after the fact, This is what you should have done. That is important to restore order. But to my mind, it also involves a good deal of pretending. I am not sure the rules would be very clear to me if it were kill or be killed."

I could have followed the lawyerly instinct and argued, especially about Kajevic, who'd created the very atmosphere she thought mitigated his crimes. But hers was a serious answer from a thoughtful person. And her reasons were higher-minded than mine had been for taking on many cases, which, generally speaking, were because crimes intrigued me a lot more than lease fore-closures, the money was great, and these engagements often allowed me to hang out with friends from the US Attorney's Office, who frequently were representing the codefendants.

"So you've signed on?"

She lifted the immense three-ring binders she'd been studying.

"I was out running when I got the call from Bozic," she said. "I went back to the office for the charging doc-ument and some background materials and haven't been out of this chair in five hours."

"And how will Lew take it," I asked, "when you tell him you aren't moving back to New York?"

Her face fell. "I do not look forward to that con-versation. It has been a week since we last spoke. Every argument is expected to end with my apology, and I will not do that this time."

I began Thursday at Nara's dentist, who put a temporary cap on my tooth, before I migrated to the Court. Goos and I had agreed to write a single joint report to all of our bosses about the last week and a half. I started the first draft.

In the middle of the afternoon my phone rang.

"Congratulations, Boom." It took me a second to place Merriwell's voice. "I wanted to thank you person-ally. I only wish I'd been there to see it. The world is a far better place today."

I told him I deserved no thanks, but assured him that the NATO troops he'd once commanded had performed impressively.

"The scuttlebutt says you and your colleague were both very brave," Merry told me.

As we'd asked, Goos and I had been omitted from the official account of the arrest provided to media outlets. But there was obviously another confidential version circulating for those in the know.

"Goos brought him down," I said. "Even though Kajevic had a pistol with which he'd shot Colonel Lothar. My act of heroism consisted in lying on the floor of an iron-plated vehicle—in full body armor."

"I was told you took his pistol."

"He was half-unconscious and his finger was nowhere near the trigger. And I was scared to death the whole time." The fact was that the more I thought about the moment I'd grabbed the Glock, the less clear it was in my memory. I remained largely astonished that I'd ever been in that position.

"That proves you're a reasonable man," Merry said. "He's a terrifying human being. Courage isn't the absence of fear, Boom. It's carrying on despite it. Hats off. The version I hear is that Kajevic was on his way to escaping when you guys cut him off."

Afterward, the soldiers had poured compliments on us. They had been frightened that Kajevic would reach the black sedan waiting to speed him back to the monastery. It was true that if Kajevic had actually gotten in that car with the monk who was driving, the aftermath might have been messier. But much as I admired Goos's quick thinking and his daring in taking on a man who'd already used his weapon, neither of us believed on reflection that there was much danger of Kajevic outrunning several men and women forty years younger than he was. As Goos said in the hours we'd spent on the plane, tirelessly recycling events that probably lasted less than a minute, the only person whose life Goos probably saved was Kajevic's, since he would have had to have been shot if he turned to fire at the troops pursuing him.

After more demurrers, I decided to take advantage of the situation and pointed out that now that Kajevic was in irons, there was less reason to withhold the intelligence reports from the effort to grab him in 2004.

Merry laughed and told me I still didn't understand the Department of Defense, but he didn't stay on the phone much longer.

When I came in Thursday night, Narawanda was dressed for our run, but she greeted me with her hands on her hips.

"Why didn't you tell me?"

"Tell you what?"

"That you guys were part of capturing Laza."

I explained that Goos and I deserved little credit and were eager to escape the blame from Kajevic's malevolent followers.

"As I hear it," she said, "you were the center of the whole operation."

I was troubled that word of our roles had already leached into civilian circles. At the ICC, the secret had held for the day, since Badu and Akemi felt it was critical to maintain a separation between our Court and the Yugoslav Tribunal. Nonetheless, there were too many people in the reporting chain for me not to have received some meaningful sideward glances and nods of recognition, even though nothing was offered out loud. I was on the verge of asking Nara, with a little irritation, how it was she'd learned about this, when I realized her source.

"You heard this from your client? He's arrived in The Hague?"

She shrugged to show she couldn't breach the wall of confidence.

"How's his nose?" I asked. I didn't even try not to smirk.

"Quite swollen. He seems more upset about that than being in jail. He is quite vain."

"I would never have guessed."

"But your role in this made for a very odd initial interview. I had to confess I knew you well, both of you. I wish I had had a chance to brief Bozic before your names came up."

I hadn't thought of that. From her perspective, I was subjecting her to some kind of conflict by keeping all this to myself. I apologized and asked how Kajevic had reacted to her disclosure. I was afraid it might cost her her role in the case, but she said Kajevic was unconcerned.

"He assumes everyone knows everyone else in The Hague. Bozic actually suggested a formal conflict waiver and Kajevic made light of that and actually scribbled something out himself. But he said to send you his respects and to tell you he would like to meet Goos and you face-to-face someday."

Nara, predictably, didn't seem to recognize the chilling import of the message. On the other hand, Kajevic's inflation of our role conformed to my impression of his grandiosity. He'd assumed he could outwit NATO forever, and would much rather think that he'd been rolled up accidentally by a couple of hapless nincompoops.

In the meantime, my conversation with Merriwell, and the unlikelihood that we'd ever get the intelligence file on the prior effort to arrest Kajevic, sparked a new idea.

"If Mr. Kajevic really wants to see Goos and me, we can interview him for our case. There are a lot of questions he could put to rest for us."

Nara responded by laughing in my face, albeit in an inoffensive way, with no scorn intended. It was the same thing I would have done if the roles were reversed.

"Bozic will never hear of it. Laza has trouble enough without talking his way into more. But I will pass the request on to both of them, so you can receive a formal no."

We went off for our run, but the skies opened unexpectedly, as they often do in The Hague, and we ended up at the Mauritshuis, The Hague's little treasure box of an art museum. The grand seventeenth-century house, built in the classical Dutch manner with a steep tiled roof and an ornamented yellow facade over the brick, is now home to some of the most famous paintings in the world, including Vermeer's *Girl with a Pearl Earring* and Carel Fabritius's *The Goldfinch*, which are coincidentally displayed in the same tiny room. We'd run past the site often, with Nara chiding me virtually every time about not having visited. With the downpour we'd decided this was the moment, inasmuch as the museum was open late Thursday nights.

I had forgotten Nara's design background and was impressed by her incisive responses to many of the pieces on display. There were paintings—a Rembrandt portrait of an old man or a Vermeer of a town scene by a waterfront—that moved me intensely with what they held of the sheer force of life. The tiny rooms of the original house had been preserved as show spaces, which lent a secret, intimate feeling to the entire experience, as Nara and I whispered to one another, pressed close in the crowd.

Once we'd circled through twice, returning to several mutual favorites, we retired to the café to wait out the rain, talking at length about the pictures. She had a lot to say about the genius of Rembrandt, who was centuries ahead in his understanding of what we actually see.

We departed at closing, walking along slowly through what had now settled to a delicate mist.

Nara sighed and said, "That was lovely." She looked up at me, tiny and ever-sincere, the rain shining on her cheeks. "Wasn't it?"

"It was," I answered.

We walked home with little more said.

On Friday morning, I found Nara standing over the coffee pot crying. I was astonished, since she ordinarily dealt with her troubles in a contained way and had been quite upbeat since I returned. She wasn't sobbing, but there was no mistaking her tears.

"Lew?" I asked.

"Everything," she answered. "My mother is on the way. She'll land at Schiphol tomorrow morning." It turned out that Nara's mother had a blood disorder, well under control, but one that nonetheless required periodic visits with a specialist in Amsterdam. She would see the doctor on Monday. "I realize I have to tell her about Lewis, but I have no idea what to say. I left messages for him today and yesterday, but there has been no response. Is that how a marriage ends? Without even answering the phone?"

I tried to comfort her. Lew was probably giving himself a break, I said. Many marriages resumed after a time-out.

She shook her head decisively. "There is little chance. The Kajevic case will keep me here for years, and I am quite happy to stay. Lewis will never accept that."

I could have pointed out that it was she, as much as Lew, who had made the critical decision, but she would probably not see it that way. There is surely no human relationship more complicated than marriage, and I knew better than to try to get inside Nara's.

Instead I asked where her mother would stay. I could see that in her anguish about having to confess the state of things with Lew to her mom, Narawanda hadn't considered that issue. Being Nara, she just told me the truth, without apology.

"Well, normally she stays here. But I suppose that will not work." She turned impish, a sideways thought suddenly lightening her mood, while, like a child, she used the back of her hand to smear away her tears. "It would be very cozy with Mum and you and your friend in your bed."

I did the chivalrous thing and said I'd go to a hotel for the weekend.

"You cannot. This is your home. Mum will be fine at Des Indes."

"No chance," I answered. I promised to tidy up tonight and be gone in the morning when they returned from the airport. After a little more Alphonse and Gaston, she accepted.

"This is so kind of you, Boom. I feel terrible tossing you out. Can I pay the hotel bill?"

"Never."

"Will you at least come for dinner tomorrow night? That would be a huge favor. Mum is a lot for me to handle alone."

I knew she meant it—Narawanda never employed devices—and I accepted. I paused on my way out of the kitchen with my coffee.

"And I'm no longer seeing my friend, as you call her. That's been kaput since the day I told you I was put out with her."

Nara reflected a second.

"I am sorry, truly. You seemed very smitten. I hope that odd scene here had nothing to do with it."

"Of course not."

Relieved, Nara smiled in her sly way. "I will never forget the sight of her, just as God made her, except that look-at-me hairdo."

The hairdo! I was always surprised by the way women saw each other.

"There was never any future," I said about Esma. "And the present, as I should have known, was much too complicated."

Nara seemed on the verge of saying more, but she stayed silent and I headed upstairs.

At work on Friday, I endured a round of meetings about how to proceed with our case. The pivotal question was whether we should even continue, since we now had to ascribe virtually no value to Ferko's potential testimony, even in the unlikely event he could be found. The conversations in the office were earnest and marked by a lot of worthwhile questions, but I was somewhat aggravated the discussions had to take place in layers—first with the division supervisor, then with Akemi added, and

finally Badu, too. Each time we all agreed that notwithstanding Ferko, the NATO records, especially the aerial
surveillance, left us with no alternative but to exhume the
Cave. The bodies were now the only likely source of additional evidence. And as Goos had recognized, having
embarrassed the United States on the front page of the
Times, we were obliged to confirm the crime. Over this
last point, Badu wound his head around sorrowfully and
said somewhat churlishly that the leak had been very ill-
considered.

The deliberations about the future of our investigation brought back a thought I'd been avoiding: I needed
to try again to contact Esma, in case she had an alternative way to reach Ferko. He was likely to have
worthwhile information, even though virtually nothing
he said could be taken at face value. For example, given
his true vocation he was likely to know how the stolen
trucks had ended up with Kajevic.

Having failed via all electronic means of communicating with Esma, I reverted to the old-fashioned method
and composed a lawyerly letter to her on Court sta-
tionery, saying that we had visited Ferko at his house
with surprising results, which I felt obliged to discuss
with her. The letter went out for overnight delivery,
addressed to her chambers in London as well as her temporary dwelling in New York.

When I was in college and law school at Easton and
brought home friends, as I'd done with Roger, I was
often torn by their reactions to my parents, whom my
buddies inevitably judged cultivated and intelligent. I
didn't mind that my friends admired my parents—I did,
too—but I was frustrated that they were unable to

recognize the emotional tightfistedness that made them so challenging for Marla and me.

Naturally, I saw the same process play out from the other side when Will and Pete brought their pals to our house, where, I could tell, Ellen and I appeared far less eccentric and annoying than the friends had been told to expect. It was another truism I'd adopted in middle age that parents and children always stood in a unique relationship to each other whose full effects were inevitably shuttered to everyone else.

Nonetheless, given Nara's agitation, I walked toward the apartment from Des Indes on Saturday expecting an awkward evening. It was a wet night, sometimes raining hard. I was in a slicker and hat, while the Dutch, as usual, were carrying on in defiance of the weather. As I strolled through the Plein, hundreds of the locals sat at the lines of outdoor picnic tables, drinking beer and huddled under the cafés' umbrellas. I realized how much I had come to admire the Dutch, with their happy communal air and their polite determination to ignore small obstacles to doing what they liked.

A block away from the apartment, I stopped in the local wine shop and bought a bottle of burgundy I knew Nara favored. Only when I offered it to her, as I was crossing the threshold, did I remember that alcohol was no way to make an impression on a Muslim woman.

"Oh, Jesus," I said, when I recognized my folly, and asked if I should hide the wine.

"Just leave it in the closet with your coat. I won't drink in front of her, but I promise, I'll have several glasses once she's asleep." Nara rolled her large eyes, then took me by the elbow to introduce me.

Annisa Darmadi proved to be bright and charming, and quick to laugh. Notwithstanding the dizzy spells that had brought her here to see her doctor, she appeared vital and healthy and, even at seventy, was a virtual look-alike of her daughter, with the same tidy form and dark round-faced handsomeness. Her hijab, which Nara said she wore more often these days, had been forsaken tonight, perhaps for her daughter's sake.

Mrs. Darmadi had insisted on cooking, as Nara had told me to expect, and she was occupied at the stove preparing several traditional Indonesian dishes. The ingredients were readily available in the Netherlands, with its large Indonesian population, and the mom couldn't understand why her daughter hadn't learned to take advantage of that. Having said as much, Mrs. Darmadi shooed Nara away whenever she even looked into the pots.

We sat down not long after I arrived. Mrs. Darmadi was a fabulous chef. There was a soup with coconut milk called *soto*, a salad with peanut sauce—*gado-gado*—and a ball of sweet rice surrounded by a pinwheel of grilled beef, whose name I never got. Over dinner, we talked mostly of Jakarta, about which I knew next to nothing, as Mrs. Darmadi brought her daughter up to date on local events. The most interesting thing to emerge in conversation was that Mrs. Darmadi, although considerably younger, was a distant cousin of Lolo Soetoro, the man who became Barack Obama's stepfather. She spoke of Lolo more approvingly than she did of Obama's mother, whom Mrs. Darmadi referred to, without elaboration, as "a hippie."

Throughout the evening, Nara kept following up her mother's remarks with explanations. This was ostensibly to augment the mom's middling English. Nara's amplifications about Indonesian culture were helpful, but very often she tried to temper her mother, who was clearly a woman of strong opinions.

"By 'hippie' she merely means unconventional," said Nara.

I smiled at her and then Mrs. Darmadi and said, "Nara, your mother and I understand each other perfectly," to which the mom responded with the same brief downstroke of her chin I had seen from her daughter a hundred times. Nara always described herself as 'sheltered.' But her mother was far more worldly than the homebound Muslim woman Nara portrayed, and I realized it was the mom's sharp judgments that had left her daughter feeling hemmed in.

I departed a few minutes before ten. When I opened the front door downstairs, I faced more rain and remembered that I'd left my slicker in the closet. I went back up, knocked several times, and finally used my key to let myself in, calling out "I'm back." They did not seem to hear me with the tap running and dishes clattering in the kitchen.

As I opened the closet, I overheard fragments of their conversation. During the evening, Mrs. Darmadi had occasionally addressed Nara in Javanese, which her daughter had answered either in English, for my benefit, or Dutch, when she didn't approve of what her mother was saying. But now the mom had succumbed and they were having a mild quarrel in Dutch. In six months, I had gotten to the point where I could understand more than half of what I heard, although it would be a long time before I dared to speak, since I was befuddled by the grammar. Nonetheless, the mom, as a non-native speaker, talked much more slowly than Nara and thus was easier to track.

The water was turned off for a moment, allowing me to clearly hear Nara's mother saying, "Nice." '*Aardig*' was the word she used, a mild compliment. "That is not what troubles me. It is highly inappropriate for you to be living with a man who is not your husband, let alone one with whom you are so obviously fascinated. You turn to him like a flower to the sun. No wonder you are having difficulties in your marriage."

"Mother!" Narawanda answered. "Mr. Ten Boom has nothing to do with the problems between Lewis and me. We have been isolated from one another for years."

The mother answered as mothers do, "*Ja, ja,*" agreeing but not agreeing at all.

I padded out like a burglar, willing myself to pretend I had heard none of that. It was only when I got back to the front door of the building that I realized I'd forgotten the slicker again. I turned up my collar and headed into the rain.

26.

New Witness—June 15–16

On Monday, we began the preliminaries required before exhuming the Cave, a process in which I again found the diplomats and bureaucrats crazy-making. Consent, they claimed, was required not only of several departments in the fractured Bosnian government, but also from the mine owners, the Rejka company, who had abandoned the site more than two decades ago and who had gone entirely unmentioned in the months we'd been crawling all over the place. As a result, I had to undertake the equivalent of a title search in Bosnia. Beyond all that, the president's office was understandably concerned about the expense of the operation, which was what had held us back from the beginning. I phoned Attila to see if she could help us find a local real estate lawyer and a deal on earth moving equipment.

"I've been meaning to call," she said. "You must be feeling pretty fucking special."

In the rush of everything else, I had not given much thought to the fact that we hadn't heard from one of the world's leading busybodies, who, in this case, could actually claim some role in these news-making events. Now she wanted every detail.

Like everybody else, Attila was impressed about Goos's courage in hindering Kajevic's escape.

"Goos keeps saying he was stupid," I told her, "because a sixty-year-old man in a dress was never going to outrun a bunch of twentysomethings. But he was really brave, Attila. I was so panicked I'd have let him dash right by."

"For twenty years in the service," said Attila, "it made my ass ache worse than hemorrhoids that I couldn't get into combat. If the jokers in the five-sided puzzle palace"—she meant the Pentagon—"ever stopped acting like having a puss was like missing an arm, I'da let Merry send me to OCS, cause I always figured I'd make a great fuckin battlefield commander. But you know, I wonder. Fact is, once the shootin starts, it's all fubar. Your brain just gets scrambled. Big props to Goos."

The longer the period since we'd returned from Bosnia, and the more mired I again became in what I thought of as ordinary life, the odder the kidnapping and the capture of Kajevic seemed, and the less connected to my natural reality. There were still instants, especially sitting alone at my desk in the office, when my heart felt like it was veering into impromptu A-fib, and I realized I was remembering the barrel of the AK at my temple. But overall, as the events receded, it was like having been on a passenger flight when there's a terrible landing—a tire blows and the plane skids off the runway and the film of your life goes by in triple speed. For a while afterward, it's hard even to look at an airliner in the sky. You recognize how much trust you're putting in everyone, the mechanics, the pilots, even Bernoulli, who discovered the principle that keeps aircraft aloft. You keep thinking about how close you came. And then, slowly, you accept the obvious: It didn't happen. You're here. You've gone on. And you head back to the airport for your next flight.

Eventually, I asked Attila about the lawyer, and then bulldozers and steam shovels.

"What for?" Attila asked.

I explained we were going to exhume the Cave.

"What kind of bullshit is that?" said Attila. "I thought you were just pretending about that so the NATO guys had a cover. Where you going with this case without Ferko?"

I didn't respond directly. Attila still had no clue what the NATO records showed, but she seemed to sense there was something important she didn't know. She asked several pointed questions about other evidence we'd gathered and I demurred, telling her that the Court's rules of investigative confidentiality constrained me, just as she'd been silenced by the need to respect the military classification of information. She sounded unsatisfied by that reply.

As for earth-moving equipment, when the troops left Bosnia, Attila had bought up everything CoroDyn had brought there to build camps and repair roads. Like many of her other business moves, it had worked out brilliantly. She'd paid only a bit more than it would have cost CoroDyn to transport the machinery elsewhere, and by her own words, she'd "made a big fat fucking fortune" leasing the equipment for the constant civilian reconstruction projects. She promised us a "friends and family price" in the quote she'd e-mail by nightfall.

Since we'd returned from Bosnia, I'd finally had the chance to carefully examine the records Attila had brought us of the truck deployments eleven years ago on the night the Chetniks appeared at Barupra. It was just as she'd claimed—there were no large contingents of vehicles checked out of either the operational or logistical pool, beyond those listed for garbage runs and other routine hauling around the base. But the documents were incomplete.

"There's nothing from the fuel depot, Attila. Nothing from the mechanics, nothing from parts supply."

"Really?" she asked. "Fuck, I didn't even look that close. I'll call Virginia and kick those cementheads in the ass. Every day, Boom, America gets to be more like Italy." She promised to have the records when we arrived in Bosnia to exhume the Cave.

I thought about Attila after I put down the phone. She was the life of the party, so to speak, wherever she went, and the logistical genius who figured out how to meet everyone's needs. But she must have been a teeming mess of justifiable resentments when she was by herself. Like a lot of well-to-do people, she'd undoubtedly learned that money, nice as it was, didn't heal the fundamental injuries of life, of which she'd endured many. Despite people like Merriwell and Attila's father, who'd tried to convince her to join the officer corps, she'd refused because, she said, there really was no place there for someone who was, in her powerfully apt and prejudiced term, 'queer.' She reveled in queerness and hated it all the same, since it had denied her, in instances like this, her proper destiny. Attila never asked anybody to feel sorry for her. But I did in the moment, experiencing some of the unrooted feelings that must have swamped her so often, especially when she was alone.

When I returned to the apartment after work, Nara was dressed for our run. Her mother, she said, had gotten a fine report from the doctor in Amsterdam.

"But I need to talk to you about something quite important," she said. She looked grave.

I prepared myself, realizing her mother had persuaded her I should move. I had already started looking at ads and stopping at real estate agents' windows to see what was posted, but I'd hoped to stay put until after we had exhumed the Cave, when I'd have a clearer idea of my future in The Hague. Nonetheless, I resolved to accept her decision with grace.

Instead, she said, "Laza wants to talk to you."

I was a second. "Kajevic?"

"I must tell you the truth. Bozic has warned him several times not to do it. And I have repeated that and challenged Laza to explain why this serves his interests at all. And I will keep trying to change his mind. But so far he insists. He is rather strong-willed."

"I imagine."

"Even so, Bojan wants full immunity from the ICC and an ironclad confidentiality agreement, so that nothing Laza says can be used against him in any court. Bozic will be here tomorrow for a hearing and wants to discuss this with you."

Those terms—exactly what I would have demanded as defense lawyer—did not figure to be challenging, especially since Bozic had all the negotiating power. I would need permission from Badu and Akemi, but they were likely to agree.

I wanted to tell Goos about this development before anyone else. He was spending the week at home, still convalescing, but I headed to his condo on Tuesday morning. His wife remained here. Fien was naturally warm and lively and kissed me on both cheeks when I arrived, which I took as a sign that Goos had spoken well of me. But we could not say much to one another since her English was every bit as poor as my Flemish. The apartment was darker than I expected and crowded, full of family photos and figurines and too much heavy walnut furniture. It was often a shock to see the dwelling space of the people you worked with, since it was frequently a venue for attitudes they would never display on the job. My guess was that Goos was comfortable here because it resembled the way Fien had decorated their house just outside Brussels and that she'd initially set her hand to this place, too. But all that implied a level of dependence between them that he seldom acknowledged with a beer in his hand.

Goos was still flat on his back, but his color was excellent. He insisted on taking a chair for our conversation, although he accepted my help getting there.

"You might be better off lying down for this," I said. "We have a chance to interview Laza Kajevic." I outlined the few details I had.

"I'll be stuffed," he said. "Stuffed. What's in this for Kajevic, Boom?"

I'd only started trying to figure that out.

"The truth, Goos, is that he'll be in prison until he dies. He can do whatever the hell he likes." That, of course, included lying his ass off when we spoke to him, for whatever malicious fun he'd get from it. We'd have to be wary.

Nonetheless, Goos smiled at me with a breadth I'd seldom seen outside the barroom.

"We are having some times with this case, mate, aren't we?"

Late Tuesday, I journeyed across town to meet personally with Bojan Bozic, who was in The Hague from Belgrade for a short hearing in Kajevic's case. We'd all agreed that Nara would make introductions and thereafter step out of the negotiations over the ground rules for the interview.

The Yugoslav Tribunal had a far plainer home than the ICC, at a site near the World Forum, where the UN flag waved outside the court. The interior resembled an old high school, and the quarters for the defense lawyers, about which Nara occasionally grumbled, were uninviting—a couple of large linoleum-floored rooms with a few desks and bulletin boards and three or four aged computers, the kind of space where you might expect to find the teachers' aides eating lunch.

It turned out, when I arrived, that Nara and Bozic had been held late in court, completing the examination of a witness who would be finishing his prison term shortly and might thereafter be unavailable. The man's testimony related to a point of jurisdiction on Kajevic's case, although only a few counts among the hundreds lodged against him. Another of the staff defense counsel showed my ICC credentials to the security person at the courtroom door, and I was permitted to take a seat in the spectators' section, behind a glass wall, while I waited for the hearing to conclude.

Although the Yugoslav Tribunal was very much the mother of the ICC, the ICTY had been established as a temporary court, and even twenty years later the courtrooms were far smaller and less grand than ours. The floor plan with the lawyers' desks and the judicial and registrars' benches was identical, with the same outcropping of black computer monitors at every seat, but the space, in what appeared to be a converted classroom, was far more confined. Here the judges' sleeves were trimmed in crimson, but Nara, who was cross-examining the witness, was in the same black robe and white lace bib we wore across town. Bozic and Kajevic, in a suit, sat at the defense table with their backs to me, while three prosecutors were making notes at another arced desk a few feet away.

I hadn't thought much about the fact that Narawanda had risen to the role of co-counsel in a huge case and must have been reasonably good in court. The woman I knew, odd and a little bit timid, did not seem to have the makings of a stereotypical trial lawyer, but in some ways neither did I, often accused of bringing a somewhat taciturn outward manner to court. The truth is that every effective trial attorney develops a style of her own, just like good painters and singers and pitchers, one that often involves capitalizing on idiosyncrasies. Nara's manner was to confront the witness in her own blankly earnest way, a sort of law-time Columbo routine in which her pose was to keep putting questions, not because the witness was lying, but due rather to her being foreign and dense. It was revealing to me to see her like this, because the laser light of a cleverness she otherwise kept to herself peeked out so clearly here in the courtroom.

The issue, so far as I could discern, was that Kajevic

had not been in the former Yugoslavia on the dates he was alleged to have committed the crimes charged in these four counts. In the US this was called an alibi and became an issue of fact at trial, but at the ICTY it was the subject of a preliminary motion contesting the court's power to try Kajevic on these specific charges. Apparently Nara and Bozic had come forward with hotel receipts and other records showing Kajevic was actually in Paris at the time of the alleged offense, but the prosecution had chosen to present the witness rather than drop the counts. It was instantly apparent that the prosecutors were so incensed about Kajevic's evildoing and his years on the run that they were unwilling to concede anything to him or his lawyers. I knew that frame of mind and had learned the hard way that it was toxic. Good defense counsel would only add to the prosecutors' frustrations at trial, goading them into angry blunders.

The man at the witness desk was a former colonel in the Bosnian Serb Army who had apparently lessened his punishment by blaming Kajevic for everything. He had the rumpled look that many of the former soldiers seemed to try to affect, sitting at the witness table in an ill-fitting suit of a strange shade of powder blue, unshaved, his tie askew. His demeanor—uncomfortably reminiscent of Ferko's—was of a simple man too feckless to do other than follow orders.

"You say you went to Banja Luka to see my client?" Nara took a moment in which she blinked at the colonel several times with no other expression.

"That is true."

"Did you ever leave the former Yugoslavia in 1992 or 1993?"

"I was an officer and we were in combat."

"You are saying no?"

"No."

"You were never in Paris in those years?"

"It was war. We were not taking Parisian vacations."

"And do you recall, Colonel, where you started when you traveled to see my client?"

"Not really, no."

"Were you driven there?"

"Yes, of course."

"And how many hours did it take?"

"I don't really know."

"Two? Ten?"

"Two perhaps, three."

"And on that date, Colonel, do you remember where the regiment you commanded was stationed?"

"Not offhand."

"You say you were in combat. Do you recall the last encounter your troops had been in?"

"We fought the Bosniaks. It must have been near Sarajevo."

"And so you went from Sarajevo to Banja Luka in wartime in two to three hours? That would be impossible now, would it not?"

"I didn't say it took only two to three hours."

"I'm sorry, I thought you said that."

"You said that."

"I apologize. But from Sarajevo to Banja Luka, during the time of fighting, that would be a journey that could take most of a day, wouldn't it?"

"Yes, it could."

"So in order to speak to President Kajevic, you would have been gone from your troops for two days at least?"

"But perhaps I was not in Sarajevo."

"I see. And I forget. Do you recall where you had been when you started out?"

"Not really. It was more than twenty years ago. How am I supposed to recall anything?"

All of this took place, as in our court, with the elaborate process of translation making it feel as if everybody was trying to run with their shoes glued in place. But despite that, with just a few questions, Nara had pulverized the colonel. The only thing he really knew was that by blaming Kajevic he could get out of prison.

They were done shortly. Nara introduced me to Bozic outside their robing room and I congratulated both of them. The Court had taken the matter under advisement, but it was clear they were going to prevail on their motion. Nara giggled like a girl when I gave her the praise she deserved for her questioning.

"Yes, yes," said Bozic, "a brilliant cross-examination." He was tubby and no more than five foot three. Despite that and being over seventy, he was quite handsome, with high color and a full head of white hair and an appealing energetic manner. He had become the go-to lawyer for all the high-ranking Serbs who'd been arrested, and he'd won acquittals for three of them. Born in Milwaukee, his American English was entirely without accent. "Four counts gone," he said. "Only 332 remaining."

Because the hearing had taken longer than expected, Bozic was now late for his plane and asked me to walk with him to the door. Nara, as promised, left us to our discussions.

"Listen," said Bozic, "my client believes he is a superhero. He has no appreciation of risk. At the end of all of this, he expects to put on his cape and fly out of prison.

An insanity defense is called for, but it goes without saying, he would fire me on the spot."

I nodded. I'd been there. We talked about the terms for Kajevic's testimony.

As a matter of character, Laza Kajevic seemed to me extremely unlikely to admit authorizing the massacre of four hundred Roma at Barupra. Nonetheless, even that remote possibility had provoked some searching conversations at the ICC in the last several hours: Was it worth it, in a case where we had no reliable witness, to make promises of immunity to the arch criminal so that we could get evidence that would lead us to others who were also responsible? It was a question every prosecutor faced from time to time, and it was usually a very tough call. Yet since Kajevic's conviction in this building, and his lifelong imprisonment, were a certainty, I was in favor.

In the event, it proved to have been a purely theoretical debate. Bozic was the kind of lawyer other lawyers loved, too busy and confident to bother with bullshit. While he was under no obligation to answer, he laughed out loud and wound his head in disbelief when I asked if Kajevic would take responsibility for Barupra. Given that, the rest of our negotiation took only minutes. The ICC by statute promised all witnesses, not just Kajevic, immunity from use anywhere of their statements against them. Bozic's remaining concerns could be addressed by agreeing that the interview would be deemed an investigative matter covered by the Court's rules of absolute confidentiality, meaning our meeting with Kajevic would remain forever secret. Having gotten everything he could want, Bozic was happy with the arrangement.

"Write it down, send it to me," he said. He was

returning to The Hague next week to confer with General Lojpur, whose case was now pending decision. If we could complete the paperwork, the Kajevic interview would take place then.

27.

Emira—June 17–19

On Wednesday, when I reached my office, the overnight envelope I'd sent to Esma at her chambers in London was lying on my desk with a notice that the addressee was unknown. I picked it up, checked the spelling and the street name, then wondered if there was any chance that Esma hadn't answered my other messages because those communications also hadn't reached her.

I went online to the sleek website for Esma's chambers at Bank Street and found no listing for her. I was stumped for a second, then concluded she must have changed her business arrangements, like successful American lawyers, who these days sometimes declare themselves free agents, akin to athletes who offer their services to the highest bidder. If she'd moved chambers, her cell phone and e-mail might have gotten screwed up in the process, accounting for her silence.

I called the receptionist at Bank Street next, but she

told me politely that she had "no information" on Esma Czarni, which is pretty much the tactic US firms utilize as an obstacle to clients who want to follow their attorney to the new workplace. So I called George Landruff, the silk—that is, senior barrister—whom Esma and I both knew at Bank Street and had spoken about for a second when we first met.

George had never mastered what parents with young children refer to as an 'inside voice.' He spoke at all times at the stentorian volume fitting for the centuries-old acoustics in the courtrooms of London. From the first blast of "Hallooooo," I kept the phone two inches from my ear.

"George!" When talking to him, my inevitable reaction was to shout, too. I reintroduced myself, but he recalled me at once. We had enjoyed a couple of dinners, one in London, one in New York, during meetings of an international trial lawyers society we'd both been honored to join. George had the kind of understated wit that escaped, like a pleasing scent, through the ventilation of his very proper British upper-class manner, offering the assurance that he was neither a stuffed shirt nor a buffoon.

"George, I am trying to find a colleague of yours—perhaps a former colleague—who kept chambers at Bank Street."

"Who might that be?"

When I told him, the phone gathered static and he finally asked me to repeat myself.

"Malc or female?" asked George.

He took one more second to think and said, "Very sorry, Boom, but can't say I recall her."

"George, she knows you. We've talked about you."

"Did you now?"

He repeated Esma's name again, then asked, "Do you mean Emira Zandi?"

I spelled her first name. "Roma heritage."

"Describe her."

"Mid-forties. Very handsome. With what other women apparently would describe as a look-at-me hairdo."

"Good man, I believe you're speaking about Emira Zandi. Read law at Caius College?"

"Yes."

"That's Emira! And what did you say about her background?"

"She's Roma."

"Gypsy? No, no. This lady is Persian."

"Persian?"

"Iranian exile family. But she hasn't been around here in more than a decade. Married an Iranian billionaire thirty years her senior and moved with him to Manhattan. Fine barrister she was, but I can't pretend, Boom, there wasn't some relief when she departed. There always seemed to be several gents after her and a lot of hissing and scratching as a result. Actually had the first fistfight I can recall in the corridors here between two fellows who each believed they were her one and only."

"And what was the name of the man she married?"

"Ah, all the tough questions. Not sure I recall. It's that metal plate they seem to have put in my head as I've grown older, Boom. I can ask around, though. Wait!" he screamed then. "His first name sounded a little like, Who's that. Hoosmeth? A bit like that. Hoosit Jalanbani. Owns a few skyscrapers in Manhattan."

I asked George to take a guess at the spelling. Something was scratching at me as I looked at what I wrote on the pad. After a few more words with George, and a promise to get together next time I passed through London, I hung up and continued staring at the paper. Then I recalled. I'd visited Esma in the residential apartment at the Carlyle of a woman she called 'Madame Jahanbani.'

When I first met Esma, I'd found no photos of her on the net, although she had a significant entry in Wikipedia, focusing on her role with the European Roma Alliance. I took it that she was like many people who are camera shy, because no photo ever captures what they see in the mirror. Attila had wanted to have a picture taken of the three of us while we were eating at that streamside restaurant after our visit to Lijce, and Esma had refused, saying it would take too much time to get her hair right.

But Emira Zandi Jahanbani was far less reticent. There were dozens of images of her, posing most often in low-cut evening gowns at fund-raisers and looking—to be a wise guy—like a billion dollars. There might have been a stylist involved: dusky eye makeup, torrential hair, face tilted to the most availing angle. Yet it was Esma, smiling toward the camera, quite often with that sealed smile full of mystical allure.

I had run without Nara on Monday and Tuesday—it was starting to be beautiful many days—but on Wednesday she wandered in as I was about to go out the door. She was completely abstracted, although when I asked if she wanted to go "for a trot," she agreed that fresh air might do her good. She dressed quickly but had virtually nothing to say as we jogged together for almost an hour. I was still far from a complete match for her as a running partner, and I often encouraged her to double-time the last mile without me, which was convenient inasmuch as it allowed her to grab a table at the fish place.

Today, she shook off the suggestion when I told her, at the usual place, that she was at liberty to canter ahead. I had thought at first it was simply our current role as opposing attorneys that had silenced her, but now I was baffled. When we started out at the apartment, she'd mumbled about going back to work this evening, saying she'd gotten nothing done during the day. Now she had no will for that. We stopped for a quick dinner at the usual place, and she had two beers before the food arrived.

I asked if her mother was okay, which she was, safely back in Jakarta.

"Lewis called me," she said finally. "While I was at work. I expect he thought I wouldn't be able to pick up."

"And?"

She played with her utensils on the steel table for a second.

"I asked him if he was seeing someone else. I was surprised I had the courage. But I have been wondering for a while."

I'd been thinking the same thing, but had kept that idea to myself.

"He gave me no answer," she said. "He said he wanted to talk about our future. And I said, 'You do not regard it as relevant to our future, if you are involved with someone there?' He said he was not 'involved,' but I knew that was semantics. When I asked him again to just say yes or no, he accused *me* of avoiding the subject. I couldn't stand it. He always has to find a way to be superior. I finally told him about Kajevic, that I could not give up a case of this importance, and said I hoped he would come home. And he answered, 'Well, that pretty much does it, doesn't it?' And hung up on *me*." She laughed, trying to find amusement as she continued to play with her fork. "Should I be crying?"

"Even if it's for the best," I said, "the end of a marriage is nothing to exult over."

"I've been thinking about hiring a detective in New York."

I made a face. I didn't know a thing about Dutch divorce law, but I was fairly sure that would be unnecessary.

"No," she answered. "It's not because I doubt that he is involved with someone. I am curious about *her*."

"To what end?" I asked.

Nara's eyes, which always seemed larger and deeper without her glasses, darted up to meet mine briefly.

"I want to know if she's like me at all," she said. That line was enough to make her well up. I watched in silence and then briefly touched her hand.

"I knew," she said.

I nodded.

"But it's still humiliating," she said.

"The exit ramps from marriages are pretty much lined with other bodies. It makes the abstract real, I guess."

"And it is *so* infuriating, too. He's running around and I have been doing *everything* to behave properly." She'd had her third beer. Her black eyes again lit on me, suddenly large with alarm, then flitted about in evident confusion. She rose abruptly and walked a good twenty feet from the table, standing with her back to me. I motioned to the busboy so he wouldn't clear our plates, then approached her. I touched Nara's shoulder, still damp from the run, but she shirked my hand in exasperation.

"I'm being an idiot," she said. She was crying again and trying to contain herself. She looked at me, attempted a smile, then crushed a hand to the center of her face. "Do you mind if I walk home alone?"

I should have spent Thursday organizing for our interview of Kajevic and speaking to the lawyer Attila had recommended in Tuzla, but there was just one thing on my mind: Esma. Twenty-four hours had only deepened my incredulity.

I searched 'Jahanbani New York City,' which brought up several hits, the most recent a small news item about the divorce of Hooshman Jahanbani from his wife, Emira. With that hint, I used the online records of the New York Supreme Court—which, confusingly, is what the trial-level court is called in New York State—to read through the ream of pleadings and briefs in the case, now eight years old.

Mr. Jahanbani, who had fled Tehran when the Shah fell, owned commercial real estate all over Manhattan. He had been married for close to fifteen years to his second wife, who was thirty-two years his junior, and whom he had originally met because Hooshman was close friends with her father, another Persian expatriate, who was in the oil business.

According to the complaint in the divorce case, Mr. Jahanbani was alleging abandonment, in that Emira had purportedly been absent from the marital home for a decade. She had—probably unwisely—countered with charges of infidelity, alleging her husband sought a divorce only in order to marry a woman from his office who was not yet thirty years old. In response, he had produced evidence of his wife's frequent affairs, involving several prominent New Yorkers—both male and female—the romances in a couple of cases apparently overlapping. The many trial sessions had apparently had their moments of drama. Emira had been found in contempt a couple of years ago for responding to one of her husband's insults—in Farsi—by smashing him over his bald head with a folding umbrella, drawing blood. From my research it appeared the case was still nowhere near conclusion.

All of this was stunning, but also somewhat comical, even if part of the joke was at my expense. Nevertheless, I was willing to entertain the thought that Emira might have regarded an alias as a logical step, given the fractiousness of everything surrounding her marriage. Yet my sense of alarm became far sharper when I moved on to searches about the European Roma Alliance. There were organizations with similar names—but that entity simply didn't seem to exist. The few entries that appeared online were all in conjunction with Esma, who was always referred to as the group's founder. At last, I phoned what online sources described as the leading Roma advocacy organization, which was based in Paris. I was passed around to several desks, but absolutely no one had heard of Esma's outfit. The European Roma Alliance pretty clearly was another piece of her fictionalized identity.

I paced around my office. I had cut my emotional connection to Esma fairly quickly. Even recognizing that our physical relationship would always give her a special place in my memory, I had processed in depth that she was no one to rely on. But this. My entire professional life as a lawyer had amounted to extended on-the-job training in making out lies. But Esma's sexual power had short-circuited my detection systems.

I had learned a dozen years ago that living two lives was neither as unusual as people might think nor as difficult to bring off. I had represented a prominent corporate lawyer, Bill Ross, who for years had left client meetings in order to trade stock in the companies whose mergers he was arranging. His brokerage account was in the name he'd been born with, Boleslaw Rozwadowski, and utilized the Social Security number Boleslaw had been issued before becoming Bill. Knowledgeable and wily, my client had been smart enough to deal in small lots so as not to attract the attention of the SEC. Infuriating as the crime was, I was more intrigued by Bill's use of the proceeds, which the prosecutors had traced. Bill's trading profits didn't go for hookers or drugs or gambling, the standard motives for many white-collar crimes. Instead, Bill sent the money to support a family he had in Poland, and whom he visited once a year. His Polish wife, a girl he'd first impregnated while they were students in gymnasium, still thought he was a house painter in the US. Despite that, and Bill's spouse and two kids in Kindle County, the Polish wife had no trouble welcoming him back when he finished the three-year prison sentence I negotiated for him.

Observing Bill, I'd realized that the principal requirement in maintaining two identities is chutzpah, and the ancillary ability to keep your lies straight. It was shocking to all of us who knew Bill, but not because the mechanics were particularly intricate. The surprise was much more because maintaining two lives is at odds with the struggle most of us endure to find one true self.

Yet it didn't take more than about ninety minutes' research to figure out how Esma had actually pulled this off. Her background—the caravan, the abusive father,

Boris with his stiff dick—appeared to have been lifted whole from an autobiography called *Gypsy Girl* by Aishe Shopati, which had been published about a decade ago to nice reviews on both sides of the Atlantic. There was an online language course, Romaninet, from which she might have mastered the basics of Romany—and a person of her wealth could easily have hired a tutor anyway. Changing the name on her existing British passport took no more preparation than filing a form called a 'deed poll' for the cost of £36 at the Royal Courts of Justice, which then would have allowed her to get credit cards, bank accounts, and a national ID in Esma's name. By exercising some care about being photographed, there was little risk that the world of a Manhattan billionairess would ever collide with that of a Roma activist on the Continent.

The mechanics of Esma's lie were nowhere near as confounding as trying to suss out how far it went. Pondering all her brazen falsehoods on top of Ferko's, I had to confront a sickening suspicion: The Barupra massacre was simply another invention to glamorize the life of 'Esma Czarni.'

Friday evening, Goos and his wife invited me for dinner. When he called with the offer, he claimed it was all Fien's idea, even though he had tried to convince her I wasn't entitled to yet another free meal.

His condition was much improved. He said he felt fully on track to return to work Monday.

We had a lot to discuss. Complementarity had informed me that the various Bosnian parties had consented to exhuming the Cave, but the president and the registrar were still asking if there was any way to reduce the cost.

"No one even cracked a smile, Goos, when I told them it was a bare-bones budget."

I knew I'd scored from the speed with which he grabbed his ribs.

We spent some time figuring out if there were costs we could reduce. There was virtually no DNA database on any of the people who had lived in Barupra, so we agreed to dispense with the team of techs to do DNA sampling on-site. Instead, we could preserve the remains until we figured out how to identify the bones. That, however, was no small point, since the skeletons wouldn't be worth much in court unless we could prove they were those of the Roma residents of Barupra.

I had passed many idle moments reviewing in my head every conversation I'd had with Esma, and I remembered now that she'd told me when we first met at Des Indes that Ferko had agreed to his first interview with her just as she'd been about to go to Kosovo to look for the families of the people who'd fled to Barupra.

"What about relatives?" I asked Goos. "If we can drum up blood relations of the people who went to Barupra, can't we do DNA profiles of them? And match that against the bones we bring back? If we get common alleles across a broad enough sample, that would be fairly compelling, right?"

Goos liked the idea. Accordingly, it would be his job when he got back to work next week to see if he could use social media and other means to find people—most likely in Kosovo—who claimed shared blood with the Roma in Barupra.

Fien poked her curly head in to announce dinner, but before we sat down to socialize, I needed to tell Goos about Esma.

"Lord, mate! You must have been ready to cark it."

I admitted I'd been upset.

"Do you think Ferko and Esma made all this up together?" I asked him. "Or were they lying to each other?"

"Mate, who knows? With this investigation, I won't be saying 'I'll be stuffed' about anything else. We have four hundred people gone walkabout overnight, and photos of them being loaded onto trucks while the Cave was still a hole in the ground. We're not going to know what to believe until we dig it all up. And if it turns out the Cave is full of gold bars or old parade confetti," he said, "I'll just nod my head."

28.

Kajevic—June 23

At 10 a.m. the following Tuesday, Goos and I presented ourselves at the ICC Detention Centre. It was situated in an old stone castle, converted to a prison by the Dutch long ago, in Scheveningen, the town adjoining The Hague that is, whatever the ironies, on the beach.

I had been reading a lot about Kajevic in the last few days and watching video, but I remained uncertain what to expect. During my years as a line assistant, I had questioned a few killers, including a contract murderer who gave off something—an aura, a pheromone—that froze my heart. But Kajevic was in a category of his own, a political leader whose charisma and rage had been enough to lead an entire nation into a realm beyond conscience. As someone whose professional life for the last thirty years had involved a sort of professional study of evildoers, I realized that today would represent a personal high-water mark. With any luck, Laza Kajevic would retire the trophy for the biggest criminal I ever met.

The detention center looked like the iso wing of many American jails, where inmates were housed who could not live in the general population, either for their protection or that of other prisoners. Along the solid white corridor where we walked, there was a line of avocado steel doors with heavy locks and tiny observation windows, too small to fertilize any fantasy of escape. Formidable-looking pay phones, twice the size of what I last saw in the US, and solely for credit card use, hung outside the doors.

But inside, Kajevic's standard-issue cell surprised me, since it was far nicer than the quarters of minimum-security prisoners in the US, who are usually housed in barracks. Even as a prosecutor, I was never in the school of those who compared federal prisons to 'country clubs.' The worst thing about prison was that it was prison: You couldn't leave, you were isolated from loved ones, and you submitted 24/7 to a regime of rules you'd never choose on your own. The additional incidents of American prison life in some institutions—the cramped double cells, the fetid air, the well-founded anxieties about beatings and sexual assaults—were punishments far beyond those provided by law. I always wanted anybody who complained about 'coddled criminals' to spend a day behind bars.

But with all that said, the prisoners of the ICC and the Yugoslav Tribunal who were housed in the detention center lived in more favorable conditions than a large portion of the people on the planet. The cell to which we were admitted was perhaps ten feet wide but nicely appointed with laminate cabinetry, an actual bed—rather than the steel shelf on which American prisoners typically sleep—a desk and chair, and a small TV. Truth told, when I'd been on the road, I had paid for motel rooms less inviting. The detention center also offered a tidy little library; a spiritual space, replete with Orthodox icons and even flowers; an educational room, where classes were taught and prisoners enjoyed access to computers; and a gym big enough for full-court basketball or tennis.

Kajevic and Bozic had elected to conduct the interview in Kajevic's cell rather than the visitor center, where prisoners received their families and others. They wanted to minimize any chance that other inmates would spread the rumor that Kajevic had turned informant. Coming to Kajevic's quarters also meant we could be evicted whenever they chose, and therefore gave Kajevic the small psychological edge of seeing us on his own turf.

Even taller than I recalled, Kajevic rose formally to shake our hands when Goos and I were admitted. The grand way he swept his hand toward the chairs set aside for us left me with a clear impression of the kind of expansive host he would have been in his presidential residence.

Kajevic took a seat at his desk, beside Bozic and a young male assistant making notes. Goos and I were given metal armchairs just inside the door, a few feet from the sink and the toilet. The uniformed guard who'd escorted us positioned himself discreetly in a corner and managed an unrelenting expression of abject indifference to whatever we said.

Bozic made a brief prefatory statement, repeating our agreement and emphasizing that he could end the questioning or decline answers whenever he or his client preferred. He also added, "As a matter of courtesy, I ask that you address my client as President Kajevic."

I replied with a preamble of my own, stating that our

promises were made only on behalf of our Court, to ensure that the interview had no impact on the charges at
the Yugoslav Tribunal. Then I looked to the yellow pad
in my lap, where I'd sketched out the areas we needed
to explore. I knew what good manners suggested, but I
couldn't stomach any thank-yous, even though Kajevic
was here voluntarily.

"We wish to ask you questions, Mr. Kajevic—
President Kajevic—about events in the first half of 2004,
especially what you know about the disappearance of
four hundred persons from a refugee camp at a place in
Bosnia commonly known as Barupra. We also want to
explore the relationship those events might have had to a
firefight between your forces and NATO troops in April
of that year. Do you understand, sir?"

"I do." His English was excellent. I expected as much,
since it had been on display during his appearances at
the UN and then in Dayton. He was reputedly fluent
in seven different languages, but with Kajevic you could
never be certain what was truth or puffery. "I have
agreed to answer your questions, because I was curious
to meet the two of you, Mr. Ten Boom, and because I
am innocent of any role in this supposed massacre. I will
tell you that now. And by saying that, I do not wish to
imply that I am guilty of any other crimes, especially the
supposed war crimes with which I am charged."

"I understand your position," I said.

"I doubt you do," said Kajevic, with a quick smile that
wavered between ingratiating and smug. "You might as
well say that war itself is a crime." He looked well, calm,
even content, although that might have been because
he was the star of the show, a role he inevitably enjoyed. He was already somewhat less paunchy than he'd

appeared running in his cassock through the streets of Madovic. Nara had told me he hadn't been eating, not as a protest of his confinement, but because he found Dutch cooking repugnant compared to the excellent cuisine of Bosnia. In the short-sleeved navy-blue jumpsuit of the jail, he seemed quite fit for a man in his early sixties, squared at the shoulder and strong through the chest. The beard under which he had hidden had been shaved, giving his face a fish-belly paleness, but he was on the way to reestablishing the monumental hairdo he'd sacrificed to remain on the loose. Darker roots had grown out below the white dye, so that at first glance he looked like he was wearing a headband. His nose might still have been a bit swollen and displayed a red lump, the size of a knuckle, near the bridge.

"In many instances, President Kajevic, wars are indeed crimes."

"On the contrary. Violent struggle is part of human nature—and evolution, frankly, Mr. Ten Boom. One tribe is smiting another tribe on virtually every page of the Old Testament. It is natural for people to want to protect their kind and see them survive. Name an epoch when there has not been war. It is part of the human condition because it breeds strength in men and is nature's way."

Kajevic's arrogance felt far advanced beyond the routine self-satisfaction of many middle-aged males. He believed he was Nietzsche's Übermensch, to whom no ordinary rules applied. He practiced law, and scrivened books of poetry I'd read a bit of, ridiculous soppy stuff that would have embarrassed any self-respecting teenager. He extolled his wife and fucked every girl he could talk into lying down. He burbled in public when he spoke about his beloved children, but was famous for publicly flogging his sons. Within his ravenous black eyes there was a Rasputin gleam, but even after a few minutes in his presence, you had to grant him his own premise about himself: He was an extraordinary fellow. Listening to him rattle on about war, I wondered instantly how Layton Merriwell would respond.

"The notion of war crimes is absurd, Mr. Ten Boom. Four hundred Gypsies are massacred and that is a war crime? How often were four hundred Serbs killed? My wife and children have existed under constant surveillance for twenty years, followed, watched through binoculars and lasers at all hours, their phones tapped. Even the sewage was inspected at one point for DNA. Believing I was inside, the Nazis of NATO blew the door off a small house and killed two children and maimed a third. But none of that is a war crime."

I had resolved beforehand not to get drawn into debates with him. But his self-justifying crap was impossible to tolerate in silence.

"And Srebrenica?" I asked. "Over a few days, more than eight thousand unarmed Muslim men and boys were gunned down one by one, President Kajevic."

Bozic now raised a hand to forbid an answer, and Kajevic responded despite him.

"I was not there, Mr. Ten Boom. And your version of what happened is nothing like what I have heard. But even pretending what you say is true, how were these Bosniaks unarmed? Most were captured as part of a military column. And if released, the next day they would have taken up guns and resumed slaughtering Christians. You know the saying, Mr. Ten Boom, that history is made by the victors? Do you?"

"Yes," I finally answered.

"So is justice. How many of the war criminals your Court prosecutes were the winners in the wars they were fighting? The Protestant West, the Americans, call me a criminal so I am a criminal. That is a matter of power, not justice. The only true war crime is losing."

"We will prosecute Americans, if that is your point, Mr. Kajevic."

"No you will not," he answered. "And if you truly believe that, you are quite dim."

He was smart. I had been prepared for that. And not without his point.

"Let us talk about Barupra, President Kajevic." Beside his client, Bozic nodded sagely.

Kajevic again denied that he, or those he commanded, had any role in annihilating the people of Barupra, adding, with his inescapable air of superiority, "I would not be here, were there any basis to believe that."

That answer begged a question that had gotten quite a bit of airtime in the prosecutorial councils at the Court in the last week. Why in the world was Kajevic sitting for questions? Leaving aside his curiosity about the men who'd inadvertently spearheaded his arrest, it seemed inevitable that he wanted to blame the Americans, whom he despised for intervening in a war he was sure he was about to win.

"And do you have any information, either direct observation or what you have been told, about what might have become of those people at Barupra?"

"I heard rumors," he said.

"And when did you hear those rumors?"

"Several weeks after. May, even June of 2004."

"And what were the rumors?"

"That the Americans had come in the dead of night, set off explosives, and the Roma were gone."

"Did you ever talk to anyone who claimed to have been present or in the vicinity when that happened?"

He turned his head several times, meaning no. "I don't believe so. I was far away by the end of April."

"Where were you?"

Bozic immediately waved a hand. Kajevic again answered despite his lawyer.

"I was nowhere near Tuzla, Mr. Ten Boom, where the Americans were searching for me in every attic and cellar, every culvert and sewer."

"And what did you make of those rumors about the Roma? Did they seem credible?"

"Of course. The Americans believe they are invincible. And so they were full of rage that a so-called war criminal had succeeded in killing and wounding so many of them."

"But why blame the Roma of Barupra?"

"Because they had provided the weapons we used in our defense." Kajevic angled his face to look at us, calm and supreme. "Surely after all your investigating, you knew that?"

When I did not respond, Kajevic beamed. He had remarkably good teeth, straight and white, for a man who had come of age with Tito-era dentistry. Beside me, Goos had stopped tapping away on his laptop. We'd had the Eureka we came hoping for: The Roma had provided the arms Kajevic used to shoot the Americans.

"No, of course, you don't know that," said Kajevic. "Because the Americans want to hide the fact that they were killed and wounded with weapons stolen from under their noses. It makes them look pathetic and inept."

Kajevic uttered a hearty stage laugh, then tapped Bozic with the back of his hand. He remarked to Bozic in Serbo-Croatian. I looked discreetly at Goos's pad, where he had written the translation, much as I would have guessed: 'I told you so.'

"You understand," Kajevic said, "that the Americans and NATO stripped us of weapons whenever they could during their occupation. Old men were beaten and deprived of their shotguns or the sidearms they had used in World War II. The NATO force left us toothless, while the Bosniaks built immense armories for the next war. Altogether, in the years after Dayton, NATO collected eight hundred fifty thousand small arms. Did you know that?"

I nodded.

"Then perhaps you know what happened to those weapons?"

"I'm sure you can tell me."

"No, I cannot," he answered. "Only a small portion. Here is what I know. Late in the winter of 2004, the American general, Layton Merriwell, the NATO supreme commander, decided he could accomplish two goals at once by transporting most of these weapons out of Bosnia. About 500,000 light arms and munitions. Do you know where he sent them?"

"No," I said.

"Iraq?" Goos asked.

"Of course, Iraq," said Kajevic. "To equip the police and defense forces, all the Sunnis the Americans had disarmed the year before. Everyone who had served in the Iraqi Army was familiar only with Soviet-type small arms, like these. So General Merriwell went about collecting weapons from all over Bosnia to ship to Iraq. Brilliant, yes?"

He was being sardonic. But it was actually a wise plan—get the guns out of Bosnia, where sooner or later they would have gone astray and been employed to disrupt the peace, while saving taxpayers the expense of arming and training the Iraqi forces with American equipment. It sounded like the combination of tactical and political genius that was part of Merriwell's legend.

"And what became of that plan?"

"You should ask your countrymen. I am told they grow very silent when that question is raised. Surely I don't know the answer. Except of course about six trucks full of light arms. That was stolen by the Gypsies."

Attila and I by now had spoken several times about the Gypsies stealing her convoy. What she'd failed to mention every time was that the trucks were full of weapons. That, apparently, was the big classified secret, although the goal, at least as Kajevic told the story, seemed to be avoiding embarrassment rather than promoting national security.

At first blush, I was inclined to blame Attila for leading me to believe that trucks were the only equipment the Roma had sold to Kajevic. Merriwell, too, had left me with that impression. I would have to review things carefully later, but after a second, I suspected that if I'd had a tape recording I'd find that both Merry and Attila simply had not corrected my errant deductions.

"And by 'Gypsies,' you mean the Roma from Barupra?"

"Who else? It is characteristic of the Americans' moral arrogance that they disregarded all warnings about employing Gypsies. And suffered the loss of their vehicles and weapons as a result."

"And you bought both? Trucks and guns?"

"Two trucks. Ammunition. One hundred assault rifles and other light arms."

"Grenade launchers?"

"Yes, yes. Those. Mortars. The armaments that proved so lethal to the Americans as we fired down from the adjoining buildings." He was trying to be stone-faced and factual, but a mean-spirited smile was tempting his lips.

"You didn't have weapons already?"

"Unfortunately, we had departed in haste from our prior refuge, making it impossible to travel armed. Once we were settled in Doboj, we needed to resupply."

"And how did you find the Roma to buy this materiel?"

"My nephew was in charge of this resupply effort. Do you have nephews, Mr. Ten Boom?"

"I do."

"And what kind of men are they?"

"Very fine. Very different. One is a medical student, the other works as a juggler and teacher. But they are both outstanding young men. My sister's sons."

"My nephew is not an outstanding young man. Also my sister's son. But he is an idiot. Yet he is my nephew." Kajevic shrugged, with the same hapless gesture most adults on earth had employed now and then in talking about certain family members. "And very loyal. He is a drug addict who claims he is cured, despite weekly relapses. But he mixes well in low elements. He bought these guns. And was very proud of himself."

"He dealt with the Roma?"

"Ah yes. Face-to-face apparently. I knew nothing about this in advance. I had no choice but to beat him once he told me the story." Kajevic added that fact with utter serenity. Violence, as he'd said, was part of nature.

"And why were you displeased?"

"Because he had dealt with Gypsies. Gypsies care only about Gypsies. It is untrue that they have no sense of honor. But it is limited to Gypsies."

"Had he told the Gypsies whom the weapons were for?"

"He claimed not. But his uncle is all my nephew has with which to impress. Girls in bars. Whoever. He has been cautioned a dozen times but is incorrigible. And even what he admitted saying was too much—how his important uncle would enjoy the fact that the weapons had been stolen from the Americans. Who else around Tuzla or Doboj would that apply to? The Gypsies are very clever. And my nephew all but gave them our precise whereabouts to deliver the goods. They would have been fools not to follow him back the few blocks. And because they are Gypsies, they would think nothing of selling weapons to us on one hand and then, on the other hand, selling information about our location to the Americans."

"So that's how you knew the Americans would be coming for you? Surmise?"

"More than surmise. Expectation. Based on certainty about the Gypsies, Mr. Ten Boom. We knew they'd betray us and that NATO would arrive. When was not clear. If we moved, we might have fallen into the Americans' snares. So we prepared. And remained hidden. I had people to watch for me all over Bosnia. You have learned that." Face averted, he again delivered a superior look of considerable satisfaction. "I had them on alert, and so learned that NATO was on the way an hour or so in advance."

I'd asked dozens of times how Kajevic had been so

ready for the Americans, but no guess, not mine or anyone else's, had been entirely accurate. As a prosecutor
and defense lawyer, I'd always loved the moment when
the defendant finally opened up. Even the most exacting
reconstruction of events before that turned out to have
missed something.

"And how did the Americans know that their troops
were shot with guns stolen from them?"

"Unfortunately, Americans were not the only persons
to die in that incident. We left our dead and their
weapons behind as we were escaping, and could remember our comrades only in our prayers. The Americans
always recorded the serial numbers of the weapons they
confiscated and usually put laser engravings on the components." Kajevic smiled again in his disturbing way.
"This is very amusing to me, your questions," he said,
"the degree to which the Americans have kept you in the
dark."

As I would have expected, Kajevic was a genius at
spotting vulnerabilities. Despite supposedly ruing his
dead, he had probably been supremely satisfied to leave
a few assault rifles behind to complete the Americans'
disgrace. It was not hard to imagine the combination of
indignation, sorrow, and rage the US forces had felt, as-
sessing the magnitude of Kajevic's triumph.

His smugness and his powerful ability to shape reality
to his liking made me eager to put him in his place.

"And yet it was you, President Kajevic, according to
what we have heard repeatedly, who sent an emissary to
threaten the people of Barupra."

Bozic's fine blue eyes rose from his pad. He'd been
taken by surprise by the question and was alarmed. He
laid his thick hand on Kajevic's forearm.

"A word with the president, please," said Bozic. But he had the client from hell, who pulled free.

"As I have told you, Mr. Ten Boom, I was hundreds of kilometers away. I did not menace anyone."

"Are you aware of any threats being made on your behalf against the people in Barupra?"

Bozic lifted his palm to call a halt. Kajevic, whose eyes never left me, again answered anyway.

"Whatever was said was idle talk. No actions were taken at my order."

"But do you know if the Roma of Barupra were informed that you would be exacting revenge against them?"

"War is not a parlor game, Mr. Ten Boom."

"Does that mean that to the best of your knowledge such threats were made?"

"I would say yes to that. Certainly I would not want to encourage others to do as the Gypsies had done." This was what Attila had explained the night I got to Bosnia. Integral to Kajevic's success in remaining at large was terrorizing anyone who might turn against him. Threatening the Gypsies for betraying him was essential.

"And what precisely was communicated, President Kajevic?"

"I would not know. I probably had no idea then, and certainly no memory now. Enough to instill fear: vengeance on any person involved—and those they cared for." He added the second piece casually, as if there was nothing special about threatening innocents.

I pondered. "But given your purpose, President Kajevic, which was to deter anyone else from helping NATO, it doesn't seem to me that what you yourself call 'idle talk' would have been sufficient."

"Perhaps," he said. "We will never know. The Americans killed the Roma."

"Before you could?"

He offered only a tiny, canny smile. He was after all a lawyer, and knew just where the lines were. To Bozic's considerable relief, Kajevic signaled with a hand that he was now done answering on that subject.

"Have you ever considered that it was not the Roma who informed against you, but someone else?"

"It was not someone else, Mr. Ten Boom. We both know that. We dealt with outsiders infrequently for just this reason. Only the Roma knew where we were and by their natures would get maximum value for that secret."

I turned to Goos, to see if he had questions. He had been typing like mad on his laptop, and pressed a button to go back.

"Did your nephew tell you the name of the Gypsy he bought the guns from?" Goos asked.

"Probably. But who could remember after more than a decade?"

"Ferko Rincic?" Goos asked.

Kajevic threw up his long, elegant hands at the uselessness of attempting to recall.

"What about Boldo Mirga?" Goos clearly was beginning to hatch a different theory about why Boldo and his relatives had died. Kajevic appeared more impressed by that name. He pulled on his chin.

"That seems more familiar. But who knows with memory?"

I glanced again to Goos for any more questions. He shook his head.

"You are surprised, of course," said Kajevic, "by what I have told you."

"Somewhat."

"The Americans, I assume, have blamed me for the deaths of these Roma."

I tossed my head in a way meant to show I couldn't say.

"No, that is how the Americans are. They love to look as innocent as schoolboys, but they are devious to the core. After our escape, we were required to make the threats we have just been discussing. Once the Americans learned that, they knew they could annihilate these Roma with impunity. And they did so. And then denied it, of course." He shook his head, sincerely amazed by the depravity of the Americans. Like every other hypocrite alive, he was very good at applying unyielding standards to others.

Bozic again straightened up to apply a note of caution.

"Once more," he said, "I remind you that President Kajevic described these threats as 'idle talk,'" said Bozic. "No action of any kind was ever taken by him or anyone he had the power to guide."

"That is quite correct," said Kajevic.

"Do you know who among the Roma received those idle threats?" I asked.

Kajevic looked upward a second to think.

"I believe it was the fellow who sold the guns. Baldo? If that's the right man. I did hear that he denied on the lives of his children that he had informed the Americans. As if we would believe that. We do not understand the Gypsies, Mr. Ten Boom. But, alas, they do not understand us."

We were all silent a second. Kajevic's serene willingness to be both judge and executioner left a weird disturbance in the quiet room.

Goos and I both took a second to search our notes, then I came to my feet. Goos, Kajevic, and Bozic followed.

"May I ask a question of you gentlemen?" said Kajevic, as we faced each other.

"You may ask, of course," I said. "If we can, we'll answer."

"When you came first to Madovic, you were there for what reason?"

"Lunch," I said.

Kajevic continued to study me with formidable intensity. He wanted to know if he'd been betrayed, if our supposed search for Ferko was a ruse. These days he could probably not fully trust anyone's loyalty. That question, I realized—and his desire to exact further revenge—was probably his ultimate motive in sitting down with us.

"We had no idea you were there," I said. "And no mandate to look for you."

"I see."

"And if your goons hadn't kidnapped us, we would have had no reason to reexamine every minute of the day to figure out why that had happened."

A philosophical look overtook Kajevic. "It was an understandable response by those men. They have served me well. They did not recognize the difference between the courts in The Hague. I, naturally, did. I had read about your investigation." Still staring at me without relent, Kajevic now added a more generous smile. "You have me to thank that you are still alive. But as happens so often, mercy was a mistake. I would not be here if those men had done what they meant to."

There was plenty of room for debate about that. At the time, Kajevic took the better bet that we'd con-

tinue to think the kidnappers were working for Ferko.
Killing us, on the other hand, would have brought in
Europol and the Bosnian Army in numbers and would
have forced Kajevic to flee the monastery. Like General Moen, I suspected that he had nowhere to go.
And I also wondered if assassinating investigators who
weren't really looking for him would have been costly
to his alliances, especially among local police. Mercy,
therefore, had had no role in his calculations. Self-
aggrandizement, however, was second nature to him.

"I am sure," said Kajevic, "you are each quite pleased
with yourselves."

"It was all accidental, President Kajevic. We both
know that."

"I don't credit your modesty," said Kajevic. "It was
your great moment. You will boast about capturing me
for the rest of your lives. I was very curious to have some
time with each of you. And I am grateful to have done
so." He looked back and forth toward Goos and me,
taller than both of us. Again, he smiled bleakly. "Because
I have seen there is nothing great about either of you."
He extended his hand to Goos. "You are a drunk," he
said, before turning to me. "And you are a very ordinary
man who wets his pants at the prospect of dying."

Predictable. He could not let us depart without inflicting some harm. Whatever causes Laza Kajevic
claimed, the flag he actually sailed under would always be
sadism.

I peered at him with his hand outstretched in mock-
ery.

"And you are the very face of evil, President Kajevic,"
I said. "Who will be punished every remaining day of
your life."

He laughed. "Five hundred years from now, an entire people will still sing my name. They will read poems of love and gratitude to me every day. You, on the other hand, Mr. Ten Boom, will be so long forgotten that it will be as if your name had never been uttered at all." Kajevic waved his chin at the guard. "See them out," he said.

As soon as we were back in the sun, Goos announced that he needed a drink. He made up for it at nighttime, but Goos didn't touch a drop during work hours, and I understood his request as a sign of distress. I was willing to join him.

We picked up our bikes and walked with them a couple of blocks to a place where there were outdoor tables and umbrellas. Goos was in a dark mood, sunk in himself, until he had downed half the beer the waitress brought.

"So what about it?" he asked. "We believe him?"

It was essential to Kajevic's compelling persona that in his presence you tended to accept every word he uttered. In reality, Kajevic could have been practicing his own reprisals by blaming the Americans for actions that, in the end, he'd not merely threatened but actually carried out. But his revelation about the guns made his account feel convincing, and I told Goos that. His opinion was the same.

"But this still has a rough feel to me, mate. The Americans have spent the last eleven years hiding the facts about those guns. Damned embarrassing to lose your troops with weapons taken out of your very hands, but it's required a lot of energy to keep that secret so long."

"You think there's more to it?" I asked.

"Something else," he said, "yay."

"A massacre by troops gone rogue?"

"Could be."

We speculated a second longer. At this stage, there was one certainty: Almost no one we'd talked to had been completely transparent.

"Let's go dig up that fucking cave," said Goos. He wrestled down his tie as a sign of resolve. "The bones won't lie."

I was with him. Goos motioned for another beer.

"And what about him?" asked Goos after a moment. "What do you make of him?" It conceded something not worth denying about the largeness of Kajevic's character that it was unnecessary even to use his name. I had noticed earlier in my life, especially after meeting people who were regarded as 'legends,' that what is called charisma, this outsize attractive power, was often rooted in madness. We experienced these people as extraordinary because deep psychic disturbances prevented them from observing the same boundaries the rest of us had learned to adhere to.

I was not surprised therefore that even half an hour later and far from the prison, Goos and I were both still oscillating from the interview. In our professional lives, as cop and prosecutor and defense lawyer, we'd each been through hundreds of encounters with criminals. Yet today we'd heard none of the standard guff —'It didn't happen that way,' 'The other guy did it,' even 'I was just following orders.' Instead, Kajevic essentially rejected our entire moral order in favor of his religion of power.

"There will always be ones like him, won't there?" Goos asked.

"Sure." I nodded. "The brilliant charismatic crackpot

who gets his hands on the levers of power and exults in mayhem? There will always be people like him."

"So what's the point then?" said Goos. He leaned toward me, bringing his whole body over his glass. By Goos's laid-back standards, he was quite intent. "Since I came up to The Hague, people in the courts always talk about deterrence: We'll put the likes of Kajevic in prison and that will be a deterrent to the next madman. Does that make any sense to you, Boom? Does it really?"

I understood his mood now. It had been a rough few weeks and it led to a bleak conclusion. We had no answers in our own case, and it didn't matter anyway, because there was some flaw in the human DNA that would always spawn miscreants like this who'd crawl out of the muck.

"Deterrence?" I asked. "Maybe I believe in it at the margins. But I don't think some guy in South Sudan with a machete, who's whacking off limbs in order to force dozens of people to jump off a ten-story building, is going to stop all the sudden, thinking, Wait, I could end up in the dock at the ICC. You know, after the years I've spent prosecuting and defending people, I've pretty much concluded that crimes, whether it's genocide or petty theft, get committed for the same reason."

"Which is?"

"The asshole thinks he'll get away with it. They all convince themselves they'll never get caught, no matter how ridiculous that is."

Goos uttered a croaky laugh, which a second ago had seemed entirely beyond him, while a hand crept down unconsciously to rub at his ribs. I'd spoken the fundamental truth of the trenches.

"So why are you here, Boom? Why come do this?"

Despite all our time together, we'd been guys and never quite gotten to this conversation.

"It was the right moment," I said. "Everything up for grabs in my life. Needed a change."

All that was true, but listening to my own words, I was instantly chagrined, because I was trying too hard to sound unsentimental.

"How's this, Goos? I know this much: Justice is good. I accept the value of testimony, of letting the victims be heard. But consequences are essential. People can't believe in civilization without being certain that a society will organize itself to do what it can to make wrongs right. Allowing the slaughter of four hundred innocents to go unpunished demeans the lives each of us leads. It's that simple."

Goos's blue eyes, watery with drink, lingered on mine and he gave another weighty nod, then lifted his beer glass and clinked it against mine.

VII.

In the Cave

29.

War and Truth—June 26–27

On Friday, the president and registrar informed us that our budget to exhume the Cave had been approved. Goos felt well enough to plan for a return to Bosnia the following Monday, and we agreed that once the initial excavation was underway, I would follow. That figured to be Wednesday of next week. In the meantime, we divided responsibilities to complete preparation.

One item, indispensable from the perspective of Fien, Goos's wife, was to ask NATO to provide round-the-clock protection. I spoke with General Moen's aide-de-camp, who promised to make arrangements. I knew the NATO troops were stretched, but I asked that the detachment to guard us come from the organization, not the Bosnian Army, and the aide ultimately agreed.

I also called Attila a few times but did not reach her directly. Instead, the registrar's office returned a signed copy of Attila's proposal for the earth-moving equipment, while I e-mailed to ask her to please set aside time for Goos and me next week. Over the months, I'd come to recognize that there was often more calculation to Attila than the blizzard of words made it seem, but I was inclined to believe what she was always implying—that it was higher-ups who were still rigidly adhering to secrecy about the details surrounding the Kajevic arrest, including the full nature of the convoy that the Roma had hijacked. Nevertheless, we had leverage now, because sooner or later we would have to file a public report with the Court, even if it was merely to close our investigation. If the Americans wanted us to avoid mentioning the weapons, they would have to explain the sensitivities, including telling us a lot more of the story than they'd been willing to so far.

At home, Narawanda continued to avoid me. She was gone before I woke and returned just before bed, when I could hear her scurrying up to her room. I left a note on Tuesday to say that our interview with Kajevic had taken place and to thank her for her role in making it happen. Beside the coffee pot, I found a very brief response. "Very welcome. Working feverishly on motions."

I understood that she had embarrassed herself painfully at our last dinner with her declaration about struggling to behave properly. Yet I'd accepted that it was best for us to keep our distance. When I returned from Bosnia, I would begin searching hard for a new place to live. Whatever fantasies about the two of us she might have been harboring—at least that evening, after three beers—were better ignored for both our sakes. I had done something incredibly stupid with Esma and had escaped with less emotional—and professional—damage than I had any right to expect. Getting involved again so soon, and with a woman who didn't have even one foot out of her marriage, was dumber yet. None of that was to deny the many appetites Nara privately stimulated. Her innate modesty was a curtain behind which she liked to hide. She had a wonderfully active mind and a sly sense of humor that frequently overcame her pose as the blank-faced foreign girl. And her physical appeal had grown on me steadily over the months. But what I was drawn to most intensely was her earnestness. She had a rare gift among humans of being able to say how she actually felt, even if that was 'I'm confused.'

Despite that, whenever I tried to consider things care-fully, I regarded myself as the party more at risk. For her, I might make a convenient spot for an emergency land-ing on the way out of her relationship with Lewis, but I was likely to be the first stop on that journey rather than the last. By my guesswork, I was seventeen years older than she was, which would look unappealing once she got around to the long view. Whereas I, especially after feeling the cold circle of the rifle barrel, was more and more ready to nest. I could fall for Nara hard and a few months along end up with a shattered heart—and nowhere to live.

All of this was the kind of thing I could explain over a drink a few years from now, after she was well situated with a new beau—or husband. For now, it rested in the chasm of things unspoken that existed in most inchoate relationships between boys and girls.

These thoughts about Nara, intermittent and gentle, contrasted with the hot anger I felt whenever Esma crossed my mind. For reasons I couldn't quite compre-hend, there seemed to have been a fundamental insult in the way I'd been duped. All of that sat side by side with the reality, made sharper by our imminent return to Bosnia, of how important it was to figure out what the hell had been transpiring with Ferko, and whether any fragment of what he'd said was true.

One striking thing about Esma—Emira—was how deeply invested she was in the lie about her Roma roots, which had required concocting those false Internet entries about herself and her make-believe organization, and the substantial effort involved in learning Romany. By Wednesday morning, it had struck me that might be a way to force her out of hiding.

I texted: Tried to reach you at Bank Street with puzzling results. No Esma Czarni???? Returning to Bosnia and still desperate to speak to Ferko one more time.

Even so, I was surprised late Friday afternoon when my cell lit up with her brief reply. Withdrew Bank Street while this case goes on and on in New York. Efforts to reach Ferko futile. Very sorry. All best E

The art—and deceit—of this bare answer after weeks of silence drove me into another spiral of rage. I went out to run by myself and carried in dinner, drinking more wine than I should have as I struggled to make sense of Esma. I understood that the Roma cause was far more righteous and appealing than the legacy of a Persian expatriate whose family history was inevitably entangled in dirty work of the Shah. But how could you start every morning with an inner recap of the long list of lies you needed to tell again today?

I was still sloshing in anger while I was rinsing my dish, when the dam broke and I thought of my father. I sank to a beaten backless kitchen stool, suddenly too flattened even to bother shutting the tap, which continued splattering in the sink. Of course. It was just like a dream when a figure turns around and now has the face of someone else. My father. The difficult seething fury that had been boiling around my heart now cooled into a glop of sadness. Since the moment atop the water tank, I'd wondered occasionally why I was more angry with him than my mother. But knowing the old-fashioned nature of my parents' relationship, I was sure who had driven all critical decisions. In fact, my mother had acknowledged to Marla that my father overruled Mom's desire to return to Rotterdam.

Comparing them to Esma, there were, naturally, differences, distinctions. Lawyers loved distinctions. My parents lied to survive. At first. But in the end, like Esma, they chose what seemed to them a more agreeable life.

Eventually, I migrated upstairs. Every day since I'd left Leiden, I'd thought briefly about a question that, in the same cagey game of unconscious avoidance, I'd never gotten around to trying to answer. The Ten Booms were still in business in Leiden. What about my father's real family, the Bergmans?

Searching the net on my tablet, I found no store by that name, but there were a number of listings in Rotterdam for Bergmans. Eventually, Googling around, I found an article, basically an advertising flyer for local jewelers that referred to a 'Meester Horlogemaker'— master watchmaker—at the shop in Rotterdam of a fancy international jewelry chain. The store was open Saturdays, and no more than three-quarters of an hour by train. I felt a fateful weight when I decided that would be my destination tomorrow.

I woke late and was ready to depart for Rotterdam, when Narawanda came through the door, evenly balanced with a small bag of groceries in each hand. We stared across the living room.

"I thought you were at work," I said. It was the kind of stupid obvious remark you make when you can't think of anything else.

"I was. I had to finish a motion. But once I sent the draft to Bozic, he called to tell me to go home. He says I will burn out if I keep working at this pace."

"He has a point."

"Yes," she said.

Neither of us had taken a further step.

"Are you on your way out?" she finally asked.

"There's an exhibit at a museum in Rotterdam whose name I can't pronounce." I tried anyway. This was not quite a lie, since I'd figured I'd stop in there for whatever refuge I needed after seeking out my father's relatives.

"Boijmans Van Beuningen. The Bosch show? I'd *love* to see that." She was suddenly alight, but that reflected her vulnerability to impulse, which in this case sprang from her joy in art. I also imagined that after several days, her embarrassment was starting to slacken. "Would it be all right if I come?"

"Please." There didn't seem to be anything else to say.

We walked to the train station. The day I arrived, I'd briefly thought I was hallucinating when I caught sight of the massive bike-parking structure outside Den Haag Centraal, a double-tiered network of steel that stretched most of a block and housed thousands of bicycles. It was now a familiar sight.

The weather was fabulous, bright, warm, with lighter wind than normal, part of the brief season when The Hague actually became a beach city. Nara said we should walk down to the sea if there was time once we got back.

Goos and I had meant to go to the shore when we left Kajevic, but had taken a wrong turn. I agreed with Nara, trying not to wonder about her assumptions.

Aboard the Intercity, I faced her.

"I need to tell you something," I said.

"Of course." Her eyes fluttered with anticipation.

"It's about why I want to go to Rotterdam."

"Oh." But she put her chin on her hand as she listened to me, her big eyes warm with feeling.

"That is very complicated," she said, when she had heard the whole story. "It has been extremely hard on you," she added, a deep truth I'd never been willing to say to myself.

"It's been difficult to process," I said, "much worse than I anticipated at first. It turns out that it messes you up to find out at age forty, when you finally think you've settled into yourself, that everything beneath you, your foundation as a person, isn't really there and never was. I've been shocked to discover how angry I am with my parents. Not for the choice—which I don't judge. But for not trusting their children with the truth when we had a chance to grow up with it."

She reached over and took my hand for a second.

By the time we arrived in Rotterdam, I was anxious and aswim, with the worst kind of anxiety, which is always about more than you can name. We exited the train station, a triumph of sleek angles, into the swarming center of the city, which was an architectural showplace. A few older buildings remained, but skyscrapers dominated, many seemingly erected in an experimental spirit. I admired the intrepidness of a business community willing to support those kinds of innovations, but several of the results invited laughter. One place had a facade of sheet metal joined by enormous rivets, as if the architect was inspired by a heating duct.

The address of the jewelry store where Bergman worked was in my hand. Feeling like somebody off the boat, I followed the navigation app and led Nara down a classy old street with trees in full leaf and century-old buildings with limestone faces. The store was easy to spot because a round clock with a gold rim, a Rolex, hung over the doorway.

A young man in a rayon short-sleeved shirt and a tie was behind the display cases. I asked for "Meneer Johannes Bergman."

The fellow looked up, thought about that, and extended his palm. It took me more than a second to realize he was asking for my watch, and rather than explain myself, I removed it from my wrist. It was a Patek Philippe that my father had given me for my twenty-first birthday, a vintage model called a Calatrava. I had always enjoyed wearing it because of its unaffected appearance, with its round face and black leather band. Over the years, when I'd had the watch cleaned, I'd learned it was quite valuable, a model that dated to 1932. For me, however, the meaning in the gift lay entirely in the fact that I'd seen my father wear the watch almost daily during my childhood. He had told me a thousand times that Patek Philippe was the world's first maker of watches. Thus when he opened the band and fastened the timepiece to my wrist, it felt like he was passing along something essential.

A few seconds after the young fellow went to the back room with the watch, a man of at least eighty swept through the curtains that screened off the rear area. On first impression, he seemed too tall to be a member of my family. He was probably close to six foot three even now, his bald scalp framed by a springy moss of long white hair. He had emerged without removing his jeweler's headpiece. The monocular lens, with multiple rings, was embedded in a leather eyepatch that was secured around his head in a scuffed band that bespoke generations of use. My father had worn a similar device, which, when I was a very young child, had made him seem as terrifying to me as the Cyclops. My watch was in the man's hand and there seemed to be incredulity both in his expression and the hasty way he'd emerged from the back.

"This is yours, sir?" His English was spoken with a heavy Dutch accent.

Even with half his face concealed, I could suddenly see the resemblance—my father's long nose and long chin and the same faint blue to his one visible eye, even though this man was handsomer than my father had ever been.

"This reference number is quite rare," he said, meaning the watch model. "But it appears to be working quite well. Is there an issue?"

"The watch was my father's. I believe he may have been your older brother. Daan Bergmann?" When I had awoken this morning, I couldn't even remember my father's birth name and had texted my sister.

"Daan Bergmann?"

"Yes."

He repeated the words, then looked behind himself to a bar-height chair and sank upon it. He removed his headgear. His mouth was parted and he looked outward for a second without appearing to be focused on anything here. He still held my watch delicately in one hand. He woke to that first and looked down, as if to assure himself it was still there. Then he spoke to me again, beginning in Dutch before repeating himself in English.

"*Your* father?" he had asked.

"*Ja*," I answered. After that, he spoke only Dutch, with Nara once or twice whispering translations beside me.

"And what name do you take?"

I told him.

"Yes, 'Ten Boom,'" he agreed. Years swam behind his eyes. "They asked my father first," he said. "To go to Leiden? But he would not abandon his family. So your father went instead. Disappeared without a word to anyone. And the Nazis took us all. All the Bergmans." He gave himself a second to consider what else to say, and then transferred my watch to the fingers of his left hand. With the right, he removed the link from his left cuff and turned up his sleeve. I knew what he was going to show me, but my heart still felt as if it had been halved by a cleaver when I saw the hand-printed numerals the Nazis had tattooed on the forearms of the inmates at Auschwitz.

I nodded once to indicate I understood.

"My mother lived and I lived," he said. "No one else. No one. I remember them every day. Twenty-two people, five children. But I try not to think of your father." He had now gathered the strength of conviction. He stood and pulled himself straight before reaching over the counter to return the watch.

"It is good to know you," he said. "But please do not come back."

We retreated to the museum, as I had planned, but I was in no state to look at anything. Nara and I sat on an upholstered bench inside the entry, just beyond the ticket kiosk at the foot of a contemporary open stairwell that led up to the exhibits. I rested my head against the wall and Narawanda held my hand.

As I had told Nara only a few hours ago, I had always exercised a strict discipline against judging what my parents had done. Yet as is inevitably true of children, I had seen all of this solely from my own perspective, out of an eagerness to understand theirs. I had been pained imagining what it was like for my father or mother when something—a musical note, a Proustian taste, a painting, a fragment of spoken Dutch—provoked a poignant memory of Rotterdam. It had to happen now and then, no matter how much will they exerted. Did they feel sorrow that they couldn't share with Marla or me what they'd once valued? Or shame about hiding their true selves? I was certain they ultimately set aside their momentary anguish with the same mantra: This was for the best.

But my sympathies hadn't run to anyone else. I had never even wondered what their choice had meant to their relatives. And so I had learned something excruciating today. My mother and father had clung so assiduously to their identity as the Ten Booms not just for the reasons I'd long understood—so that US immigration wouldn't discover that they'd entered the country under a false name, or to ensure that they were always taken as gentiles when the next Inquisition began. It was also the final unapologetic renunciation of their families, a way to tell themselves that they had learned the lesson of Lot's wife and would never look back. They were no longer Bergmans and would not accept blame. At last, I fully understood why they had spurned all things Dutch.

I was grateful to have had my time on earth, although

that, like death, is so elemental that it is difficult to ponder the alternate state. But it had never dawned on me that there was an entire shattered community in Holland that regarded my father and mother with scorn.

"That was why they didn't want us to know," I told Nara.

"I'm sorry?"

"My parents. It wasn't that they were Jews—that wasn't what they wanted to keep from us."

"What was?"

"They didn't want us to realize they had betrayed their families." I faced Narawanda as I said that. "I never thought of them as cowards."

"Nor should you," she said without hesitation.

"He does. Johannes."

"He is bitter—that he suffered, that those he loved suffered, and that your parents did not. But if he spoke to you longer, I suspect you would also find that some of his anger, whether he could stand to say it or not, is with his father, for making a choice that inflicted such pain on him and the rest of his family. And that is what your parents understood. What would it have accomplished, Boom, if your parents refused that chance? Do you think it would have helped anything if the Nazis counted two more victims?"

She was making sense. But there was reason behind Johannes's indignation as well. There are no rules, no order, no civilization if everyone is simply out for himself. I told her that.

"This is the same conversation we had a couple of weeks ago," she answered.

I'm sure my expression in response was completely blank.

"When I told you that I have never known what I would do in wartime?" she asked. "People do horrible things, but often because they face horrible choices. We can admire heroes who put principle over peril to them-selves. But their behavior is not normal. He--Johannes— might wish to believe that if your parents had stayed, they could have helped avoid what happened, but we both know that is magical thinking. The will of millions was not enough to stop the Nazis. To me, saving two lives was the best your parents could accomplish. And many peo-ple, starting with your sons and including me, are grateful they did that and that you are alive."

She looked at me fearlessly as she added the last thought, her chin raised, eyes clear. There was no flirta-tion intended, just facts.

We walked back to the station, without saying much. Once we were on the Intercity, I reached over for Nara's hand and held it for the half an hour plus it took to again reach The Hague. Aboard the train, we agreed we would take the tram out to Scheveningen and the beach, a ride of no more than ten minutes, which felt to me like a good place for continued reflection.

During the winter, life in The Hague goes on as if this neighborhood was far inland, but with the arrival of sum-mer, the huge sandy beach was bustling, with restaurant tables set up outside the seaside cafés, and families play-ing at the edge of the cool water. The North Sea, usually a leaden green, had turned blue in the sun and rolled in calmly in the soft wind.

We sat on the sand. Nara had worn a long dress and rolled it up and extended her pretty brown legs in the sun. Eventually, we removed our shoes and walked at the water's edge, hand in hand again.

What is happening? What are you doing? I wondered. But I was caught in the unfolding of time. Given what I'd experienced in Rotterdam, and Nara's unhesitating comfort, I was impelled by a momentum I felt no will to control.

Still barefoot, we walked up to the yellow tables of one of the cafés for a simple meal. We both drank wine, which sharpened my appreciation of the sea light and the sheer pleasure of breathing.

Around four, as it started to turn cooler, we took the tram back to the Fred and walked home, communicating in isolated words. I entered the dimmer light of the apartment feeling the weight of all that had transpired since we departed a few hours before. I plunged down on the sofa and Nara sat on one of the little square coffee tables, so she was directly in front of me with her knees against mine. She reached forward and took my hands between hers and fastened on me with her immense dark eyes.

"May we please get this done with?" she asked.

I laughed for the first time in hours. I had not been completely sure whether Nara had been holding my hand only to offer consolation as a good friend. I was grateful and I felt far closer to her than when we'd walked out the door seven hours ago. Yet in my imagination, we were going to return home and find some separation. Our coming together, if that was to happen, would require more thought and more time. But Nara was herself, sweetly subject to impulse, and impossibly direct in her communications, and I was glad she wanted to make this easy on both of us.

So our moment came, and again, as in Tuzla, I experienced the drama and definitiveness of a first kiss.

Whatever it is that will occur between a man and a woman is more than half done the first time their lips meet in earnest. The wall that separates us from everyone else dissolves, and from then on, the two stand on different ground. And so we did.

About ten that night I woke with Nara layered against my side in my bed. Well spent, we had dozed for an hour. The shade was up and I could see flecks of stars in the black sky, a rare sight in The Hague, where nightfall so often brings clouds. From the pace of her breath on my neck, I could tell she was awake, too.

"Are we just lonely?" she asked suddenly in a small voice.

I took a second.

"No," I said then. "It doesn't feel like that to me. Does it feel like that to you?"

"This is such an immense step that I am still in shock, especially with myself. I am not sure of anything, except that my life after tonight will never be the same. But for many weeks now, when I have dared to be honest, I have thought I was falling in love with you."

"But now you don't know? That's high praise for me as a lover."

She poked my side hard in reprisal for the teasing. Against my expectations, we'd both had a grand time. For all her occasional timidity, this was one arena where Nara had proved to have no trouble letting go.

"You are changing the subject," she said. "Do you love me, Boom? A little?"

"At this moment, yes. Far more than a little."

I was afraid she would regard my answer as hedged, but instead she giggled.

"A friend of mine, an older woman, once told me that every man is in love for an hour before and after each orgasm."

I laughed, too.

"This is more than orgasms, Nara. For both of us. Of that I'm sure."

She pushed herself up to an elbow to peer down at me with her essential earnestness.

"And what will happen?" she asked. "With us?" She was trusting me as a sage older person to be able to tell her. "Do you know?"

"No. Not yet. But I'm not prepared to worry about it. We'll breathe. We'll live."

"But I'm not even sure what happens next." She meant on Monday or Tuesday when better sense invaded us both.

I pulled myself up in the same posture as her so I could face her. Then I smiled.

"That much I know," I answered.

"Really?"

"Let me show you what happens next," I said and gently eased her down on the bed again.

30.

The Cave—June 29–July 2

Goos called from Bosnia about noon on Monday in what was, for him, a fairly agitated mood.

"Any word from your cobber Attila?"

"You mean today?"

"Today, yesterday. I've got my whole professional staff out here, ready to go fossicking about in the Cave, and there's none of the heavy equipment he promised."

"She."

"She, he. Nothing. And not one of the hired blokes we were looking for either."

"Did you call her?"

"Constantly, mate. Just finally spoke with her office. Back in the States, they say."

"Maybe there was some emergency."

"Not so, buddy. They say she's been planning a vac since last week."

As had grown common recently, I was having a difficult time discerning motives. Perhaps Attila had been instructed to stop being so helpful by the people she relied on for business at the Department of Defense. Or perhaps that direction had come from Merriwell.

"Doesn't sound like she's on our side anymore, does it?" I asked.

"That might not be a change, mate."

I understood why Goos was saying that, but the person who picked us up from the salt mine seemed, within the limits of recent acquaintance, a genuine friend. Attila's fundamental delight in life seemed to come from thinking she'd been helpful. It was hard to square that with the notion that she'd been playing us false all along.

Goos and I signed off and spoke again around 5 p.m. He had reached the construction company that had helped him and the Yugoslav Tribunal exhume some of the hundreds of mass graves near Srebrenica eighteen years ago. The firm was still in business and said they could have equipment on-site tomorrow afternoon. Their price was actually lower than Attila's. As for laborers, with 25 percent unemployment in Bosnia, Goos wasn't worried. He'd called one of the desk clerks at the Blue Lamp, who said she could organize a team of workers by nightfall. Digging would begin late Tuesday. Unless I heard otherwise, Goos and I agreed I would come Wednesday as we'd projected originally.

I had told Nara I would be going back to Bosnia, but she was unhappy receiving the news as we were dressing to run Tuesday evening. I emphasized that armed troops would guard us at all times.

Our new life together, now in its fourth day, did not seem all that different from our old life. We went to work. We came home. We ran. We ate seafood and drank wine and talked, except that now it was between bouts in bed. Whatever caution I had meant to exert evaporated in the heat of our bedroom and the clutch of intimacy. I trusted Nara Logan. I knew she would never harm me intentionally. As important, she had seen too much of me, over the months in which we'd dwelled in the same space, for me to engage in the attempts to conceal weak points in my personality that were typical at the start of a relationship, when people were waiting to find out how much love could change them. Nara's guileless honesty sometimes exceeded sensible boundaries—as when she compared Lewis and me as lovers, naturally giving the prize to me, even though as a male I was apparently no match for Lewis's generous proportions—but overall I relished being with a person so free of calculation. With Nara, I was as much myself as I was ever going to be in the company of someone else.

Over time, we would see whether that would endure and how far it could take us, but by Tuesday I'd faced the fact that I was utterly mad for Nara. Somewhat perversely, I was glad to be leaving town, just to see how much of my consuming hunger for her would remain when we were apart.

At the Sarajevo airport, where I arrived around 1 p.m. after a stop in Munich, I had no trouble spotting my two NATO escorts. Just beyond the secure area, they awaited me in the full combat gear of the Danish Army, including flak vests, helmets, and M10 carbines. The sight of assault weapons in the airport attracted a fair amount of attention, but General Moen was clearly making an emphatic statement to anyone who might want to revenge Kajevic's capture.

An SUV was at the curb with the blue NATO flag, sporting its four-pointed star, mounted over each headlight. We sped into the Bosnian hills that I had first seen deep in snow, and which were now dressed in the heart-lifting green of summer. Mid-journey, I felt a brief spurt of terror when something in the mountains, a shape or even the angle of the light, ignited a memory of my last trip to this country. For the most part, though, I was calm and strangely pleased to be back.

I asked the driver to take me straight to Barupra, as I wanted to get there before work closed down for the night. We arrived a little before four.

Looking down from the edge of the former refugee camp, I saw that the site of the Rejka mine was a hive. Heavy equipment had been inched perilously down the narrow dirt road. Two bright yellow backhoes had climbed up the face of the Cave on their treads and were clawing into it. Goos had told me the night before that he had checked with Madame Professor Tchitchikov, who was confident that the original hollow in the rock formation, the result of stripping out the vein of coal, would not collapse while the new rubble was cleared. After easing off the rock pile, the backhoes emptied their buckets into the beds of two red articulated dump trucks, which then wove down to the valley floor, depositing the contents through their liftgate onto huge green tarpaulins. There, a cadre of workers in orange hazmat suits was sorting every rock individually. Much farther from me, I could see a collection of blackish objects—bones, I guessed—that had been segregated onto smaller blue tarps. Other workers in orange were photographing what lay there.

As usual, I avoided focusing on the remains. It was

not easy to see that far anyway. The dust being raised by the digging rode on the air, a brownish fog with an acrid odor and bitter taste. Everyone was wearing white face masks, including the NATO troops who were positioned at the corners of the site, with rifles across their bodies.

My NATO driver went through an elaborate back–and-forth on his radio. Apparently, the mining road was barricaded by a huge construction crane whose operator couldn't be located. I assured everybody that there was no reason I couldn't walk. I had worn jeans and hiking shoes and I tromped down to the site of the dig, while my two bodyguards watched from above. More than half of the Cave appeared to have been excavated now, leaving the outer edge of original overhang visible, a darker brown than the surrounding rock.

A dump truck driver was leaning out of her cab when I got that far.

"Becl?" she called. She motioned to her passenger seat and ferried me down to the valley floor, where Goos in his white mask was waiting. He pulled it up to his forehead and took a swig of water from a bottle in his hand. The flesh the mask had covered was several shades lighter than the rest of his face.

I asked how he felt, but he backhanded the question like a fly.

"And what about the digging?" I asked.

"I'd say we're about two-thirds of the way. Come have a look."

I followed him toward the blue tarps, a walk of several hundred feet. I wrestled my phobia, but when I finally dared look up, I could see that what had been laid out was not bones.

I stopped dead, grabbing Goos's arm. "Guns?" I asked.

"Yay, weapons," he said. "And bits of trucks."

On each tarp, there were a couple of hundred small arms laid side by side, a virtual armory that, all told, covered an area nearly the size of a football field. There were the green tubes of antitank weapons, shoulder-fired missiles and their launchers, grenades, carbines, sniper rifles, submachine guns and pistols, drab mortars with their attached tripods, and, most frequently, Zastavas. Here and there the workers had also laid out lines of helmets and body armor. The most distant tarps held cases of ammunition and bands of machine gun bullets.

"Gonna be around five thousand guns, I'd say," Goos told me. "Today, getting into the rear of the Cave, we've been digging up some truck parts, whole gamut from fenders through engine blocks. Like maybe they had some kind of small warehouse back in there."

"And how many bodies?"

"So far as I reckon, nil," said Goos. His blue eyes were narrowed in the dust but fixed to me to await my reaction. "Late yesterday, we found a couple of bones and were barracking about for a few minutes, quiet like, not that it would be anything to celebrate. Turned out to belong to a fox. So far, those are the only biologic remains."

"You're sure?"

"We've got two blokes putting an eye on every speck of dust. It's the same protocol we used near Srebrenica, Boom. We've found the usual kids' junk—wrappers, bottles, a busted beach ball. But no clothing, no bones. We're spraying with Luminol at random, but no blood either. Only decent discovery is here." He led me over to another blue sheet, where pieces of electronics had been isolated. They were dust-covered and usually no more than tidbits of wire and semiconductors and metal, but on a corner, about a dozen square old cell phones, each the size of a dinner biscuit, were segregated, largely intact.

"It's the devil's own dance getting into these things anymore, but at NFI they may be able to do it. Might be some photos, messages, something to help identify the people who were here. Hardest part will be finding chargers."

"And that's the best we've got?"

"How I reckon, Boom, this here, the Cave, was some kind of arms depot. The weapons are mostly Yugoslav made, with a few old Soviet items here and there. They've got marks engraved on the components. We'll need to check with some military types, but I think that signifies that the stuff was in NATO custody at some point."

"Are you thinking NATO buried these weapons here?"

"Truth told, Boom, I haven't even begun to think about why these arms are here. Still stuffed that there aren't any human remains."

"Could the bodies turn up?"

Goos tilted his face up at the mine.

"Well, like I say, Boom, we still have a third of the way to go, but how I figure, fitting four hundred people in a space of that size, we should have found something already. My guess, we've got Buckley's chance any bones will turn up."

Like Goos, I looked to the Cave, where the powerful engine of the crane had just fired to life, farting black smoke. The bitter dust in the air was already gathering at the back of my throat and there was some irritation in my lungs. But my principal reaction was emotional, somewhat dizzied that this was what the last months had amounted to.

"So Ferko was a stone liar?" I asked. "It was *all* bullshit?" Even now, I'd expected to discover some truthful elements in his testimony, but Goos solemnly turned his head one way, then the other.

"Sheer rort," he answered.

General Moen and Colonel Ruehl journeyed to Tuzla for dinner that night. Ruehl's arm remained in the cast he'd be wearing for several more weeks, so an aide intervened whenever he needed to cut something on his plate.

The dinner was meant to be a celebration. Goos and I weren't really in the mood, and as it turned out, the NATO people weren't either. It was a good thing for the world that Laza Kajevic had been captured, and an achievement for the soldiers who'd been hunting for him, but even the thought of Kajevic and his crimes was enough to dampen emotions.

Goos brought several of the weapons we'd recovered to dinner in a canvas bag, and both Ruehl and General Moen examined the contents, discreetly enough that only a few of the diners took notice. Neither of them was familiar with the markings, but Moen's aide had been here in 2004 and confirmed that the laser engraving was typical of what NATO, especially the American forces, had done when they seized weapons stocks in Bosnia.

While we were eating dessert, General Moen asked if we'd heard any reports in The Hague about how Kajevic was adapting to confinement. I said only that I'd been told he did not care for Dutch food.

On Thursday morning, I sat down for breakfast with Goos before I flew back to The Hague. Goos was staying on until the excavation was complete and all the arms and truck parts had been photographed. He preferred to bring everything he'd uncovered back to The Hague, but transporting weapons would require permits. Goos planned to go to Brussels on Sunday, to help Fien pack. With their youngest grandchild now school-age, Fien had decided to move to The Hague, at least for the rest of the summer, perhaps permanently.

"Told her I'd give the program another burl," Goos said. He didn't quite allow his eyes to meet mine.

I had noticed that he wasn't drinking last night at dinner and was afraid he wasn't feeling well, maybe from all the dust the exhumation had raised. I nodded now, just to show I had heard him. There was a lot of information in his last sentence.

"If it takes," Goos said, "then I'll have to give Kajevic his due." I wasn't sure whether Goos was referring to Kajevic's insult, telling Goos he looked like a drunk, or the moment of reflection the Tigers had provided for us on the top of the water tank. It didn't make much difference either way.

We shook hands, which wasn't customary for us with our comings and goings, then I stood up to get ready to leave the Blue Lamp. We'd had some eventful times here.

31.

Fallacies—July 3–6

I returned to The Hague Thursday. Friday morning, as I approached the entrance to the Court, I was astounded to see Roger, in his twenty-year-old suit, a narrow-brimmed felt hat protecting him from the sun. I bounded up the last step to hug him.

"What the hell?" I asked. "What brings you here?"

"You, actually. I've been flying all night. Can we have a cup of coffee?"

It was easier to go back under the concrete underpass of the Sprinter to Voorburg than to try to get Roger approved as a guest at the Court, where the security team required at least a day's notice of any visitor. As we walked over, we exchanged briefings on our families. Rog was going to have them all together at the Eastern Shore for the Fourth. I smiled imagining Roger pottering around out there in his über-WASP attire, displaying his skinny legs in lime shorts, wearing a long-sleeved white shirt and penny loafers without socks.

Once we were on some old wood-slatted folding chairs outside a café, Roger got down to business.

"You sort of interrupted my holiday plans," Rog said. Today was a federal holiday in the US.

"Me?"

The wind ruffled the red feather in his hatband, and he had to keep his fingers on the brim to keep the chapeau from blowing away.

"There's a story circulating that you didn't find any bodies in Bosnia."

I looked at him for a second.

"Rog, aren't you guys embarrassed about keeping an eye on me? Go protect the embassy in Benghazi or something. I'm not worth this kind of trouble."

"There are people in the Pentagon who think you've been a lot of trouble. That massacre story in the *Times* left them spitting whenever they hear your name."

"I told you—"

"Right, it wasn't you. Spare me. Anyway, there are plenty of them who think turnabout is fair play. They want to tip the *Times* that you didn't find any bodies."

I shrugged. "They're entitled to the follow-up. The exhumation was a public event."

"But they want to wipe out the original story. I mean, punish it. The narrative they're pushing is that a prosecutor, eager to return to the limelight, starts sleeping with the Chief Allegator and checks his judgment at the door, doing her bidding instead of smelling out pure bullshit. I wanted you to hear this."

My fingertips were ice cold. There was no point asking where the Pentagon people were coming up with these details. I'd just chided Roger for the way the spooks had kept an eye on me. He'd started referring to Esma as my girlfriend a couple of months back.

"Once fucking is part of a news story, Boom, there's not much room for nuance. You know that. They'll throw you under the bus at the Court, I imagine. Fire you. I know I got you into this. And you meant to do the right thing. Instead, you're going to go home in disgrace. I'm really sorry, Boom. I mean it."

Esma had played serpent and I'd bitten the apple. It would get worse when the reporters caught wind of the fact that she was actually playing make-believe. They'd give me the trophy as World's Biggest Idiot.

You always think you don't care what people say about you, until it's something like this. Attila had told me that about Merriwell. I finally uttered a deep sigh.

"It doesn't sound like there's much I can do," I said, "except warn the press people at the Court and then hand Badu my resignation."

Roger let his fingers come off the hat.

"Well, wait. Wait. What are the chances that I could go back to these guys and say, 'You don't need to do anything. The Court's going to announce this week that it's closed its investigation, acknowledging that there was no massacre.' Is there any chance of that?"

I considered a second.

"We can't say there was no massacre," I told Roger.

He made a face. "You know there was no massacre. I've told you from the git-go there was no massacre."

"I still don't know for certain there wasn't a massacre. All I know is that the allegation about four hundred people being buried in that coal mine is completely unfounded."

"And there is no evidence of a massacre."

I weighed that one. Four hundred people gone overnight, but last seen being loaded into trucks by the US Army, didn't quite qualify in my mind as 'no evidence.'

"We'd have to massage that a little," I said.

"Well, let's get the client on the table and do the massage right now and give him a happy ending. I've got to get back to these guys with something definitive. Or they're going to strip you naked in public, Boom, and laugh at your pecker."

I grimaced a bit but managed a laugh. Roger was always colorful. I tried to get out the lawyer's toolkit to think about how we could lay our scalpel on the words. Roger was waiting with his lips rumpled. Looking at him, not changed all that much by the years, I recalled our last conversation, when he was furious at me and I had recognized that our friendship, durable as it had been, was marooned for a while on neutral ground while we both had jobs to do.

But with that memory there was abruptly a dawning of some kind, accompanied by a small bloodrush as thought labored toward solid form. And then I saw it, the way you suddenly make out a form in the dark: Roger wasn't here to protect me, no matter how clever the posturing or how blunt the appeal to my self-interest. He was here to kill the case.

But what did that mean? Were the Roma in a trench somewhere else with American rounds in their heads? Or was there another secret my government wanted to keep? I went with instinct.

"So our press release would say nothing about the arms we found?"

We hadn't spoken a word yet about the weapons. I wanted to see if Roger would bother feigning surprise.

"I don't know exactly what the fuck you found, but it's beside the point, isn't it? There aren't any bodies. No?"

"No bodies," I said. "But whoever was watching us, Rog"—and I realized that his source was almost certainly within NATO—"had to have told you we found a large arms cache there."

"What's the diff, Boom?"

"Well, Rog, those guns we found, they all had NATO markings. Was that a surprise to you? That we found weapons in the Cave?"

"It was a big surprise."

"And no idea how they got there?"

"Nothing definitive. And I couldn't care less at this point. I just need DoD off my back."

I had it now. It was what Kajevic had said. Of all the people in the world, we'd gotten the truth from Laza fucking Kajevic.

"Well, Rog, here's the thing. I have the feeling those weapons are of great concern to you. And if it's not how they got there that bothers you, then it has to be where they came from. So I'm wondering—actually I'm suddenly pretty sure: They were part of five hundred thousand arms that were supposed to be shipped in April 2004 from Bosnia to Iraq."

Roger, my friend, always had a very short fuse. His nostrils flared and his color changed.

"Where did you hear about that? From Attila, that blabbermouth? I'll tell you right now, she's not going to have a security clearance by the end of the day." He used a nasty word about her.

"It wasn't Attila," I said. "I've gotten nothing from her but the company line."

"Then who?"

"Then what? What's such a big deal about five hundred thousand guns, Rog, that it has to remain classified eleven years later? That you're ready to fly all night to keep me from finding out?"

He stared, with that screwed-up intense face Merry had imitated the first time I met him.

"You're playing mumbly-peg with a two-foot sword," Roger said.

"Any press release about what we didn't find in the Cave that also includes what we did find—those small arms—that's a disaster for you, isn't it? Because some intrepid reporter will ask how those weapons fell into Roma hands and then—this is the big one—what happened to the five hundred thousand or so other guns headed for Iraq. The investigation you don't want us to do gets done by the *New York Times* instead. And I'll be curious about the answers." I looked across the table. "You're bluffing, Rog."

"The hell I am."

"You're bluffing. And you're pretty close to lying. Let me think." I did that, right in front of him, as another gust blew a small aluminum spoon off the table. I reached down to retrieve it. "So it's been the guns all along, right? You always knew that Kajevic killed those American soldiers with stolen guns the Roma had sold him. But it's the arms that didn't get stolen you *really* don't want to talk about. Right? Because you guys—you and Merry and Attila and the Army—you've been playing rope-a-dope: Accuse us of a crime we didn't commit, massacring four hundred Roma at the Cave in Barupra. Maybe we'll even provide some evidence that tends to support that. Because it helps to conceal our actual crime."

"A crime?" Roger sat back. He was trying to look outraged, but he was clearly alarmed. "What crime?"

"I can't tell you that, Rog. Not yet. But generally speaking, people don't tolerate getting accused of atrocities in front of the world unless they're hiding something else. And the secret they're keeping usually isn't that they have bad table manners. It's something that would get you guys in real trouble."

"Nobody committed a crime," Roger said. "And unless you just got reappointed as the United States Attorney, it's none of your fucking business anyway."

"Okay," I said. "Just tell that to the *Times*. But it's bad juju, isn't it, Rog? Did the weapons actually get to Iraq? You were part of it, right? You were the intelligence liaison on that deal, whatever it was. You're hanging out somehow. You and Merry, too. I think you and Merry, you're the guys who are going to be naked in public, you and your peckers, once people start asking about those guns."

He didn't answer, just stared. He needed a haircut. The wind was pushing around the scruff of gray hair that had grown over his ears.

"You took the wrong approach, Rog," I said. "You should have told me you needed a huge favor."

Calculation quickened his light eyes now that he'd been exposed.

"I need a huge favor," he said.

"Too late," I answered. "Chips fall where they may. Burn me up, if you have to. But I'm going to point the reporters straight at the rest of the story if you do. Your best chance is that we finish our investigation about what happened to those people, say whatever we should say in public, and leave the rest of the details in the file. If I have any discretion, Rog, I'll exercise it the way you were sure I would when you recruited me for this gig. You knew if I had any choice I'd protect you. And, believe it or not, I still will. Because you used to be a really good friend."

I walked away and turned back with a parting thought over my shoulder.

"Enjoy your holiday."

While I was in Bosnia, Nara had gone to Belgrade to meet with Bozic. She didn't return until Friday night. I lit up like a rocket when I saw her, and we were in bed as soon as she dropped her suitcase. It rained Saturday, but we were content inside.

Often, as Nara dozed beside me throughout the weekend, I thought about my case. I'd been surprised often in the last several months, but if we ended up closing the investigation, I had to figure out what would come next for me professionally. My appointment at the Court was nominally permanent, but the gallant thing would be to offer to resign, since I wasn't sure anyone envisioned me staying on if the Barupra situation didn't culminate in charges. I thought I'd made a good impression at the Court and could probably sign on to one of the trial teams, if that was what I really wanted to do. Alternatively, I could return to the US, which didn't feel right at the moment, or I could take off for my endless summer. But after a gut check, none of these ideas about leaving held any appeal for one principal reason: Narawanda could not come with me, given her commitment to the Kajevic case. So that meant I was staying in The Hague, at the Court or with another organization.

If I'd had a chalkboard four or five years ago on which

I listed the qualities of the person I thought I'd end up with, Nara would never have matched. I pictured myself, for example, with someone more socially graceful than I am and with greater natural warmth, someone who'd be able to supplement shortcomings I rued in myself. But I had accepted the glory of the future, which is that it is unknown, and had never bothered with a list. The truth was that for reasons that surpassed understanding, I was at home with Nara, not only in love, but also at peace. God only knew if it would last. But I couldn't leave until I found out.

On Sunday, it turned beautiful once more and we took the day by the sea. Returning to the apartment in the late afternoon, we were full of summer ardor, that sensation when the sun seems to bring all your nerves to the surface of your skin and desire becomes more urgent after the long touch of the light winds. We ended up in her bed for the first time, a location that seemed somewhat symbolic.

Afterward, as the light leaked from the room, I put a question to her that had long lingered unspoken.

"Do you want to have children?" My tone was neutral and curious, as if it was just one more thing I needed to ask to know her better.

"Lewis is against it now. He says it is too dark a world to bring children into."

"And where will the light come from?"

"It is an excuse, I know. He is reluctant to distract himself from his career and what is important to him."

I noticed that Lew still occupied the present tense.

"And are you willing to accept that?" I asked.

"Unclear. I have not come to the moment of not accepting it. Yet I have never agreed. It has been something—like too many other things—that we put off. My mother keeps hinting, naturally."

I finally asked how old Nara was and she became cutely evasive.

"Guess," she answered.

"Be careful now, *chérie*," I said, a phrase that had been spoken several times a week on the Trappers' radio broadcasts when I was a boy, at moments when the opposing team was threatening to score.

She giggled.

"On looks?" I asked. "On looks you could pass for twenty-three."

"Brilliant," she said, although I meant it.

"But doing the arithmetic on your education and career, I thought you were about thirty-eight."

"Thirty-seven. I was ahead in school."

I repeated the number. "It might be time to think about whether you want to do this."

"Have children?"

"Yes."

"I always thought I did, while I was growing up. Most of me probably still feels like that. What do you advise?"

"About whether you should have children? I think I should have no views on a question like that. But if you ask me about my own life, it's unimaginable without my sons. For me, becoming a parent completely changed my idea about what it means to walk on this planet. Most people would say the same thing. It's as if the world has gone from flat to 3-D."

"So you would say I must."

"The one 'must' is for you to decide what is best for you. But as someone who cares for you deeply, I would wish for you the same profound connection my children brought to my life. I didn't even completely know how badly my marriage was working until the boys were out of the house, because I had been so happy they were there."

"And would you have more children?" She asked that as lightly as I had about her desire to have kids.

I had never thought about that issue in much depth. Instead I'd more or less answered by action. In my dating life, I'd been unattracted to women with young children, or those whose biological clock could be heard ticking.

So now, in her bed, with Nara pasted to my side in the sweat we had generated, I shone the light on myself: Could I be a father again at fifty-five? That didn't seem to be too late for movie stars and CEOs. I knew at least one man back home in Kindle County, the Prosecuting Attorney, Tommy Molto, who'd married at fifty-two and then had a family, and he seemed like a tulip blooming midwinter in a greenhouse, even though he'd once told me that with his worn looks, he was often mistaken for his sons' grandfather.

But Tommy did not have grown children who would be completely disoriented by this decision, especially Pete, who was not all that far from starting a family of his own. Nor had Tommy, in the crudest terms, been there and done that. At first blush, having kids at my age seemed to be one of those acts like Icarus's as he flew too close to the sun. It felt as if I'd be trying to live twice.

"I need to think," I said. "We both do."

"We do," she answered and pulled herself even closer.

On Monday morning, Goos and I worked together on a joint report about the exhumation of the Cave. In Bosnia, we had felt merely befuddled, because we still had no idea where the people who'd lived in Barupra had gone. But here we had to confront our institutional responsibilities. The plain fact was that we had consumed a lot of the Court's resources on allegations that were unfounded. At this stage, it was a blessing that Ferko's testimony had been presented in public and that three judges had voted to authorize the investigation. But now what? Our conclusion, after noodling together for a while, was that because we still did not know if a war crime had been perpetrated, we were obliged to do some limited follow-up, even if continuing meant conducting what amounted to a four-hundred-head missing persons investigation.

A few hours later, in the waning hours of the afternoon, Goos entered my office and closed the door, a standard sign that something was up. The jolly air that he generally brought with him, and which had been much in evidence this morning after bringing Fien back to The Hague, had evaporated. He appeared, if anything, upset.

My first thought was that Roger had carried through on his threat.

"Is my name in print?" I hadn't told Goos yet about my meeting with Roger, which had seemed embarrassing to me for many reasons, particularly because Goos knew I counted Rog as a friend.

"How's that?" he said.

"I didn't tell you I nearly resigned on Friday."

As I related what happened, Goos tilted his head like the RCA dog looking into the bell of the Victrola. He didn't get it.

"You know, Goos, I probably need to think about quitting anyway. Sooner or later that story about Esma and me is going to come out around here. And people will say that's why we believed Ferko and got into this whole investigation. I'll be the scapegoat."

"No, you won't. The Pre-Trial Chamber approved the investigation. And that story about Esma and you? No one will even follow up." He took the other chair in front of my desk and looked up at my blank walls as if there was actually something there. His lips were bunched and his mouth moved a couple of times on the verge of words.

"Just say it, Goos."

"Well, if you believe the wags, you weren't the first person at the Court to root her."

By now, with Esma, nothing surprised me.

"And who was before me?"

"Akemi. Last fall. Suspect that's why the investigation got approved, even with the Americans braying and carrying on."

"Akemi?"

"So they say. I don't have color photos. Quite the furphy hereabouts, but one never knows. Didn't bother me ever. Investigation should have been approved a long time ago."

Despite Esma's denials, I would never have bet much that I wasn't part of a parade—and the fact that women were also marching along had been reported in my readings about her divorce. The part that bothered me most was seeing ever more clearly that I—and poor Akemi—had been a means to an end.

"And what became of the happy couple?" I asked.

"Story is Esma called it quits and broke Akemi's heart. Suspect that's her way."

That would explain why Esma was upset when I pulled the plug. She regarded it as her imperial right to exit the stage first.

Goos was still hunched, watching me with evident unease. My instinct was to to ask why he hadn't said something before, but I recognized that was stupid. Half the people on earth had probably told someone they cared about, 'She isn't going to be good for you,' and the number of times those warnings hadn't backfired was a lot smaller.

"And no drum from your mate about what happened to those five hundred thousand weapons?" Goos asked about Roger.

"No info," I said. "I'd love to find out."

"Not our business to investigate that, though, is it?"

"No," I said. "Our business was to investigate the massacre of four hundred people who were supposedly buried in the Cave and who're now AWOL."

"Yay," he said, "but I've got some good oil on that. Was that I'd come over to tell you."

He put several screenshots from Facebook on my desk.

"Am I supposed to read this?" I asked.

"Not that you'll enjoy it much."

"Goos, this is in Serbo-Croatian."

"Right, right, right," he said and spanned his forehead with his hand. "Should I translate?" he asked.

"I'll take the gist."

"Remember our makeshift DNA database?"

"You mean to identify the relatives of all those people we thought we'd find in the Cave?"

"Right. So I put out a request on Facebook: Love to hear from blood relations of the folks who lived in Barupra from 1999 to 2004. Here's two girls, both of them new to Facebook, saying they were born in Barupra."

"Born there? And where are they living now?"

"Mitrovica, Kosovo. It's where the Barupra lot came from, mate. One, the fifteen-year-old, she's answered my messages today a couple of times. Says she and her friends, how they grew up, parents were such that you couldn't even say the word 'Barupra' out loud. Not in the whole camp where they are. Plenty of her friends don't even know they were born there. And I mean, Boom, I've tried 'Barupra' before on the net. YouTube. Facebook. Crime Stoppers. Whatnot. And nary a word from anyone saying they ever lived there."

"So what changed?"

"Figure I better go there and ask, don't you think?"

"But these girls, they're saying their parents lived in Barupra, too? And other people in this camp she's in now. Right? That's the implication, isn't it?"

"That's the implication, Boom. Sounds like after all this, our Roma just went home."

The Investigative Fallacy is assuming facts you want to believe. Goos and I had been trained to take nothing for granted. But the unquestioned disappearance of four hundred people, as well as Ferko's testimony, had somehow never allowed either of us to consider the alternative that they had all simply moved away. There were reasons for what we believed. The Roma had departed with no word to their few friends or relations in the area, not then and not in the last eleven years. And beyond that, they had no means of transportation for four hundred people. Unless, I realized suddenly, the US Army had arrived in the middle of the night with dozens of trucks to carry them home.

32.

Home?—July 6–7

I came in from work on Monday, after my meeting with Goos, in a sour mood. I was prepared to tell Nara that I didn't feel like running, but I could see at once that she had troubles of her own.

"You should never try a career playing poker," I told her.

"What does that mean?"

"It means you're not very good at hiding it when you're worried."

"Truly? People always tell me that I am so difficult to read."

I would have said the same thing months ago. It was a plus, I supposed, that to me she was now transparent.

She motioned me to the sofa, so we were sitting side by side, and she touched my hand in her prim way.

"Lewis," she said.

"What about him?"

"He called and said he would like to come home to discuss things."

I hesitated. "Discuss what? Divorce? Reconciliation? Where to send his clothes?"

"I do not know, Boom. I asked all of those questions and he said he thinks it is a good idea for us to sit down face-to-face and talk it all through."

"And what did you say?"

Her large eyes were suddenly darker with some faint disappointment.

"Boom, he's my husband. I cannot refuse to speak to him."

"Of course not," I said. But I felt everything inside me stalling out, as if I'd swallowed poison. "When's he coming?"

"This weekend."

"Ah," I said. I held my breath emotionally for a second and then plunged again into the deep water. "And where will he stay?"

She looked down at her hands. "We didn't talk about that."

I nodded. "I'll go back to Des Indes."

"You don't have to do that."

"It's in my interest to leave another bedroom available."

"Boom, please. I'm sure he's thinking he'll sleep on the sofa."

"You guys deserve your privacy." Gary Cooper, or some other highly honorable movie hero of the past, couldn't have uttered that line with greater resolve, but I hated saying it. You knew better, I thought. You warned yourself: Nowhere to live. And a shattered heart.

There was not much more to say right now, and so we

ended up going for a run. That night we ended up again in my bed.

On Tuesday, I found myself more wallopingly depressed than I'd been since my mother died. The last five years of my life, my grand adventure, as Ellen called it sarcastically from time to time, were not going to amount to much. Lesson taken: You gamble, sometimes you lose.

After lunch, I went down the hall to Goos's office, which to almost every appearance could have been mine. He was leaving for Kosovo tomorrow. By now, he'd identified at least a dozen people in Mitrovica who said they had lived in Barupra. None had explained where they had been for more than a decade, or why they had seemingly rematerialized only now. Goos thought it was better to ask those questions in person, a judgment I shared.

"What if I told you," I asked him, "that while you're gone, I'm going to head to the United States?" The idea had been growing on me all day. The worst part of how I felt was my sense of utter futility concerning everything we'd done for the last several months. And of course, it would be best to leave The Hague while Nara and Lewis were hashing things out. It would drive me insane to be a few blocks away. A dark night of the imagination.

"For what reason, Boom?"

"To try to corner several people who owe us some answers. Starting with Esma."

Goos pulled a mouth.

"Think you might be breaking the law," said Goos.

"Not if I'm there as a private citizen. If I'm asking questions for my own sake, with no intention of using the information here at the Court, that can't be illegal.

We have this thing in the US called the first amendment."

"You're the lawyer, Boom."

"You keep telling me that."

I thought about it a little more and got on the Internet. *Jahanbani v. Jahanbani* was listed for a hearing Thursday at 2:00 p.m. A Delta flight at 9:30 a.m. that day would get me to JFK before noon. I e-mailed Akemi and asked to take personal time for the balance of the week. Then I called DC.

"How would you like to take a huge step to restoring a friendship that's lasted nearly three decades?" I asked Roger as soon as he picked up.

He took his time before he said, "I'd like that a lot."

"I need a favor," I told him.

He said "Okay," in a chastened tone.

"I lost my passport in rather difficult circumstances a month ago that you probably know all about." They'd been tracking me much too carefully to have missed the kidnapping, especially once it was reported to NATO.

"Without commenting on your assumptions, I may have heard about a nasty encounter you had. On top of a gas tank?"

"Saltwater tank."

"Right right right," said Roger.

Coming and going from an EU country, with a pocketful of documents issued by the government of BiH, I'd had no trouble at the Bosnian or Dutch borders, but, ironically, I'd have a much harder time entering my own country without my passport. I'd applied for a replacement, but given the distance, the wheels were turning slowly.

Roger asked for the relevant numbers, then put me on hold.

"Do you know where the embassy is?" he asked, when he returned after several minutes. I did, although because of my role at the Court, I'd avoided the place. "If you present yourself there late tomorrow afternoon and ask for Reeda James, she will have your passport."

"Thank you."

"May I ask if this has anything to do with your investigation?"

"I won't be acting on behalf of the Court, Rog, if that's what you're worried about. I may ask some questions for my own sake. Starting with my former girlfriend, as you like to call her."

"Ah," said Roger.

"I suspect you know this, but her name isn't Esma Czarni, and she isn't a Gypsy. She's Iranian."

I didn't hear Roger's breath for a second.

"Iranian?" he asked then. "Ir-*ranian*? You mean all this bullshit traces back to Tehran?"

"Rog, I have no idea where it traces. She's probably just a sui generis crackpot."

"Jesus Christ. Why didn't I know this? Have you got any idea about those people, the delight they take in embarrassing the United States? She's Ir-*ranian*?"

We shared a moment of continuing mutual shock, albeit arising from much different sources.

"Roger, you're not actually telling me that the intelligence services of the United States get their information about people they're concerned with from Google and Wikipedia, are you?"

He didn't answer that. "We need to have a word with her," he said. "What's her real name?"

"I expect to see her on Thursday. Once I do, you can have at her." I didn't want Roger ruining my surprise.

Esma/Emira would have a lawyer after a visit from the
FBI. He groused about the delay, but knew he had no
choice.

"As long as I have you," he said, "may I ask about the
future of your investigation?"

"I'd say it appears to be wrapping up. I'll know for
sure by the end of the week. There are still lots of
questions, but being frank, none of them appear to be
appropriate concerns for the ICC. I take it that you aren't
the Answer Man?"

"I can't, Boom. We probably know less than you think
about the matters that concern you. Perhaps someone
who's not in the reporting chain any longer could speak
a little more freely. As long as it's completely off the
record."

He meant Merriwell. I paused to think and Roger
filled in the silence.

"I handled things badly last week, Boom. I'm sorry."

"Apology accepted," I said.

I thanked him again for his help with my passport and
promised to get back to him about Esma by the end of
the week.

"Iranian," said Roger one more time before we got off
the phone.

When Nara arrived home, I was in my room. I'd gotten
out a suitcase and was throwing a few things in, as I tried
to figure out what I needed to wash for the trip. She
looked stricken at the sight of the bag.

"Are you leaving me?"

"Just back to the US for a few days. Tie up some loose
ends on my investigation. It's a good time, in any event,
to get out of your way."

"I don't need you out of my way. I was actually thinking it might be a good idea if you were here when Lewis comes."

"That is definitely not the right approach. Nara, you need to do what is best for you. For your life."

She sat down on the bed shaking her head.

"Please don't talk like we're in a play."

"I mean it. If you can salvage your marriage, you should think seriously about doing that."

She tilted her small face to look at me, manifestly displeased.

"Do you truly believe that Lewis is the best thing for me?"

I faced her with a couple of T-shirts in my hand.

"Truly? No. He seems like a dick. No offense."

"And do you not honestly think that you are better for me? Honestly?"

"Honestly, yes. I vote for me. But there are roughly three and a half billion other men on the planet and there's a fair chance that one of them is even better for you than both of us."

She gave me that tiny impish grin.

"I think my life is complicated enough with two men in it," she answered. "I must skip the other three billion for the moment."

We went out to run, but rain started halfway along. Ordinarily, we might have kept going, but we caught each other's eye and went straight home, where we climbed into the shower together.

"Don't give me away so easily, Boom," she said as she clung to me afterward in my bed.

"I'm not giving you away, Nara. But one of the worst moments a person can have is to look up years later and wonder what you did with your life."

"You say these things as if you have no stake in them. How would you feel if I say, 'Okay, you are right, I am going to look for someone else, someone who's certain he wants kids,' or something like that?"

"I'd feel shattered, frankly. But I'd try to understand. I think I would. And I'd move on. I'd have no choice. Only—"

"Only what?" she said.

"Nothing," I said. I had no wish to guilt her, which would have been the result. And I was a little surprised at myself anyway. I'd been about to say, 'Only I'd worry whether I'll ever feel this way again.'

VIII.

Breaking the Law

33.

Foley Square—July 9

I dropped my suitcase at a boutique hotel in Nolita that I'd chosen off the Internet, then walked through Chinatown to Foley Square and 60 Centre Street, the original home in New York City of the State Supreme Court. I had never set foot in this building, although I'd spent more time than I'd liked at the federal courthouse across the street. There, the zesty fuck-you air of New York had left relations between the prosecutors and defense lawyers so permanently embittered that I might as well have introduced myself to the Assistant US Attorneys I had to deal with as the Snake from the Garden.

Like many other courthouses erected in the nineteenth and early twentieth century, 60 Centre was intended to be a temple of Justice, fronted by an imposing Corinthian colonnade. Within, I found what I regarded as standard New York building stock, which is to say a structure with gorgeous bones—marble footboards, graceful arches, grand beaux arts chandeliers on huge brass chains, delicate stenciling on the plaster, and a brightly restored mural over the rotunda featuring such all-stars of justice as Lincoln and Hammurabi. All those glorious details were overcome by weak light, years of grime, scaling paint, and decades of uncompleted repairs, accounting for the frequent use of duct tape on doorways, vents, and some furnishings.

Part 51, the Matrimonial Division courtroom where the Jahanbani case was being heard, was in the same mood as the rest of the building, two and one half stories tall, with pressed panels of oak wainscoting and a lovely turned railing separating the well of the court from the straight-backed oak pews for spectators, where I took my seat. The beauty of the design appeared to be entirely lost in the rush of the day-to-day. A blue plastic recycling bin sat beside the jury box, while decades of justice had taken their toll on the handsome oak furniture on which the finish was splintered along the edges. This was especially true of the long table in front of the judicial bench at which I recognized Esma, seated beside a young woman whom I took to be one of her junior attorneys. At the other end of the same table, the opposing associate and client were also seated, a practice I hadn't seen before and which seemed fairly injudicious, given the hot-tempered nature of divorce litigation. Looking at this arrangement, I suddenly understood how Mr. Jahanbani had gotten batted across the head. He looked none the worse for it, dignified and straight backed, a slender handsome elderly man, bald headed, with a vein beating visibly at his temple.

According to my reading, *Jahanbani v. Jahanbani* now had a procedural history as complex and irregular as the growth pattern of some cancers. In the last few years, the Jahanbanis had been referred out three different times for trial of different issues before hearing officers, called 'referees' in this system, but were back before the beleaguered judge for an evidentiary hearing about whether certain assets of Mr. Jahanbani—of which his wife wanted a piece—were within the jurisdiction of an American court.

Listening now, I could hear the principal lawyers for Mr. and Mrs. bickering before the judge about the order of witnesses for the day. At this stage of my life, I had come to accept that I was basically a law nerd who could sit in virtually any courtroom and be drawn in. I was inevitably engaged by the nuances of the lawyers' performances, and even more by the way the judges, who had heard it all before and, far worse, were going to hear it all again tomorrow, absorbed the speeches and complaints. Probably because the judge's role was the only one here I hadn't played, I was always fascinated by the demeanor each brought to the silent duty of listening. Some displayed visible boredom or churlish impatience, some sat expressionless as a zombie, others evinced a trace of whimsy or—the most admirable, because they were doing what I could never manage—avid interest in every word.

Among trial lawyers, there was always a group who dismissed divorce cases as not litigation at all. I never saw it that way, although it was almost always true that the anguish of the parties dominated the proceedings. No matter what the lawyers' art, you always heard the same agonized lament playing in the space between words like the muffled screech of a violin—'S/he doesn't love me anymore.' That was an injustice for which the law had no soothing response.

The judge, named Kelly, a middle-aged African American woman, had followed the idiosyncratic local practice, sometimes adopted as a bow to democracy, and wore no robe. Seated on the bench in her mauve business suit, Judge Kelly was in charge nonetheless, pleasant but efficient. She ruled without much elaboration in behalf of Esma on the latest dustup. With that, the justice, as judges were called here, announced a recess and exited. All stood, and Esma, chatting with her main lawyer, who'd returned to counsel table, faced my way as they proceeded toward the corridor. I waited just beyond the dark rail.

Catching sight of me, Esma came to a complete halt. Although her eyes never left me, she eventually reached for her lawyer's elbow to send the woman ahead. After another second, Esma exited through the gap in the rail to approach me.

"Bill," she said. She seemed somewhat breathless from surprise. She was again dressed down for court: a simple gray dress, less jewelry, her overgrowth of dark hair tamed by a ribbon tied at the back of her head. She looked well and, as always, beautiful. "This is quite a surprise."

"I need to speak to you," I answered.

"Bill, I'm sorry I never returned your calls. But I don't need to explain, do I?"

"Not that," I said. "Perhaps a few other things."

She pointed and we went into the dim corridor with its marble-clad walls. All in all, she seemed far more poised than I could have been after being discovered in a lie of this magnitude.

"And how is it that you find me here?" she asked.

"A little scouting around. You'd described this case to me."

"Ah yes. You can see it's as I said, bitter and interminable." She was walking me down the hall, out of earshot of anyone else. "By the way, your last message mentioned Bank Street?"

"They claimed to have no information about you, Esma."

"That's just Kayla, the receptionist," she said lightly. "She's protective of everyone's privacy." I was startled for a second, then suddenly comprehended her strategy. Assuming I remained none the wiser, she was continuing to pretend she was the lawyer in the Jahanbani case rather than the client. "And what is it that you need to know, Bill?"

I was wrathful, but personal rebukes would predictably end our conversation. My priority had to be learning what I could about Ferko and her arrangements with him.

"Do you know anything concerning Ferko's current whereabouts?" I asked.

"I don't, Bill. And I don't believe I would tell you if I did. We both know that's information he doesn't want shared. And he's quite put out with you at the moment, as well as me, I might add."

"You've spoken to him?"

"Once. A few weeks ago. After one of your round of messages asking to see him, I rang him. Or tried. When I found his line out of service, I used a number I had for his son. Ferko was quite angry. He thinks you led Laza Kajevic's Tigers to him. Said they cuffed him about and asked questions concerning Goos and you. Is that possible?"

"It was quite inadvertent," I said, although Ferko's answers had probably ended up saving our lives.

"But you accosted Ferko at home?"

"We did."

"Well, that's very much against the rules of your Court, Bill. I'm not surprised he wants nothing to do with you. He was promised that would never occur."

I made no response. I was not going to take instruction from Esma about ethics.

"So you're saying you never even saw his house?" I asked.

She tossed around her head and laughed.

"Never. I had not so much as an address for him. I promised him from the start that I would keep no records that would allow anyone to locate him and punish him for giving evidence. When we met, I reached him by mobile and arranged to see him most often at my hotel." That was how Ferko could perpetrate this hoax. As I'd realized, the very nature of being a protected witness meant no one ever investigated the basic claims he'd made about himself.

"Do you care to know what we found, Esma?"

Accepting that Esma was a studied composition at all times, her surprise, as I described what Goos and I had discovered in Vo Selo, appeared genuine. As she listened, she drew her chin back and pulled her face aside, finally looking behind to find a seat on a stone bench along the wall.

"This is all very strange," she said. "Are you suggesting he was playing a part?"

"More or less."

"How awful," she answered. Then she gave her face a quick little shake to show she didn't quite accept what I was saying. "But you corroborated his testimony. I was there to see the bones in Boldo's grave."

From a seat at the other end of the bench, I offered an outline of what Madame Professor Tchitchikov had concluded concerning the soil in the grave and what the forensics had shown about the bullets Goos recovered.

"But to what end?" Esma asked. "What gain is there to Ferko in planting bullets or claiming his wife is dead when she is alive?" Those were the right questions—even though the logical answers seemed to involve Esma. "I can't make sense of any of this," she said. "We know there was an explosion. We know four hundred people from Barupra disappeared without a trace."

"We exhumed the Cave last week, Esma."

"Finding what?"

"No bodies."

Esma's features were reduced by incomprehension.

"They are buried somewhere else?" she asked.

"No, Esma. What proof was there ever that four hundred people are dead, aside from Ferko's word? Nothing he said is true. In fact, we now believe that a number of the Roma who were living in Barupra at that time are in Kosovo."

"*Kos*-ovo?" She laid one finger on her chin. As I had known her, Esma did not often appear entirely puzzled. She usually had her own goals in mind at every moment, and a strategy for achieving them. "What on earth would impel Ferko to make up such a thing?"

That remained the pivotal question. I gave her my best guess.

"The only alternative that really makes sense to me is that you put him up to it. Paid him perhaps. All for the good of the Roma cause."

"*Me?*" She recoiled so far that she nearly rolled off the stone bench. Sharp anger was also not something I'd witnessed often from Esma. What she'd pulled off required mad skills as an actress, but even so, she was doing a superior job of appearing startled, uncomprehending and now indignant. "Me? What good is it to the Roma cause, as you put it, to trot out such an elaborate lie when it is bound to be ultimately exposed? Really, Bill. I know I disappointed you at one moment, but I am not completely daft. Or entirely disingenuous."

I dragged a hand down my face. I was ready.

"Well, it doesn't surprise you, does it, Esma, that someone would tell elaborate lies and live them out for years, for whatever gratification it offers?"

"I should say I'm very much surprised. Even more so than you, Bill. I've believed all of this about Ferko for nearly a decade."

I held a beat.

"Have you ever heard of a woman from a Persian exile family whose maiden name is Emira Zandi?"

She jolted visibly again. Her eyes were wide and still and she'd drawn her shoulders around herself protectively. Despite her makeup, I thought there had been a change in her color. Most telling, all her wondrous brio was gone, replaced by the flickering arrival of an expression that was the rarest of all the new looks that had come over her in the last few minutes. She was scared.

"Not really," she said. "And what would that have to do with Ferko?"

"Well, Emira Zandi bears a startling resemblance to you, Mrs. Jahanbani."

She waited for a thought. Her mouth twitched over words.

"Mrs. Who?"

"You're a liar," I said. "And a gigantic crackpot. You

could spare me some trouble, not that you would care about that, if you told me why Ferko and you cooked this up?"

I had suddenly given her a handhold, something relatively genuine to hang on to again: angry denial.

"I cooked up nothing with Ferko. I persuaded him to give evidence to your Court, Bill, which required some cajoling. But that is because I so wholeheartedly believed him."

"And weeping over that photograph of his family, Esma." I could still call her nothing else. "Whose idea was that?"

She nodded several times, as if building up inertia to make a concession.

"Yes, I suggested he bring a photo to court, Bill. And I surely told him that it was not worth the anxiety and effort of taking the stand if he did not do his utmost to be sincere. But I did not instruct him to cry crocodile tears. I prepared him, Bill, as you have prepared hundreds of your clients over the years when they were about to go under oath."

It was an essential part of advocacy to rehearse your witnesses to be effective on the stand. Yet there were limits, admittedly subtle ones at times. Yet I never told anybody who was dry-eyed that it would be a good idea to cry.

"Again, Bill, I had nothing to gain by any of the lies you say Ferko was telling."

"Except to call attention to the plight of the Roma."

"The plight of the Roma is painfully obvious on its own. Their suffering, which has gone on for centuries, is not a pretense. And I am not pretending either."

"I have no doubts about the miseries of the Roma. But I will never believe anything you say."

She stared, calculating and doing her best to appear not calculating at all.

"It would take too long to explain this, Bill. But it is Emira Zandi who is a creation. I am who I have told you."

"I only wish. Because I actually liked Esma a good deal. She wasn't the right gal for me for the long run, but she's someone I enjoyed and admired. In some ways she was a dream come true." A wet one, my inner wise guy would have added, but that was not to diminish the depth or the importance of the longing. "But there is no barrister at Bank Street, or in all of the UK for that matter, named Esma Czarni."

"I was called to the bar in my maiden name."

"You told me you were never married. Now I find you and Jahanbani have been involved in a protracted divorce here in New York."

"I knew you were far too respectable to become involved with a married woman, Bill, even though my marriage has been functionally dead for a decade."

She had reconnected with her skills as a liar, leveling her chin and steadying her eyes for the last declarations about Esma. We could leapfrog our way through her fabrications forever, with me exposing one and her answering by making up another, switching identities as need be. She was exorbitantly unhinged. And equally gifted. There was no point.

"You lured me to your bed, Emira, so I would believe all this bullshit. Which I did. It was very exciting."

She responded sternly.

"You wanted to be 'lured,' Bill, as you put it."

"True that. I did."

"But I was never going to be any more to you, Bill,

than a playmate with big tits. You were never going to love me."

The boiling nature of that accusation struck me at first as another of the gambits a savvy fraud employed to put the other party on the defensive. She'd tried this before, casting me as the wrongdoer and herself as the victim. I was ready to remind her that it was she who'd warned me against falling in love.

But again, none of this was about what was rational. It went without saying that someone who lived a made-up reality did so to experience what she wouldn't otherwise. Given that, she had warned me against what in some ways she must have most wanted. Who, after all, ever feels she or he has had enough love?

"I have always suspected you were in love with someone else," Esma said. "I can see that I am right—the signs are all over you, the way you stand apart from me, so defiantly. That's why you're here in the US, isn't it? It's been coming for months. You have gone back to your ex-wife, haven't you, Bill?"

I gripped my forehead instinctively.

"I would have hoped, Esma, Emira, whoever you are—" I stopped. "I would have hoped that whatever else, you would have actually learned something about me. Apparently not."

"You are covering up. I know what I know, Bill. You are now sure you are in love, and not with me. Go ahead, Bill. Go back to your wife and your silly little life in Kindle County."

I stood up. "Are you going to tell me why you did this? Why you engaged in this lengthy charade?"

"The Roma people are entitled to justice, Bill. Whatever you think of me, or wish to believe, the Roma have never had justice. I wanted to bring them some. And in my zeal, I was taken in by Ferko, just like you and Goos."

That, I supposed, was the best I was going to get from her, as much as I would hear from beneath the mask.

"Good-bye, Esma," I said.

I started down the corridor past her, and she laid her hand on my arm as I brushed past. She spoke in a low voice, her eyes again radiating some of their familiar power.

"I never lied to you in bed, Bill," she said.

Outside, it had become an overcast day of jungle humidity. I looked for a place to gather myself. After making a wrong turn, I ended up on an avenue behind the jail, strung with the neon signs for bail bondsmen, where I found a hole-in-the-wall bodega. There were a couple of chipped linoleum tables beneath a clanging window air conditioner, and I sat at one, downing half of a soda from a waxed cup. The floor here hadn't been mopped since the turn of the millennium, and the place had the faint stink of grime and bad plumbing. Several of the hustlers going to or coming from court dates filtered in, speaking too loudly to the Pakistani guy behind the cash register as they purchased lottery tickets or cigarettes. That man, presumably the owner, made no effort to be friendly. One of his hands never came above the scratched Plexiglas counter beside him, a display case of candy and gum bearing a makeshift padlock. I was relatively sure he was holding a weapon of some kind, probably a bat or a crowbar, out of sight.

Pondering now, a few blocks and a few minutes away from Esma, I found myself less enraged than I expected. My parents, especially my father, were never far off whenever I started condemning her for her make-believe life. In truth, many of us did lesser versions of what she had done, settling into new selves at times. Only six months ago, I'd thrown over the life I'd spent a quarter of a century making in Kindle County, because I felt something more authentic calling to me from The Hague.

The one thing that had continued to baffle me was why she wanted to be Roma. But going through my haphazard research about her again before departing for this trip, I'd noticed that probably the most famous person of Rom heritage in the academic world, Professor Bavel Wilson, an outspoken advocate for Roma civil rights, had been for decades a fellow at Caius College at Cambridge, where Esma passed her university years. He was a magnetic and inspirational figure in his YouTube videos, and it was not hard to imagine his effect on the younger Emira. But without the psychological excursions of a biographer, I would never fully comprehend her inner motivations. Did she feel deeply injured or abused for some reason? Probably. Why else would she want to present herself as a member of what Roger had appropriately called the most screwed-over group of white people on earth?

But that remained speculation. The one thing I felt surer of, as I instinctively kept an eye on the lurking types who slid in and out of the bodega, was that Esma's seductive power was rooted in her dual personas. Whoever she was being, some fragment of her consciousness had to be reserved for the other personality, so she could escape to it when need be. Except in the bed. The line of hers that would always excite me most in memory was when she urged me to experience that moment 'when there is nothing of you but pleasure.' For her, the bedroom was a place of purification, where, at peak moments, she was one soul, without reservations or ambiguity. Thus it was probably true that from her perspective she had never lied to me there.

And for that reason she'd been able to recognize a kindred yearning in me. Digging through the layers of her lies and what they meant about the case, about her, and about me, I hit that locked chest that explorers in stories inevitably found when they hunted buried treasure. Within it was my own dirty little secret. No matter how baffling her motives, I would always have to acknowledge this: I had gotten exactly what I wanted from her anyway.

34.

OTR—July 9–10

From the bodega, I tried several calls, connecting with no one. For Nara, it was too late; she'd already silenced her phone. Goos seemed to be out of range in Kosovo. And after getting Roger's voice mail, I texted him all the contact info I had for Emira Jahanbani. In a few months, Rog and I would have dinner and a lot of wine in Kindle County or DC and decide yet again that we'd been friends for too long to turn away from each other now. Finally, I left a message on Merriwell's personal cell, where an out-of-office recording said he'd return tomorrow.

The one person I did reach was Teresa Held, one of my former litigation partners here, whom I met at my hotel for a drink. Teresa had been recently nominated for the federal bench in Brooklyn. She wanted my advice and help about making it through the Senate Judiciary Committee. The bipartisan fan club Roger thought I enjoyed on the Hill had its sole shadow of reality in Judiciary.

My home state's senior senator, who'd made me US Attorney, was now the committee's ranking member, and I also had a friend on the other side of the aisle, my freshman dorm counselor, an R who was the junior senator from Kentucky. Todd remained a wonderfully decent guy, even though my jaw sometimes fell open listening to what he said on TV. I promised to call both senators for Teresa.

Then I went upstairs to order room service and deal with my e-mail. I found a very sweet note Nara had sent before going to sleep, and a couple of messages Goos had forwarded while he was in Kosovo or on his way. Before looking at them, I sent him an e-mail offering a brief précis of my confrontation with Esma. "She claims ardently that Ferko duped her, too. God only knows why but I tend to believe her. She seemed sincerely surprised about his wife and his house and the grave. That said, I wouldn't wager even a keim that there's not a lot more to the story than she acknowledged."

The e-mails Goos had forwarded proved to be from NFI. The first was a report analyzing the explosive residues on the stones Professor Tchitchikov had first collected at the Cave five weeks ago. Given Goos's physical condition, it had taken him a while, once we returned after Kajevic's capture, to deliver the samples to the lab. The Dutch scientists then found it necessary to confer with the FBI. The report they'd finally prepared included a lot of terminology that was beyond me—'fragment range and dispersal,' 'shock wave reflection'—but the conclusion was intelligible: The black stuff was characteristic of a small explosive device, such as a hand grenade, utilized by the United States military. Interestingly, NFI reached this determination based not on the chemical composition of the explosive material, but rather of the metal from the hand grenade wall that was melted into the residue.

Given the NATO aerial surveillance photos, the result was unsurprising, although I still had no idea why US troops wanted to bury five thousand weapons in the Cave. I was mulling that over, when my phone buzzed. It was Merriwell, calling from the limo on his way back home from Dulles.

We talked for a second about baseball. I had paid exorbitantly for seven field box seats for Sunday's Trappers game, to which I would take two sons, one fiancée, one girlfriend, and, as an appreciation of their generosity, Ellen and Howard.

"So you're in the US then?" Merry asked.

"I am. And I was hoping to make a stop in DC to get some more of your time."

"Official business?"

"Not really. Related perhaps, but definitely personal."

"Sounds intriguing."

"I'll explain when I see you."

He weighed that for a second, but said he would have time tomorrow afternoon.

Once I hung up, I booked a seat on the noon Acela and returned to the second e-mail Goos had forwarded, which attached NFI's findings from several of the cell phones that had been recovered from the Cave. The lab had identified four of the cells' owners, although the names meant nothing to me. One of the phones was equipped with a camera. That was still an innovation in 2004, and given the dismal living standard in Barupra, the device might have been acquired by means other than purchase. But whoever was using it had taken pictures of everything—kids, dogs, clouds, cars, and many of the neighbors. The photos were often touching, showing people, even in the midst of agonizing poverty, enjoying what they could.

The most interesting pictures for our purposes had been snapped on the night of April 27, 2004. There were probably a dozen of them. They'd clearly been taken on the sneak, and many were unfocused and often quite dark, but they were still revealing. The first showed a line of Chetniks entering Barupra, weapons in hand. Next were a couple of stills of what I assumed was the Chetnik commander, standing with a flashlight shining on him and with the electric megaphone raised to his mouth. The most dramatic photograph in the bunch was of the same officer, a moment later. The megaphone still hung from his neck but he'd dropped to one knee, his assault rifle raised and flame, like a lizard tongue, jumping from the barrel. Following in the sequence was a photo of the soldiers tearing the old plasterboard sheeting off one of the dwellings, and then several images of the residents marching off toward the trucks at gunpoint, their arms crowded with things precious to them, while young children carried dolls or, even more pathetically, walked with their hands in the air. The last shot was fairly blurry, and it required a minute to make out the forms: the bodies of Boldo and his son. The boy had fallen faceup on his father's chest, as they lay together on the ground brown with blood.

I had visualized and revisualized what had happened in Barupra so often, based on Ferko's account, that I was instantly comparing what was here to what I'd imagined. Having dismissed Ferko as largely a con, I was startled that so much of what had been captured in these images bore out his testimony. Yet I also felt exhausted by the constant chase for the truth with Ferko and cautioned myself against trying to reach conclusions. Some of the hardest words for an investigator, especially after lots of work, are 'We'll never know.'

Once I set that aside, I found myself nagged at by something else, a sense I might have known the commander. His form—his posture and narrow physique—in the three photos in which he appeared seemed familiar. I couldn't place him, although I had a visceral memory that he was someone I liked. My best guess was that he was one of the soldiers I'd met under General Moen's command.

Merriwell was CEO of Distance Communications, a job he'd held quite successfully since leaving the service in scandal. The corporate campus was in northern Virginia, not far from the Pentagon, on a piece of land with hills and big deciduous trees, surrounded by a fence of steel spears at least fifteen feet high. At the guardhouse, I gave my name and waited for the back-and-forth until I was admitted.

For a company I'd literally never heard of before I met Merriwell, Distance had headquarters whose size astounded me. At least fifty acres served as a security perimeter for a network of low functional-looking buildings, designed with little regard to the lush hills behind them. The reception area was all marble but there was a hush to the place that seemed unnerving, especially in combination with the cameras that hung from most corners of the ceiling. After I signed in with the stoic receptionist, one of the cameras rotated to follow me back to my chair. I was sure I was being processed in facial recognition software against a database of terrorists. After a while, I received a clip-on badge, and one of Merriwell's assistants emerged to escort me back.

The office to which she led me was vast. When I was US Attorney, I used to make jokes about the size of my office, saying that because the government didn't pay much in salary, you were rewarded instead with square footage. But the space Merriwell inhabited had to be at least three times as large. You'd literally have trouble hearing someone on the other side of the room unless they shouted. Because the space was so huge, it had a somewhat barren quality. The furniture, for example, appeared to have been left over since 1960, teak Danish Modern, although I knew that stuff was coming back. Even so, Merry could have done more to warm the place up. Aside from the lone photo of his grandchild, there was not a picture in the place. The only decorations were awards the company had received over the years from DoD. I'd represented another defense contractor during my days in private practice and had been impressed by the deliberately nondescript character of the employees' workspaces, especially the battleship-gray walls. I took it now that was an industry practice.

Merriwell, in his white shirt and sedate tie, greeted me warmly, then showed me to a twelve-seat conference table that absorbed a corner of the room. He looked even better than a few weeks back and now had that vital windswept color that comes from lots of sailing. He said he'd been spending quite a bit of time at his place on the Eastern Shore. That was where Rog's weekend home was, too, and I suspected they passed time together.

I asked if they'd spoken this week.

"We've been missing each other. He told me he

wanted to have a cup of coffee, but I was in West Africa until yesterday. I assume I'm about to find out what he has on his mind?"

I shrugged.

"The one thing he told me on the phone," Merriwell said, "was that your investigation is nearing its end."

"It is. We exhumed the Cave."

"With what result?"

"Well, I guess from your perspective, Merry, I'd probably say it was good news and bad."

"Okay," said Merriwell. He thought. "I'm feeling more optimistic lately, so I'll take the good news first."

"No bodies."

He nodded many times with his mouth pursed.

"Forgive me, Boom, but I have told you more than once to expect that."

"Based on what?"

"I'm sorry?"

"What made you so confident that the Roma of Barupra weren't all massacred?"

"I was promised that emphatically. I told you I spoke to my senior officers before you and I first met."

"Which of your senior officers assured you the Roma weren't murdered?"

I received Merry's scowl, his faint brows drawn into his eyes.

"You know I can't answer that, Boom."

"I say it was Attila. She had control of the trucks that ended up taking the Roma from Barupra."

"Well, now you seem to know more than I do."

"I doubt that, Merry."

"If you have questions about Attila, she's probably the best person to answer them."

"If she will."

"Why wouldn't she?"

"I was hoping you'd be able to explain that to me."

He gave a slow, ponderous shake of the head to show he had no idea.

"And I suppose," he said, "I should ask for the bad news."

"We found about five thousand light arms—assault rifles, grenades, ammunition, RPGs, mortars—a true armory. The bulk of them were of Yugoslav manufacture, but bore laser markings indicating they'd been in NATO's custody. Am I telling you anything you don't know?"

"That there were five thousand weapons in what you call the Cave? Frankly, I'm astounded."

I considered whether I believed him.

"Well," I said, "I think we're verging on things you do know about. If my deductions are correct, those weapons were stolen by some of the Roma from a convoy that Attila was running to the airfield at Camp Comanche. About a hundred of those stolen arms were then sold by the Gypsies to Kajevic, who ended up using them to wound or kill twelve of your troops. That fact, I sense, was not only tragic for you, but problematic. Because all of those arms—the ones Kajevic used, the ones in the Cave, the ones in the convoy—were part of about 500,000 weapons you were collecting to ship to Iraq whose ultimate disposition seems to be quite mysterious."

Merry had watched me with his lead-gray eyes absolutely still.

"Perhaps I'm helping you understand, Merry, why Rog wants a coffee date?"

"Boom, I thought you told me this wasn't official business."

"It isn't. The ICC prosecutes crimes against humanity, not weapons trafficking. Besides, you and I both know that it's against the law for me to be investigating on US soil, or for you to be helping me. This is just one of those conversations between two guys that isn't even happening."

Merry looked at me askance as he continued reflecting.

I said, "You had to have known within hours of the casualties in Doboj that those soldiers were shot with weapons that had been stolen from NATO. Originally, when I learned that, I thought you had kept that information to yourself because it was so embarrassing—our only combat fatalities in Bosnia coming with ammo and small arms that had been taken out of our hands. Then, over time, I reconsidered and wondered if you were suppressing that information because the Roma's theft and sale of those arms gave American soldiers such a strong motive to play vigilante and to go kill the Gypsies."

Merriwell shook his head and said simply, "No."

"We'll come back to that," I said. "But more recently, I've become aware of something else, which is why I referred to the guns in the Cave as bad news for you. The problem with acknowledging that our soldiers had been killed with light arms stolen from one of our convoys was that somebody—the press, the parents of one of those slain soldiers, a representative in Congress—one of those somebodies would inevitably ask why in the hell a convoy of NATO-seized weapons was headed to Camp Comanche in the first place. Where were those weapons being flown? Because those arms—the guns that killed our soldiers, the guns buried in the Cave, the guns in the convoy, all 500,000 small arms headed to Iraq—were what you guys really don't want to talk about."

"I understand what you're suggesting," said Merriwell.

"But?"

"But the disposition of the Bosnian weapons sent to Iraq remains a highly classified matter."

"It's eleven years later, Merry."

"Revising security classifications was never my job, Boom, and it certainly isn't now. I'm sorry. It goes without saying that this business"—a finger circled the room—"depends on not overstepping those boundaries."

I'd heard a lot of that bullshit by now. I folded my hands on the table. I was never under the illusion that Merriwell and I had become friends, despite sharing some personal moments. I think we respected each other, but we'd always recognized that our roles were in some way antagonistic.

"I really didn't come here to threaten you, Merry."

I got an unwilling smile. "But you're going to threaten me anyway. I'll tell you right now that if you truly think I was engaged in arms trafficking, then you have no leverage at all."

"Well, I'll tell you one thing I *do* know, Merry, one of those pieces of criminal law trivia you learn as a federal prosecutor, which I suspect you know, too: There's a wartime exception to the federal criminal statute of limitations. Anything that might be regarded as a fraud against the US government will be prosecutable for at least five years after the last troops left Iraq, which means Roger and you remain in the crosshairs until the end of 2016 at least. I don't know exactly what you guys did, but I'm pretty sure that your mutual anxiety attack isn't just about face-saving. The efforts you've made to hide this have been too sustained and energetic. And nobody grits his teeth through an accusation of war crimes on the front page of the *New York Times*—especially an accusation that's untrue—unless silence is required to hide something real."

I got a very tough look from Merriwell. He was a soldier.

"So, Merry, consider me like many other successful fifty-five-year-old lawyers. I have lots of friends on Capitol Hill, people who'd be happy to see me on short notice, including the senator who named me US Attorney. People in office always enjoy getting their names in the paper as champions of the truth—and American taxpayers. My goal isn't to embarrass Roger or you. But I'm not going to be stonewalled either. I've just wasted six months of my life investigating a crime that didn't happen, so you guys could avoid an investigation of what did. I'd like some answers. Call them hypothetical if you like. But if I was imagining that 500,000 small arms were going to be shipped to Iraq, should I be thinking they got there?"

Erect in his chair, in a posture he'd probably first assumed by the time he was five, Merriwell drummed his fingers on the tabletop.

"All OTR?" he asked. Off the record.

"Deep dark OTR," I said.

Nonetheless, he took another instant.

"They were sent in two shipments," he said then. "My belief is that they all arrived at the airport in Baghdad. What happened after that is somewhat opaque."

I smiled. That was the same word Roger had used in January when he visited me in my law office.

"And why opaque?"

"There were documents that showed that officials of the Iraqi Ministry of Defense signed for the weapons. But the Iraqis claimed subsequently those signatures were forgeries."

"So the weapons never got to Iraq?"

"No, they were definitely in Iraq."

"If the guns were in Iraq, why did the Defense Ministry deny they'd received them?"

Merriwell, cautious by nature, watched me, clearly weighing what to say next.

"Many of the weapons were recovered on the battlefield," he said at last.

I didn't get it for a second.

"From the enemy?"

"Yes."

"He sold them to Al Qaeda in Iraq? The defense minister?"

"Or they were stolen from him. Or they were diverted before reaching Baghdad, which is what the Iraqis claimed."

"So you shipped hundreds of thousands of weapons to Iraq that were then used to kill US soldiers and Marines?"

Merriwell declined to react. His face was granite.

"It would have been very embarrassing, Boom. No question about that. But there were no witnesses, at least none who would talk to us about seeing the weapons shipments in Baghdad. Ultimately, the White House and DoD decided this had to remain a top-secret matter, because of the lasting damage it would have done to our relationship with the new government of Iraq.

"You must remember the context, Boom. After the

invasion in 2003, we disarmed the civilian police and the armed forces because they were Saddam's proxies— almost all were Sunnis, like Hussein. But they were also the only forces trained to maintain order. By the time we realized we had made a catastrophic mistake and wanted to give those folks their weapons back, a Shia-dominated government was in power, whose members recoiled at that prospect. So if the Iraqi Shia government misdirected a weapon or two for every assault rifle given back to the Sunnis, we had no choice but to accept it. Weapons in this world are like currency. They are in demand everywhere." Merry hitched a shoulder. "Al Qaeda would have bought arms from someone else."

It was bribery, of course, of a sophisticated form: Help the defense minister and God knows who else loosen their objections to rearming the Sunnis by allowing him and his cronies to pad their Swiss bank accounts.

"Merry, I doubt the American taxpayers would have been philosophical about the Iraqi defense minister selling the weapons killing our troops. No wonder DoD and the White House didn't want that story to get out. It would have devastated support for the war."

Merriwell pulled his lips into his mouth.

"You know that I never favored that war, Boom. But the task that confronted me once I arrived was to salvage the remnants of an entire society. We'd destroyed their government and every public institution. We were stuck, unless we wanted to leave and hand the Iranians title to the whole country."

As Nara insisted, there were often no good choices once a war begins.

"And why are Roger and you so squeamish if the White House and Defense were onboard originally?"

He displayed a sardonic little smile.

"You probably know how the blame game goes in this town, Boom. Memories fade. Fingers point. You can't find ten people who were in Congress who'd say they would invade Iraq again today. A lot of this would come down to what was documented, in a situation in which no one ever wanted to put anything in writing. Roger was the top intelligence officer. I was the senior commander. As they say, Shit rolls downhill. And over the years, Boom, there were several congressional briefings and inquiries where someone might say Roger and I chose our words a little too carefully."

I closed my eyes to think it through. If I was Merry's lawyer, I'd see the perils very clearly. The people above Merriwell in the chain of command would bob and weave. They'd say they didn't know in advance that the Iraqi defense minister was going to divert the weapons, and certainly not to Al Qaeda. And in a fluid situation, where the truth moved like quicksilver and calamity was always at hand, it was possible, even likely, that Roger and Merry hadn't waited for all the right approvals. Even eleven years later, there would be fury, starting with the families of every soldier who died in Iraq in that period. It would get really ugly, really fast.

And Layton Merriwell—who even tried to help me in order to avoid further damage to his name—was clearly not up to another scandal. Or to shredding one more career. Or years of grand juries and lawsuits, or even prosecution. With his government pension, Roger had a special vulnerability. I didn't need to reread Title 18, the US criminal code, to figure out if arming the enemy was an offense. The second shipment, after Merriwell and Roger knew the guns were likely to go awry, would be very very hard to defend—which was why the officials above them were bound to maintain they never had the complete picture.

"Three years later, in 2007," Merry said, "the Administration and I were no longer on the same page about the war, as you know. I was just starting to read my name in the papers—"

"As a presidential candidate?"

He nodded. "There was suddenly a flurry of congressional inquiries about the weapons we'd gathered in Bosnia. I understood it was a shot across the bow. Eventually, senior Administration figures intervened to convince a couple of committee chairs that this was Pandora's box for many people besides me."

"Is that why you decided not to run? To end that investigation?"

He laughed a little.

"I had many reasons for not running. Florence was completely against it. My chances were slight. For the most part, I couldn't imagine spending every day begging for money like a monk with a tin cup. But yes, my announcement that I was staying in the military certainly encouraged everyone to let the sleeping dogs lie.

"One odd development, though, was that the compelling Ms. Czarni showed up in Bosnia asking about Barupra at almost exactly the same time. I've always assumed that was a coincidence, but I could never convince Attila."

"Speaking of Attila—she was the one who told you that the people of Barupra were alive?"

"Hypothetically."

"When?"

"A few days before I first met with you."

"Did you ask where they were? Or why someone couldn't just tell the Court that?"

"Attila said they had been promised complete confidentiality concerning their whereabouts. It was like the Witness Protection Program on a large scale."

"Because?"

"Because Laza Kajevic wanted to kill them. He'd sworn revenge on them after the firefight in Doboj. They would always be in mortal danger as long as Kajevic remained at large."

A surprised sound escaped me, although now that Merry said it, I realized I should have put that together on my own. That was why people who'd been AWOL for the last eleven years were suddenly out in the open.

"Attila's explanation made some sense, Boom. But certainly, under the circumstances, it wasn't my secret to tell you. Nor was it my right to put those people at risk. I did my best to lead you to the NATO records, thinking they'd provide you some clues. Once I saw those aerial surveillance photos, I admit I got a sinking feeling. I hoped Attila had some role in moving those people. It was possible, of course, that she had lied to me, and the Gypsies in the pictures were instants away from their deaths. But I could never make myself believe that."

"You didn't ask Attila?"

"I learned a long time ago, Boom, that when it came to the intelligence services and the civilian contractors, I was very much 'need to know.' I stayed between the lines. And, by contrast, I never discussed the materials I turned over to you with Attila. It was your job to get to the bottom of all that, not mine."

I understood the eyes-forward mentality, but I didn't really approve when the question Merriwell avoided asking Attila was, Did you commit a crime against humanity? But his logic was that there was nothing to gain. If Attila said no, Merry would still be unsure whether she was speaking the truth. And even worse, what would Merriwell do if his former top NCO answered yes?

"And what about my witness, Ferko? Any idea what he was up to? Was he protecting the people of Barupra by testifying they were dead?"

"Same answer: I never asked. My assumption was that his testimony was a contrivance of Ms. Czarni's, but your guess is as good as mine. Maybe he was being heroic."

Lawyers and judges, who placed a sacred weight on testimony, seldom saw perjury in that light. And as Goos and I had acknowledged, it was hard to conceive of the man we met in Vo Selo, with his little castle and a ring on each finger, as a bold protector of his people. But perhaps. What had Merriwell said? With their need to live in an ever-changing present, the Gypsies don't really see it as lying anyway.

I closed my eyes again to concentrate and conjure up my remaining questions. I'd made notes on the plane, but it didn't seem sporting to take them out.

"And in 2004, what did you understand about the Roma's role regarding Kajevic?"

"Less than you seem to think. I knew that the Roma had provided the intelligence on Kajevic's whereabouts. My information was that they sold his people black-market goods—car parts, something like that—and recognized only later whom they'd been dealing with. But even after our soldiers were killed and wounded, I didn't know that the Roma had stolen the weapons or sold them to Kajevic. I admit, Boom, that those arms were a sensitive issue that we didn't want the press or Congress to explore for fear of where it would lead. But, as you point out, the identity of the thieves was not central to that concern."

"So who did you think stole the weapons?"

"I'd been told at the time that those trucks had been hot-wired in the middle of the night by thieves who escaped unseen. Because of other information, Army Intelligence formed a theory that the thieves were jihadis who wanted to get the guns to the Middle East. That's why we were so unprepared for the firepower Kajevic had acquired. I left for Iraq two days after the raid, when no one yet had an explanation for how Kajevic got his hands on the weapons—or the trucks, for that matter."

"When did you learn about the Roma's role in that?"

"I think it was 2007 when Ms. Czarni showed up in Bosnia. Attila told Roger, and Roger told me, that the disappearance of the Roma had some relationship to the weapons Kajevic used. Again, I didn't ask for details."

I took a second again to piece things through. In the interval, Merriwell hiked across the room to speak to his assistant on the phone. I could tell that his next meeting was ready to start. I promised him not to be much longer, but he took the time to refresh our coffees from a black plastic Thermos before he resumed his seat in his leather chair.

I asked the question I'd been saving for last.

"Any chance Attila sold the weapons to Kajevic?"

Merriwell did me the favor of briefly reflecting on the possibility before shaking his head emphatically.

"Her behavior has been a bit odd. I imagine you could see that I was surprised when you thanked me at your ex-wife's house for encouraging Attila to assist you. The day before that, she'd been on the phone, raising her voice with me and insisting I was crazy to turn the NATO records over to you. And she was very put out when I told her that I couldn't describe the documents. Attila hates no answer more than, I can't tell you. But selling weapons to Kajevic? There isn't money enough to make Attila Doby betray her country or our soldiers."

"She's back in the US apparently," I said. "Do you have her address?"

"I'm sure." Merriwell crossed the office again—he really needed a backpack and a walking stick in here to go end to end—and eventually phoned one of his assistants, who, he said, would provide me with all of Attila's domestic contact information on my way out.

At the door, Merry again offered his hand. I remained impressed by how hale and confident he looked with his summer tan. He was a complicated guy, like most of us. But I felt he'd told me the truth today. For the most part, he always had, at least about what concerned me: There was no massacre.

"I hope you will stay in touch, Boom. I still look back on that dinner we had as a transformative moment in my life."

"I take no credit."

"You gave me hope," he said. "Which was borne out. You'll have to come to dinner again to take a look at my place next time you're in town. Jamie's redecorating. I'm sure you saw that it needed it."

I could feel my face fall.

"Oh." Merriwell smiled hugely when he saw my expression. It was probably the most amused I'd ever seen him, grinning broadly enough to reveal a lot of gum recession. "I guess the American gossip rags don't reach The Hague."

"I don't keep track of them, that's for sure."

"Jamie's come back to me." He was referring to Major St. John. "She left Rick. I would never have had the courage to reach out again were it not for you."

I shook his hand once more, and on my way out accepted a piece of paper from Merriwell's assistant, but I remained dazed. I could not imagine what Merriwell heard in my advice to move on that he reinterpreted to fit his own needs. But he had what he wanted, at least for a while. I had told him, 'Stay happy,' as I departed, but I left feeling the man was probably doomed.

35.

Foreign Voices—July 10–11

I stayed overnight in DC at the Huntington and managed to reach college friends, Melvin and Milly Hunter, for dinner. The Hunters—he was black and she was white—were both physicians, Milly an ENT and Melvin an oncologist. We talked mostly about our kids, but the subject turned to race, everything from Obama through Michael Brown. When I first met Melvin, he did not like to mention in public that he was black, but he seemed increasingly desperate about how inescapable color was in America, particularly for their kids, whom they'd idealistically brought up to check 'Other' on forms asking about race.

I was asleep early, but left my phone on, hoping to hear from Nara. We'd been exchanging voice mails, but still hadn't connected. As I was leaving The Hague, she appeared just a little uneasy that I was going to see Esma, although her discomfort was minor compared to my apprehensions about her visit with Lew.

Near 4 a.m., my phone pinged and I roused myself and turned on the light, sitting at the edge of the bed with my hands on my thighs while I tried to remind myself where I was.

The text was from Goos. He'd positioned himself at an Internet café and wondered if we could speak by Skype. He'd attached several photos of the people he'd interviewed in the last couple of days.

His image swam a bit on the screen and shattered into uneven lines before it cohered. We ended up starting with a rundown on my conversation with Merriwell.

"Think we're lucky he's taken a liking to you, Boom."

"Maybe. He knows I'm reluctant to burn Roger. But I think he was afraid not to tell me the truth."

Like me, Goos could see how Merry and Roger would be left holding the bag if the Iraqi weapons shipments became a subject of public discussion. Even if they ended up pointing fingers at the White House to save themselves, it would make a grim end to their public careers, with no guaranteed outcome.

Eventually, we turned to the results of Goos's efforts in Kosovo.

"Talked to about forty people in the last two days," Goos said. "Some by themselves, some in groups. Have a couple folks standing by, if you've a mind to ask questions yourself."

"What's the executive summary before we do that?"

"Making it very skinny, the 386 souls who used to live in Barupra arrived here on April 28, 2004."

"And here is Mitrovica? The refugee camp where the locals tried to burn them out in 1999?"

"Right you are, Boom. Not much more popular now hereabouts, I'd say. A hundred thousand or so Roma in Kosovo back then and ninety thousand ended up as refugees. Usual story. Everybody hates them."

I was experiencing some difficulty sorting out my reactions. I was supposed to be happy these people were still alive.

"And what happened to them once they got to Mitrovica?"

"Well, I sent you photos, but here, this café is just across the street."

He swung his laptop around. What I saw was not much better than Barupra, shacks with corrugated tin roofs, sided in canvas or bare planks. As in Barupra, there were dwellings under blue tarps and, in one case, the old drab tenting of the UN relief agency. Clothing hung on wash lines, and as always there were piles of metal refuse everywhere. The place was deep in mud.

"The reason there was still room in the old camp here," Goos said, "was there'd been a lot of whinging that folks were getting sick. Turns out it's right down the hill from a lead mine. Place was finally closed a few years back. But there's still thirty, forty of the Roma from Barupra squatting here."

"What about lead poisoning?"

"What about it? There's dead kids, blind kids, kids with all manner of problems. Some of the grown-ups have got nerve conditions. But there's nowhere else to go. Most from Barupra are over in a better camp, former UN barracks, little white buildings. And a lot have fallen back in with the Roma community in town, the Mahalla. But aren't a lot of them here, Boom, wherever they're living, that've got a piece of piss for a life—it's all damn hard."

"No happy endings for the Roma?"

"Not in this movie."

On my tablet, I navigated to the photos Goos had sent: kids in cheap dirty clothes, most of them in short pants, as seemed to be the custom without regard to the season. The adults had the insular weathered look I'd seen before. They wore Crocs and no socks and polyester jackets and surplus T-shirts with ridiculous slogans that had caused the garments to go unsold until the Roma bought them for pennies. The sight was starting to have a disheartening familiarity.

"Was it easy getting them to talk?"

"Not easy. The younger ones were better. A couple months back, before Kajevic was captured, I'd have had Buckley's chance with any of them." That was more or less what I'd pieced together with Merriwell.

"How it turned out, Boom, I was a bit tin-arsed." He meant he'd been lucky. "Recollect Sinfi from Lijce, the other Roma town? You told me all about her."

I wouldn't forget Sinfi soon. She was the thin beautiful young woman who first informed us about Kajevic's threats, while holding her nine-month-old on her hip.

"I was having a squizz around the camp here," Goos said, "when I saw this sheila and thought to myself, Must be she's Sinfi's sister." He had to be referring to the withered arm. "So I asked her, you know. Turned out I was right. I lent her my mobile to call Lijce. No one here's got international service. Happy times, Boom. Tears of joy. I was everybody's mate after that. Only thing was the lot of them wanted to be double sure Kajevic was in irons. Had a couple NATO photos to show them."

"So you're the big man on campus?"

"Could say. You know, Boom, I suspect some of them are looking to have a lend of us. Just their way. They'll

stick their hands out soon enough. Reparations? Whatever they can get. You understand, Boom. They're poor."

I didn't need to tell Goos how to steer around that:
Make no promises but, on the other hand, don't tell
them now that their hopes were unrealistic. It was almost
impossible to deal with the Roma without screwing them
over in some way.

"So here's our man Ion." Lacking directorial skills,
Goos forgot to re-aim the camera, which I assumed was
in his laptop, perched in turn on a café table. But eventually Ion was at Goos's side. Ion was chunky, with a full
face and wiry black hair and brown as an old penny. He
was a good-natured sort, smiling often, despite his den-
tition, in which his two front teeth appeared to be alone
in his upper gum. The sight of him took me all the way
back to childhood and a puppet called Ollie, a dragon
with a single tooth that overlapped his lower lip.

Ion spoke quickly in Serbo-Croatian and also knew
a few words of English, since he was another former
CoroDyn employee. But Goos frequently held him up so
he could translate for me.

Ion had worked on Boldo's crew and drove regularly
for Attila and CoroDyn. In mid-March 2004, he was
deployed on several convoys, picking up stores of
weapons at various facilities around Bosnia and delivering them to Camp Comanche for what I now knew was
air transport to Iraq. The final convoy did not follow
the pattern.

"They went down toward Mostar and picked up the
load of weapons, twelve trucks, but when they got back
toward Tuzla, Boldo suddenly tells half of them, Ion
included, to take the arms and the trucks to Barupra.
Boldo had them steer these rigs down that road to the

Cave in the middle of the night, which didn't make any of these blokes especially content, but Boldo is mean as cat's piss. In the morning, Ion and a dozen of them from the village unloaded the weapons from the trucks. Boldo is strutting around, grinning like a shot fox, saying how he had a customer for some of this."

"Was this new?" I said. "Did Boldo deal in stolen guns regularly?"

"Boldo," Goos told me, after he'd asked, "was pretty good at boosting cars and chopping them. But weapons, so far as Ion knew, that was a new lurk for Boldo."

Goos and Ion again chatted for a minute. In the afternoon, after all the arms were unloaded, Boldo and Ion and the other drivers were taken back to where the rest of the convoy had waited. Then they proceeded to Commanche, where Boldo reported the hijacking. The next day, the men working for Boldo warehoused the weapons in the Cave.

"Ion was up top of the ridge for a rest when he sees a car raising dust across the valley. Looked like a jet with a vapor trail, doing 150 kilometers at least."

Ion was a vivid storyteller like so many other Roma. He was in the midst of rolling himself a cigarette but was able to do a pantomime illustrating the speed of the car, even while Ion held the unsealed paper, lined with tobacco, in his other hand.

"Sedan parks in front of the Cave, and even on top, Ion can hear Attila screaming, cross as a frog in a sack. 'Where's Boldo? *Where's* Boldo?'"

"Boldo comes sauntering down and Attila gets up in his grill. Quite the blue."

Ion made a shooting gesture.

"What's that?" I asked.

"Says if either had a sidearm there'd have been bullets fired, that's how mad they were."

"Did Ion hear any of the argument?"

"He and quite a few others started down the road to watch. But mostly it was in English, with some Bosnian at times. He remembers Boldo saying to Attila, 'When generals steal they are heroes, and when Gypsies steal they are thieves.'"

Ion added something then at which Goos drew back. He was clearly asking Ion to repeat it.

"Ion also recalls Boldo saying to Attila, 'You said we should steal these weapons.'"

I took a second.

"And how did Attila respond?"

Ion took the time to light his cigarette, then made the shooting gesture again with his thumb and his fore-finger.

"And what's the conclusion to this argument?" I asked.

"Attila gives a bunch of orders. Boldo is all sulky. Attila is standing there, like a mom over a kid, while Boldo gets out his acetylene torch and starts parting out one of the trucks."

"Chopping it?"

"Yay, they get done with a couple and put the pieces back in the Cave and call it a day."

I asked Goos, "Do you understand what was up with Attila?"

"Nary a clue."

"Okay."

"As soon as Attila is gone, Boldo starts mocking her, how no dyke is gonna be telling him what to do. Eventually, Boldo slinks off to town. Usually does some dirty business in the clubs outside Tuzla, them that will let a Gypsy in."

Goos turned back to Ion to listen.

"Right," Goos said. "Next morning this pimply bogan, kid maybe twenty, druggie-looking, gray teeth from meth, shows up, so much cash it doesn't fit in one pocket. Ion gets called back down to the Cave, and he and several other blokes load up two of the covered cargo trucks that haven't been chopped, with a hundred assault weapons, body armor, ammo, RPGs, mortars. Very big score for Boldo. About 40,000 keim." Roughly $20,000 American. "Boldo is going to deliver all that after dark."

"Did Ion make the delivery?" I asked.

In reply, Ion was emphatic with Goos.

"No. For that, Boldo sent three of his regulars who helped him boost cars, including our friend Ferko. Ion and Ferko were mates in those days, so Ion heard about this from Ferko afterwards. Apparently the trucks and weapons went to the wrecked part of Doboj that took a lot of hits while the Serbs were driving out everyone else.

"Now Ion here doesn't know exactly what Ferko heard or saw, but Ferko, when he comes back he's all ropeable and gets into it with Boldo. Boldo puts a pistol on Ferko in the end to shut him up. Afterwards, Ferko is still spewin, tells Ion that Boldo is dealing with Satan and this all is never gonna come good: Between NATO and the Bosnians, every person in town who so much as looked at those weapons is gonna be at the bottom of a dungeon somewhere. Made enough of an impression on Ion that he didn't go back down there to the Cave again."

"And when is this exactly, Goos?"

"Could only guess, Boom, but maybe April 1."

"Two weeks before the firefight with Kajevic?"

"I'm guessing, yeah." Goos shook with Ion, while Goos waved in a woman he introduced as Florica. Her arm was held close to her body. A tiny cramped hand, dark and skeletal, protruded from her sleeve. This had to be Sinfi's sister. She was much shorter than Sinfi and quite round, wearing a long skirt and head scarf. She was a smiler, though, and instantly appealing. Ion continued lurking in the background.

Goos asked her to repeat what he'd heard from her before.

"About three weeks later—" Goos said.

"April 20?"

"Thereabouts. A couple soldiers show up in Barupra from Republika Srpska. Boldo, you know, he's on commercial terms with many of the local gendarmes, and she thinks these two are here for the same reason, but no, these two tell Boldo in front of Florica and half the camp that they have solid info that Laza Kajevic intends to kill every greasy Gypsy in the place for dobbing him in to NATO."

"And how did Boldo react?"

Unbidden, Ion moved back into the frame to act out the scene between Boldo and the soldiers, falling to his knees with his hands joined in prayer.

"Boldo is swearing that's a lie. He gets two of his children and, on their lives, says he did no such thing. No one in Barupra is such a dill as to speak against Kajevic."

"But someone in Barupra did exactly that, right? Informed?"

"Bloody oath, Boom. You and I missed a lot of this

story, but we got that right a while ago. One of the Roma told NATO where Kajevic was."

"Like maybe Ferko?"

"How I'm thinking."

"And what's the reaction in Barupra?"

"Panic, Boom. Kajevic, you might have noticed, cunning as a dunny rat. He doesn't threaten anybody who can run and hide. This way he gets a giggle out of putting a knife to their throats. Truth is they're refugees already. These folks have nowhere to go and no way to get there. They can't ask NATO for protection, because NATO and the Americans would lock up half the village for stealing the weapons in the first place. All the trucks are either sold or chopped by now."

"And what does Boldo say to this threat?"

Goos put the question to Florica.

"Boldo is all like, No worries. The soldiers believed him, he says, that he never told NATO. Besides, if they ever see Kajevic's Tigers coming, they've got five thousand weapons down in the Cave and can defend themselves. In the meantime, a different family will stand sentry every night, just in case."

"Boldo hasn't sold the rest of those guns yet?"

"No no. Seems like Attila warned him off that. Florica here says some people in Barupra wanted Boldo to hand out weapons to every family, but he wasn't hearing that."

Ion offered a sardonic interjection with a bitter smile.

"Ion here thinks Boldo was afraid if he handed out rifles, someone in town would shoot him and bring the body to the Bosnian Army as proof that Kajevic didn't need to kill anyone else. Boldo, for all of that, he started in sleeping with his AK."

The scene around Goos, especially Ion's theatrics, had

begun to attract a small crowd, mostly kids. Naturally, some of the children began to stick their faces in front of Goos's camera, and both Ion and he had to shoo them away. Florica actually swatted one of the boys in the back of the head, not a serious blow but enough to make a point.

"And where are we in time now, Goos?"

"Well, we've got to be in the last week in April 2004, because a few nights later, Ion and Florica say they woke up to find armed Chetniks going house to house in the village."

"What happened to the sentries?"

Goos asked Ion. I could make out the word 'Ferko' in his response.

"Ferko was the sentry?" I asked.

"Ferko and his sons and his sons-in-law."

Ion rattled on again for a minute. "He says," said Goos, "that was the last they heard tell of Ferko until about a month ago when he showed up here again. There's to be a *kris* in a week or two—you know, the Gypsy court—to decide whether to expel him. Ferko is saying he saved all of their lives. And they're thinking he sold all of them out."

"Any opinions on that, Goos?"

"Well, we know Ferko more or less assumed Boldo's business."

I took a second to ponder Ferko, who was still not coming into focus. I'd never sensed in him the kind of guile these manipulations with the Americans required.

I asked Goos to direct the witnesses back to the entry of the Chetniks into the village close to midnight on April 27. In the interval, another person, Dilfo, had intruded onto the screen. He was an old man, rotund, with a face like a potato. He was Florica's father-in-law and the father of Ion and Prako, Florica's husband. All three began talking and Goos held them up at times to translate.

"These Chetniks are very well organized. First thing Ion and Dilfo see is they encircle Boldo's house. And there's a commander outside who speaks good Serbo-Croatian using an electronic megaphone to tell Boldo to come out with his hands up. And Boldo instead comes flying out with a Zastava and they gunned him down when he was not more than four steps from his door. Commanding officer fired first, and then there were shots from each side."

Goos and Ion conversed for a while in Serbo-Croatian.

"Ion says anyone who knew Boldo would know he wasn't gonna be raising his hands. It all happened very fast. Boldo goes down. Then the son runs out and grabs his father's AK and another soldier shoots him. Then the brother arrives, screaming that Boldo never talked to the Americans and how can you kill him? They try to disarm the brother, pretty much like Ferko testified, but the brother, Refke, he gets shot, too. I mean, I heard about forty different versions of this part of the story in the last couple days, Boom. None of them tell it quite the same."

"The usual," I said. Few humans cultivated skills of cool observation while they were watching people get killed.

"In the meantime, the Chetniks go house to house, rousting everyone. The Roma are all begging for their lives to start, assuming this is Kajevic come to kill them, but the Chetnik on the megaphone is saying, 'You're safe, you're going back to Kosovo.' The soldiers search everybody and take the cell phones from the few of them who owned such back then. And load the Roma on the trucks at gunpoint. No one is fighting now that Boldo and his kin have been shot."

Dilfo, in the center of the picture, suddenly propelled his hands in the air.

"The explosion?" I asked.

"Exactly," says Goos. "Last truck is maybe eight hundred meters out of town when they hear the explosion down below." Goos translated Dilfo directly for a moment.

"'We are in the trucks about eight hours until we arrive in Mitrovica. Seeing what we've come back to, the People are crying and carrying on. And the Chetnik commander, who's still wearing the balaclava, gets on top of the truck and says in Serbo-Croatian, "We brought you here for your own good. Because sooner or later Kajevic and his Tigers would have killed every last one of you. He's sworn a curse on the whole village of Barupra."' Roma, you know, Boom, they put a lot of stock in curses. And they heard the Bosnian soldiers deliver Kajevic's threat anyway.

"The commander goes on: 'No one can know you are here. That's why we took your cell phones. As far as Kajevic is concerned, you're all dead back in that Cave, and it's up to you to leave him thinking that way. Some of you will want to let your kin know you're alive. But you can't. If Kajevic finds out that the people of Barupra live, he will hunt you down. Every last one of you.'

"Most of them, of course, Boom, they're with their families anyway, they don't have a lot of people back in Bosnia to tell. The Big Man, new one after Boldo, goes around and has a heart-to-heart with every family. Everyone signs on: 'Barupra' is a word none of them will ever speak. They don't like telling the non-Roma—"

"The *gadje*?"

"Right. They don't like telling the *gadje* their secrets anyway."

"And do they know who these men in balaclavas are?" Goos asked, which caused the three of them to talk over each other and quarrel among themselves.

"They argue to this day," said Goos.

"I can see."

"Some people think they were Kajevic's Tigers who were pretending not to be. Or some other paramilitary, like the Scorpions, doing the Tigers' dirty work. Boldo's family is sure of that, that they came to kill Boldo." Florica interjected something and Goos nodded. "Florica, she says the Chetniks had NATO papers to get across the border to Kosovo. She was peeking out of the truck. So perhaps they were Germans or French."

"But the people on the trucks recognized nobody?"

"One," Ion answered in English.

"The Chetnik commander," said Goos. "Some people say this Chetnik was a man. But people like Ion say otherwise."

Ion looked into the camera.

"Atee-la," Ion said.

"Attila? In person?" I asked.

"Yay, Attila. Look close at the photos I sent. Dinky-di, I say. That's Attila."

"Shooting Boldo, right?"

"That's my guess."

Goos thanked the three witnesses and let them go on their ways. Then he took a seat so his face filled up the whole screen.

Largely as an act of intellectual discipline, I tried to figure out if we had any kind of case left. The Roma clearly had been forced to return to Kosovo at gunpoint, although it was hard to calculate whether they or I would be more reluctant to see any of them near a witness stand.

"You know, Goos, forced migration is designated as a war crime in our governing statute."

"Well, you tell me, Boom. Is it a forced relocation if you bring people back home? Especially to save their lives?"

I was at that hinge point where a lot of good prosecutors become bad prosecutors, trying to justify months or years of hard work and bad assumptions by hammering the facts into the shape of an established crime.

"We're done," I said. "Agree?"

"Carked for sure, mate."

"I still have a plane reservation to Cincinnati in the morning."

"For?"

"I'm going to try to find Attila. She's got a horse farm in northern Kentucky. Remember the pictures?"

"To what point, Boom?"

"Well, there's a lot we don't know. Like who put up Ferko to lying through his teeth? Why did Boldo say Attila told him to steal those guns? Mostly, I want to look Attila in the eye and tell her I don't care for the way she blew smoke up our ass."

We talked a little more. Nara had texted while I was on with Goos, and I was anxious to speak to her.

"Make sure you send me a selfie," Goos said, "when you get to Attila's. Not being a larrikin. Just so there's proof of your last whereabouts. There's more to Attila than we reckoned."

That sounded extreme, but I agreed.

At that moment, Dilfo wandered back into the picture to deliver some parting thought to Goos.

"What was that?" I asked.

"Wants us to get them out of Kosovo. All the People. Says Kajevic made them prisoners here for a dozen years. Now they deserve to go someplace better." Goos looked into the camera and added, "Some place they're welcome."

"I just wanted to hear your voice," Nara said when she picked up.

"Should I read you the phone book?"

"I was thinking of something like, I love you."

I obliged.

"I talked to Lewis. He will be here in an hour."

"Any clues about his state of mind?"

"He said that he was reconsidering everything." She took a second. "I told him about you."

"Was he upset?"

"Very. But I didn't want him to walk in not knowing."

Overall I saw her point.

"And what about your state of mind?" I asked, even though I was certain she'd know nothing for real until her husband was standing in front of her, in the home they had shared.

"I am trying to follow your advice and consider everything. But I do not believe that is how people make choices in these situations. As if it was a decision tree. Falling in love is not easy, Boom. Certainly not for me. If you say to almost every person on earth, Would you like to live with love or without love, what do you think they would say? People don't choose against love, Boom."

She was a smart girl. But that misstated her choice. Seeing Lewis, if he said the right things, she might feel something else, a rekindling of whatever brought them together to start.

Nara said, "But I have thought a lot about what I said the other night. About you giving me away?"

"And?"

"I think I am correct. You want me to walk away—"

"I don't want you to walk away."

"A part of you does, so you do not have to deal with the difficulties. How can you deny someone you love the experience of children? But how can you parent a child if you lack the will? So you tell me I should think, so you are not forced to choose."

I didn't know how to calculate the duration of our relationship, given the months we'd dwelled together platonically beforehand. But by my quick arithmetic, Nara and I had been lovers for all of three weeks. Couples often said, when things worked out, that they'd known it from the first instant, but I suspected there was a lot of retrospective reshaping in those declarations, no matter how clear it all seemed looking back. The wiser part of me knew that even if Nara sent Lewis packing, it would be a long time before the two of us would have a sure view of our future. But on the other hand, as a man who'd flunked out of every relationship before this one, I'd learned that it was never too early to calmly say, This will never work—if you were certain that was the case. Narawanda was right to require me to answer her question, even though a truthful response seemed far more elusive than my feelings about her.

"Do I actually have the right to make that choice?" I asked her. That might have sounded to her like a way to buy time, but to me it felt like the proper order for decision, what my contractor clients liked to call 'the critical path.' I would never be able to reach conclusions in the abstract.

"I think you do," she said. "But I will tell you for sure after the weekend."

36.

Bad Person—July 11

In Attila's office, I had seen the pictures of her place in northern Kentucky, but in the height of summer, the farm and the surrounding landscape had a lushness and serenity that photography could never reflect. She lived about an hour from the Cincinnati airport, halfway to Louisville, outside of Carrollton. The site overlooked a tranquil stretch of the Ohio River, closely resembling the River Kindle beside which I'd passed much of my life, a bluish satin ribbon between the low green hills. Following GPS to the address I'd received from Merriwell's assistant, I found myself at a call box beside yet another set of gold-tipped iron gates.

A woman answered, her accent distinct even as she said hello, and I gave my name, adding I was a friend of Attila's. I was prepared to be refused—She's not home, She's busy, She's sick, She doesn't know you, Go way—but the motorized gates swung open, and I proceeded up a drive of fancy French pavers a good quarter of a mile. The house, all white stone but with Georgian looks in the grand McMansion style, was at the top of a knob behind several acres of velvety lawn, amid areas of deep woods.

Attila's beautiful wife, a stately-looking woman even in her jeans, made her leisurely way from the house to greet me. She had straight black hair, shining like ravens' wings, halfway down her back, and blue eyes that stood out from fifty feet.

I left the car and introduced myself. She was Valeria.

"Attila at store," she said. "Back soon." She sounded Russian or Polish, and not long from the boat. "You funny name. Remember from Attila."

She offered coffee while I waited, and showed me in, past the stout oak doors at the entry, which were tooled with a coat of arms that I'm sure had nothing to do with Attila or her. The sleek kitchen, with its marble counters and appliances hidden in the sycamore cabinetry, was straight from a design magazine, and rivaled the luxe features I'd seen at Ellen and Howard's.

Valeria produced a cup of coffee from a chrome device across the room, then seated herself on a black leather stool on one side of the counter and pointed me to another. The air grew a little thicker as I tried to figure out how to start a conversation.

"How did you meet Attila?" I asked.

She smiled thinly. "Bought me," she said.

It had to be the accent, I figured.

"I'm sorry, but I thought you said she bought you."

Valeria managed a grimly ironic smile. The story, even as she struggled with language, was riveting. Valeria was from Tiraspol in Moldova, where the post-Communist transition to a market economy had created a desperate time of cascading inflation, no work, and little food.

"Woman, Taja, say 'Come Italy, be waitress.'" Taja took Valeria's passport, supposedly in order to obtain Italian work permits. But once Taja had possession of the document, Valeria, along with four other girls, was forced at knifepoint into a horse van, in which they were driven for hours. Eventually, they found themselves on a small boat, making a nighttime passage into Bosnia. There she and approximately twenty other young women were taken to a barn and at gunpoint instructed to remove all their clothing. After inspection, they were sold. The woman who bought Valeria owned a club near Tuzla.

"Very mean, this woman. All the time she say her sons, 'Bitter, bitter.'" Beat her, I realized. "Still hear when sleep."

The first time Valeria was told to have sex with a patron, she refused. As it turned out, the bar owner had a customer who paid well for the right to be the first to beat and rape each of the women.

"We live four girls in room behind bar. This also place for meet with customers. Smells? Dirty rubbers on floor. Never wash sheets. Sleep six hours maybe. One time each day food, but four, five man. And she, boss lady, she say, 'Escape? You got no work paper. I call police, they take you jail.'"

Valeria was told that after six months the debt she supposedly owed the club owner for the cost of bringing her here would be considered repaid and her passport returned. Instead, as the date approached, the owner informed Valeria that she had a new boss, who'd paid 3,000 deutsche marks for her.

"Was Attila. Seen before around bar. Was man, I'm thinking." She again briefly deployed her taut smile. "Attila take me her house. Give me clothes, food. Say, 'You want leave, leave. But you so beautiful, I cry.' I say, 'Okay, few days.' Attila good. Very good. Very kind. Love very much. Here now, have everything." She raised her long hands toward the kitchen and heaven above.

I pondered the obvious question, but after you screwed to stay alive, I would imagine tenderness made a big impression.

"Do you have friends here?"

"Some. Church. But Skype now all day with Moldova. Attila say, 'How you learn English, talk all day Romanian?' Understand English good. But can't speak."

I told her about my struggles with Dutch in the last several months. The front door slammed then.

"Hey, baby, who's here?" Attila sang. She sounded lighthearted, but hung on the threshold when she saw me.

"Boom," she said. She approached very slowly and shook my hand without the usual vigor. Her odd complexion was sunburned and her fashion sense had not improved. She wore plastic flip-flops, jeans cinched with a rope, and a T-shirt that did a good job of obscuring any sign of gender. "What the fuck you doin here, man?"

"I wanted to ask you some questions."

"I thought you guys couldn't investigate in the US."

I had already guessed why Attila had headed for home so suddenly.

"We can't," I said. "This is for my own sake."

"Just you and me?"

"I'll tell Goos."

"That's all? Like it never happened? I just don't want

to get my dumb half-black, half-Hungarian ass in any deep roughage."

"Did you do something wrong, Attila?"

"Well, fuck yeah, I did. You probably know that by now, don't you, Boom?"

I wasn't ready to give her any clues.

"I know you gave me a pretty good line," I said.

"Not really," she answered. "Mostly it was about what I didn't say. I like you, Boom. I told you all along those Gypsies weren't dead."

"But you didn't tell me you hid them."

I had her with that. She didn't stir for a second as she watched me.

"It was that fuckin GPS, wasn't it?" She meant the one transponder that had briefly showed up on the aerial photographs. "Tell me true, Boom. Do I need to get myself a damn lawyer?"

"Look, Attila. If I report what you tell me, either at the Court or to anybody in the US, I'm the one who'll end up in trouble, because I have no permission to be here asking questions."

She considered whether that was good enough. I threw down my ace.

"I spoke with Merry yesterday."

"Huh," she said, then went to what proved to be a refrigerated drawer in the huge central island and poured an ice tea in a mason jar. After making another for me, she led me outside to the screened porch. The air was thick here, far more humid than I'd felt in a while, but a breeze rose off the river, and there was a lovely view of the serene water idling below. We were high enough that the birds and dragonflies zagged over the trees at eye level.

I told her some of what I'd discovered: the light arms, Iraq.

"I have lots of questions," I said. "But maybe we should start with a simple one. How the hell did a bunch of Gypsies end up with guns to sell to Kajevic?"

"Who told you that?"

"Is it untrue?"

"Fuck no, it ain't untrue. I'm just tryin to figure how you found out is all. You're good, Boom. You and Goos. You're good at your job."

"I'm too old for you to tell me how pretty I am, Attila. How about just letting me hear the whole story."

She looked at her mug, while using her nail-bitten index finger to draw a figure in the moisture gathered on the glass. Her gaze was still there as she said, "You know, I ain't a bad person, Boom. I'm really not. I was tryin to do right by everybody. You'll see that's so. Sometimes you just get deeper and deeper in shit."

I nodded, but hesitated to provide any spoken comfort. I'd heard a lot of similar excuses in my law office.

"You know," she said, "Merry takes the blame for this whole arms-to-Iraq thing, but I'm still believin it was your buddy Roger's idea. Whoever, it was purely fugazi, man. All this top-secret crap. The whole operation was run on the intelligence side with private contractors. Our armed forces never touched those weapons, probably so they'd have deniability.

"And don't you know, two days after the first transport takes off for Iraq I'm getting all these freaked-out calls from the Green Zone in Baghdad about where in the hell did the weapons go? And it's not two weeks before a telex arrives from Army Intelligence. They're recovering assault rifles from Al Qaeda in Iraq, which have either the serial numbers we'd recorded or our laser engraving, usually both. You know, the Iraqis tried to torch off the identifiers before they sold the firearms, but they were as good at that as they were anything else.

"Okay. So bad enough we sent 200,000 small arms to Iraq to kill Americans, but no more than two weeks later, right after I start hearing about where these weapons are endin up, Roger calls me to say we've got to send a second shipment, 300,000 more. And I'm like, Fuck you, I'm not in business to kill US soldiers, or Canadian soldiers or British soldiers or anybody else on my side. And he's like, You don't understand shit about what's goin down here. It's bedlam. We need to reestablish the police and the military, and if 50,000 guns walk away, then that's what happens. And besides, did you ever hear about following fucking orders? I can replace your worthless ass with one phone call." Attila paused to wag her chin. "Hate that prick," she said.

"I thought you were explaining how the Roma got the guns they sold Kajevic."

"I am."

"How's that?"

"Cause there was a bunch of Gypsy drivers standing around in my office when I got that last call from Roger."

"Why were they in your office?"

"Payday. Those Roma don't know from bank accounts, so I had to give them their wages in cash. And Boom, I'm a big boy—how I run my company, I'm the only one who handles large amounts of currency. Just fact."

"And who exactly was there with you when you had that argument with Roger?"

Attila lifted her face and squinted at me.

"Have you got that jackass Ferko in your pocket?"

"Attila, just answer me."

She pouted briefly.

"Well, I argued like that with Roger more than once, and I can't say who-all was there for sure, but it must have been six, seven of them. Boldo. Ferko, I imagine, and Boldo's dumb brother, Refke, cause they was almost always with Boldo. Three or four others who'd driven that week."

"Remind me about Boldo. How did you know him?"

"Boldo? You go on the Internet and you Google 'anus,' there's gonna be a great big picture of Boldo right there. He'd been in Dubrava prison in Kosovo up until maybe a month before the Roma got torched out in Mitrovica in '99."

"What was he in prison for?"

Attila shrugged. "How I heard, he sliced up some guy in a bar. Maybe it was thievin. He was a real thief. Anyway, NATO bombed the prison and the Serbians overran it and let the non-Muslims go. So Boldo was with the whole Gypsy mob when they came to Bosnia. And pretty much the Big Man there. Over time, Boldo got into chop-shoppin, and stealin cars, too."

"And you employed him anyway?"

"That's *why* I hired that whole lot, Boom. Do I want them rippin my trucks? I had them on payroll so they'd leave my shit alone. Plus that kept anybody else from boostin my equipment, seein as how Boldo was the main place you'd go to move it. I mean," said Attila, peeking at me, "it's business."

"And how many of them were in this group?"

"There was maybe ten in all I'd see from time to time."

"Names?"

Attila scratched her chin and looked upward to recall. She came up with about six names, Ion among them.

"All right," I said. "So we're in your office. You get a call and you and Roger have this intense argument while these Gypsy drivers are standing around waiting to be paid."

"Right. And when I get off the phone, I just lose my shit. I mean it's a real and total hissy fit. I'm rattling on in English, throwing shit at the wall, while these guys are just starin with no clue. 'Fuck me if I'm gonna send guns to Iraq to arm Al Qaeda, even for Layton fuckin Merriwell. Fuck me if I'm gonna let the fuckin Iraqis steal this shit that thousands of NATO soldiers have risked their lives to collect. Fuck me, fuck me. If I had any real stones, I'd steal those fuckin guns myself and send them someplace where they wouldn't be shootin Americans.' I went on and on how Merriwell had lost his mind. Only I forgot one thing, Boom."

"Which was?"

"Boldo spoke English. He was the only one. The rest of them didn't even speak Bosnian well. But Boldo, he understood every word."

"Ouch," I said.

"Yeah, ouch," said Attila. "Like there goes my clearance if anyone hears I was so loose with all that classified shit. I mean, Boom, I told you a long time ago: I talk too much. I've been stepping on my dick like that my whole life. I just always think I'm so fuckin entertaining." She stopped with her narrow shoulders drawn and seemed to reflect for a second about herself.

"Any rate, I finally done like I was told and pooled another 300,000 or so light arms. And the last transport is about to fly off for Iraq from Comanche. We actually held it for a couple hours waitin for the final convoy, and these Gypsy so-and-so's drag in tellin this tale bout how six of the trucks got hot-wired overnight and are gone. I didn't think all that much of it at first. I wanted to get the planes off the ground. I telexed Roger and everybody else in Iraq, and we reported this to the Bosnian police and the NATO criminal investigators.

"But a day later, it ain't sittin right with me. I looked at the reports that were taken from Boldo and Ferko and the rest of the crew, and they hadn't even bothered to match out their stories. No two of them said the same about where they were overnight, or what the bad guys looked like, or even how the six that had their trucks stole got back to Barupra.

"So I go tearin off for the refugee camp to find Boldo. I come the back way into the valley and I hike up to the Cave, and you know what I see? Merry's weapons. Thousands of them. Zastavas. And ammo. Mortars and RPGs.

"Boldo comes down like he's a king and we really got into it. And the jagoff, you know what he says? 'You told me to steal these guns. All these guys heard you.'

"And I'm like, 'If I tell you to go fuck yourself right now, are you gonna do that, too?'

"And he's like, 'I'll give you half what I get. I think I already have a customer for some of this.'

"And I'm like, 'You numbnuts moron, you may know all about stealing cars, but you don't know shit about this stuff. These weapons are marked. You try sellin them and the first guy who gets caught with one, he'll be giving law enforcement your name faster than he says his own. NATO will be up your rectum with a router and a flashlight. You're going straight back to prison.' All of which was true.

"But Boldo hears all this, and smiles and says, 'Yeah, but you said to steal 'em.'

"He was screwin with me, naturally. But he wasn't stupid. If I turned in Boldo to the Bosnians or NATO, he would repeat everything he overheard on the phone, about Al Qaeda and the Iraqis and Merriwell, and say I was the one who decided to steal a few weapons to do what little I could to stop that. So the upshot would be I'd end up fuckin Merriwell, I'd lose my job and my clearance, and I'd have to deal with Boldo and his gang lyin on me."

I lifted a finger to interrupt.

"But you didn't tell him to steal the guns, right, Attila?"

She bolted back from the table.

"Fuck, Boom." She scowled at me.

"Is the answer no?"

"No. The answer is Fuck No. Never. You don't believe that, do you?" In her vulnerable moments, Attila was easy to read and she clearly was wounded, but I still took a second to be certain about what I thought.

"I don't," I said then. I reminded her where she was in the story, which was her confrontation with Boldo outside the Cave. Attila's narrow shoulders trembled with a sigh before she plunged back in.

"So okay, gotta make lemonade out of lemons, right? I tell Boldo, 'Fuckjob, you bury these guns right here. Right in the Cave. That's the last you or me or anyone else ever sees of them.' As for the trucks, that's more trouble than it's worth, if they turn up again. So I say to Boldo, 'This is all you're gettin out of this. You can chop these trucks and sell the parts. But you assholes are done driving for me. That's over.'

"I actually stand there for a while to watch Boldo start piecing out the first vehicle.

"Anyway, no more than three days later, I get a message on my cell from Ferko, who's just about wettin himself he's so scared. He literally wants to meet in a cellar and makes me swear on the lives of the children I don't have, that I'll never let any of this bounce back on him. Apparently, Boldo encountered some scumbag kid in one of the sex clubs outside Tuzla and agreed to sell him two trucks and a hundred AKs, and Boldo sent Ferko and a couple others to deliver the shit in Doboj.

"But the guys who received the equipment, every single one of them had the Arkan tattoo—it's a roaring tiger—right on their hands. And more than one is laughin about how 'the president' loves that he got these weapons off the Americans. And the kid is some kind of relative to Kajevic and keeps talking about 'Laza.' And I mean, Ferko, he ain't no intellect, but he's a survivor.

"Ferko goes runnin back to Boldo and says, 'I think we just sold shit to Kajevic,' and Boldo laughs in his face. 'Who cares? NATO and the Americans won't know anything about this. They haven't caught Kajevic for ten years and there's barely any of them left to catch him now.'

"Now Ferko, there's a lot here he don't like. First off, he don't like Boldo. Nobody does. He especially don't like Kajevic, who killed lots of Gypsies. And he don't like losin his job with me either, since I pay better than Boldo. But worst of all, what he really don't care for is gettin caught. Because he knows that if the Bosnians ever get wind that he had to do with sellin weapons to Kajevic, they will peel the flesh off him one square inch at a time and fill each wound with that famous Tuzla salt.

No exaggeration. None at all. And thanks to Boldo, he, Ferko, is the guy everybody in Doboj saw deliverin that shit."

"So you got Ferko to tell Army Intelligence about Kajevic?"

"No, Boom, I went to Intelligence. Was *me*. I said, 'I have this Gypsy driver who swears some of them sold some black-market shit to these guys hiding out in Doboj and he's sure it's Kajevic.'

"Of course, Intelligence, they're like, 'Well, we gotta talk to him,' and I'm like, 'Negative on that. Gypsies don't rat out Gypsies. The Roma won't just drown this bird in Lake Pannonica. They'll excommunicate his whole family.' Which is true by the way. 'Here's the coordinates,' I tell them. 'Do a surveillance and see for yourselves.'"

"But you didn't mention the weapons Ferko delivered?"

"Never. I said the guy I heard this from was a car thief, and that's all I know. I was tryin to cover Ferko. And Merry. Even that prick Roger. And me. If they balled up Boldo, he'd blame it all on me. After all, I'm a fuckin white man."

"So to speak."

She smiled. "So to speak." She took a second to raise her thumb to her teeth. The determination with which she bit and tore at herself was not pleasant to watch. "But, Boom, honest to God, it never dawned on me that Intelligence wouldn't realize Kajevic and his Tigers were armed to the teeth. How fuckin stupid do you have to be to know an arms convoy has gone missin thirty kilometers away and not wonder if Kajevic got some of that shit? But it's the military, Boom. One hand don't know about the other. The NATO guys who are looking for my trucks have decided it was jihadis who stole them. And to this day, I don't know why. Some hot tip they had.

"So Kajevic was waitin for Special Forces with firepower they flat-ass never figured on. We got four dead Americans and eight more in various states of blown-to-shit, and I'm in deeper now than I could ever imagine.

"And within a week, it gets worse. First, Kajevic has sent word that he's shootin every Roma in Barupra, and Ferko is givin me that I gotta protect him and them.

"And Intelligence, they are just beside themselves. They don't need nobody to tell them they screwed the pooch, and they're tryin to figure how. And they come back on me sayin, 'No bullshit now, we gotta talk to your source.'

"So instead, after about a day I tell them the truth. Sort of. I say, 'I looked a little harder, and them damn Gypsies spun me. They stole weapons from that convoy and sold them to Kajevic and they still have thousands more. And now, because my guy did the right thing and told me about Kajevic, him and his Tigers want to come back and wipe out the whole camp.'

"And of course, the Intelligence guys at first, they're saying, 'Sounds like a good idea, fuck those fuckers anyway. We sure as shit ain't gonna protect a bunch of people who sold out our troops.'

"I'm like, 'Understood, only we got some very big problems here. Which are gonna undermine our whole mission in this country. First, if those guns the Roma stole get sold to the Tigers or the Scorpions or some other paramilitary, who knows what hell they'll raise? Or who gets killed or wounded tryin to disarm them?

Maybe those Gypsy fuckers do what NATO thought and deliver those weapons to a bunch of jihadis who send them to Hezbollah. Or imagine Kajevic actually does go into Barupra and kills them all. How does all this peace-keeping shit look after that? There ain't no happy ending here. We gotta do something and we gotta do it quick.'

"And the guys I'm talkin to, they say, 'Well, we'll take this to HQ,' and I'm like, 'You kick this upstairs and they'll all pull their puds for a week, and somethin bad will happen in the meanwhile.' Merry had just left and the new NATO commanders, they were still scoutin around for the latrines.

"Naturally, the intel guys ask, 'Well, you got a better idea?' And I do. 'Let's get rid of the weapons and get rid of the Gypsies, too,' I say. 'Take the fuckers back to where they came from. We'll let my guy—'"

"Your guy is Ferko?"

"Exactly. Let my guy stay here and say these masked men came in there and killed the rest of them.

"And you know, Boom, it wasn't such a bad plan. It had to be a vigilante kind of thing, cause no one in command would ever sign off on it. But it was no lack of volunteers from Intelligence.

"So here I am finally directing an armed operation. Everybody had creds as CoroDyn civilian employees, and typed orders from NATO to cross the border. We timed it so Ferko and his sons and sons-in-laws were the sentries that night. We drove in from the back, on the mine side, and glided down into the valley, then secured the Cave and double-timed up into the village on foot. I knew Boldo would be sleepin with an AK, literally, so we surrounded his dumpy little hut to start. But Boldo, man, Boldo wasn't hearin this Hands-up shit."

"Who shot him?" I asked.

"Me. First, at least. I didn't wait long neither when I saw that assault rifle in his hands. Twenty years in the Army, Boom, and I never shot at anything but a target before that. I probably could have waited another second, probably. I mean, I hated the fucker. But still. I don't know. But once the bullets start flyin, people get nervous." She peeked up at me. "This combat shit is way overrated," she said. She reflected a second on that.

"And you know, once one guy pulls the trigger, everybody wants to. And that's how that poor boy got shot. By some lame-ass kid not much older than him. And Boom, I just stood there thinkin, Okay, now, you're the one who figures everything out, figure out how you're gonna make this good. It just didn't seem possible there wasn't some way to turn around something that took just a skinny little part of a second." Attila shook her head for a long time.

"What about the brother?"

"He was the same kind of jerk as Boldo. He wouldn't *let* his damn life get saved. So there he goes, too.

"Joke is, the rest of it after that went down totally excellent—movin the Roma out, blowin the Cave. We had them in Kosovo and were back before Taps. And the Roma all took that stuff about Kajevic looking for them as gospel."

"And Ferko's reward for snitching was that he stayed and took over Boldo's business?" I asked.

"Right. Somebody had to stick around to say, This is what happened. We needed the word to go out that the Roma were dead and gone."

"And Ferko wasn't worried about Kajevic?"

"You kiddin? He'd start to whimper whenever he

heard Kajevic's name. I wanted him to say Kajevic's Tigers killed all the Roma, but Ferko was afraid to draw that kind of fire. Kajevic got what he wanted anyway. The Roma were gone. He probably thought the US had buried all them in the Cave."

"I believe he did."

"So it was what it was, sad and all: The Roma were gone and so were the arms Boldo stole. Until 2007 when your Gypsy honey showed up and said she'd heard these terrible rumors about a massacre and wanted an international investigation. I told Ferko just to blow her off, which he did several times, but then she says she's got this idea about building up a circum-stantial case, going to Mitrovica to find the relatives of the people in Barupra so they, the relatives, can say the Barupra people haven't been heard from by any of their kin for years now. Well, that just sucks. If she starts in walkin round Mitrovica, jabberin in Romany, sooner or later she'll know the whole damn story. And she's no ordinary Gypsy."

"Hardly," I said.

"She's going to start in demanding records and raisin hell in the newspapers. I called Roger."

"You were back on speaking terms?"

"Not really. But he wasn't about to ignore my call."

"And what did you want from Roger?"

"I thought maybe he could get the Kosovars to keep her outta the country. Which he couldn't. At least, that's what he said."

"And did you tell Roger then that the Roma from Barupra were alive?"

Attila stared down, pinching her thighs as she was thinking.

"I started, but he didn't want to hear any of that. He told me the Gypsies were my problem. But he didn't mince no words that what happened with the shit we sent to Iraq still had a top-secret classification. People were talkin about Merry bein president, so all the ins and outs with those weapons, who stole what when, would get a lot of attention that would probably sink us all if reporters or the GAO got hold of it.

"So we couldn't let Esma get to Kosovo. I told Ferko, 'You gotta talk to her and convince her everybody in Barupra is dead.'"

"What was in it for Ferko?"

"Well, I paid him for one thing. But there wasn't anything he'd done he wanted to go braggin about neither—waylaying a convoy of weapons, or sellin to Kajevic, or tippin me off? There was plenty he needed to hide. So best for everybody if she bought that story."

Attila had been pretty shy about looking at me, but she faced me now, as she continued fingering the mason jar.

"So, okay. Do I sound like just the biggest dick so far?"

"Keep talking, Attila. I'll tell you what I think when I've heard the whole story."

Attila caught sight of one of her dogs outside doing something naughty and she got up to yell at the pooch. Through the screens, the black dog came into view, slinking off in shame.

"Can I jump ahead a little?" I said, when Attila again sat in her wrought-iron chair. "I understand that you didn't want Esma going to Kosovo. But why in the hell did Ferko have to testify in my case?"

"I told him not to. There was nothin to gain from

that. Nothin. But, you know, over time, man, he got to be sort of fascinated with the Gypsy lady. Real interested in makin her happy. He never quite said so, but I was pretty convinced she was lickin his lollipop now and then, when there was something she wanted."

Goos had overheard Ferko saying to Esma in Barupra, 'I want what you promised.' I thought I had her figured out the other day in Manhattan, but with Esma you never got to the bottom. In bed, she lied to no one. She could make Ferko—or Akemi—or me believe what she needed to, because she could abandon herself to it. That was one of the great advantages of having a personality without real boundaries. She was compelling, as Merry said. The sociopaths always were.

Attila said, "I told the dumbfuck, 'If you're really gonna testify, you better do it well. You get up there and lose your shit, we're all in deep—including your people back in Kosovo. Kajevic will have a team of Tigers on the first train if he knows they're all alive. You better do just like she tells you.' Seems like he enjoyed all the rehearsing." Attila rolled her lips into her mouth to suppress a lurid little smile. "Still and all, I can't believe folks were dumb enough to believe a Gypsy."

"Like me, you mean."

"Your dick believed him," Attila said. I was inclined to quarrel, but there was no point.

"Did Ferko actually bury Boldo and his relatives in Barupra?"

"Nope. We carried those bodies with us to Kosovo. Boldo's people, you know, they were the only ones we were afraid wouldn't stick with the program. But they were terrified. They knew Kajevic would be lookin to kill them first. And I gave Ferko money to send them every month, sayin it was their cut of the business. When your investigation started, Ferko found a couple grave robbers to bring the bodies back to Barupra."

"And who reburied them?"

"Ferko. He wanted me to help, but I'm like, 'This is on you, dude. This is all because you wanna testify.'"

"And he tossed a couple of rounds in there to make it look good?" I asked.

Attila's murky eyes rose to the ceiling.

"I think I told him to do that." She nodded, and bit again on her fingernails. She was bleeding from one of the cuticles. "So whatta you say, Boom? Am I just this big douche who got away with all kinds of stuff? I really was tryin to do good every step of the way. I was. But there were seven people dead in Bosnia inside of a month on account of me and those bang-bangs, and eight more wounded. And I know it. I really do. I ain't proud or anything. I fucked up. I think about it all the time. But I ain't a bad person, Boom. I'm really not."

Attila liked to present herself as a hard case, but her tiny eyes were welling as they searched me for my appraisal.

I had heard this declaration—I'm not bad—in some form from many clients over the years, and I often used the preacher's piety about not judging any person by his worst acts. But Attila was speaking from a deeper place of need. She had been told much of her early life that there was something wrong with her, and she wanted my comfort.

But justice is supposed to be unsparing. She'd empowered me to pronounce judgment and I was going to do it.

"First, Attila, you can wrap yourself in the flag and

talk about the troops in Iraq and protecting Merry and Roger, but this was about you, first and foremost. Your security classification. Your company. Your money. I know all that means a lot to you, and I understand why. But that's no excuse."

She chucked her head around, seemingly agreeing. I wasn't sure she really thought I was right, but she wasn't going to argue.

"Second, I don't buy that you were surprised you ended up having to kill Boldo. I think you went to Barupra expecting that. You knew Boldo would believe the Tigers were there for him, and that he'd be better off making them shoot him, rather than getting captured and tortured."

Attila rubber-mouthed a second. This time she shook her head.

"If he'd have come out with his hands up, Boom, he'd be fat and happy in Kosovo, stealin whatever he could. But I wasn't gonna count to three and see how many of us he could kill. The AK was loaded, Boom. You sayin you wouldn't have shot him?"

"No, I'd have shot him, too. But I'd have realized when I hatched this plan that it probably was going to involve killing a man, and I hope I would have thought twice about the whole escapade for that reason. I know Boldo was an asshole, Attila. But generally speaking, that's not a crime punishable by death. Let alone for two more people who were basically blameless."

She looked down at the table like a second grader. I had the feeling my evaluation had taken her by surprise.

"And third, and most important to me, Attila, very few of the people in Barupra had done anything to deserve getting deported at gunpoint. NATO could have guarded that camp from Kajevic. But you wanted to get the Gypsies and what they knew the hell out of Bosnia to keep them silent. So the Roma are getting lead poisoning in Kosovo for two reasons: First to cover your ass. And second to give a bunch of Intelligence guys, who were sore and ashamed that they hadn't figured on Kajevic being heavily armed, a chance to take out their sorrows on somebody else. And the Gypsies have always been useful for that purpose."

"I fucked up, Boom. Like I said. I'm not really askin you to forgive me."

"I don't forgive you, Attila. You're walking away from this with no punishment. That's as much comfort as you're going to get from me. I won't pat you on the back and say you can just forget about it now."

We locked eyes at that point, a long look, until she suddenly rose in her herky-jerky way and fled the table.

I stood to look at the river and the bluff. The dogs, both black labs, were chasing around in the yard. I could see a far-off pasture with a fence where several horses, Appaloosas, were standing around, flicking their tails at the flies. I enjoyed the full air and the richness of summer for a minute or so, then I followed Attila into the huge kitchen, where I found her with her back to me and her arms around her wife, who was a good head taller.

I stood a moment, then said, "You have a good woman, Attila."

She started nodding, while she picked up a paper napkin from the counter, using it to wipe her nose and eyes. When she turned my way, her face was bright red.

"We can agree about that, Boom. Good woman's hard to find. Hope you have some better luck. I warned you about the Gypsy lady, didn't I?"

"That you did."

Attila invited me to stay for dinner but I meant what I had said. I wasn't going to sit at her table and pretend nothing was wrong. I sent more than one person to the penitentiary whom I ended up liking for their honesty or their humor, or even because they were at core far better people than they'd been in a weak moment when they'd given in to impulse or the influence of someone else. And I liked Attila. And felt for her. And accepted that things had gotten away from her. But she'd wreaked havoc in many lives.

I kissed Valeria good-bye. Attila saw me out and we shook hands beside my rental car in her driveway.

"Where you go from here?" Attila asked.

The question startled me, because I realized only now how hard I'd been avoiding it. I still had no long-term answer. I could feel a pit starting to open in my chest, a bit of it nerves, but most of it absence.

"I'm taking my sons to a ball game tomorrow. After that, I'd prefer to return to The Hague," I said. "I like the Court. I believe in what they do. But I'm not sure the stars are in the right place for me to go back."

I could see Attila's inner busybody calculating, but she seemed to recognize that we were no longer on a footing where she was free to ask.

"Hope it all works out," she said. She gave me another brooding look, still yearning for the forgiveness she wasn't going to get from me, then slapped my shoulder and headed back inside.

When that beautiful front door of hers slammed, I more or less slid into the emotional sinkhole that had begun to trickle open inside me a second before. I had arrived at that moment I'd feared a few months ago in

The Hague, confronting the reality that my extended efforts at renewal had gotten me nowhere. I was approaching fifty-five years old and had done my level best to give myself a chance to be happy. I'd tried to do the right things and figure out what mattered. But here I was. The bad guys, whoever they were, weren't getting punished. The people of Barupra were suffering in Kosovo. And I was still without a home. What the hell, anyway?

I touched the auto's start button beside the wheel, but my phone, in my shirt pocket, began to vibrate. My heart spurted and I was suddenly high with hope.

It was Nara.

Author's Note

So how much of this is true? Every novelist wants to answer that question the same way: All of it—and none.

I'll be a little more straightforward. I was often inspired by real-world events. Yet this is a work of imagination. No character is a representation of anyone who has lived. That is because even when I started from actual occurrences, I altered them for dramatic effect or to serve the larger purposes of my story.

For example, despite the deplorable history of abuse of the Rom people, including during the Balkan Wars, there never was a Roma refugee camp on the outskirts of the real Eagle Base. I am not aware of a massacre of hundreds of Roma, actual or alleged, in Bosnia after the war, let alone one in which American NATO troops were suspects. In fact, the reputation of the US troops who served at Eagle Base, as I

heard it, was outstanding, although I cannot say the
same about our private military contractors. (See,
for example, Human Rights Watch Report, Vol. 14
No. 9 (D), "Hopes Betrayed: Trafficking of Women
and Girls to Post-Conflict Bosnia and Herzegovina
for Forced Prostitution" [New York: Human Rights
Watch, 2002].)

On the other hand, the shipment of hundreds of
thousands of weapons from Bosnia to Iraq in August 2004, including the fact that the disposition of
those arms has never been accounted for, is well documented by, among others, the Government Accountability Office and Amnesty International. (See Glenn
Kessler, "Weapons Given to Iraq Are Missing," *Washington Post*, August 6, 2007; Amnesty International
and TransArms, *Dead on Time: Arms Transportation, Brokering and the Threat to Human Rights*
(London: Amnesty International, May 2006); see
also "Bosnian Arms Donated to Afghanistan Probably in Taliban's Hands—Researcher," BBC Monitoring International Reports, August 14, 2007; and
Stephen Braun, "Bad Guys Make Even Worse Allies,"
Los   Angeles   Times,   August   13,   2007,
http://www.latimes.com/la-oe-
braun13aug13-story.html.

In the same vein, I acknowledge that I've sometimes played loose with the geography of Bosnia.
The description of major cities was intended to be
accurate. However, the small towns I mention are
generally fictitious, as is the monastery at Madovic,
even though it bears some resemblance to other
monasteries elsewhere in BiH.

Rather than turn this Note into a law review article, with endless citations cataloging the pieces of reality that were my starting places, I have posted on my website (www.scottturow.com) a series of page-by-page endnotes describing some of what inspired me. I have also included there a bibliography of the many written works central to my research. I am deeply indebted to those writers.

Readers will not be surprised to learn that writing this book took me to Europe a number of times, including trips to the Netherlands and Bosnia. I will never be able to adequately thank the many persons who shared their time and impressions with me. Everyone spoke to me without precondition on what I was going to write, and I suspect that in many cases they will disagree with the opinions I—or my characters—have expressed. None of the people mentioned below are responsible either for my views or for the errors I undoubtedly made despite their efforts. (And to the many who preferred to stay unacknowledged, I remain mindful of your help and deeply grateful.)

First, the International Criminal Court. Like any institution, the ICC has its strengths and its weaknesses. But I share with Boom the belief that, given the enduring reality of wartime atrocities, the ICC is indispensable in making the world more just. I hope that in time the United States lends its moral authority to the Court by ratifying the treaty we signed. Given the legal foundations for the Court's exercise of its authority, I regard US fears of the Court, while far from fanciful, as misplaced and at odds with the US's long-term interest in supporting the rule of law around the world.

I was received at the Court by a number of officials: Presiding Judge Cuno Tarfusser; the Prosecutor, Mrs. Fatou Bensouda; and registrar Herman von Hebel. I also talked with many current or former members of the OTP. Professor Alex Whiting of Harvard Law School was extraordinarily generous with his time and made many introductions; I spoke also with Sam Lowery, Julian Nicholls, and Claus Molitor, among others.

Marie O'Leary, Dan Ivetic, and Vera Douwes Dekker helped me understand the lives of defense lawyers in The Hague, at both the ICC and the ICTY.

The wonderful novelist Jean Kwok and her husband, Erwin Kluwer, introduced me to Indonesian cuisine in The Hague and answered countless questions over the next two years about life in their home city. Both read an earlier draft of this book and corrected errors large and small, including a couple that would have proved downright comical.

My understanding of The Hague and the surrounding diplomatic environment was greatly enhanced through my conversations with my friends, our former ambassador to the Netherlands Fay Hartog-Levin and her husband, Dan Levin. Ambassador Tim Broas was also kind enough to see me at the embassy. Many of the connections I made in the diplomatic community occurred with the help of my dear friends Julie and David Jacobson, David being both my former law partner and our recent ambassador to Canada. I am also indebted to Andrew Wright and Thea Geerts-Kuijper for their hospitality while I was in The Hague. Thanks, too, to Retired Judge Thomas Buergenthal of the International

Court of Justice, who talked to me informally about global legal issues. Last regarding Holland, a shout-out of deep thanks to Hague resident William Rosato, who offered intrepid suggestions for the plot of this book.

My comprehension of Bosnia was enlarged by many people. My high school classmates, our former ambassador there (and in Greece) Tom Miller and his wife, Bonnie Stern Miller, provided invaluable insights. Scott Simon was kind enough to share some of his recollections of Bosnia from his time there as a reporter (and as the author of a superb novel, *Pretty Birds,* which also informed me in many ways). I spoke several times to Christopher Bragdon, who runs BILD, an NGO committed to Bosnian re-building and reconciliation. My fellow Chicagoan, the renowned author Aleksandar Hemon, offered periodic advice about his homeland while I was writing and kindly corrected errors in an earlier draft of the book. I must offer not only words of gratitude but also of apology to Husagić Mesnur and the officials of Rudnik soli Tuzla ("Tuzla Salt Mine"), who welcomed me warmly, with no idea of the evil that can take place in a novelist's imagination. All events that Boom describes at a different—and entirely imaginary—salt mine are completely fictitious. Great thanks to Edin Selvic for the day he spent with me, including showing me the site of Camp Bedrock. My gratitude to Professor Eric Stover of the UC Berkeley School of Law for our e-mail exchanges about human rights issues and forensic anthropology, including one sad story that I wove into this novel.

In the town of Poljice, Nazif Mujić, known to the world through his role in the prizewinning film *An Episode in the Life of An Iron Picker*, welcomed me to his home, and with his family and friends spoke to me at length about Roma life in Bosnia. Thanks, too, to my friend Michael Bandler, who helped expand my understanding of international issues concerning the Roma.

No one was more helpful in deepening my understanding of Bosnia than my incomparable guide there, Dajana Zildzic. Dajana drove me around her country for days, spoke to me candidly about Bosnia, and translated for me in several interviews. She also reviewed and corrected a prior version of the book. Finally, she helped with a small humanitarian project we undertook together, with the assistance of Chris Bragdon.

Changing hemispheres, the esteemed Australian author, authors' advocate, and editor Angelo Loukakis helped Goos speak better Australian. Angelo also offered discerning comments on the manuscript.

Closer to home, I received valuable feedback on early drafts of the book from Julian Solotorovsky and Dan Pastern; my agent at CAA, Bruce Vinokour; and from my daughters, Rachel Turow and Eve Turow Paul, as well as my son-in-law Ben Schiffrin.

Eternal thanks to the world's greatest literary agent, Gail Hochman. And big applause and gratitude to my editor Deb Futter, who deserves extra-special mention for being willing to bet on a book with a largely foreign setting in an unfamiliar legal system, as well as for her tireless editing that put me through my paces on several drafts.

Last, love and special thanks to my wife Adriane, who read and commented on several drafts. More to the point, she put up for years with my sudden vacant looks and half-finished sentences when, in the midst of our conversations, my mind flew back to Boom.

About the Author

Scott Turow is the author of eleven bestselling works of fiction, including *Identical*, *Innocent*, *Presumed Innocent*, and *The Burden of Proof*, and two nonfiction books, including *One L*, about his experience as a law student. His books have been translated into more than forty languages, sold more than thirty million copies worldwide, and have been adapted into movies and television projects. He frequently contributes essays and op-ed pieces to publications such as the *New York Times*, *Washington Post*, *Vanity Fair*, *The New Yorker*, and *Time*.

ELKHART PUBLIC LIBRARY

3 3080 01699 5311

ELKHART PUBLIC LIBRARY

GRAND
CENTRAL
PUBLISHING

A BOOK FOR EVERY READER.

Your next great read
is only a click away.

GrandCentralPublishing.com

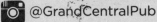

GrandCentralPub

@GrandCentralPub

@GrandCentralPub

GRAND
CENTRAL
PUBLISHING

FOREVER

L&S
LIFE & STYLE

TWELVE

VISION